COPYRIGHT

ISBN 9780648480525

SHATTERED DREAMS

PORTRAITS IN BLUE - BOOK TWO

PENNY FIELDS-SCHNEIDER

PFS

PROLOGUE

*J*ack's head bumped against the window for the third time, this time waking him. He repositioned his long legs, now tingling with numbness after the extended immobility. Sleepily, he gazed at the blur of trees against the rock face as the ancient train swayed around a tight bend, enjoying the comfortable feeling of Sofia's body, warm against his, as they traversed the spectacular, if not terrifying, mountain range - the Iberian System - their destination: Madrid. Snow-capped peaks towered overhead, while seemingly bottomless crevices gaped only yards from the track's edge. Jack instinctively moved back from the window as if, by this small shift of his weight, he could avert disaster.

For the hundredth time in the last twenty-four hours, he felt he should pinch himself. A glance at his watch confirmed that, at this very minute, he was supposed to be arriving at Aunt Elizabeth's and Uncle Robert's house in Surrey, and he hoped they'd received the telegram he'd hastily sent from the Cerbère Railway Station when they'd swapped trains, allowing them to continue the journey that had begun in Paris, across the Spanish border and onto Madrid.

He felt guilty, knowing the bewilderment that his words would have created.

CHANGE OF PLANS STOP HEADING TO MÁLAGA WITH SOFIA AND ANDRÉS STOP WILL BE IN TOUCH ASAP STOP

Jack's attempt to reassure himself that it would have been far worse if he'd failed to turn up, without giving his aunt and uncle advance warning, did not help. They would have been counting the hours until his return and he hated to think of their surprised expressions when they heard the knock. Their eyes would rise towards each other enquiringly – 'Is Jack early?' – then, on answering it, they would have been confused by the presence of a postman on their doorstep with a telegram in his hand.

Certainly, he was not a young child – almost a man, really – but Jack knew they would have been feeling the weight of responsibility for assuring his safety. Jack was, after all, their only nephew, and had been entrusted in their care when he'd had travelled across the world to stay with them on his 'great adventure' – a journey which was supposed to have started and ended in England. The sudden diversion he'd taken, to attend an art school in Paris, had created ripples of anxiety that extended all the way to his parents in Australia. Probably a tidal wave, Jack thought wryly. Even so, both his aunt and uncle, as well as his parents, had reconciled themselves to his decision to enrol in the Académie Julian for four months of art lessons.

These days, Jack found it hard to recall his life in Australia. Even though barely six months had passed since he'd originally boarded the *Ormonde* and travelled to London, it felt like a life-time ago. There he'd been, just turned eighteen and finished with school, about to take up a position at Goldsbrough Mort & Co, where his father had worked for almost three decades. Jack had not been looking forward to it at all. His father may have found happiness in an office where his life was all about adding up figures, maintaining enormous ledgers and providing recommendations for the company's investments, but Jack could not imagine it for himself.

The problem was, unfortunately, that Jack simply had not known what he wanted to do with his life. He had envied the lads at school who were clear on their plan: Mark and Steve, off to Melbourne University, one to study medicine, the other, law; Keith, excited to be joining the Australian Army; and Davo, returning to Shepparton to help his family manage their sheep station. However, Jack's mind had always drawn a blank whenever he'd thought about his own future.

The overseas adventure would be good for Jack, his parents had decided. When he returned home, he'd be ready to settle and embark on his career. Being quite good at mathematics, Goldsbrough Mort & Co offered good future prospects for him. The company was, after all, one of Australia's largest wool exporting businesses. With hard work, Jack could be a financial manager, like his father, in under a decade.

Emitting a sigh, Jack refocussed on the scene outside the window. Just thinking about the job awaiting him made his chest tighten. The truth was that, if Jack had dreaded the thought of working in the offices of Goldsbrough Mort & Co before he'd embarked on his adventure across the world, now, after the freedom he'd experienced in the last few months, the very thought of it was intolerable. Like being admitted to prison for a life sentence.

The only thing that had ever interested Jack was painting and there was no living to be made in that. Or was there? Maybe not in his parents' eyes, but his experiences of the last few months suggested otherwise.

Their birthday gift of tickets for the *Ormonde*'s voyage to London had proved wonderful. Jack had loved walking the decks of the great ship, sketching and painting, morning and afternoon. Relishing the freedom of being on his own for the first time in his life.

Barely a week into the sea voyage, he'd met a fellow painter,

Margaret. She'd thought that his sketches were amazing and insisted that Jack's future simply must be that of an artist. So much so, that she'd arranged for him to meet her family and show his paintings to her uncle, Roger Fry. Perhaps not her real uncle, but a life-long family friend, the man was an influential art critic – and he had contacts. Contacts that had paved the way for Jack's Parisian adventure, and all that had followed.

~

While the point of his visit to Paris had been to spend three months gaining insight into the world of modern art, what no one had anticipated, least of all Jack, were the life-changing wonders that Paris had offered. The friendship that he'd developed with a fellow art student, Andrés. The consequences of his meeting with Andrés' sister, Sofia. How much the Spanish-born twins had come to mean to him. And no-one could have imagined the allure of life in Paris.

Jack's days had started with morning classes at the academy, where he'd learned modern painting techniques under the guidance of Monsieur Simon. Jack knew that his works, always pleasing, had improved significantly from these lessons. His understanding of colour theories and interpretation of scenes had developed and now, when he put brush to canvas, his work was underpinned by knowledge, rather than mere instinct.

~

Each afternoon, when lessons were finished for the day, he and Andrés, along with Sofia, had explored Paris. They'd wandered the streets and alleyways of the Parisian arrondissements, treading cobblestones that were centuries old. They'd sipped hot chocolate and coffee and tasted every variety of crepe the cafés had to offer. Late afternoons, and many an evening, they'd drank kirsch and brandy in the smoky cafés of Montparnasse, brimming with artists and writers from all over the world, all hoping to achieve fame and fortune, or at least to gain inspiration from the churning vortex of creative energy that was Paris – the madhouse, bohemian art capital of the world.

Together, they'd visited the tourist sites. Museums and galleries. The Louvre, of course, and Notre Dame. They'd climbed the Eiffel Tower, wandered along the Champs-Élysées, visited the beautiful parks and gazed out across Paris from the heights of the Arc de Triomphe. They'd spent hours walking, even fishing, along the Seine, usually with their drawing books in hand. Sofia had detailed their daily trips in her notebook and tracked their journey on her well-worn map.

Best of all, there had been the magical experience of falling in love. Jack smiled to himself, recalling his efforts to hide the feelings he had rapidly developed for Sofia. Battling the trembling that overcame him when she'd drawn him close, each afternoon as they'd ventured onto the streets for sightseeing, her left arm hooked through his, her right arm through Andres'. Controlling the feelings of exhilaration that overwhelmed him, in response to her enchanting, ever-present giggle and sparkling smile when she'd looked up at him, teasingly. Ignoring the warmth that had coursed through him as she'd extended to Jack the nurturing affection that she held for Andrés, worrying about his health and making sure he ate properly and even cooking for him.

Jack had never met anyone like Sofia, and right from the beginning, he had been besotted with her and yet had struggled to deal with his feelings, convinced that she was unavailable. He twirled the ring – the glittering, tiny, culprit – on the third finger of her left hand resting in his, that had been responsible for misleading him into believing that she was engaged to another man. How glad he'd been to discover that Spanish custom would have placed an engagement ring on the third finger of her *right* hand, not the left, as was the tradition in Australia. Jack knew that he was the luckiest man in the world when he'd learned that there was no other man , and furthermore, that Sofia had cherished the same feelings of love for him as he did for her.

And then, of course, those wonderful nights when he'd finally held her close to him. Jack tingled at the memories.

～

Much to his amazement, Jack's painting had achieved unexpected heights in Paris, thanks to Margaret's far reaching connections, bringing his and Andre's work to the attention of Gertrude Stein. A friend of Roger Fry's and well-known for her capacity to spot new talent, the influential patron had agreed to organise an exhibition showcasing his and Andrés' work to her own contacts - Americans and British collectors, writers and other artists - who had attended, admired, and even bought, their paintings.

Who would have thought? Jack mused. He realised now that he had not fully recognised or appreciated the extraordinary opportunity that he'd been presented with. His paintings set before prominent people - even the media! Andrés had understood immediately, and been ecstatic; it was the break that the young Spanish artist had dreamt of when he had come to Paris to attend the Académie Julian, unlike Jack who'd merely been swept along with the arrangements. Now, they each had paintings hanging on walls in London and Paris. America, even.

The exhibition had, thrillingly, led to a meeting with Pablo Picasso. The notorious artist had roots in Málaga, the twins' hometown, and he'd been generous with his encouragement to both Jack and Andrés, even inviting them to his home. Jack had no doubts that Pablo's advice had influenced his painting of Sofia, inspiring the attention of the judges who bestowed him with the Académie's Annual Student Exhibition's esteemed Portrait Prize, two weeks after the Stein exhibition. Jack would never forget Pablo's wisdom: *let each brush stroke speak, not of colour or line but rather, of truth* - words that had surely guided Jack as he'd told the story of his love for Sofia on canvas.

It hadn't all been wonderful, though. There had been the crisis which no one had anticipated. The night when Andrés' health, always precarious, had failed him. Jack felt a pang of guilt, recalling the shocking event, and glanced across the aisle to where Andrés rested, his eyes closed and head falling awkwardly against the window. Andrés' hands looked unnaturally pale and delicate - almost feminine - as they lay across his spindly thighs. Considering how weakened Andrés was, Jack hoped he would endure this long journey, from the northern tip of Spain through to its most southerly reaches, without mishap. Had he and Sofia been so caught up with each other that they neglected the warning signs of Andrés' failing health? Certainly, Andrés had been pushing himself, working day and night to prepare his paintings, first for the Stein exhibition and then for the academy's annual student show, determined to leave his mark on the Parisian art world. And that Andrés certainly did, not only with Miss Stein's patronage but also by winning the Académie Julian's esteemed gold medal. How terrible it had been that the joy of Andrés' success had ended with him, collapsing, breathless, on the floor of Carrefour Vavin, from where he'd been transported, by ambulance, to the Hôpital de la Pitié.

Jack had been meant to return to Australia that very week, following the Académie's student exhibition, but how could he have left Sofia alone in Paris, with her brother so ill? So, he'd extended his stay and sat with her, hoping and praying for Andrés recovery.

Now, over a month later, with Andrés cleared by the doctor to travel back to Spain, Jack's parents were expecting him to be returning to London and booking his passage to Australia. He could only imagine their shock when they, like his aunt and uncle, received the telegram he'd just sent, that revealed that he was journeying to southern Spain.

Jack shuddered, thinking about how close he'd come to leaving Sofia, not just once, but twice. The first separation, of course, was postponed by Andrés illness and hospitalisation; however, no such excuse had arisen to allow a second rescheduling of his trip home. Throughout the last week, their pending separation had hung over them like a rain-cloud, smothering their conversation and scotching the enthusiasm they'd shared for the plans they'd made for his visit to Spain the following year. Doubts had set in. Would Sofia's love for him endure time and distance?

He and Sofia had each, separately, become captive to their own misery. Unable to articulate the dark fears that had emerged, they'd transferred their time and attention to other issues: Andrés' release from hospital; organising the twins' journey back to Málaga - his own to Australia; a final round of visits to the galleries that held his and Andrés' works on consignment, visits where he and Sofia had chosen to offload the remnants of their paintings, instead of carrying them as luggage, and where they'd provided forwarding addresses for ongoing communications to the galleries. There had been the packing and the farewells.

Was it only two days ago that the twins' Aunt Christina had arrived bearing two heavy baskets, crammed with bread, cold meat, cake and an assortment of jars for their respective train journeys? She'd hugged them each in turn as she'd bravely fought back tears, promising to visit Málaga sometime soon, although the demands of running her café, coupled with caring for an elderly husband, suggested this was more of a hope than a likely plan.

～

Finally, the day of departure had arrived and Jack thought about yesterday morning, when he'd escorted Sofia and Andrés to the Gare de Nord, his heart heavy with despair. Days of busyness, undertaking the preparations for their respective journeys, had failed to obscure the hollow ache within his chest whenever he'd thought of their separation. Even the very act of breathing seemed difficult as the days became hours, and hours became minutes, before their final farewell.

Then it arrived.

The final moments, where he'd dragged Andrés and Sofia's suitcases onto the train. The last quick shake of hands with Andrés. The hurried kiss with Sofia that had been rudely interrupted by the call of the porter – '*ALL ABOARD*!'— demanding Jack's return to the platform. He remembered standing beside the chugging, spluttering train, an aching sense of emptiness overwhelming him, even as he'd held Sofia's hand, wishing for something that might compensate for their lack-lustre farewell. The train's deafening whistle accompanied the porters' loud warning – '*STAND CLEAR!*' – as though directly commanding Jack to step away.

So, he had stood – she, in the carriage doorway, he, on the station walking alongside the moving train, still unable to relinquish her hand, quickening his pace as the carriage began to move. And then, amid the billowing smoke and the engine's slow chugging, escalating as if to garner the energy required to haul the carriages out of the station, up mountains and across plains, transporting Sofia far, far away, Jack's purpose had suddenly crystalized with radiant clarity, as a voice in his head cried urgently – 'Get on the train. Now!'

And without a second thought, he did.

Gripping Sofia's warm fingers, Jack felt as though he'd been granted a reprieve. He wondered at the whereabouts of the basket Aunt Christina had given him – abandoned, along with his own suitcase and art satchel on the station platform – hopefully, now in the hands of a starving artist who'd be thankful for a sudden change of fortune.

While he and Sofia hadn't really spoken of his sudden change of plans yet, he knew from the way that she'd clung to him when he'd leapt, her grip so tight that he thought she would never let him go, that this was exactly where he belonged. Knowledge confirmed by Andrés' broad grin, depicting his pleasure – perhaps, even relief – that his new 'Aussie mate' was not leaving them yet.

Andrés had confided that, worse than his battle with illness, was his concern for his sister.

'What will happen to Sofia if I die here, in Paris?' he'd asked Jack in the very first days, when his life was hanging in the balance. More recently, in a lighter moment, he'd joked that if he was going to succumb to a silly malady, it should at least be in the twins' own home, surrounded by friends who would offer Sofia shoulders to cry on and help her to pick up the pieces of her life. Andrés had added with a sly smile toward Jack that perhaps one of the town lads would console Sofia should he die before Jack had a chance to get to Spain. Jack had not been amused.

So here he was, overwhelmingly relieved that fate had directed his actions. No clothes, not even a toothbrush to his name, and yet Jack knew that he had everything he'd ever wanted, seated right here beside him. Gently positioning Sofia's head against his neck, Jack rested his own against the headrest as the train accelerated into a final descent off the mountain range and onto the flat fields stretching as far as his eyes could see. He hoped sleep would help while away the afternoon as they approached Madrid, where they planned to rest overnight before continuing their journey to Málaga the following morning.

PART I

SPAIN

CHAPTER 1

*L*ater that afternoon Andrés and Sofia, now fully alert, leaned forward alongside Jack as the train approached Madrid. They watched the city's silhouette sharpen into focus, the sinking, blood-red sun reflecting vibrant gold off the centuries-old buildings. They were relieved when the carriage finally arrived in the railyard, inching at a snail's pace through the tangled mass of criss-crossing steel tracks until, with a metallic screeching of brakes, it came to a standstill on Platform Eight of Madrid Railway Station.

'Sofia, how about you and Andrés wait at those seats? I'll get the bags,' Jack suggested, glad to be active at last.

Sofia nodded. 'I'll get Andrés settled and then find the taxi rank – the driver should be able to recommend a decent place for us to stay that's near the station. We need to be back here early tomorrow. The train to Málaga leaves at seven.'

The taxi driver – José, his name badge indicated – was a fine-looking man whose lithe figure moved rapidly, as though he much preferred to be physically active than constrained in a motor vehicle all day. Leaping out of the driver's seat, he loaded their suitcases into the cab's trunk and saw them comfortable before navigating through the

busy peak-hour traffic to arrive, within minutes, outside the broad glass
doors of the Hotel Paseo del Arte. Leaving the engine running, he
assisted them to unload their suitcases. However, after glancing at
Andrés, he directed a comment in rapid-fire Spanish to Sofia: *You
worry about him.* Even Jack understood the gesture when José waved
towards Andrés, who leaned against the open door of the taxi,
breathing heavily.

Jack helped Sofia guide a protesting Andrés into the foyer, where
they seated him. José followed and placed their suitcases beside them
with an expression of kind concern.

'You are leaving for Málaga early, sí? I will return in the morning –
6.15, yes?' he offered.

'That is very early. Are you sure you will be here?' Sofia asked, but
José waved her concerns aside.

'Certainly, Señorita. It will be my pleasure. I will be here, waiting.'

'*Merci.*' Jack found the French response instinctive after months in
Paris, realising his error when José chuckled.

Jack remained with Andrés, relieved to hear his breathing settle
into a normal rhythm as they sat and watched Sofia negotiate rooms
with the hotel concierge, her hands gesticulating rapidly as she spoke
assertively, outlining their needs. He did not understand a word Sofia
spoke, however; her confident demeanour reminded him of the way
she had stepped forward to clarify the details of his and Andrés' exhibition that had been organised by Roger Fry and Gertrude Stein, and he
felt proud to be with her. She was certainly a woman to be reckoned
with.

Within minutes, they were ensconced in a hotel room, neat and
comfortable, its windows overlooking a broad avenue along which
couples strolled arm in arm beneath glowing haloes as the streetlights
flickered into life. A colourful neon light pulsated red and green on the
building directly across from the motel, and the clipping of horse
hooves against the cobblestones drifted in through the open window.
The window was immediately closed; Sofia would take no chances that
Andrés might catch a chill from the cooling evening air.

'How about we see what the hotel offers for dinner?' she asked.

Jack agreed, suddenly realising how hungry he felt, despite having nibbled, throughout the train journey, on dried ham and pickled gherkins and other assorted goodies, from the basket that Aunt Christina had given Andrés and Sofia.

'Go out, you two! Find a restaurant – have dinner. I'll be fine. Enjoy Madrid!' Andrés insisted.

'No, Andrés. We're not leaving you,' Jack replied, as the Parisian doctor's stern insistence that he 'look after his friend' sprang into his mind. Not that he needed anyone to tell him what he should do. Perhaps the doctor assumed they were just another bunch of irresponsible young artists who spent their time intoxicated, carousing the streets of Paris!

'It has been a long day and we need to be up early in the morning,' Sofia reasoned. 'Besides, I know how hard it will be to get you two organised in the early hours! There will be time enough for us all to be gadding about in Málaga soon. Perhaps, in a few months, we might bring Jack back here to Madrid, Andrés. We must take him to the Museo del Prado!'

'Museo del Prado?' Jack asked.

'Spain's national gallery. It's huge and simply wonderful. Has the most amazing collection of paintings from all over Europe. Centuries-old works!'

Andrés nodded, adding, 'You have to see Goya's work, Jack. You'd love his portraits – they are extraordinary. Goya had a sad life... and like Picasso, he painted things as he saw them. Wars, lunatics, fantasy! Strange things, not always nice. Many people do not like his work. Our father... he found it fascinating. He always brought us to the museum whenever we came to Madrid. And he would tell us about Goya – his life – the techniques he used. Sof and I - we, too, think he's amazing.'

Jack nodded with interest, although an unnerving feeling rippled through him. Andrés' description of Goya reminded him of Picasso's experiences and his comment to Jack that, one day, he too would experience grief and sorrow. That then his paintings would not be so 'nice'. That one day he would be able to paint Truth.

Did truth have to be borne of tragedy? Jack wondered. Couldn't nice things be true too? Why did sadness so often surround the lives of artists? Did one really have to experience sorrow to be great? Surely not!

Jack was more than happy to remain in the hotel for dinner for his own reasons. It had been a long day, and in honesty, he looked forward to ensuring that Andrés was comfortable and settled, before joining Sofia in her room for a very long goodnight. It seemed like forever since they had been alone together. And since that moment of madness, when Jack had launched himself onto the train at Gare du Nord, they had much to catch up on. Best done lying close together, he thought, with Sofia held tightly in his arms.

In the end they decided to eat in the hotel's dining room: albondigas - small meatballs in a rich tomato sauce - accompanied by soft, round bread rolls, which they ate with relish, washed down with glasses of Garnacha, a fruity wine that Jack liked instantly. Fatigued by their long journey, their dinner conversation was quiet, and immediately after finishing his meal, Andrés declared it was bedtime for him. Waving away Jack's and Sofia's offers to escort him to his room, he made his way to the lift.

Finally, alone together, Jack found himself a little nervous about what he should say to Sofia. Was she really pleased with his sudden change of heart? Of the way he'd launched onto the train at the last minute and imposed himself into Andrés' and her lives? All of the doubts that had clouded their last week in Paris suddenly resurfaced.

Jack's dark thoughts were quickly dispelled when, upon returning to her room, Sofia leaned up to him, placing her arms around his neck. 'Thank you, Jack. Thank you for staying.' She snuggled against him. 'I don't know what I would have done without you.'

'It's okay, Sofia. I'm sorry. I was dumb. I should never have even planned for you and Andrés to travel alone. I don't know what I was thinking.'

'Well, Jack, you have your job waiting. Your parents will be worried.'

Listening to her words, Jack felt that he must seem like a child to her: he sure seemed to act like one, always worrying about what his parents were thinking.

'They'll just have to worry for a bit longer, Sofia. It will be okay,' he said with conviction. 'Getting you and Andrés home safely is all that matters.'

Sofia's nod of relief was everything Jack could have hoped for, and without thinking, he gathered her into his arms and carried her to the bed. Laying her down, he looked into her eyes, wanting to be sure of her feelings before he continued. Reassured by her smile and the touch of her hands stroking his face, Jack gently undid the buttons of her dress, one by one, following the trail of his fingers with searching lips, his tongue flicking and teasing the fine soft skin. His hands roamed across her shoulders, sweeping the soft fabric of her dress loose before caressing the curve of her breasts. He loved the feeling of her satin-smooth skin against his fingers.

'Sit up, Jack! Let me help,' Sofia said, and he sat forward, allowing her to tug his shirt free, laughing as her soft kisses burrowed into his neck and moved to tickle his ear lobe. As she fumbled with the buttons, he inhaled deeply, tingling at the feel of her hands trailing across his bare chest, before he could stand it no longer. After firmly lifting her from him, Jack settled Sofia onto the bed, and together, their hands took on a mind of their own, searching and caressing each other's bodies, delighting in the closeness of being together. Jack knew with certainty that there was no place in the world he wanted to be more than here, with Sofia in his arms.

CHAPTER 2

*J*ack was relieved to see José chatting to the concierge at the desk when they exited the hotel lift the next morning. Noticing them immediately, the taxi driver stepped forward, reaching for the case that Sofia held. Jack saw the look of concern José cast towards Andrés, and when they stepped onto the pavement where the taxi sat waiting, the attentive driver immediately positioned Andrés in the front passenger seat before helping Jack and Sofia lift their cases into the trunk. It was then that Jack realised that, although he and Sofia were accustomed to Andrés' thinness, his appearance – so pale and gaunt, with the dark shadows under his eyes – was a shock to unsuspecting strangers. José must have drawn his own conclusions as to why three young people would acquire the services of his cab rather than walk the short distance to Málaga Station, clearly visible in the early morning quiet, barely a block away.

Arriving at the station, moments later, José grabbed a stray luggage trolley, unloaded their luggage onto it and wished them a safe journey to Málaga. He shook his head when Sofia offered payment for the cab fare, shrugging and saying that it was hardly worth turning the taxi meter on for such a small distance. Jack marvelled at the kindness of this stranger, who'd gotten out of bed early to ensure that they were safely delivered without mishap. Grateful, they thanked him profusely before turning to join the commuters who were now streaming onto the station's broad concourse. They were well in time for their seven o'clock departure, beginning the final leg of their long journey to southern Spain.

As they travelled to Málaga, the thing Jack noticed most about the scenery were the olives. Ancient, gnarled trees were visible in every direction: extending row-upon-row, across dry, stony flats and perched on the sides of hills. Single trees were positioned as centre-pieces in the front yards of houses. The southern Spanish countryside was a patchwork of small farms connected by narrow ribbons of gravel, along which an occasional donkey-pulled cart moved slowly. While not as spectacular as the snow-capped peaks and plunging valleys in the north, the landscape was still incredibly diverse and picturesque, with its hills and flats punctuated by jagged rock formations that seemed to rise steeply out of nowhere. Some hills were crowned with tall, narrow buildings clustered together, towering steeples rising from their centres, a declaration to the world that the village inhabitants were proud, God-fearing people.

As the train mounted the final slopes to arrive at Granada Station, Sofia pointed out a dust storm rising below them, where two carts converged on the narrow ascending gravel track.

'This will be interesting,' she remarked. 'Some drivers are so stubborn they'd rather fall over the edge than give way on the roads.'

'Roads!' Jack snorted. 'They are scarcely wide enough to take a car! You need to have legs of two different lengths just to stand upright.'

Truly, every road invariably ascended or descended, including those that ran through the village centres. He looked out the window as the train chugged along, fascinated to see people going about their daily tasks. The surrounding buildings reflected multiple hues of white - from blinding sunlit reflections to the purple and grey of those walls in shadow - which were contrasted by a multitude of shutters and doors painted in yellows and greens and blues. Explosive splashes of red and purple erupted from the geraniums and bougainvillaea which cascaded from terracotta pots and spilled over the walls of rooftop terraces.

He was surprised to see an imposing building that rose from the forested area on the edge of the town. Clearly ancient, its pinkish walls glowed in the midday sun, high walls that rose majestically above the town.

'The Alhambra. She's very beautiful, isn't she? "A pearl set in emeralds," they call her.' Andrés' voice, his tone of awe, penetrated Jack's musings.

'Amazing. It's enormous!' Jack replied.

'Very ancient. Ninth century. Once a fortress, then a palace, lived in by sultans and kings, and then, due to neglect, even poor squatters were able to call it home. We saw it only two years ago. Papá said it was a place he had to see before he died and so we came here and it did not disappoint him. Utterly beautiful. Full of amazing artefacts. It's...a little bit of everything. Papá and I made many sketches. I must show them to you.'

'Remember the Moorish inscriptions, Andrés?' Sofia joined in. Turning to Jack, she continued, 'Thousands of tiny symbols lined the walls, the roof, everywhere. And there are domes, walkways and gardens filled with intricate details. Carvings, fountains, pools. So magical! We really must bring Jack here, Andrés!'

'Yes, a place for me to see again before I die!'

'Stop it! You are not going to die! I am not going to listen to you if you keep talking like that.'

Andrés winked at Jack and turned to the window, leaning his head against the backrest. 'Sofia, Sofia. Death comes to us all. You have to accept that.'

'Maybe so, but you and I... We've already had our share of deaths. Now stop talking about dying! Let's be thankful that you're alive after all that we've just been through, not fantasising about your death.'

Jack noted Sofia's sharp response, sensing that Andrés was not actually teasing her, but rather, preparing her for a time when he may not be around. Sofia, her mouth pursed tightly, had shut her eyes. The glimmer of a tear appeared in one corner and he squeezed her hand.

Of course, she does not want to hear of a life without her brother, he considered. She had already lost both of her parents. Andrés was the only family she had. For Sofia, life without him would be an agony beyond contemplation.

CHAPTER 3

*S*ofia and Andrés' excitement was contagious as they entered the outer regions of Malaga in the early afternoon.

'The orange trees will need pruning ...'

'Aunt Jovita said she would leave the key in the pot in the courtyard.'

'I think I'll make up the blue room for Jack.'

All of their conversation was focused on the home they loved, and while many of their comments meant little to Jack, he was pleased to see them so happy. Finally, they stepped off the train at Malaga Station to be greeted by a salty southerly breeze - air that felt lively and fresh after the heavy city odours of Paris and Madrid. Here he was, in the Costa del Sol - Southern Spain, of all places. Andalusian country, Andrés had told Jack only half an hour earlier, explaining the distinctions between Spain's various regions.

'We Spanish have had many influences over the decades – Phoenicians, Romans and Moors – and although sometimes this causes problems, it also makes our lives... interesting. Our beautiful horses, ceramics, tapas and fiestas have their histories. And then, of course, there is the Romani, who share with us their love of singing and dancing.'

And here he was, Jack thought, looking around in wonder. It was incredible, unbelievable even, to know that he was here, so far from home. However, Sofia had no intention of lingering to enjoy the scenery or act as a tour guide. With rapid instructions in the Spanglish to which he was rapidly becoming accustomed, she led them through the turnstiles towards a line of waiting taxis. Her stride was purposeful, and Jack suspected that she was determined to avoid any chance meetings with old friends – her sole focus, rather, to get Andrés home and rested.

In no time at all, they were motoring up a steep incline, twisting around tight bends and passing small groups of oncoming hikers that were making their way down the mountain. Jack held his breath as the vehicle skirted close to the narrow edge of the gravel road, their driver determinedly overtaking a slow-moving wagon that creaked under its load of urns, the enormous contraption hauled by a pair of panting, sweating mules. He returned waves to men and women at work in their yards, who raised their heads and shaded their eyes with leathery hands, squinting curiously at the taxi that was motoring up the hill.

He looked with interest at a golden rock face towering above them which became clearer as they approached it, realising that it was not a natural formation, but rather, stony walls high on the hill that had been built centuries earlier. Another fortress? This must be the castle that Andrés and Sofia had spoken of - the one that they had ran around in, when they were young. Not nearly as imposing as the Alhambra that he'd seen in Granada but, nonetheless, intriguing.

Glimpses of the Mediterranean took on spectacular proportions as their elevated position offered expansive views of the sea, its calm surface dotted with dozens of small boats. Jack searched their decks, sure he could see ant-like movements – evidence of fishermen at work, perhaps.

Gradually, the vehicle slowed and Jack focused his attention on the immediate surroundings. From the roadside, the first indication of the gallery was a small stone wall with a distinctive, colourful sign swinging from an iron stand that marked the entrance gate. Jack recognised the work of Andrés in its bold design - modern, semi-abstract, almost Picasso-like. The minimalist scene portrayed a winding pathway ascending a steep hill towards a small building, a castle behind it, and the words *Toulouse Galleria* printed above in colourful letters.

Turning right, the taxi came to rest in a small area under a sign, *Automovilismo*.

Alighting, Jack looked around. His eyes landed on a shed beside the parked vehicle.

'Suzie lives in there,' Sofia said, catching Jack's gaze, and then turned to Andrés. 'She hasn't been out for a while. I hope that she behaves... You might have to check her...'

Jack tried to recall any mention of a woman called Suzie. Perhaps an aunt? Seeing his puzzled expression, Sofia laughed.

'She's our car, Jack! A huge spluttering, cantankerous *señora* that always pretends she is going to breakdown any minute, but she never has yet. Just keeps us on edge and costs us precious pesetas! A Hispano-Suiza that Papá fell in love with just before he got ill. That's why we call her Suzie.'

Jack nodded as though he understood, but the truth was that now, standing on the threshold of the twin's finca, halfway up a mountain, in the shadow of the castle that loomed above, everything felt unfamiliar and he suddenly, overwhelmingly, felt like a foreigner. Determined to fulfil his mission and be helpful, he grasped a suitcase in each hand before following Sofia through a quaint archway, glimpsing aged stonework behind the tendrils of sweet-smelling jasmine which covered it. They entered a rectangular courtyard, enclosed at the front by the roadside fence and by the white-washed walls of buildings on the other three sides. Jack inhaled deeply - the sweet aroma lingering in the air came from a magnolia tree, he realised - the centrepiece of the small garden, whose limbs extended in every direction. Three wooden tables sat nestled in the shade created by the tree's enormous boughs.

'I won't be a minute. I just want to check the gallery,' Sofia called over her shoulder and fumbled in a pot plant.

'*Voi-la!*' she said, victoriously waving a keyring, and having selected a large iron key, she inserted it into the ancient lock with a deft wiggle. The door swung open and Sofia beckoned Jack to enter the darkened room. Deceptively small from the outside, the low-set gallery's interior was large and open, barn-like, with rustic timber beams criss-crossing high above. Jack looked out through leaded windows into the courtyard they had just left – a delightful setting just waiting to be painted, he thought.

Rows of paintings filled the walls and the four large tables distributed through the centre of the room were loaded with brightly coloured ceramic bowls, leather belts and baskets. After glancing around, Sofia turned, evidently satisfied that the gallery had not succumbed to any disaster in her absence.

'We'd better check the studio, too,' she called over her shoulder.

Andrés looked at Jack and shrugged. 'She's mad about the place,' he said. 'Thinks the gallery and studio are more important than the house, really. Look at her – she's forgotten all about me - an ill man, gasping for breath out here, exhausted after days of rattling through Spain!'

Sofia looked at him sharply, and he laughed.

'Go on,' he said. 'I'm all right. I'll survive another five minutes, I suppose!'

'I'll only be one minute, Andrés. Are you sure you're okay?'

'I'm fine... Don't you worry about me...worry about Jack! He looks like he might collapse, lugging those cases about after you!'

Sofia laughed. 'Put them down, Jack. You don't need to keep carrying them!'

'Ma'am, I am at your service. I came to carry your bags and that is what I'll do, even if my arms get dragged out of their sockets in the effort.'

Chuckling, Sofia led the way to the second white-walled building. Slightly smaller in overall dimensions, it mirrored the first in design.

Clearly, this was the art studio. Sofia looked around approvingly, although she did not comment, still on a mission to ensure that the buildings that they had left over six months earlier were safe and sound.

'This old building was once a storage shed. Almost in ruins, when we were little. Papá was teaching at the time, determined to fulfil his dream to have an art school here. So, he put a new roof on, built some shelves and was in business.' Jack could hear the pride in Andrés' voice.

'Didn't the children love him?' Sofia said softly. 'He was such a good teacher. "Paint me a masterpiece," he'd say to the children. And they did. He'd frame their best paintings and hang them all in the gallery. Invite their parents up for *exhibicións*.'

Andrés nodded. 'Hundreds of children came here. See their little easels?' He pointed to a pile packed against a wall in the corner.

Jack imagined those happy days in the twins' lives, not so many years ago, when the children of Malaga had ventured up the hill to learn charcoal drawing and oil painting from the man with a gift for developing a love of art in the very young. He'd never thought of teaching other people's children how to paint, but often imagined how good it would be to have a child of his own to show everything he'd learned.

Leaving the studio, Andrés finally succumbed to fatigue, resting on a bench in the courtyard. Jack sat with him while Sofia went hunting for the key to the house. Shutting his eyes, Jack tilted his head back and inhaled the sweet smell of the magnolia flowers, revelling in the sensation of their intoxicating aroma. Insects chirped and warm sunlight filtered through the leaves and onto his face. He thought that this place was, perhaps, the loveliest he had ever known.

Sofia's call jolted Jack back to reality. 'It's open!'

She turned her attention to her brother. 'Are you okay, Andrés? Do you need to rest? How about I freshen up your bed and you have a sleep?'

'Ah, now my matron finally worries about me! I could have

collapsed in the courtyard and you wouldn't have even noticed, fussing about the gallery and studio as though they were the most important things in the world.'

'You were all right, Andrés. Jack was looking after you,' Sofia said, even as she looked a little guilty. 'He would have come to your rescue if you needed anything. Would you like a cup of tea?'

'No, I'm fine... I want to see what's been happening in the orchard while we've been away. But first, we must show Jack the house!'

Leading him through the downstairs living area, Andrés was talkative, clearly delighted to be back in his own home. 'Here is the lounge... and here is the kitchen. This is Sofia's palace. We have to do what she tells us to do here!'

'I'm always happy to help in the kitchen, especially if it means I get to eat Sofia's *tortilla española* and *croquetas*,' Jack replied.

He was conscious of the coolness and light that filled the rooms. An aroma of citrus permeated through the air, and the gleaming surfaces suggested that the rooms had been cleaned, recently. The floors captured Jack's interest. The deep red clay tiles were set in a diagonal pattern, broken by a scattering of heavy cotton rugs. Rugs that were woven in intricate, colourful designs unlike anything that he had ever seen.

'The trees should be full of oranges... Ours are the juiciest in all of Spain, Jack. You will love them!' Reaching the back door, Andrés indicated for Jack to follow him outside, where together they stood, silently absorbing the view. It was breathtaking. Beyond the small level area along the back of the house, the land fell away into a deep valley. The small orchard of orange trees he'd heard so much about clung to the left side of the steep decline, and as Andrés predicted, bright oranges could be seen, nestled amongst shiny green leaves. To the right were rows of gnarled, scraggly trees – the finca's olive plantation.

Joined by Sofia, Jack followed Andrés along the first row of orange trees. It had been cut into steps, which made picking the fruit a lot easier, Jack guessed. Selecting a couple of oranges from the branches overhead, Andrés tossed one to Jack. Its thick skin was warm to touch and when peeled, exposed golden segments that dripped with juice as soon as he separated them. Turning, Jack passed a piece directly into Sofia's mouth and then followed with a piece into his own, leaning his head back and savouring the taste with pleasure. 'So sweet! And juicy! You may be right, Andrés. Perhaps they are the best oranges in Spain... maybe the world! They are definitely the sweetest that I have ever eaten.'

'Papa was forever growing things,' Sofia said. 'Anything. He always was keen to try exotic vegetables and herbs – collected seeds everywhere we went. He and our mother planted the orange grove when they first bought the property back in 1903. The olive plantation was already here – it was decades old when they came.'

They returned to the back of the house, where vegetable gardens - their edges defined by lengths of timber - filled most of the level area. Utterly overgrown, they had obviously been neglected in the twins' absence. Sofia squatted and she began removing weeds with unconscious ease and a wry expression.

'Just as I expected,' she said, shrugging. 'I keep these going for Papá. Andrés and I don't need this much food, but...well...I like it out here. It is when I'm here that I feel Papá most.'

Andrés nodded. 'Yes, he certainly loved this garden. I think it was to here he came, to clear his head. Especially when we were young! It was his quiet place. I always felt that Papá must have been thinking of Mamá when he pottered here in the cool of the evening.'

'Yes,' Sofia continued. 'I used to think he seemed sad, but somehow complete, when he was gardening. And I felt like I was interrupting him if I ever needed to bother him for something. It was like he was having a conversation with someone inside his head.'

'Probably asking Mamá how to manage us!' Andrés suggested. 'It must have been hard at times, rearing us two children, on his own.'

Jack listened, conscious of the nostalgia that had settled over Andrés and Sofia. He felt an intruder on their thoughts, even though it was to him that they were speaking. Yes, it would have been difficult for their father, he imagined; however, it also must have been hard for

Sofia and Andrés. Growing up, envisioning the mother they'd never seen, her presence lingering in their father's memories and throughout the rooms of their home, and yet never having had a chance to know her.

'What do you grow here?' Jack asked, thinking perhaps he could lend a hand to Sofia to get the garden cleared and planted again.

'Oh, spinach, carrots, potatoes, onions. Beans. Strawberries, sometimes. Anything, really. And just like Papá did, we always put any excess produce on the table out by the front gate. Most of it for free, or perhaps for a few pesos. Occasionally we take a load down to Malaga. "There is always someone who can use a few extra vegetables," Papá always told us.'

They returned inside. Sofia put the kettle on and was thrilled to discover the biscuit tin that had been left out on the bench was filled with fresh churros, which she immediately set out on plates to accompany their tea.

She read aloud from the note propped beside the tin.

Welcome home, Sofia and Andrés,
I hope that you have had a comfortable journey and expect that you are both exhausted and ready to collapse after such a long trip. I will call by tomorrow morning and update you on the gallery news. In the fridge you will find a bowl of gazpacho, some chicken paella and some torrijas. Also, there is a jug of milk in the refrigerator and a fresh loaf of bread in the urn. That should get you by for dinner.
Sleep well. I look forward to hearing all about your Paris adventure and checking to see that you, Andrés, have made a full recovery.
Love,
Aunt Jovita xx

'Oh, she is so kind, isn't she, Andrés?' Sofia said as she opened the fridge door to reveal the contents as described in the note. She explained to Jack, 'All our lives, Aunt Jovita has looked out for us. We are very thankful to have her. Plus, she loves to care for the gallery at any opportunity, which is wonderful – she and our cousin, Stefan. It makes our lives so much easier if we ever need to be away. I would never have been able to go to Paris with Andrés if it wasn't for them.'

'And that would have been terrible,' Jack agreed, smiling at Sofia, meaningfully.

Immediately after their tea, Andrés agreed that he would go to his room and rest for an hour, in which time Sofia prepared a bed for Jack in the second of the two small rooms beside the stairwell. Together, they lay on the small single mattress, holding each other tightly as they drifted off to sleep, waking over an hour later to find the room bathed in the deep red of the setting sun, to the sound of Andrés descending the stairs. Rising, they joined him and Jack helped Sofia prepare the table for dinner.

The next morning, as Jack helped Sofia tidy the kitchen following their breakfast, the sound of voices drifted across the courtyard through the kitchen window.

'Andrés, it's Aunt Jovita and Stefan,' Sofia called before running outside. Jack smiled as he listened to her incomprehensible torrent of Spanish words as she greeted the visitors. Within seconds, Sofia returned, her arm around a sweet-looking older lady whom she introduced as Aunt Jovita, Papá's sister, and following them, their cousin, Stefan, who was a tall good-looking man with shiny black hair and a broad smile. It was obvious from their enthusiastic chatter that they'd enjoyed their time tending to the gallery, opening its doors from Tuesdays through to Sundays, from ten am to two pm, and that there was much to catch up on. Although they glanced with curiosity at Jack, it was the sight of Andrés, with his pale skin and weight loss, that dominated their conversation as Sofia made a fresh pot of tea. Jack politely escaped into the garden, where he found a small hoe and started hefting weeds from an overgrown bed, allowing Sofia and Andrés to catch up on gallery business and share the details of their time in Paris with their relatives, without feeling the need to maintain a constant flow of English translations for his benefit.

∼

Very quickly, Jack adjusted to the new rhythm of living with Sofia and Andrés and was sure that he'd never been happier. He watched with pride as Sofia commanded the day-to-day affairs with efficiency – meals, shopping, bills and decisions about maintenance of the finca all came easily to her.

Each morning, she rose from the small bedroom below the stairs at daybreak to fry potatoes and onions, to which she added beaten eggs, pepper and salt to make the *tortilla española* which had quickly become Jack's favourite. It was obvious how much Sofia loved her kitchen, relishing her role as its mistress, and enjoying nothing more than to set to work at the large benches, combining fresh ingredients to create meals for the three of them, or to cook for the gallery. Rising with her, Jack had developed his own morning ritual of going out to the orchard to select eight oranges, which he would cut and squeeze for juice to accompany their breakfast. During the first week, Sofia carried a glass of the juice upstairs to Andrés, encouraging him to stay in bed for a little more sleep; however, in no time at all, Andrés began appearing outside, helping Jack to collect the oranges. 'I am right, mate,' Jack said to him. 'Have a bit of a lie in. It will do you good.'

'Jack, I will get all the rest that I need when I am dead, but for now, I'd rather be up, enjoying the mornings, while I can.' Jack nodded, uncomfortably, not sure what he should say.

Over breakfast, their day would be planned – for the first couple of hours Andrés and Jack dedicated to work on the finca, while Sofia prepared fresh food for the gallery's café. Without doubt, it was she who provided practical guidance for the farming activities.

'I think we need to set the stakes for the tomatoes,' she'd suggest to Andrés and Jack, or she would ask, 'Andrés, have you seen the pruning shears? I'd like to tidy the jasmine in the courtyard.'

Always easy-going, Andrés accepted Sofia's direction, winking at Jack as he playfully grumbled at her bossy manner.

Following breakfast, Andrés and Jack helped Sofia tidy the kitchen before heading out to the garden and Jack was surprised to find how much he enjoyed working on the terraced landscape, amid the rows of trees. The large steps, Andrés explained, not only allowed for easy movement as Jack had thought, but they also conserved precious moisture in the ground and encouraged the growth of legumes – clovers and vetches - which improved the land's fertility by fixing nitrogen into the stony soil.

Jack quickly become adept at balancing on the ladder, his shoulders bearing a canvas bag which he filled with oranges. Their tantalizing aroma combined with the tangy smell of sea salt on the autumn breeze made for pleasant work, and as he reached for the ripe fruit on the upper boughs of the trees, he and Andrés maintained a happy banter, calling back and forth to each other. Andrés, in his convalescent state, was resigned to pottering at ground level, picking up fallen fruit, shifting the small stepladders, inspecting the trees for signs of insect damage and making Jack laugh with humorous depictions of his and Sofia's childhood.

Where Sofia was very practical with the day-to-day decisions around the finca, Andrés was clearly more of a dreamer, his art his priority and his mind no doubt occupied by thoughts of his next painting. Jack was quite sure he would forget to eat if Sofia did not prompt him. However, to Jack's surprise, Andrés revealed a deep interest in Spain's political news as well as the local Malagian community events. Over breakfast he read *El Debate*, the newspaper delivered to the finca each morning, and laughingly recounted amusing stories, such as a donkey's frenzied dash through the streets of Frigiliana during their village festival, half a dozen men in hot pursuit - a spectacle that ended when the distraught beast finally turned into the courtyard of a local bakery, where the shrewd baker's wife had the foresight to shut the gate on the men's faces and calm the donkey by feeding it apples. That week, customers would not be buying the *empanada de Manzana*, the delicious apple pies the baker was famous for, the article concluded in a sombre tone, as though relaying details of a national tragedy.

Spanish politics was an unwelcome topic at the breakfast table, for Sofia refused to listen to tales of gloom. This however, did not stop Andrés from expressing his thoughts. Declaring outrage at the tales of poverty or snorting in disgust when reading stories about Miguel Primo de Rivera, the Spanish prime minister who had ruled Spain for the last seven years – badly, Andrés believed – and who was now trying to deflect the rise of Republicans who were demanding improved conditions for the Spanish working classes.

'It will be okay, Andrés, don't be so upset,' Sofia would say when his passion escalated, but he would shake his head.

'It is all very well "not to get upset," Sofia. That would be good for everybody, sí, but staying calm is not going to feed the poor, nor pacify the military nor satisfy the elitists, that is for certain.'

Jack could not comprehend the complexity of the Spanish regions or the issues that mattered to Andrés, but when he asked Sofia, she just shrugged and shook her head. He soon realised that her mind was on the world of the orchards and gallery, not concerns that stirred beyond the boundaries of the Toulouse Galleria.

Between ten and half-past each morning, Sofia called Jack and Andrés from the garden to the kitchen which, by this time, was usually infused with the aroma of freshly baked *tarta de Santiago*, a moist orange-flavoured cake, or *almendrados*, the sweet almond biscuits they loved. The ritual was always the same.

'No! No more!' she'd say, feigning annoyance and slapping their hands away from the trays. 'You are meant to be carrying them over to the gallery for our customers, not eating them!'

'Well, you've been making us slave away in the garden...' they responded, making a show of rubbing tired muscles, lamenting that their delicate artists' hands were being damaged by the manual labour that Sofia – *la jefa* – had ordered them to do.

'Hah! Two hours in the garden and you complain you are tired! What is the world coming to?' she'd say, tutting and shaking her head.

After helping Sofia to carry the trays across to the gallery, they all sat at a table under the magnolia tree for their own morning tea, which inevitably included treats from her baking. They'd discuss the progress of artwork and gallery business. Plans were made: they'd move the centre display tables farther to the left, which would allow for two more small tables inside the café area for diners who preferred to escape the heat of summer; Andrés wanted to update some of the paintings he had displayed in the gallery; they'd create some wall space for Jack's paintings. Following morning tea, it was time for Jack and Andrés to head into the studio to start their day's painting, while Sofia busied herself opening the gallery to visitors.

CHAPTER 4

*W*orking alongside Andrés, Jack could not help but notice the changes in his friend since they'd arrived home. He sensed an aura of completeness. Peace. Safely home, and despite a lingering weakness, Andrés had regained his command. He diminished Sofia's fussing when he coughed or yawned, chiding her by saying, 'I am not dead yet, Sofia. Time to worry about my coffin later. For now, let me live.'

With great pride, he showed Jack the body of artwork their papá had accumulated over three decades, now carefully stored in large flat boxes. Jack admired the paintings that had been completed by the twins' father – a legacy of a man with extraordinary talent. Brilliant landscapes, portraits which captured subtle moments of daily life: a farmer nudging his dairy cattle along a gravel road; small children – possibly Andrés and Sofia – with sleepy eyes, heads close together as they read from the same book; the same two children, this time flying a kite in the yard. Seascapes and landscapes. Paintings of a laughing woman, her face glowing with the same delicate beauty as Sofia's. In one, her left arm held a basket of freshly picked oranges, her right hand outstretched towards the artist, offering a peeled segment, its juice dripping from her fingers. Their mother? Perhaps an orange from their first crop?

In the second box were works by other Spanish artists, layers of paintings separated by transparent sheets. Jack, far more schooled in critiquing artworks these days, recognised the quality and diversity of the collection. There were some Picassos, which did not surprise Jack - given the friendship between that great artist and the twins' father, decades earlier. A pair of paintings caught Jack's eye - strange abstract figures unlike anything he'd seen. These had been purchased in Barcelona years earlier from Joan Miro. Andrés told him. They were in the style of Surrealism, deliberately expressing images that were ridiculous and random. Surrealist art was born of dreams and imaginings, Andrés, ever-knowledgeable of the modern art movements, explained to Jack. He explained how many surrealist artists followed the theories of the psychoanalyst, Freud, and shared a belief in the power of the unconscious mind. Surrealists opposed society's rational ideals, which they blamed for leading the world into war and destruction.

Jack shrugged as he listened to Andrés' explanation, sure that there were some things about art that he would never understand.

However, one series of works captured his attention so much that he could not stop looking at them, convinced that he'd seen no paintings more beautiful. Women and children strolling along the beach and playing in the waves. The settings of these extraordinary scenes reminded Jack of the beach in Brighton where his parents used to take him swimming on hot summer days when he was a child. He looked at the name in the corner – Joachim Sorolla.

Andrés agreed that these paintings were special, very much loved by his father, who had developed a friendship with Sorolla many years earlier. The paintings were of the artist's own family, painted on the shores of Valencia where they'd a holiday home. Jack marvelled at the delicacy of the brush strokes, sure that he had never seen paint reflect brilliant light and glimmering water so well, and he determined that one day he would create paintings of his own family, equal to these.

A series of bright modern works on the wall of the gallery also captured his interest. He accurately guessed these to be made by Andrés, who, in response to Jack's request, showed his full portfolio, demonstrating the changes his work had taken over time in both techniques and influences. A series of paintings that Jack now easily identified as Cubist was outstanding. Depictions of Malaga from all angles – viewed from above, from the shoreline looking back towards the town, in streetscapes and landscapes. Although Picasso's influence was evident in these semi-abstract canvases, the vibrant combinations of colour were Andrés' own: warm-bodied reds and oranges set startlingly against purples and blues. Andrés admitted that they sold well to the tourist trade. Jack looked at him with renewed respect. He had long understood Andrés' earnest commitment to his painting. Notwithstanding, to see the tangible fruits of Andrés' labour laid out before him was inspiring – evidence of years of hard work and passion, ever seeking to trial techniques and improve.

In comparison, Jack felt like an amateur and was desperate to pick up his brushes and advance his own skills. Certainly, his lessons with Monsieur Simon and visits to galleries across Paris had opened his eyes. Jack felt he could now write a thesis on the techniques, both historical and contemporary, that artists had available to them. However, he knew that being a master artist was not about what he knew, but rather, about applying paint to paper. Jack itched to put all that he had learned into serious practice; to create masterpieces of portraiture that had the beauty and finesse of Sorolla's paintings.

In the first week, Andrés had cleared a space in the studio for Jack to work beside a large window where natural light poured into the room. He found an enormous free-standing easel that would hold the largest of canvases, as well as a smaller one for Jack to position on the bench. Opening cupboards and drawers, he'd then shown Jack where stores of canvas, stretching timbers and tacks could be found, as well as tubes of oils and bottles of spirits. Jack nodded appreciatively, but was determined to travel into Malaga and purchase some supplies of his own at the first opportunity. Paints were expensive, by any standard, and he did not want to be using Andrés' precious supplies while he was here.

He noticed a series of paintings, matadors teasing large bulls, that appeared half-finished and had evidently lain dormant for the last few months.

'You were painting these three at once?'

'Yes, it is easier, really... I can move between them, adding a dab here and there. It is quicker and the overall effect tends to look better when the paintings are finished and on the gallery's wall. Saves me mixing up the same colours all of the time. Tourists love them. We sell them by the hundreds! Sofia hates me painting the bull-fights but these, as with the dancers, are the paintings that pay our bills.'

He showed Jack dozens more, laid out neatly between tissue paper in a large drawer. The subjects were classic Spain: flamenco dancers with colourful skirts twirling, flying feet kicking, hands aloft bearing castanets – the blur of blue and red, merged together, creating a sense of motion; enormous bulls with rippling muscles and powerful shoulders, pawing the ground, ready to charge; matadors in bejewelled vests who taunted the magnificent beasts with waving capes; the Castillo Gibralfaro, bedded into the side of the ancient mountain, an enduring symbol of defence for the residents of Malaga, its high stone walls appearing solid despite the ravage of centuries. And then of course there were seascapes featuring the endless, blue, cloudless sky and hot sun hovering over the sparkling turquoise of the Mediterranean, colourful boats dotting its surface.

Jack nodded with interest as Andrés explained how the paintings could be rolled into small transportable cardboard tubes. The fact that they were easy to mail home or be carried in luggage without being damaged made them the ideal souvenir for tourists.

～

Determined to contribute to the gallery stock, Jack had wandered along the dusty track and across the hillside, searching for suitable subject matter. Of course, there were the sea and the castle, but already Andrés was working with those subjects. Catching sight of a large rooster, splendid with its deep red and gold plumes, meandering along the road edge pecking at grubs, he suddenly knew exactly what he'd paint. Roosters, donkeys and horses.

His drawing skills made this easy work and he enjoyed experimenting with strong, bold, earthy colours that were fitting for the rural landscape, bathed in the glow of Spain's bright sunlight. Showing these paintings to Sofia a few days later, Jack was pleased when she responded with delight. 'They are wonderful, Jack! Just the sort of pictures that our tourists love!'

Andrés looked on, nodding. 'Huh. Soon you will be selling more paintings than I do,' he grunted with a smile.

Jack was also determined to bring the quiet beauty of the courtyard to life with pen and ink, and in the late afternoon after the gallery had closed its doors to tourists, when Andrés was resting and Sofia busy with paperwork, he created small drawings of the stone walls, arches, terracotta pots and jasmine spilling onto mosaic tiles.

'They're so sweet, Jack. Draw me some more,' Sofia insisted, claiming them and immediately setting them up on the gallery's broad counter.

'Guess what just happened?' she said the next afternoon, bursting into the studio where Jack and Andrés were painting. 'Your postcard – it's been sold!'

'Sold?'

'Yes, five pesos!'

'You are giving my masterpieces away for five pesos! How is that ever going to make me a famous artist?' Jack asked with a frown, at the same time thrilled to be contributing to the finca's finances.

Sofia took in his frown with a concerned expression. 'Jack, it's a postcard.' she said feebly.

'No, Sof, I'm joking. That is great news. I guess I can put up with sitting in the courtyard every afternoon, getting fat on your churros while I slave away with pen and ink to keep the tourists supplied with postcards!'

Encouraged, Jack continued with his small sketches, including the charming sign swinging over the front entrance as well as an expansive view of the gallery as seen from a hill just down the road. They immediately proved popular. Some visitors even purchased half a dozen at a time. While seated at the courtyard tables, sipping tea and eating sweet biscuits or savoury tapas, they would write messages to their friends and families far away. Jack was chuffed to have his postcards sent across Europe and beyond.

Even though it was late autumn, the sun remained pervasive, its grasping tentacles reaching through bedroom windows and prompting residents into wakefulness and activity at an early hour.

At two PM each afternoon, Sofia closed the gallery for siesta – the time when the population of Spain called children indoors, closed blinds, shut their shops and retired to their beds for a brief nap. Jack was incredulous when he heard that workplaces shut their doors in the afternoons, every day.

'Why?'

'If you knew the scorching heat of summer, Jack, then you would not be asking 'why?'' exclaimed Sofia.

'Well, Victoria gets pretty darned hot, too,' Jack retorted, remembering days when temperatures soared above one hundred degrees Fahrenheit. 'Nobody there goes and lies down! Mind you, many a time as schoolchildren, we wished our teachers would go home. Trying to learn maths and write Latin verbs with perspiration dripping off our brows was not fun at all.'

However, he had no trouble adjusting to the tradition of siesta, enjoying the afternoon rest with Sofia wrapped in his arms, Andrés resting in his room upstairs. On particularly hot days, Jack and Sofia took the blanket from Jack's bed and spread it under the trees at the top of the orchard, where the swaying boughs offered welcome relief from the blazing sun.

~

Spain's rustic earthiness appealed to Jack's senses. He never tired of gazing at the rugged landscape interspersed with rocky outcrops springing from rubble. The sun on his back enlivened him when he stripped his off shirt and worked with Andrés in the orchard each morning, inhaling the air that seemed infused with the dust of a parched earth, its taste like iron in his mouth. However, by lunchtime the afternoon breeze infused a tangy saltiness into the air. The smell reminded Jack of summer days on Brighton Beach back in Australia.

There was a dairy half-way down the hill. Not the milking-cow type of dairy that was common around Victoria, but rather, a dairy that milked goats, something that Jack had never heard of.

'Goats! Can humans even drink their milk!' It just seemed so strange.

'Yes, Jack. Of course, we can. I have been drinking it all my life. And we eat cheese from the dairy, too. Goats are far better suited to Malaga's dry, rocky, mountainous surrounds than cows would ever be. In fact – Malaga is quite famous for its dairy products.'

The dairy was owned by a kindly old couple, Salvador and Jacinta who loved to chat with Sofia, and every second evening, they'd walk hand-in-hand along the road with the milk urn, watching the sun as it drifted low into the sea, sending the water ablaze with reds and pinks and mauves and deep crimson, dappled with blinding streaks of silver.

All manner of wildflowers erupted haphazardly along the fence-lines. Sofia frequently picked them for the tables in the courtyard.

'Weeds,' Jack insisted as he trudged beside her, the heavy milk urn in his arms.

'Wildflowers,' she replied, filling her arms with as many as she could manage.

Jack mused that the colourful glory of flowers littering the roadside would never be tolerated on the suburban streets of South Yarra. There, flowers were ascribed to neat rows in thoughtfully designed garden beds that were edged with strips of concrete or brickwork to demarcate their rightful place. 'Any plant foolish enough to peep out of a cracked pavement or outside a fence-line would have its' head lopped off in an instant,' he explained to Sofia, with a clap of his hands to emphasise the brutality of the slaying. However, he could not help thinking, the gardens of South Yarra felt somehow poorer for the absence of these charming intruders erupting from cracks and crevices along the roadside.

At least once a week, Andrés revved up Suzie's engine and the three of them piled in, then veered down the windy road into Malaga to do their shopping. It was an enjoyable drive, albeit very steep, and Jack was always fascinated by the sights along the route: cows tied along the roadside to graze where the grass was a little sweeter, huge sows laying in the shade with a dozen piglets scrambling over them, an assortment of fowl pecking the ground as they wandered freely, oblivious to the wagons drawn by mules and assortment of motor vehicles traversing the narrow gravel road.

CHAPTER 5

*J*ack had been in Malaga for almost seven weeks when their morning tea break was interrupted by a light honk from the postman's van.

'*Buenos días, señor,*' the postman said, appearing through the gate and approaching Jack with the excited tone of someone who had particularly good news to share. He continued in a rush of Spanish, which Sofia rapidly interpreted for Jack, who was struggling to keep up with the speed of the story. The postman had remembered his meeting with Jack, here at the *galería*, a few weeks earlier, and by Jack's fair hair, he had known, *instantáneamente*, he was a newcomer to this part of the world. From that chance meeting, he'd been able to solve a *rompecabezas* - puzzle-, deducing the destination of a mysterious well-worn envelope that had sat at the Malaga post office for the last week, intriguing many with the *sellos* that revealed its long, convoluted journey from Australia.

The postman's co-workers had almost returned the letter, reversing its voyage all the way back to Australia – indeed, the word *desconocida* was visible - scrawled across the envelope in red ink. However, the quick-witted postman standing before them had intervened, retrieving the letter, convinced that he knew where it belonged.

Clearly thrilled with himself, the postman no doubt anticipated admiration and praise for his sleuthing skills, perhaps even a tip to reward his quick thinking. Instead he was compensated with a startled expression on Jack's face that quickly transformed to one of guilt and an awkwardly muttered *gracias*.

The letter felt heavy in his hand, and aware that Sofia's eyes were upon him, Jack felt self-conscious. For weeks he'd blatantly disregarded the nagging voice within his head, reminding him that he needed to write to his parents and update them on his movements. That was the problem - there was no plan at present, and that was how Jack liked it. Living from day to day, oblivious to the responsibilities awaiting him at home. No, not oblivious to his responsibilities, for indeed they had prodded his consciousness from time to time. Rather, he'd deferred acting on them, and now he was suddenly confronted with the fact that, in procrastinating, he had totally overlooked the shock his parents would have experienced when they'd received the telegram, hastily written from Cerbère, announcing that he was delaying his return for yet a third time. Ignored that such news would have been both alarming and embarrassing to them. Furthermore, Jack felt guilty in the knowledge that his telegram had been a lie. Not the part about delaying his return – that was certainly a fact – but the reason for the delay. Yes, he had supported Sofia as she transported Andrés home. However, the undisclosed truth of the matter, the honest reason that he'd gone to Spain, was because he was in love and could not have left Sofia even if he'd wanted to.

'Are you okay, Jack?' Sofia asked, interrupting his reverie. 'Is there a problem?'

'No. No, it is okay. I think I will find a quiet spot to read this.' Jack felt like a child suddenly. One about to be told off by his parents and he decided that he'd prefer to avoid an audience as he absorbed his mother's reprimand.

Making his way to the back of the finca, Jack settled on the bench at the top of the orchard and examined the tattered envelope.

The original handwriting was barely decipherable; the postage stamps on the upper right corner of the envelope, a poignant reminder of the world that Jack had, to all appearances, abandoned. These images of King George had been defaced by a series of additional inky stamps, evidence of its well-travelled life: from Australia to the Passage Dantzig, where Mimi would have faithfully forwarded it to his aunt and uncle's in London, the contact details that Jack had provided to her when he first arrived in Paris, and from there it had been re-addressed in his aunt's neat handwriting: C/O Malaga Post Office, Spain.

Opening the envelope and reading, his mother's words, although vastly obsolete given Jack's changed circumstances, cut through time and distance. Clearly, she had not received his telegram announcing his trip to Spain at the time of writing, nor either of the brief messages that he'd sent to them since – barely a page each, saying little more than that Malaga was a pleasant city with beautiful views of the sea, Andrés was slowly recovering, and some polite questions about how things were at home. This letter, its words simmering with remonstrations, was a response to the first letter he had hastily written almost three months earlier, the one where he'd advised his parents of Andrés' illness, and were so vivid that she may as well have been standing before him.

'How on earth can you, a foreigner who speaks neither French or Spanish, be of any real support to the poor twins? Surely they have family on hand who are far more suited to assist them?' Jack fought back a stab of guilt as he absorbed her neatly written words. *'When Andrés is fit and ready to return to his home in Spain, you must book your passage on the Ormonde and return to Australia immediately. Mr Gilmore has kindly agreed to hold your position at Goldsbrough Mort & Co through to October. We are extremely grateful for this as the*

troubles in America have spread across the world and many workers here have being laid off.'

Jack had heard about the world-wide economic woes, having listened to Andrés' accounts of stock market crashes, businesses closures and high unemployment. However, the Spanish version of American problems, translated in Andrés' accented English, had held little significance to Jack. Furthermore, he and Sofia, whose mind was firmly fixed on finca business, were happily distracted by the joys of their romance and it had been easy to disregard Andrés' postulations of the doom that was sweeping the world, as well as those he believed were about to befall Spain.

Continuing to read his mother's words, Jack's conscience prickled uncomfortably.

'You must realise, it has been a little awkward for us to ask Mr Gilmore to hold the position open for you a second time. Please do not delay your return any longer than necessary.'

Jack shuddered, knowing that, since writing this letter, his mother would have received the telegram announcing his spontaneous decision to accompany the twins on their journey home. Even so, he doubted that they would have a picture of his present existence: residing high above Malaga, painting his days away and living a simple village life, with no immediate thoughts of returning to Australia.

Jack reflected that now, with the twins settled in their finca, Andrés' health stable and a host of friends on hand to provide support to the twins if it was needed, there was no reason why he couldn't embark on the long trip home. He could even be back by October if he made haste. That was if he wanted to return - and he knew for certain that he didn't.

He would have to write a reply. Immediately. The trouble was that he had no idea what to tell them. Furthermore, Jack felt embarrassed by the tone of his mother's letter. Later that afternoon when Sofia asked him how his parents were, he simply said that they were well and missing him. What else could he say?

CHAPTER 6

O ver the next week Jack sensed a change in Sofia's manner - so subtle, he thought he was imagining it at first. At night, she continued to come to his room and hold him tight. However, her kisses seemed to have an urgency that confused Jack. He, in turn, loved her back, although he found himself increasingly tongue-tied, convinced that she was using the passion of their nights together to bid him goodbye without saying the words.

Hoping that he was just imagining things, Jack tried to push his fears aside. He loved Sofia, and she, him.

But, for as much as Jack tried to behave normally, a feeling of awkwardness crept into his conversations with her and his words started to feel forced and unnatural. Simple discussions about harvesting olives or handing over a fresh pile of postcards that he'd completed seemed strained. Periods of silence followed their lovemaking. Where he'd once reached for Sofia's hand naturally as they lay together, he started to hold back, unsure of what she wanted. The silence rattled him. But even more distressing were the things that Sofia said.

'So, Jack, your parents will be expecting you home soon?' she queried towards the end of his ninth week.

Jack started at the bluntness of her words, and then shrugged in response, overwhelmingly aware that his parents most certainly were expecting him home. However, he was surprised to hear Sofia echo their expectations.

'What are you thinking you will do...?' she'd continued. 'You have your job waiting for you. Your parents will be thinking something has happened if you don't contact them.'

'I'll contact them soon,' Jack replied, a flatness descending on him as he contemplated the return journey. More than that, though, it was Sofia's hint that he should be going home. What was she saying? Did she want him to go? Was he overstaying his welcome? Perhaps now that she and Andrés were back on the finca, together in their own home, she'd had second thoughts about their future together.

Certainly, there seemed to be no shortage of young Spanish men who would love to take Sofia out. Every week, one old friend or another had popped by the finca to welcome Sofia and Andrés home. Friendly women, their dark eyes flashing, who were clearly curious about Jack's relationship with Sofia. Their pealing giggles and comments spoken in Spanish, indiscernible to Jack, rang through the open windows of the studio while he and Andrés worked. Andrés occasionally smiled at him and shrugged, and Jack wondered what they were saying that was so amusing.

Then there were the male visitors, stylish with their pleated pants and snowy white shirts, blue-black hair slick and gleaming, their smiles dazzling as they hugged both Andrés and Sofia in turn and warily shook hands with Jack. He felt their eyes upon him, summing up his presence. Suspicious of him, the foreigner? Questioning his motives? Jack could not tell, and while he did his best to maintain the open, friendly manner that came naturally to him, he did feel uncomfortable. At times, he inwardly smouldered at their comments, incomprehensible as they were to him.

One man, Mario, had visited three times now, and here he was again, today. Jack found himself seething, just thinking about him. What did he want? Initially Jack had assumed Mario was Andrés' friend, since he'd hugged Andrés close and patted him on his back when he'd first arrived. However, on each visit he'd made his way over to the gallery and chatted with Sofia before leaving. Stayed for far too long. Right now, Jack could hear his booming laughter drifting from the kitchen through to the garden, and then silence. What did the silence mean?

Fuming, as he watered the spinach seedlings he and Sofia had planted two weeks earlier, Jack heard a scrape of boots on the brick path behind him. Refusing to turn, he continued watering.

'So, Jack. You are an…Australian…yes?' Mario's English was halting.

'Yeah, mate.' Jack turned and met Mario's gaze, replying with what he hoped was relaxed ease, even as his hands clenched. *Of course he was Australian.* Hadn't Mario been told that, the very day that Andrés had introduced him to Jack. He forced back a sudden desire to hit someone. He who'd never been in a fight in his life. 'South Yarra, Victoria. Australia.'

'What brings you to Malaga? You're a…very much…long distance…from your family. True?'

What business was it to you? Jack thought, but tried to be polite, wondering why he was explaining himself to this man. 'Just wanted to make sure Sofia got Andrés home safely.'

'They are safe now. No need to worry. We'll look after them.'

Suddenly, Mario turned on his heels and departed, leaving Jack gobsmacked. It sounded to him like he was being ordered to leave. Was Sofia aware of Mario's views? Did she know of this conversation?

Jack plummeted into confusion. Suddenly, it dawned upon him – Mario was interested in Sofia. Did Sofia want to be with Mario? Was this why she'd been talking about him leaving? Why her manner had become withdrawn? He was suddenly reminded of those final, awful days in Paris - days when they were planning their separation, he to Australia and her to Spain.

That night, as they lay in bed, Jack was quiet, searching for words, overwhelmed by the thought that she did not want him there.

He decided that there was nothing for it but to be strong. The truth was that neither he nor Sofia had made any commitments to each other. Certainly, in Paris he'd made plans to visit the twins in Malaga as soon as he could, but even that was proposed as a holiday. Neither had been ready for their romance to end, so it had seemed like a good idea. And here he was, in Malaga, and for Sofia, the feelings were evidently not as long-lasting as he'd hoped. Certainly not as durable as his own. Jack had been certain that he could have loved Sofia forever if she'd let him. He still was, but if their future together was not to be, he could handle it. He'd just have to.

Jack pictured his departure, formulating a mental image of himself farewelling Andrés and Sofia at Malaga Station. Shaking hands with Andrés. Turning to Sofia and giving her a final embrace. A kiss. Would it be a peck, or would he make one last bid to assure her that he loved her? That he was the one that she should choose? Not Mario – that smooth-talking ladies' man. Jack wished that he had hit him while he'd had his chance. Or at least said something menacing. He should have told Mario to back off.

Jack decided that the very next time he was in Malaga, he would enquire about his trip to Australia – find out if he needed to go via London, or if there was a quicker route.

Having resolved that he was going home, Jack struggled to find the words to discuss this with Sofia. He did not trust himself to speak them without his voice breaking and he knew that he could not face her agreement; helping him to organise the return trip in her efficient manner. Instead, he decided to practise the conversation with Andrés as they collected tools from the garden shed the next morning.

'I suppose that I'd better be heading back soon…'

'Back? Back where…?'

'You know…back home. Australia….' The lump in Jack's throat seemed to enlarge and he found he could not continue speaking. The shed suddenly felt airless and he left without further comment.

Morning tea was a quiet affair following which he and Andrés painted in the studio, although today they painted in silence, each lost in their own thoughts. Jack found it near impossible to concentrate and was relieved when Sofia called them to help her carry the bowls of *salmorejo* which she served with *pan con tomate*, the crusty garlic and tomato bread which he loved, followed by sweet wine-soaked peaches and coffee. Today, he found swallowing difficult, and afterwards, when he and Sofia retired to the coolness of the house for siesta, Jack knew that he needed to talk to her. Sofia beat him to it, however.

'So, Jack? You are thinking of leaving?' she asked softly.

'How do you know? Did Andrés say something?' Jack was disconcerted and his sense of being an outsider escalated. He had thought that Andrés would respect that it was Jack's business to tell Sofia, but of course, why should he? Andrés' concern would be for his sister.

'No. Andrés has said nothing. Why should he? Does he know something that I don't?' Sofia's sharp reply stung like a barb to Jack's heart.

'Yes. I thought it was probably time. I don't want to wear out my welcome. You and Andrés are all settled now. You don't need me anymore.'

Sofia looked at the ceiling and her hand, which had been settled loosely in his, was suddenly withdrawn. Jack could barely look at her, so miserable did he feel.

Good grief. Surely, he wasn't about to cry! He took a deep breath and attempted to explain himself. To sound like a man in control, not a heart-broken boy. 'Well, the job at Goldsbrough Mort & Co has been held open for months now. If I get back quickly, perhaps it might still be available. Apparently, lots of men are losing their jobs in Australia. I suppose that I should be glad to have one.'

'But what about your painting, Jack?'

'I can't spend my life painting. That's not going to get me ahead. I need a serious job, where I can earn good money and buy a house one day.'

'What about Spain? Paris?'

Jack turned and looked at Sofia, determined to make this as easy as he could for both of them. 'It's been wonderful. I have loved every minute of it. I have learned so much and now I am painting better than I could ever have imagined. But it's time to go home.'

The truth was that Jack would have happily thrown all of his paints into the Mediterranean Sea at that moment if it meant Sofia could be his. Picasso had been right. He'd said Jack would experience heart-break, even grief, and that in doing so, his paintings would improve. However, Jack had no intentions of using pain to become a better artist. In fact, he had no intention of becoming any sort of artist at all! He resolved, at that minute, that he would never paint again. How could he? His best painting memories were firmly tied to his adventures this year. His time spent in Paris. To his life here at the finca - working in the garden, their morning teas in the courtyard, laughing with Andrés and Sofia as they dipped freshly fried *churros* into *champurrado*. Days spent in the studio with Andrés, where palette-loads of azure blue, alizarin crimson and burnt umber were transferred to broad creamy canvases, creating lively scenes with knives and brushes. Paintings inspired by nights of holding Sofia tightly in his arms.

Now, just to imagine returning to his parents' home, weekends spent painting scenes of strangers on the banks of the Yarra, filled him with dread. He felt as if his creative fervour was exhausted – reduced to blackened coals of an abandoned campfire that had once blazed with life, heat and iridescent colour.

Jack lay with his eyes closed, even as he felt Sofia rise from beside him. He listened as she quietly straightened her clothing. He sensed her eyes upon him as she stood at the doorway; and then his heart sank as he heard her bare feet departing, padding away from him, along the hallway to the kitchen, until he could hear them no more.

～

'Hombre, what are you doing here?'

Andrés' words jolted Jack out of his reverie. It was almost dinner time and he'd been sitting in the courtyard, making a poor show of sketching the postcards that had been selling so well in the gallery.

'I was drawing, but must have nodded off.' Jack nodded towards the blank postcard-sized sheets next to him, his ink pen capped, unused, beside them.

'You are tired? Not sleeping?'

'No. I'm all right.'

'You need to talk to her…to Sofia.'

'I did talk to her!'

Of course, he'd talked to Sofia. What was Andrés thinking? That Jack would just leave without saying anything? Sneak off in the early hours of the morning? Jack was disappointed. Miffed, even. Surely, Andrés thought better of him than that.

'You told her you were leaving!' The shock in Andrés' tone surprised Jack. 'Did you explain *why* you are going? In fact, I am curious about why you are leaving, also. I thought that you were happy here.'

'*Why*? Because Sofia wants me to leave! She told me so!'

'Jack, no! This does not sound right. You must talk to Sofia again.'

'Well, I can hardly beg her to let me stay, can I? She wants to be with Mario!' Finally, it was out.

'Mario? Mario!'

Andrés repeated the name that spurred waves of jealous fury through Jack's being. Yet the air was filled with his friend's incredulity.

'Jack, we Spaniards can be primitive, granted. But we stopped marrying our cousins decades ago. I am fairly certain that Sofia does not wish to marry Mario.'

Mario was Sofia's cousin? 'But Mario warned me off. He as good as told me to leave. And then Sofia asked me what my plans were.' Jack felt so wrung out with emotion that he was too exhausted to feel hopeful. And Mario may well be Sofia's cousin, but he'd seen the sparkle in her eyes as Mario had teased her. And the menace in Mario's eyes when he'd told Jack, in no uncertain terms, that he would look after Sofia.

'Jack, you are surely wrong. Sofia loves you. I am sure that she does not want you to go.'

'Jack can go anywhere he likes.' Sofia's words resonated with a harsh undercurrent as she approached the table, slamming down a tray of plates and cutlery. 'There are glasses and a jug of orange juice on the bench. Or a bottle of wine if you would prefer. Jack, can you please fetch the pot off the stove? It is a little heavy.'

A few minutes later they sat at the table, polite conversation falling into awkward silences until Andrés took the lead.

'Well, if this is to be our last supper, we'd better enjoy it. Wine, Jack? Sofia?' He extended the bottle to their glasses with an overly cheerful smile.

'I'm all right, mate.'

'No, Andrés, thank you.'

'Well, if you two would like to bask in misery, go right ahead. I might just take me a plateful of this wonderful food, a glass of this divine red wine, and find myself some more stimulating company, even if it is just myself, the moonlight and the bats that have invaded the olive grove.'

Jack and Sofia watched in surprise as Andrés collected his plate, fork and glass and retreated to the back of the house, pausing to balance the items in one hand as he fumbled with the gate's latch.

'I want to hear you two talking,' he called. 'Definitely no throwing of plates, Sofia.' His departing chuckle remained audible even as he vanished from view.

'Jack, why are you leaving?'

'Sofia, do you love Mario?'

Their words collided mid-air.

'I don't want to go.'

'Mario!'

Sofia's single word conquered Jack's sentence by its sheer volume. Surely the neighbours at the dairy heard her.

And was that Andrés' chortling laughter in the distance? Jack began to feel a little foolish.

'Well, you asked me when I was leaving.' The words sounded ridiculous in his ears, now that they were said. Petulant, even.

'No, Jack, I asked what you were thinking of doing. You received a letter from your parents. They wanted you home, si? They would have asked you when you were going to be home. You have a job waiting for you?'

Yes, yes and yes. Jack could not deny Sofia was right on each count.

She had not finished. 'You never said anything to me, Jack. I *asked* what you were thinking of doing. I was not *telling you* to go!'

'But Mario! He told me… He warned me…' Jack could not find the words to finish either sentence.

'Pah – Mario is a busybody. He worries about me. He thought that you were going to leave me here, pregnant and heartbroken. I kept telling him you were not like that. And then, suddenly, it seemed that he was right!'

Heartbroken. Sofia, heartbroken. Jack had thought it was he who had the broken heart. He shook his head, wondering how things could ever have become so confused.

'So you don't want me to leave?' he asked. 'I've been so miserable, Sof…'

'Jack. I love you. I don't want you to leave. I love having you here with Andrés and me. Andrés loves having you here, too.'

The sound of Sofia's voice, rising on each phrase, evidently captured Andrés' attention by the sound of the heartfelt '*Gracias a dios,*' that filtered across the back fence.

'Can I come back now? It is getting a little dark out here… I can barely see the food on my plate.' Andrés emerged out of the darkness and slid back into his seat. 'Pour me another glass of wine, Jack. I am sure I need one. Perhaps one for you and Sofia also, si? A little celebration for *crisis evitida*. And maybe, next time, we just have a little clearing of the air each day, instead of turning molehills into mountains.'

Jack found himself laughing with relief as Andrés continued. 'Now, can we move beyond your combined dispositions for foolishness and discuss more important matters? I am thinking we should plan our trip back to Paris, perhaps in March next year. There is a lot to be organised. If we focus on this, perhaps you two might control your riotous *imaginaciones*.'

'Andrés, *si*. That is a wonderful idea,' said Sofia, and Jack found himself nodding in agreement. To go back to Paris with Sofia and Andrés would be wonderful.

The excitement of planning their return trip proved the best remedy for the turmoil that had beset Sofia's and Jack's relationship over the last week. When Jack rose from the dinner table later that evening, he felt invigorated with hope, secured by the knowledge that his and Sofia's love for each other was firmly intact and overwhelmingly reassured that she wanted him to stay here in Malaga with her.

What Jack was not expecting, on a Wednesday morning in his third month in Malaga, was the sound of his parents' voices in the courtyard of the Toulouse Galleria.

CHAPTER 7

*F*or Jack, the day had begun like every other. Following breakfast, he had worked in the garden, digging through a small plot of hardened earth that was over-run by weeds, at the far end of the house. It had once been used to grow a variety of potatoes, although - according to Sofia - none too successfully, and had been neglected since they'd come home. At the breakfast table, he'd offered to dig out the weeds and prepare it for the herb seedlings that Sofia was keen to plant. Meanwhile, Andrés had repaired the leak that had suddenly sprung in their garden tap, wasting their precious water. Following their outdoor work, they'd shared a pot of tea and plate of *alfajores* with Sofia before heading for the studio, while she finalised her preparations for the gallery.

An hour later, Jack had just finished stretching a rectangle of canvas over a particularly large frame and was dissolving pellets of rabbit-skin glue in hot water, a solution that he would then apply to the canvas to ensure the painting's longevity. He chuckled to himself, hearing the voice of Monsieur Simon ringing in his ears. *Surface preparation is as important as the painting! What is the good of painting your masterpiece, only for the paint to flake off in ten years?*

And this, Jack was sure, was going to be his masterpiece. After the glue dried, he intended to apply two coats of a ground – a durable foundation coat on which he would paint – made from linseed oil, silver white and a tinge of golden yellow. He'd decided that it was time to create a very special portrait in the manner of Sorolla, whose style he so admired. A portrait of Sofia, of course. Jack could see the image he planned to paint, fully formed in his mind. Not just the design, but the emotion that he planned to portray: Sofia's essence, the joy she exuded when she worked at her kitchen bench, her hair loosely tied back, stray curls springing from the scarf that she liked to wear while baking. Her hands strong and confident as they rolled dough into small rounds, later to be flattened with her metal 'squasher', as Jack called it, the implement that left the pleasant, criss-cross indents on the surface of her biscuits. Already, he had made sketches of the proposed scene and developed some colour samples – all that remained was to execute his masterpiece.

'Hello!' The voice was male and hesitant. The flattened syllables suggested an accent that could only be Australian. Jack looked at Andrés in surprise.

'Anyone about?' the voice persisted.

With a combination of nervousness and excitement, Jack walked to the door of the studio and was astounded to see his parents standing in the courtyard before him. An avalanche of thoughts cascaded through his mind as he approached them.

'Mum! Dad!' The words sounded astonishingly alien as they left his mouth, while his hands performed the more familiar task of grabbing a cloth that reeked with the heady odour of turpentine to remove imagined paint from his fingers. As Jack crossed the courtyard, he could feel the eyes of Andrés on him as he leaned against the studio's doorway watching, his curiosity roused.

Attempting to appear as though living in a finca in Southern Spain and painting his days away was the most normal thing in the world, Jack forged on. 'What a surprise! How are you?'

His mother reached up to him. Her tight grip around his neck revealed her relief. It had, after all, been eight months, Jack quickly calculated as he returned the embrace, his arms tightening also, suddenly overcome with delight at seeing her. Somehow, she seemed smaller and older than he remembered. Frailer, even.

'Look at you, Jack. You've grown,' she said, and he was relieved to see her smile as she stepped back to gaze at him in the familiar way she had done, ever since he was a tiny boy.

Jack laughed self-consciously, knowing that his growth had nothing to do with his height, which had settled at six foot, two inches when he was barely fifteen years-old. He felt self-conscious, aware that his hair must appear somewhat straggly and well overdue for a cut, and that his whiskers were in competition for neglect. Even his clothes would surely appear untidy to his parents, his dress more suited to this rural environment than the sleek-fitted shirt, tie and neat slacks he had worn as a city dweller in Melbourne for most of his life.

William's greeting was more subdued and a certain gruffness infused his tone as he shook hands with his son. 'Well, well. So, this is where you've been hiding.' He glanced around at the buildings and courtyard with an inquisitive air.

Jack caught himself also looking around, visualising the courtyard through his father's eyes. It must appear somewhat worn – even rundown – to William's neat and ordered mind. Feeling ashamed of himself for his own critical appraisal, Jack was suddenly acutely aware of multiple signs of neglect that he'd been oblivious to until this very minute. A broken paling on the trellis, uneven flagstones which could do with some weeding and chips in two of the terracotta pots resting against the gallery wall - the combined effect a collusion of tangible evidence of Jack's lapsed state.

Catching sight of Sofia standing quietly next to Andrés, Jack made hasty introductions. 'Mum, Dad, this is my friend Andrés. And' – turning towards her – 'his sister, Sofia.'

At the sharp look she cast his way, Jack felt a piercing stab of remorse. Caught off-guard, this important introduction had come out wrong. He tried to make up for his casual, understated reference to

Sofia. 'This is their home. Sofia manages the gallery.' He waved his hand to the right, stumbling awkwardly over his words. 'Would you like to see it?'

Sofia stepped forward with a welcoming smile, encouraging William and Marian through the doorway as she'd done with hundreds of tourists who found their way to the gallery. Stretching her English vocabulary to its limits, she explained how her parents had purchased the finca near thirty years ago and how her father had combined his work in the orchards with his life as an artist. She pointed out craftworks consigned from local artisans, pottery and leather, and in response to William and Marian's polite questioning, described the fresh produce bought up to the gallery each morning and the recent addition of the gallery's cafe. Sofia then ushered them into the courtyard, suggesting Jack sit and talk with his parents while she prepared a pot of tea.

Jack fidgeted uncomfortably, knowing that explanations were due, but hoping to delay them. Their conversation awkwardly meandered around William and Marian's decision to visit. Concerned about his extended absence, they'd wanted to see first-hand that he was well. Marian described the sea voyage they had undertaken and her joy at catching up with Aunt Elizabeth and Uncle Robert in London. The rough overnight crossing of the Channel to Paris that had left her and William quite ill for a day. They'd thought that the train ride from Paris to Madrid and then on to Malaga was never going to end.

Listening as they described their extensive journey, Jack again felt pangs of remorse. Marian and William may well have crossed the world as a young couple decades earlier, but he did not perceive his parents as adventuring types. He knew they had only travelled because of their extreme concern for his safety. He pictured Marian's anxiety escalating daily, until William eventually succumbed to her fears, finally agreeing that, if Jack was not coming home, they needed to see with their own eyes that he was safe and well. They did not say this in so many words, instead stating they had always planned to return to the 'Mother Country' one day and make a trip to the continent. Now, with

Jack in Spain, it seemed as good a time as any, and William had managed to combine their trip with important business affairs in London on behalf of Goldsbrough Mort & Co, who had been adversely affected by the recent stock market crisis that had created chaos across the globe. Perhaps Jack had heard about it?

A discussion of where William and Marian were going to stay arose and Sofia quickly offered them the second room tucked below the staircase next to Jack's, essentially a storeroom, but it had occasionally served as a guest bedroom over the years. They politely declined, insisting they had booked a room at one of Malaga's guest houses that was more than adequate. However, they did accept Sofia's invitation to see indoors, nodding in approval at the delightful, sunny home that was about a quarter the size of their own house in South Yarra. Jack showed them his room under the stairs and noticed relief on his mother's face when she saw the small single bed and his belongings set out neatly on the timber chest of drawers.

Andrés had said little for the duration of the visit, except to politely thank William and Marian when they'd inquired after his health and expressed their gladness for his recovery. Despite his quiet manner, Jack noticed how Andrés' keen eyes observed his parents and wondered what Andrés was thinking.

Somehow, they got through the morning, and as the first wave of tourists began to arrive at the gallery, William and Marian excused themselves, stating that they were very tired from their week of travel and would go back to their guest house for a rest.

'Jack, how about you meet us for dinner tonight? We will be able to have a good talk and make some plans then.'

The invitation was more of an instruction and clearly directed to Jack alone. In an instant, he guessed that not only had his parents travelled across the world to see if he was safe and well, but very likely had the intention of taking him home with them! Thinking that this was one conversation best held in the absence of Sofia and Andrés, Jack agreed to meet them at six PM in the foyer of their guesthouse.

After William and Marian left, Sofia looked at Jack enquiringly.

'How lovely for your parents to visit, Jack?' she said, her words more a question than a statement.

'Yes, yes.' Jack took her by the hand, and pulling her close to him, brought it up to his lips and kissed her palm. 'Sofia, I am so sorry. I'm stupid. It was such a surprise to see them. I knew they had a lot to take in, just seeing me here…living in Spain…painting. It is all so different for them. Hard for them to understand. Still, I should have told them about you…us.'

'It's okay, Jack. They are your parents. You will tell them when you are ready. When they are ready. Do not worry,' Sofia said with conviction.

However, Jack sensed in Sofia a return of the vulnerability that he had first witnessed in Paris, and again, when he'd received that letter from his mother. She'd be thinking he would want to go back home. That his parents might talk him into it. However, Jack had no intentions of letting poor communication create a wedge between him and Sofia this time. He determined that he would follow Andrés' good advice – talk through times of confusion rather than let molehills become mountains. Here was his home, now. Sofia was his home.

That evening over dinner with his parents, Jack described the life-changing events that he'd experienced since he'd left home. Beginning where it started, he told William and Marian about his meeting with Margaret on the *Ormonde*. How she'd discovered him, really, prompting Marian to giggle and touch his hand. 'Son, you make it sound as if you were lost.'

Ignoring her words, Jack continued, explaining that Margaret had thought he was talented and had insisted he show his paintings to a friend of hers, Roger Fry. They listened in silence as he enthused about the painting classes Roger had arranged for him in Paris - what a wonderful opportunity it had been - and explaining how much he had learned. Even as he spoke, Jack could see the lack of comprehension in his parents' faces. He continued speaking, describing his success at Gertrude Stein's exhibition as well as the portrait prize at the Académie Julian. Marian offered the familiar exclamation, 'Good for you Jack. That is wonderful!' with the same enthusiastic delight she'd expressed when he'd won school art prizes. William nodded in agreement, but could not resist offering fatherly words of caution. 'That is all very well, Jack, but winning art prizes and selling a few paintings are not going to set you up for the future. You have a job waiting for you in Australia.'

Ignoring his father's cool reaction, Jack described his meeting with Andrés and subsequent friendship with the twins, the seriousness of Andrés' illness and how close to death he'd been, hence his desire to remain in Paris until Andrés was well, and then the last-minute decision he'd made to assist Sofia as she escorted her brother on the long train journey to their home. None of this was news to them – Jack had detailed the same information in the letters he'd sent from both London and Paris – but, in telling his parents to their faces, Jack hoped that he could impart the significance of these events. However, the more he spoke, the more he realised that his words were meaningless to them. Regardless, he forged on, describing his current work helping manage the finca and painting each morning with Andrés. Earning a small but growing income from his works at the gallery.

'But not a real income,' responded William. 'You need to be saving for your future. Thinking about buying a home. Paying for your children's education one day!'

'And you can't live with Andrés forever,' said his mother. Excluding any reference to Sofia seemed a deliberate omission. 'Besides, he is not a well man. I don't mean to speak ill, but you said yourself that Andrés' future is uncertain,' she continued. 'Remember Jack, Mr Gilmore is still holding a job for you. We can't keep him waiting forever!'

Jack knew that, as unpalatable as it would be for his parents, he needed to spell out his intentions for his future with clarity.

'Mum, I'm not planning to come home any time soon. I won't be taking up the job at Goldsbrough Mort & Co. You will just have to apologise to Mr Gilmore. In fact, I will write to him myself, thanking him for his generosity in holding the job open for so long. However, I love my life here. I love Sofia... I am not going to leave her... I am going to marry her!'

Jack was not sure who was more amazed, himself or his parents, when these words left his mouth.

'*Marry* Sofia!' William spluttered, his face reddening. The sudden display of anger emanating from his father shocked Jack and immediately he knew that it was not a job waiting in Australia, nor the importance of saving for his future, that concerned his parents. Rather, it was Jack's relationship with Sofia that had them worried.

'What are you talking about, son? You cannot marry her. She is...a...foreigner. A Spaniard. That would not do. How on earth will she fit in? No one will speak to you.'

Aghast, Jack's anger escalated to match his father's and his voice took on an uncharacteristic harshness.

'What do you mean, I cannot marry her? Sofia is beautiful. She is the sweetest, kindest girl I have ever met. She loves me and I love her. We will get married and I don't care what people think!'

This response surprised all three of them. Anger was rarely displayed in the Tomlinson household and never, ever, had Jack directed it towards his parents. However, as he sat looking at them, his father appeared haughty and snobbish, his mother, nodding her agreement beside him, small-minded. Jack felt he could not relate to them, nor did he wish to. As he stared back at his father in stony defiance, his jaw clenched with frustration.

'For once I am happy, really happy. I love painting, I love Spain and I love Sofia. I never wanted to work at Goldsbrough Mort & Co. That was your plan, not mine. I will not be returning home any time soon, and I will be marrying Sofia.'

Marian, ever the peacemaker, intervened, her words coming out in a rush as if to prevent any more words from being spoken in anger. 'Jack, of course, she is a lovely girl. Very sweet. And she takes such wonderful care of that beautiful home and gallery. I can see why you have feelings for her. Her brother is very nice, too. So sad about his health. I can see why you are happy here. Let's not rush into anything and let's not be angry.'

She patted both Jack's and her husband's hands as if, by simultaneously touching them, her body would act as a conduit, connecting them together in a spirit of peace. It seemed to work.

'We won't talk about this now, son,' his father stated gruffly, though Jack knew that the conversation was not over. Changing the subject, William expounded on Goldsbrough Mort & Co's plan to expand their business interests into northern England, possibly even Wales, as soon as the financial crisis settled. They would be seeking agents for the newly established offices. Jack felt sure the pause that followed this news was deliberate, an opportunity to volunteer his interest; if he could not be lured back to Australia, perhaps he might be attracted to the more civilised shores of Great Britain.

Maintaining their tenuous quest for peace, the conversation turned to Jack's time in London with his Aunt Elizabeth and Uncle Robert. How taken they'd been with Jack, enjoying their card games and sightseeing together. How they'd loved having a young person in the house – it had made them feel young again, they'd said. Allowed them to see London through new eyes. Marian asked about the bright young Australian woman Elizabeth had spoken about, Margaret. Again, Jack suspected their motive, guessing they were clutching at alternative love interests for him. Anyone other than Sofia, with her unsuitable foreign blood. Again, he felt irritation rising at their closed-mindedness.

CHAPTER 8

*W*illiam's and Marian's schedule allowed for ten days in Malaga and Jack and Sofia planned a series of sight-seeing activities for them. Rising early each morning, Sofia hurriedly completed her day's baking, setting out the trays of biscuits and snacks on the broad benches of the gallery. Aunt Jovita was thrilled to once again step in as manager, if only for a short period. Freed, each morning Sofia and Jack drove Suzie down the hill, collected Marian and William from their guest house and headed out to view the sights of the region. Andrés elected to stay at the finca, as he often did these days, declaring he would be on hand to help his aunt should she require assistance. Jack, aware of the increasing signs of fatigue Andrés displayed as they worked in the garden and studio, suspected that the real reason he chose to remain at home was so he could conserve his energy, avoid crowds and minimise any risks of contracting an infection.

Sofia, enjoying her role as tour guide, led Jack, William and Marian on excursions around the immediate area. First, she took them to the ruins of the Castillo Gibralfaro, and as they'd walked the ramparts she shared details of its history, describing how, as children, she and Andrés had spent hours playing hide-and-seek around the fortress with their friends. Later, they'd accompanied their father when he'd taken groups of students and instructed them on the skills for painting *plein air*. The view from the castle's highest point, the lookout, was breathtaking – the deep blue of the Mediterranean swept to the horizon, snowy white puffs of cloud high in the sky mirrored by the white ripples flashing in the sea and colourful fishing boats dotting the expanse of water.

Driving down the hill, Sofia steered Suzie sharply to the left, toward the road that led to an ancient fortress, the Alcazabar. Jack had been here once before, in his first week in Malaga, and as they looked around, he was sorry that he hadn't returned. The site was an artists' dream, with dozens of ancient buildings set in picturesque gardens. The elegant beauty of bygone days was present wherever they cast their eyes – keyhole archways, ornate doorways and buildings with domed ceilings inscribed with thousands of Islamic symbols – mysterious messages from a time long past. The buildings were interconnected by pathways; intricate works of art in themselves, created from arrangements of colourful pebbles to form overlapping circles or brickwork laid in geometric patterns. Weaving amid intriguing statues and exotic foliage, the pathways were bordered by enormous pillars, interspersed with delightful nooks. The sound of running water was everpresent and Jack was fascinated by the engineering feat created by a series of tiny canals adjoining the pathways, fuelled by cascading fountains, and which, provided a continuous supply of water throughout the site.

The next day they travelled to Malaga's seaside, and despite the cool winter breeze, Jack was amazed when his father removed his shoes and socks, rolled up his trousers and waded into the frothing waves that lapped the shoreline.

'Come on, Marian,' he called. 'We can't be close to the Mediterranean Sea and not have a dip! If I had my togs I'd go right in!'

'But William, it must be freezing!' his mother replied, even as she abandoned her shoes and slid off her stockings before joining him.

Jack and Sofia wandered hand-in-hand along the water's edge, enjoying the winter sunshine.

'They are having a good time?' Sofia asked.

'I'm sure they are. They do love the sea. We often used to go down to the local beaches near home - Melbourne is located right on Port Phillip Bay, and its many beaches are very popular.'

'Are they expecting you to go home with them, Jack? I got the impression that they weren't so happy to see you living with us at the finca, painting your days away.'

'They would take me home if they could. But I told them that I won't be leaving any time soon.'

'Oh, Jack! What did they say? Are they happy about that?'

Jack felt himself tightening up, remembering his father's attitude towards Sofia's Spanish origins. He couldn't possibly tell her about that – she would be devastated.

'They'll just have to be happy, won't they?' he replied, more tersely than intended. He reached for her hand to reassure Sofia that his annoyance was not directed at her and was relieved when she stopped asking questions.

Eventually they turned and walked back towards town, rejoining his parents. They left the beach and soon found a café with a large sign swinging at its entry, the colourful English letters boldly claiming that it offered the freshest seafood to be found in all of Malaga. The marketing ruse targeting the British and American tourists who increasingly converged on the Costa del Sol was evidently successful, for loud English-speaking voices filled the room.

Insisting that lunch would be his treat, William asked Sofia if she would make a selection on their behalf. Without a second thought, she recommended that they share a *fritura malagueña*, advertised as the best fried fish in all of Spain, promising that it would be the finest they would ever taste. The enormous platter arrived at the table promptly, its tantalising aroma wafting throughout the room, and the rice dish, infused with mussels, octopus and large portions of glistening white fish that had been caught by Mediterranean fisherman that very morning, bathed in a lemon sauce, did not disappoint.

'Sofia, this tastes wonderful,' Marian said.

'Yes, our fishermen, they take great pride in their catch and our chefs love to create special meals. They are … mouth-watering … you say, Jack?'

'Definitely mouth-watering,' William agreed, smiling. 'It is a real treat to be eating freshly cooked seafood straight out of the Mediterranean.'

'You should taste Sofia's *paella de mariscos*! It's even better than this!' Jack said, enjoying the opportunity to highlight Sofia's talents.

After their meal, Sofia wandered across the room to a notice board and returned to the table, excitement in her voice. 'Tomorrow we must go to Nerja – it is their festival! It's quite a drive, but it will be worth it!'

She looked at Marian and William and continued. 'It will be a treat for you to experience a Spanish festival. They are always so much fun… It will make a special memory for you to take home…'

'That sounds lovely, Sofia. What do you think, William?'

After collecting William and Marian at seven o'clock the following morning, Sofia spoke in Spanish, her voice uncommonly strident, the words directed to no one in particular, as she climbed into the driver's seat.

'Is everything okay?' Jack asked in surprise.

Sofia laughed at the quizzical expressions on the faces of Jack, William, and Marian.

'I just told Suzie to behave. She is making a growling sound… She needs to be quiet and do as she is told! Yes?'

Thankfully, Suzie must have heard the menacing tone in Sofia's voice, for they weaved along the coastal road to the east of Malaga, arriving at the bustling village of Nerja, just after nine, without mishap. William and Marian gasped with delight as Sofia parked Suzie. The panoramic view before them was spectacular: a string of headlands dotted the coastline, each peppered with charming buildings on land so steep, surely they would slide into the sea someday, the blue water lapping against stony cliff faces, extending as far as the eye could see. Already the market was seething with activity - men, women and children jostling for position around the timber trestle tables to make their selections: toys, leather belts, hats, scarves and aprons, hair ornaments, and delicious-looking, sweets and jars of spicy pickles and sauces were laid out enticingly. They sampled all manner of local produce, including dozens of olives – red, green and black, stuffed, doused in spicy marinades or mashed into salty tapenades, fine slices of ham and hot roasted almonds in small paper cups. Then there were the sweets, Jack's favourite was the hunks of sticky nougat that were chipped from an enormous slab with a chisel and hammer before their eyes, hewn by a cheerful man with a thick black moustache, his expression nervous as he watched them taste the sample he offered.

'You like this, *si*?' he asked, as if fearing their response.

'Love it!' Jack replied, selecting a large bag to purchase for himself and a second to take home for Andrés.

At eleven, they were carried along by the tide of what felt like the entire population of Nerja. The human river flowed towards the main street, lapping its edges and waving as they called out to children, friends and family participating in a colourful, noisy street parade.

Sofia's knowledge of Spanish customs was extensive and she provided a constant stream of explanations about the events around them in answer to Jack's and his parents' questions. These festivals were reproduced, she told them, each with their own regional variations, right across Spain.

Clapping, they watched local schoolchildren marching past them. Rows of giggling young girls were adorable in their colourful '*traje de flamenco*' – dresses decorated with rows of ruffles, flounces and enormous sleeves made from puffy balls of lace. No two girls looked alike for, as individual as their dresses could be, so was their hair, ornately braided and adorned with ribbons, fancy combs called *peinetas*, or pointy cone-shaped attachments topped by silky *mantillas* that floated in the breeze. At frequent intervals, the girls, led by their teachers, broke into a dance, feet twirling and arms high, clicking small castanets above their heads for a few minutes before collapsing into giggles and reforming their lines to continue their march.

A group of boys followed, and Sofia laughed, pointing out to Jack their serious expressions. Resplendent in their fitted jackets, broad waistbands and wide-brimmed hats, they refused to be distracted by the waving crowds, keeping their eyes forward. Sofia suggested they would have been given stern warnings and threats of punishment for anything less than perfect behaviour.

The parade continued with a brass band marching in unison - loud drum beats marking their timing - frolicking clowns that teased embarrassed onlookers and twirling flamenco dancers who combined their forward motion with a continuous array of complex dance steps.

Sofia, Jack and his family cheered with the rest of the crowds as a tall, skinny man on a horse passed them by, closely followed by a fat man on a small donkey. Sofia explained the comical couple were playing characters from the Miguel de Cerva's story of *Don Quixote*, the crazy nobleman from La Mancha who elected that he would be a knight, accompanied by Sancho Panza, his appointed 'squire,' who was forever forced to rescue his master from outrageous adventures.

After the parade had finished, Sofia led them to the town square, where wooden benches and tables were arranged, now filling with hundreds of Spaniards in high spirits, revelling in the fine weather, the simple pleasure of gathering with friends and neighbours, and the success of their festival. The air rang with loud voices calling and laughing as platters of dried, salted fish and soft bread soaked in olive oil were freely distributed by young men and women, also wearing the vibrant *traje de flamenco*.

Jack and his parents were transfixed by the loud music that suddenly erupted from a stage, drowning out all speech. A quartet, dressed for the occasion in ornate black jackets, impressively thick, groomed moustaches and smiles as broad as the brims of their flamboyant hats, commenced a lively tune, fingers flying over guitar strings, notes weaving and cascading in a joyful melody of celebration. Dozens of couples rose, drawn onto the dance floor. Jack was both surprised and pleased when a kindly couple sitting alongside them persuaded his parents to join in the dancing, their friendly smiles overcoming the language barrier, their outstretched, beckoning hands sending a clear universal message.

'Oh, no…we couldn't!' exclaimed Marian, tittering with pleasure.

'Of course – it is the *sevillina*! Anyone can dance the *sevillina*,' boomed the twinkling-eyed gentleman, whose English was better than most Spaniards' Jack had encountered. Sofia nodded encouragingly towards Marian and William, and Jack was delighted by the sight of his parents giggling as they allowed themselves to be led onto the dance floor. The man immediately took Marian's arm and began twirling her, while the lady took William's hands and commenced sashaying her hips, encouraging him to do likewise. Sofia looked questioningly at Jack before taking his hand and leading him to join in.

Together they laughed and danced the afternoon away, sipping on the varieties of deep crimson wine that were served in tiny glasses, tasting morsels of savoury and sweet delicacies and enjoying music delivered by a range of performers throughout the afternoon.

All agreed that the late-night visit to Señora Maria's Den was the highlight of the week. Arriving at nine pm Jack, Sofia, Marian and William, along with a crowd of hushed tourists, sat around the edge of a small, darkened room, its walls decorated with fans, castanets and posters.

Jack pointed out the grainy photographs of past performances to his mother. She smiled at him with a nervous expression and he imagined how strange she must be feeling, seated among dozens of strangers in this room – den – at this late hour when she would normally be preparing for bed. He patted her hand with a smile as the audience's quiet murmuring stilled into silence when a young man with the shiniest hair Jack had ever seen, splendidly adorned in an intricately embroidered vest, began plucking at the strings of a guitar and crooning a heartfelt melody.

As the song's haunting first verse came to an end, four young women emerged from a partition. With their ruffled polka-dotted dresses swirling, arms high, they moved as one in a slow, swaying motion, flirtatiously responding to the guitar's seductive rhythm. Then, just as the gentle flow of notes lulled Jack's senses into a quiet restfulness, the tempo changed and he gasped with surprise.

In an instant the music was transformed, its notes rapid, the volume increasing, the room reverberating as waves of deep, menacing chords tumbled over each other, bouncing off the walls, a humming vibration felt through their chairs. Jack was spellbound and felt Sofia's hand tighten in his as an extraordinary-looking woman entered the stage, although she remained separate from the other dancers. She must have been at least sixty, he thought, her body somewhat heavier than the slim figures of the younger women, her face commanding, heavy-lidded eyes rimmed with black eyeliner, full lips red and sensuous, golden hoops dangling from pendulous earlobes. Unquestionably, the lead dancer.

Throwing her head back, she struck a dramatic pose, and then, with barely a movement of her upper body beyond the clicking of fingers, she stomped her feet, a sequential pounding that she repeated over and over, escalating in speed, forewarning a threat, heralding that some unspeakable drama was about to unfold. The music pulsated, tumultuous notes roaring through the room like thunder erupting from storm clouds. Light-footed, the four younger dancers created a ring around the woman before deftly launching into a display of complex steps.

The music's volume increased further, becoming a deafening cacophony as four young males launched onto the floor. Each partnered a young woman, their movements punctuated by cries of "*Olé!*" The couples reeled around the edges of the floor while the lone central figure swayed softly, a spellbinding presence, captive to a haunting melody audible to her alone. Then, pair by pair, the couples retreated, finally leaving her still figure, as the sound diminished and the crowd erupted into applause.

Released from her trance, the majestic lead dancer smiled as she receded to the background and the room quietened, before the spellbound crowd erupted into noisy applause for her. The audience settled quickly, stilled as a lovelorn guitarist emerged and strolled across the small space. His voice resonated with despair as using, English, he described a tale of homesickness and lost love. His mournful cry seemed to call down the sorrow and heartbreak of the ages, evoking an atmosphere of melancholy so acute that Jack shivered and took Sofia's hand into his. Thankfully, not wishing to leave the audience depressed, the soloist then launched into a bright, happy tune, smiling broadly, nodding to each person in turn by way of thanking them for coming to the show.

As the final notes lingered in the air, the audience paused for a moment, as if collectively captivated by the spell of Maria's Den, before erupting into appreciative clapping. On cue, the dancers reappeared, bearing trays of red wine in small glasses which they distributed with broad smiles. Jack and his parents were breathless with the excitement and tension of the performances.

Following the break, the older dancer again took to the floor and the room darkened until a single lamp highlighted this grand woman of the flamenco. She introduced herself as Maria, and told a story of the many generations of her *gitano* family – of their Romani heritage and subsequent settlement into Andalusian country, centuries earlier. She described their love affair with dance and their very own Malagian version, the *fandango*. After outlining the traditional story behind her earlier performance, Maria introduced the dancers one by one, explaining how they not only performed nightly shows for tourists, but also kept *fandango* alive by teaching the young girls of Malaga.

To Jack's surprise, Maria suddenly beckoned to Sofia, insisting that she come forward in a tone so commanding that Sofia had no option but to obey. The audience was enchanted as she instructed Sofia to join the four women in a performance of the fandango, a dance she had learned as a young child. Jack grinned, his eyes shining as he watched with pride while Sofia performed the steps expertly. Marian grasped his hand and whispered, 'She's every bit as good as they are, isn't she!' and Jack agreed.

The dance soon ended and Sofia returned to Jack's side looking jubilant, energized by the thrill of dancing. He spontaneously kissed her.

Returning his gaze to the stage, which was suddenly silent, Jack realised that Maria's eyes had fallen upon him. Reaching out, she firmly grasped his hand and he had no choice but to go with her. Walking around the room, she beckoned with a barely perceptible but no less commanding flick of her wrist towards three other young men. Not knowing quite what to expect, Jack stood nervously until suddenly the floor become crowded as the four male dancers re-entered the room. It was to be a dance lesson and Jack could not stop laughing as he and his fellow captives duplicated a series of flying leaps and graceful twirls that had the audience in stitches, so badly did they perform.

It was eleven o'clock when the audience spilled out onto the street. William and Marian chattered non-stop, thrilled by their experience. They thanked Sofia profusely for organising the evening and complimented her on her fine dancing. Bidding his parents goodnight at the entry to their accommodation, Jack was warmed to see his mother kiss Sofia on the cheek before following William through the glass doors into the dimly lit foyer.

All over Malaga, posters advertising a bull fight to be held on Friday night were plastered across walls, doors and even posts. Celebrated bullfighters from across Spain were converging to the Plaza de Toros, the enormous sixteen-sided building that had fascinated Jack each time he'd gone into town. William suggested to Sofia that perhaps a bull-fight could be an interesting experience.

'No, William. I will not go. Many Spanish people love bullfighting; however, equally many think it cruel. You go, if you wish, but I won't join you.'

'I thought all the Spanish loved bullfighting,' said William.

'No, many like Andrés and I abhor bullfighting. We'd like to see it banned. The organisers say it is a fair fight, but it's not. They use cruel tricks to weaken the bulls and make sure that the matador wins. I hate to see the beautiful animals killed while everyone sits watching and cheering. It is so wrong!'

So passionate was Sofia in her opposition to bullfighting that Jack and his parents agreed they did not wish to attend, either.

On the day of William and Marian's departure, Jack hitched a ride down the hill on Salvador's milk truck, to accompany his parent's to the train station. They had a long trip ahead of them, back to Madrid and on to Barcelona, Cerbère, Paris and London, reversing the trip they had undertaken less than two weeks earlier. Deliberately arriving early, taking no risk of missing their train, they settled into the station's small café and ordered cups of tea and toast.

'Jack, we have had a lovely time. I can see why you love Spain so much,' Marian said, her voice quiet.

'But, son,' William continued, 'Spain is a place for a holiday – not a place to build your life in. You will need a good job to get ahead. You can't bury yourself up there on the mountain, painting pictures for the rest of your life.'

'Dad, this is not about Spain. It is about Sofia. I love her and I am not leaving her.' Jack breathed deeply, trying to control his emotions. The last thing he wanted to do was argue with his parents now, after they'd all had such a wonderful time together this last week.

William persisted as if he had not heard. 'It's just not that simple, Jack. Yes, Sofia is lovely. She is very sweet – your mother and I can see that. We have had a wonderful time in Malaga and that is largely thanks to Sofia's thoughtfulness in planning our days.'

Jack's shoulders stiffened with tension, for he knew what was coming.

'However,' William continued, 'in Australia, Sofia would be very unhappy. Lonely. Australia has a policy, you know: white people only. English speaking. People with foreign accents have a hard time. They are not easily accepted. You really need to think about Sofia's happiness. Plus, what if you have children? Our society would ignore them!'

At Jack's stony expression, Marian patted William on the hand, implying she felt that he'd said enough.

She tried a different approach. 'Jack, why don't you come back to Australia for Christmas? Andrés is so much better now. You can get your bearings. Make a decision from home, and if you decide you want to live in Spain, come back next year.'

This was met with equally stony silence, broken when Marion erupted into tears, declaring her fear that she would never see him again. Jack stirred, softened by his mother's weeping, and he hugged her, knowing her fears were genuine.

'Mum, don't say that. Of course, you will see me again. I'll be home in no time. Sofia and I will come for a holiday.'

As Jack saw his parents onto the train, he felt a stab of sadness. The reality of Australia, and his family being on the other side of the world, suddenly engulfed him. He stood waving as the departing train, carrying his parents on the first leg of their long journey home, became a small dot in the distance.

Turning, he looked out on the streets of Malaga, now busy with businesses opening for the day. He walked towards the sea, noticing the fragrant air, as always, pungent with the saltiness that was unique to seaside villages – today additionally tainted with the unmistakable dank odour of seaweed, which Jack knew would be bunched up on the sand, its looped, glistening tendrils forming a thick carpet. *Must be low tide*, he thought. He watched a flock of gulls swooping on the roadway opposite him, their screeches ringing as they fought over scraps that had been left outside the very same café he and Sofia had taken his parents to earlier that week.

Jack belonged here now. Here with Sofia, and together they would build a happy life. He would work hard creating paintings to sell to tourists. He also hoped to increase his income by entering competitions which would help to establish his name as an artist of repute and so allow him to increase the price of his paintings. Hopefully, he'd even get commissions for portraits. And when they returned to Paris the following summer, while Andrés took up his position at the Académie Julian, he and Sofia would reconnect with the contacts who had shown interest in their works. Just this week, a welcome cheque from one of the Parisian galleries holding their works on consignment, accompanied by a letter asking if any more paintings were available, had arrived at the finca. It was exciting news, and Sofia had helped him and Andrés make some selections from their growing collections, which she'd already wrapped, ready to be sent to Paris.

Fate had a cruel way of dictating reality, however, and it was only a few short, happy months after Jack had waved his parents off at Malaga Station that Andrés' health again showed signs of deterioration.

CHAPTER 9

They'd had a quiet Christmas celebration, using Andrés' vulnerable health as an excuse to decline Aunt Jovita's invitation to join her and Stefan for lunch. Instead, they'd enjoyed the enforced restfulness of a day indoors, remaining in bed later than usual and then sharing a long brunch of omelettes, followed with a platter of cold meats, and then, as mid-morning became late morning, they'd decided to open a bottle of cava, which they drank accompanied by a range of sweet treats – Toledo's finest peanut marzipan that Sofia had bought, as well as Jack's contribution to the feast, a large box of Matías López chocolates that he'd found in a delicatessen in Malaga. Eventually, they'd agreed that too much of eating and doing nothing was exhausting, and so Andrés returned upstairs for a nap while Jack and Sofia rested in the living room. He read his Christmas gift from Sofia, Hemingway's *A Farewell to Arms*, a reminder of the American author whom they'd seen writing furiously in the cafés of Montparnasse and who'd arrived at Gertrude Stein's exhibition for Andrés and Jack.

Whilst December showed all the promise that winter would be mild, in late January the weather turned for the worse, with a run of particularly cool days where the wind swirled around the orchard and rattled the windows in their frames, and the normally warm house offered little relief from the blistering cold. The studio and gallery were even colder, freezing during the mornings and taking until mid-afternoon to reach a comfortable temperature. Andrés constantly wore his jacket as well as a scarf, and he repeatedly rubbed his hands together in an effort to warm his freezing fingers. Worse than Andrés' chilled bones, though, was the cough that he developed. A subtle clearing of his throat at first, by February it had worsened, causing fitful nights of sleep, his coughing echoing down the stairs. Sofia sprang into action, sending Jack to the Malaga pharmacy for cough mixture and brewing herbal teas which she insisted Andrés drink, claiming that he would be better in no time at all if he rested and took his medicine.

Although, Andrés' cough eventually settled, he developed a breath-lessness when walking even short distances, and tired easily, often heading indoors for an early siesta. His usual one-hour afternoon rest stretched into two - and even three - hours.

More and more, Jack found himself compensating for Andrés' increasing weakness. 'I'll grab that, mate,' he'd say, stepping forward to lift the larger canvases around the studio or carrying the heaviest of Sofia's trays of cooking to be transported to the gallery.

It was early March when Andrés who put into words that which no one else dared. Jack had just finished preparing a frame for him to paint on. Normally, for the larger frames, Andrés would have helped by unrolling the canvas while Jack lifted the rectangular timber frame onto the bench, and together, they would tack the heavy fabric into place. However, today Andrés was particularly tired and he watched quietly as Jack worked, smiling when Jack joked that he'd done a much better job preparing the canvas alone than he'd ever done with Andrés' assistance.

'Jack, we both know that I was lucky to get through this winter. Who knows what the future may bring.'

The words came out in a rush and caught Jack by surprise. Jack turned and looked into the soft, dark eyes of his friend, which today reflected fatigue and sadness. He took a deep breath, barely trusting himself to speak. While his instinct was to refute Andrés' words with banter, Jack knew that this moment needed to be about honesty, and to deny Andrés the opportunity to speak his mind, would be disrespectful.

'Yes, mate,' he replied quietly. 'You let me know what you need me to do. Anything.'

'I'm okay,' Andrés replied. 'I have been to see Father Sebastian. Our priest. We've known him our whole lives and he is a good, kind man. He'll know what to do. He is ready and I am ready. It is Sofia I worry about. So unfair for her to lose her whole family so young. It is she who'll need support. She'll be devastated.'

The tremor in Andrés' voice caused tears to spring to Jack's eyes. 'I will be here for Sofia, mate,' he promised gruffly. 'I promise you that I will look after her.' He took another deep breath and tried to ignore the lump forming in his throat. 'You know I want to marry her?'

'That is wonderful news, Jack. Has she accepted?'

I haven't asked her—or you, yet,' he corrected himself.

'Why ever not?'

'Because I haven't got anything to offer. As her husband, I'll need to support her. Provide for our future. Maybe I should get a job some-where, so you and Sofia are not supporting me.' Speaking in a rush, Jack was relieved to finally share the concerns that had been keeping him awake at nights.

Andrés shook his head and smiled broadly. 'This makes me very happy, Jack. It is what she would want, I know. And people would talk if you don't marry. While I am here, it is not so bad, I am her brother and people know that if you were to be…ungentlemanly…I would have to shoot you.'

Jack shuddered guiltily – Sofia's nightly sojourns to Jack's bedroom had never been mentioned between them, but he relaxed when he saw the amused glint in Andrés' eye.

'But once I'm gone, it will be awful. That will not be good for Sofia. All villages have their gossips and you can imagine that, even now, plenty are wondering what the bedding arrangements are here at the finca. They are just harmless busybodies with nothing else to talk about. Yet you must get married soon, or you would have to leave.'

Jack nodded, pleased that Andrés was so determined that a wedding should take place. He hoped Sofia would feel the same.

'There is no need to worry about a job. The gallery is enough for now and there is plenty to do here to keep you busy.' Andrés' expression took a serious turn, and with some urgency, he said, 'But when I am gone, you need to sell the gallery. Take Sofia from here. To Australia. England even. Spain is...what would you say?... very troubled. There are problems coming. Strife. I fear for what may come here to Malaga.'

Andrés' insistence that they should leave Spain surprised Jack. Certainly, he had watched Andrés pouring over newspapers and had listened to his comments to Sofia, more recently his voice becoming agitated – at odds with his usual calm demeanour. Sofia would reply, 'No, no ...*Va a estar bien*,' but Andrés would shake his head stubbornly. Occasionally, he'd attempted to explain the issues to Jack – both political and economic - that were threatening Spain, the words spilling out in an emotional rush, his sentences, a blend of English and Spanish that escaped Jack's grasp. Jack understood that Andrés bore fears for Spain's future, in particular, the influence of aggressors. Increasingly, Andrés spoken of Francisco Franco – his belief that Franco would bring bloodshed to Spain, his concern that Malaga may well become a battleground. Like Sofia, to him Andrés concerns seemed highly improbable in the light of their beautiful Spanish summer days on the finca. Jack was astounded to hear Andrés' tell him that a day would come when he must take Sofia across the world, away from the home she loved. How on earth could Andrés even imagine Sofia willingly leaving the finca. What was Jack supposed to do – drag her by the hair!

'Ask her to marry you!' Andrés said, bringing Jack back to the present. 'Ask her soon. We can have a wedding here at the finca. It will be wonderful. And it will give Sofia something to look forward to. No need to sit and be morbid, waiting for me to die,' Andrés said ruefully. 'It will give me something to look forward to, also!'

CHAPTER 10

*E*ncouraged by Andrés' enthusiasm for the idea, Jack decided not to waste any time and he immediately began planning the monumental event of his marriage proposal. He pictured himself on bended knee, his mind formulating the words that he would say. The lack of a customary engagement ring bothered him for a minute, but he disregarded that obstacle, determining that he and Sofia would pick one together. Jack knew exactly where the proposal would take place.

He and Sofia had continued their habit of resting under the orange trees during the siesta when the weather allowed and that afternoon, as they walked from the house, Jack took Sofia's hand and led her along the path to the farthest edge of the finca. Here, a high spot provided a view of the Castillo Gibralfaro above, and the expanse of the Mediterranean below, the olive plantation falling away on the slope before them. This was the location that he always pictured when his mind had turned to fanciful notions of asking Sofia to marry him. Its spectacular scenery was surely the perfect backdrop for such an auspicious occasion. Today was no fanciful imagining though; but rather, the real event and Jack could scarcely contain his excitement. On reaching the wooden seat that had been built for the very purpose of enjoying this magnificent view, he pulled Sofia to him. Holding her close, he looked into her eyes and words tumbled out of his mouth like a cascading waterfall, all thoughts of his well-planned proposal speech forgotten. 'Sofia. I love you. I want to marry you. Will you marry me ....? Wait…stop…'

Jack shook his head and dropped onto one knee. 'Sofia, will you please make me the happiest man in the world by agreeing to be my wife?'

Her eyes lit up. 'Oh, Jack... My love. Of course, I will. Of course, yes. Yes!'

Jack barely believed his ears and relished the joy of the moment. Here he was, in a foreign land, living a life that was beyond anything that he could have imagined a year ago. With the sweetest girl in the world, whom he knew without a doubt loved him as he loved her – and she had just agreed to marry him.

'Come on, Jack – stand up!' Sofia laughed as she pulled him up and reached her arms around his shoulders.

'Jack, this is so wonderful! We can have a wedding in spring! We need to go and see Father Sebastian…Andrés will be so thrilled…'

At the mention of Andrés' name, Jack took a deep breath, recalling this morning's conversation. Pleased to see Sofia's excitement about wedding plans, he was at the same time overcome by depths of sadness for her, knowing what was ahead. Speechless with emotion, he cradled her in his arms, silently vowing that he would do everything in his power to make her happy.

Later that afternoon, glowing with pleasure, they shared the news with Andrés. Feigning total surprise, he offered congratulations and wished them the best, slapping Jack on the back and hugging Sofia. He declared with mock woefulness that he supposed he would have to start washing his own clothes and cooking his own meals now that she was going to have a husband to care for. Sofia laughingly replied that perhaps he could find himself a wife, suggesting some of her own friends in town who frequented the gallery.

Andrés asked when the marriage would take place and suggested they place bans the next day, give the perfunctory four weeks' notice and have a wedding ceremony at the small church at the bottom of the hill, followed by a reception at the art gallery. To Jack's surprise, Sofia was in total agreement, confident that she could organise the wedding within a few weeks. It made him wonder if she was more attuned to Andrés' failing health than she ever admitted.

The next day, Jack and Sofia drove Suzie down the hill to discuss their plans with Father Sebastian and it was clear that Sofia shared her brother's fondness for the priest.

'He has been there for all of our lives – always looked out for me and Andrés. '

'So, he's Catholic?' Jack asked.

'Jack, all of Spain is Catholic. Is that a problem?'

'Not at all… I'll jump a broomstick if you want me to…'

'Broomstick? What do you mean, jump a broomstick?'

'Nothing. Don't worry. We will get married any way you like. I just want us to be married.'

In no time at all they arrived at the presbytery, a whitewashed building positioned beside the small stone cathedral that Jack had noticed in passing on previous occasions when they had traversed the mountain road.

The door opened, even before he and Sofia had reached its entrance, and the priest, looking decidedly unpriestly in gardening overalls, greeted Sofia with a warm hug.

'Dios mío, ¿a quién tenemos aquí?'

Looking at Jack, he continued in surprisingly good English, albeit with a distinct British accent.

'Sofia! Sweet girl, tell me…how are you?' Before she could answer, he then turned to Jack and extended his hand. 'So, this is the young man Andrés has been telling me about?'

'Andrés? Andrés has been here?'

'Oh, we men have a chat occasionally.' The priest's glance at Jack reflected concern, no doubt at Sofia's surprise. 'I have known this girl since… well, since before she was born. Married her parents, oversaw her baptism, confirmation… the happy and… unfortunately, the sad.'

'How do you do.' Jack imagined each of these occasions would have been bittersweet, underpinned by the lingering melancholy of her mother's untimely death. And more recently, Father Sebastian would have supported Sofia and Andrés while their father lay dying. Looking at the gentle lines on the priest's face, his expression revealing a kindly fondness for Sofia, Jack immediately understood why Andrés had turned to him to discuss his own ailing health and to prepare him to be on hand to support Sofia through the dark hours ahead.

'So, Jack. You are from Australia, I hear?' Jack did not get a chance to reply before the priest continued. 'And you are here to stay…not just going to "love her and leave her", as they say?'

Although the priest's tone was light, no twinkle glimmered in his eye when his piercing gaze met Jack's, who knew that he was being challenged.

'No, certainly not. I love Sofia and am thrilled that she has agreed to marry me,' he replied.

'That is very good. Sofia does not need any grief from a broken love affair.'

'Father Sebastian! No! Jack is not like that! We want you to marry us. Soon!'

'Soon! Is there something that I should know? Or perhaps it is best that I don't know?'

Laughing, Sofia patted the priest's garden-soiled hand. 'Father, we love each other. We want to be married, and no, there is no little surprise on the way!'

Jack chuckled guiltily at the subtle side-step to the question of his and Sofia's carnal relations. No, there was no baby on its way … a not unrealistic event that he'd actually raised with Sofia, himself, recently, but she had discounted his fears. *Do not worry Jack. The women in my family do not get pregnant so easily. My mother - she took three years before falling pregnant with me and Andrés. I will let you know the second I am late that our little bebé is on its way!*

'I am happy for you both, then. Congratulations! This is wonderful news! Come in and we will talk over a pot of coffee.'

It took a few minutes for Jack's eyes to adjust to the room, lit only by a small window. Father Sebastian ushered him and Sofia to a cluttered table, where he hastily gathered an assortment of papers, a large Bible opened at the Gospel of Matthew and pens, amid a scattering of cutlery on one end, before going to the sink to fill a large enamel kettle. He settled it on a gas burner and went to a desk in the corner. After fumbling there, Father Sebastian returned to the table with a large notebook, which he opened to a new page, and carefully charged his old fountain pen with ink.

For the next half-hour he recorded details – date, religion, parents' names.

'Jack is Protestant – is that okay?' Sofia asked.

Father Sebastian shrugged. Jack glanced at his open notebook, but the canny priest's hand lay casually over the page, concealing the words that had been recorded.

'It will be all right, my dear. Don't worry. Let's look at my diary for the next few weeks – and decide on a date for your special day.' After a brief discussion the words - Sofia and Jack: Wedding 3 o'clock - were penned into Father Sebastians diary.

An hour later, Jack and Sofia waved farewell to Father Sebastian, who stood watching them from his gate. They would have been pleased to know that the priest had been reassured by his meeting with Jack. His instincts predicted that the young Australian was just right for Sofia, as Andrés had asserted, and if there was one thing Father Sebastian had learned after years of dealing with people, it was to trust his instincts. They would have also have been interested to know that, with Jack a non-Catholic, endless counsel and special permission from the bishop would normally be required prior to their wedding to ensure their union was sanctified. And they would have been astonished to learn of the unhesitating sleight of Father Sebastian's hand, less than an hour later, when, as he transcribed his notes onto the formal documents required by authorities, his upcast eyes accompanied his prayer asking forgiveness for sins committed for the sake of expediency. His flurry of hand movements – from forehead to heart and shoulder to shoulder – ensured potential impediments had been eliminated, and as the inky Spanish words, recorded with a swirling flourish, dried on the page, Jack and Sofia were blissfully ignorant of the shrewd Father's bungle that had identified Jack as a Catholic.

As they returned up the hill to the finca, Jack was startled when Sofia emitted a sound of dismay.

'Jack, what about your parents? I never thought about them! We have not allowed them enough time to travel. Will they be upset to miss your wedding?'

'No – I am sure it will be okay. It really is too big a journey for them to come all the way back to Malaga again.' Jack imagined his parents sitting at the front of the church, their expressions dour, and was thankful that distance would exclude their presence – not to mention his father's work commitments. 'We will be doing them a favour by taking their choice from them.'

The truth was that, as much as William and Marian had warmed to Sofia, acknowledging that she was beautiful, kind and intelligent, it did not mean they would be agreeable to her being wedded to their only son. However, he had long decided that this was their problem to deal with. He was marrying the woman he loved, and so be it.

'I will write to them this afternoon and let them know of our plans. I'll send Margaret a letter, too. She would kill me if I forgot to tell her that we are getting married. Wouldn't it be wonderful if she could come!'

CHAPTER 11

Over the next few weeks, it seemed as if wedding planning took over every minute of their lives. Andrés enthusiastically discussed guests, food and wine, and Jack knew that, beyond his brotherly delight in seeing Sofia marry, Andrés gained additional comfort in seeing Sofia happy and loved in the light of his own poor prognosis.

He and Andrés were given a job list that seemed to grow every day - activities to beautify the courtyard and gallery in readiness for the feast. They moved old, chipped pots to the back garden, cleared weeds that crept through the mosaic pathway and tidied edges. And then there was the painting: walls, garden gates and even the tables and chairs, whose shabby charm borne of years of neglect was no longer accept-able in Sofia's suddenly very critical eyes. Washing duties emerged, including attention to the gallery, studio and the walls and windows that surrounded the courtyard. Jack and Andrés laughingly called Sofia 'Boss Lady' as they worked, asking if she wanted the broom cupboard cleaned and the back fence, two hundred yards down the hill, painted. Ever grumbling that their artists' hands were being destroyed by menial labour, they worked well together: Andrés provided the know-how, while Jack happily followed instructions and completed tasks under his supervision.

～

Jack shook his head as Sofia set off down to Malaga to visit Aunt Jovita for the third day in a row. 'What on earth do you have to talk about?' he asked, and received the stock reply to anything that he or Andrés asked Sofia whenever she met with her aunt: 'Serviettes!'

'In Australia we just have roast lamb, baked vegetables, pavlova and a piece of fruit cake at weddings! There's no need for days on end discussing *serviettes*,' Jack grumbled playfully, although in truth, he'd never attended a wedding in his life, and consequently, was no more knowledgeable about Australian celebrations than he was of Spanish customs. Nonetheless, the hours Sofia dedicated to preparations for their wedding astonished him. Furthermore, beyond the major planning for the reception, several secret rituals seemed to be taking place. For instance, sewing had become a part of Sofia's day, her needle and thread tucked into her bodice and jabbed into fabric at every opportunity – a heavy calico sewing bag accompanying her wherever she went.

'What on earth are you making?' Jack asked, angling his head to make sense of the material held in a taut circle by the embroidery hoop.

'Nothing, Jack…a surprise…you must wait!'

'Well, when shall we buy our wedding rings? It will be a big surprise if you are standing at the altar and I don't have a ring for you! Plus, we still need to buy an engagement ring.'

'Yes, we do need to buy wedding bands. But, I've been thinking … I would like to wear my mother's engagement ring, if that's okay with you. I'll show it to you – it's beautiful! Taking only a few minutes, Sofia returned with the ring her mother had worn for barely five years. It was pretty, a ruby, surrounded by diamonds, set in a fine band of gold. Jack agreed with Sofia, wearing it was exactly the right decision, before pausing, positioning himself on bended knee, and dramatically repeating his words of proposal, to which Sofia laughed hysterically and he declared that he might just withdraw his proposal altogether, since she thought it all such a big joke.

While Jack was happy enough for Sofia to wear her own mother's engagement ring, he decided that he would make his own gift to her. Two days later, with Andrés at the wheel steering Suzie down the hill into Malaga, he undertook a journey that piqued Sofia's curiosity, generating a barrage of questions that Jack absolutely refused to answer.

'But Jack, what did you buy?'

'Nothing.'

'You must have bought something!'

'Not really…nothing that you would be interested in.'

'I could be interested. How do you know what I am interested in?'

'Okay, then: they are fine, white and very pretty!'

'What, Jack? What have you bought?'

'*Serviettes*!'

Jack was amazed to learn that more than a hundred people would attend their wedding, the majority of whom he'd only met by way of brief greetings, but that did not worry him at all. He did experience pangs of disappointment when he received the envelope addressed in Margaret's scrawl, containing her apology for being unable to attend their wedding, and he knew that she too would be equally disappointed. He smiled, thinking about the demanding self-appointed mentor and adopted sister who'd 'discovered' him on his sea crossing to London, and how her relentless interference had been the catalyst for all of the wonderful things that had happened over the last year. She had come to mean a lot to him.

Margaret was also very special to Sofia, as a result of the times that she'd spent with them in Paris. Her role in introducing Andrés' paintings to Roger Fry, leading to their inclusion in Gertrude Stein's exhibition alongside Jack's; her presence when Andrés had won the Julian Academy Student Exhibition annual prize; and of course, she had been right beside them when Andrés had collapsed and rushed to hospital on that same evening. It was Margaret who'd provided a sense of order amid those terrible circumstances. Her quiet support and focus on the practical needs during that awful time would never be forgotten by himself or Sofia.

Jack reread the words on the page before him –

My Dearest Jack and Sofia!!!
I am so excited to hear that you two are tying the knot. How wonderful!
Congratulations! I am sure that you will have years and years of
happiness together, lots of squawking babies, and you, Jack, will get
fatter by the day eating Sofia's amazing Spanish tucker.
Sadly...oh so horribly, terribly sadly, I am not going to be able to make
the trip to Malaga for the nuptials! I've committed to being in Edin-
burgh for almost a month to help Freddie assess the art collection of
some old lord or duke or some such person of Great Significance. It is
an enormously important contract for him – been arranged for months
now, and I cannot let him down. Oh, words cannot describe how disap-
pointed I feel!!! If only Malaga was not so far away! Paris I might
have managed, but not a trip to the deep south of Spain!
Please take lots of photographs, save me some wedding cake and I
promise that I will get to Malaga as soon as I can to swig champagne
with you both in celebration of your marriage.
Much love!
Margaret xxxx
P.S. Love to you also, Andrés. I hope you are behaving yourself,
following Sofia's instructions for good health and painting master-
pieces ready to take to Paris with you when you return to the Académie
Julian.
P.P.S Have you arranged a date to take up your scholarship prize? We
must all coordinate our timetables and I will make sure that I am with

*you all for at least a month. It will be so much fun! The four of us in
Paris together!!*

Jack felt a tremor of nervousness as he read the final paragraph,
addressed to Andrés. Conversations about their return to Paris had
subsided over recent weeks. Certainly, the wedding had dominated all
their thoughts, yet there was a more ominous reason, for as Jack
worked each day alongside Andrés, he was acutely aware of the
increasing frequency with which Andrés was forced to stand and wait
while he regained his breath.

'Curse the damned Spanish Influenza,' Andrés had said recently,
when Jack had entered the studio to find him leaning over the table,
gasping and succumbing to a rare moment of ill humour, as he'd
berated the disease that had left his lungs damaged and vulnerable to
recurring infections.

And, of even greater concern, a moment when Andrés was
suddenly so overcome by weakness that Jack had found a chair and
assisted him to sit. Andrés' hands visibly trembled and the colour
drained from his face. Jack had wanted to call Sofia or the doctor
immediately.

'No, Jack - just let me sit. I'll be all right. This is not the first time.
It will pass soon.'

'But Andrés - remember what happened in Paris! What if you
collapse again?'

Andrés shook his head. 'I promise to be good. If we call the doctor,
Sofia will just worry and it will ruin the fun she's having planning the
wedding.'

Jack shook his head doubtfully, feeling very apprehensive even as
he gave in to Andrés' insistence that he promise to keep the event from
Sofia. Unquestionably, the day of the wedding could not come quickly
enough.

∽

In the final days preceding the wedding, the kitchen's oven seemed to blaze continuously. Sofia rose early, and by mid-morning she was joined by her aunt and other young women - friends and cousins, Jack was never sure – who all laughed together as they beat eggs, sieved flour and added assorted ingredients, creating concoctions which were spread or dolloped or rolled, placed onto the enormous trays and then baked, cooled and stored. A process that continued well into the evening.

Jack and Andrés dared each other to go to the kitchen door, hoping for a cup of tea or a bite to eat, but more often than not, they would be given a job at the sink, asked to remove waste or simply chased out because there was no room for another body in the small space.

Happily, Jack carried a dozen clay pots into the courtyard and filled them with branches of orange blossom collected from the trees in the yard. Orange blossom was essential to Spanish weddings, Andrés explained, bringing both good luck and good fortune. The scent soon filled the courtyard and gallery, becoming infused in Jack's hands and clothing, and inhaling it, he felt his lungs might explode with happiness.

Andrés teased Jack about his obligations, warning him that he'd better sell a few paintings, because as custom dictated, he must provide Sofia with *las arras* - thirteen gold coins during the wedding ceremony or risk having a very unhappy bride.

'Put the coins in this, Jack – it will mean a lot to Sofia.' Andrés handed over a small wooden box, beautifully decorated with a finely-carved olive tree set on a hillside. Andrés explained that this was the very box his father had given to their mother as he'd carried out his wedding duty of *las arras* when he'd married her. The custom symbolized Christ, together with his apostles, and reflected Jack's own promise that he would provide for Sofia and their family in years to come.

It was in such moments as this that Jack sensed, for all of his brotherly bantering and good-natured support as they prepared for the wedding, Andrés' role was also that of a father, overseeing his daughter's suitor, ensuring that proper respect was shown, customs honoured and that Sofia's happiness was protected.

~

Finding a quiet moment to escape, Jack and Andrés drove Suzie into Malaga for some final shopping. Men's business, they told Sofia, refusing to explain their purpose. 'You have your secrets, and we have ours!'

They picked up the two identical suits that had been ordered the previous week and purchased shiny patent leather shoes to match. There was no need to buy shirts, for Sofia had surprised them by presenting them each with a parcel the previous evening, her eyes alight with anticipation of their reaction.

'So now we finally see the fruits of the mystery sewing,' Jack had said, admiring the full-sleeved shirts the packages had revealed, each extraordinarily ornate with thousands of tiny stitches forming decorative bands across the collar and over the chest. Sensing the love Sofia had infused into every stitch, Jack was moved by her attention to detail.

'Yes, and they nearly wore my fingers away,' Sofia replied, beaming with satisfaction at the results of her handiwork.

The absence of both Jack and Sofia's parents at the ceremony necessitated a reshuffling of some customs. Where Jack would have walked down the aisle with his mother and waited together for the grand entrance of the bride, in her absence it was agreed that Aunt Jovita would play that part. Furthermore, where traditionally the bride's father escorted his daughter down the aisle, there was no question – Andrés would undertake that task.

Ever happy to submit to all of Sofia's instructions for the wedding, Jack was determined to add his own custom, and on the night before the ceremony he surprised her with a small gift, the object of mystery that had been purchased on his trip to Malaga weeks earlier. Sofia giggled as she carefully peeled back silver tissue paper to reveal a small red leather box, ornately embossed and decorated in gold. Opening it, she squealed with pleasure when she found an oval-shaped locket, rose gold, engraved with floral swirls, lying on a bed of velvet.

'Oh, Jack! It is so beautiful,' she said, and insisted that he help her put it on immediately. Fumbling with the clasp, Jack was reminded of a day on the Champs-Élysées over ten months ago. The day that his trembling hands had draped a cheap coral necklace, spontaneously purchased from a street vendor, around her slender neck. The day that he and Sofia had released the pent-up avalanche of feelings they'd held for each other. He considered how far they had come, sure that he was the luckiest man alive.

CHAPTER 12

*A*s agreed, Jack and Andrés rose early, excitement in their steps and bantering playfully as they lifted their heavy suitcase, neatly packed with their clothes for the wedding, into Suzie's trunk. Andrés gave a departing honk of the horn as the car veered onto the road, signalling to Sofia that the coast was clear – she could now arise. She had been so serious when insisting that she and Jack must not see each other before their wedding ceremony the next day, for fear of bad luck, that Andrés had visibly stifled his laughter, while Jack resisted the urge to comment on the not-so-traditional nightly visits that had been taking place ever since they arrived in Spain.

He and Andrés planned to spend the day at Aunt Jovita's house, while their aunt, in turn, would spend the day at the finca with Sofia, tending to last-minute preparations - setting food on benches, ready for warming and serving, placing lanterns at the ready for lighting at the first sign of darkness, and loading a table with crockery and cutlery for the wedding breakfast. Sofia had been very clear in her instructions for the men: to unpack the suitcase and hang out their clothes as soon as they arrived at Aunt Jovita's house; to relax, but not allow Stefan to ply them with too much wine; and finally, a non-negotiable direction for

Andrés to drop Jack at the church at precisely 2:30, return to the finca to collect herself at exactly 2:45 and to have her standing at the church entrance promptly, at 3:00.

For Jack, the day took on the aspect of a dream, so surreal he was barely able to comprehend the momentous events that would take place in the early afternoon. Nervous anticipation caused his hands to tremor and his legs to feel like someone else's. At the same time, a sense of quiet dread washed over him at unexpected moments. An irrational fear that some catastrophe might befall himself or Sofia, crushing their wedding plans before they could even take place. He counted the hours to when he would be reunited with Sofia – finally to be her husband – and as he contemplated their future together, he knew that he had never felt more complete. It seemed everything in his past before Paris was disconnected, irrelevant to their life together here in Spain. Barely fifteen months ago, when he'd received the ticket for the *Ormonde*, the proposed journey to visit relatives and see Big Ben and the London Tower had thrilled him. His place in the world was firmly established – the son of Marian and William Tomlinson, reluctantly committed to taking up a position in his father's company as a junior clerk. A career plan that Jack had dreaded, but in the absence of any other ideas, his future had been mapped out – working in finance, on a trajectory towards accounts manager, and possibly a financial advisor for Goldsbrough Mort & Co, like his father. There he would stay, for the next forty years, with job security in a respectable position that would provide a sound income to meet the needs of the family he'd hoped to call his own one day. Beyond his personal fondness for drawing, his life had been predetermined as an extension of his parents'. He had been modelled in the image of his father and destined to follow the well-trodden pathway to affluence and respectability, to marry a girl in the image of his mother, who would keep a fine home, attend morning teas and host dinners to help him strengthen business ties. They would have two or three children, who would have gone to the right schools, played foot-ball and cricket, and possibly joined a rowing club to meet on frosty mornings on the banks of the Yarra River. Perhaps one of his children might have enjoyed drawing also, and Jack would have treasured afternoons in the sun as he showed his youngster the rudiments: how to shade to create three-dimensional images, to blend colours and apply paint.

However, in that world, drawing was a passion for children to enjoy, not a pursuit that parents of young men bragged about as they might sporting or academic achievements. Certainly, a painting could be shown to guests and admired for its detail - never was it viewed as the path to a career!

Today, Jack knew he was a very different person from that boy who'd left Australia. Whole in a way he'd never imagined. He'd experienced the joys of being independent, and was about to be bound with Sofia in marriage; henceforth, creating their own destiny. Every day would be spent with each other; meals, long lazy mornings, talking, planning, working side by side to build a home. And one day, there would be babies. His and Sofia's children.

While he loved his parents, the truth was that he now viewed them through the foggy veil of distance and time. Their values and ambitions were no longer his, nor did he feel bound by them.

Now, he appreciated simple joys: time passed working in an orchard, creating paintings in brilliant hues and loving the sweetest woman in the world. And increasingly, he understood life's woes. The poverty and hardship of the artists of Montparnasse, the losses Sofia and Andrés had borne with the deaths of their parents, the illness that threatened Andrés' life, and the perils Andrés believed Spain faced. With a deeper understanding of the world, Jack felt responsible for keeping Sofia safe, honouring the promise he'd made to Andrés many times during their hours of quiet conversation in the studio. Should the time come, Jack knew that Andrés expected him to take Sofia to Australia, regardless of her determination to stay. Repeatedly, Jack had listened when Andrés had tried to warn Sofia with his predictions about Spain's future; however, Andrés' concerns always fell on deaf ears. Sofia stubbornly insisted that the troubles arising in Spain between the workers, military and church would be temporary, in just the same way as she insisted that Andrés' health would improve.

~

Three o'clock finally arrived and Jack waited at the altar of the beautiful little church, now filled with dozens of people. A few faces were familiar amongst the majority of whom he'd never met before, their heads wobbling as though on swivels, alternating between smiling encouragingly at him and rotating towards the doorway. It seemed that everybody was determined to be the first to see Sofia when she arrived. As planned, Aunt Jovita stood beside him, smiling and squeezing his arm. All of a sudden, the voices in the room quietened, eyes focused on the open door at the back of the church.

Spellbound, Jack's heart quickened as he gazed towards the arched entrance where Sofia stood, her arm lightly resting on Andrés'. The black wedding dress, complete with a gossamer-fine lace veil draped across her face, had been recreated in the style of her own mother's, and was less of a shock to Jack than he expected, although he was glad Sofia had the foresight to explain that Spanish brides traditionally wore black – especially in her mother's day. Truly, she looked beautiful, and his eyes never left her as she gracefully walked down the aisle towards him, a silent communication of love, tenderness and joy passing between them.

Jack straightened as Sofia approached him, instinctively reaching out to grasp her right hand in his. He nodded to Andrés, and as their eyes met, Jack hoped Andrés felt his assurance – his promise to care for Sofia in the manner he knew Andrés expected.

Andrés responded with a faltering smile and a subtle nod, and that briefest, almost imperceptible exchange held the significance of a shaking of hands, of a contract written in blood, of an edict delivered by a judge. Jack knew he was making a vow this day not only to Sofia, but also to Andrés.

Taking Sofia's left hand, Jack positioned her squarely in front of him, certain it could not be possible to love anyone more than he loved her at this moment.

Over the next few minutes, words were uttered; the congregation stood, sang, sat, and murmured responses at the priest's prompts. Jack, however, may as well have been in an empty room with only Sofia before him. She smiled when he passed the small box of coins to her, nodding her appreciation and whispering *gracias* and all seemed to be on track. Then came a moment of distraction when he sought her left hand for the placement of the wedding ring and he could hear laughter from the congregation as she withdrew it, placing her other hand towards him. Confused, he again reached for her left hand.

'No, Jack, the right hand. This is the Spanish way,' she instructed, laughing at his puzzled face when she repositioned her right hand in his.

Shrugging his shoulders and shaking his head as if to say 'you Spanish are very odd', Jack pushed the gold wedding band firmly onto her right ring finger. Finally, on cue, he responded, 'I do' to Father Sebastian's prompting to take Sofia to be his wife and then, abandoning all formality, in a moment of sheer exuberance, he pulled Sofia towards him and lifted her in a firm bear hug, kissing her deeply and swinging her around in a full circle before settling her to face the congregation, who were now laughing, cheering and applauding.

'And now I suppose we had better pronounce them man and wife,' came the chortling, belated response from Father Sebastian.

Following the ceremony, Jack and Sofia made their way along the aisle amid a cascade of congratulatory kisses and hugs, and as planned, they walked up the hill to the finca hand-in-hand. The twenty-minute journey provided time for the advance crew of Sofia's friends and cousins, led by her aunt, to undertake the final preparations for the courtyard and gallery in readiness for the wedding breakfast. A carnival atmosphere prevailed as dozens of high-spirited friends and relatives joined them on the walk, chattering, laughing and intermittently erupting into boisterous and somewhat bawdy singing accompanied by rapid clapping, while, adding to the chaos, others rained a constant stream of rice at the newlyweds. At regular intervals the whole parade stopped, laughing hysterically while Sofia made a show of pulling at the folds of her dress, groping into her bodice, and shaking out the grains that had slipped through her neckline and into her undergarments.

Finally, they reached the roadside entrance of the gallery. Together, he and Sofia waited beside the picket gate, accepting congratulations and welcoming each guest to the reception, before ushering them through to the courtyard, now bathed in the soft glow of candles and kerosene lanterns. The gallery doors were set wide open, revealing a stunning transformation - from its usual layout to that of a beautiful reception room. Pottery and craftwork had been carefully packed and stored, and now three neat rows of trestle tables were visible in the flickering candlelight. Orange blossom petals were scattered across them amid green foliage and orbs of bright polished, perfect oranges. The lively sound of guitars filled the air, skilfully played by three young men – the local *mariachi* band. While their rippling notes provided a delightful ambiance, the trio were, in fact, warming up, preparing themselves in readiness to play the lengthy *seguidillas manchegas*, the traditional Spanish wedding dance. When Sofia had told Jack about this particular custom, he'd been firstly horrified, and then abundantly relieved to find it was Sofia, the bride, who would take the main role, and he could stand back and watch. For all of the enjoyment they'd had on the dance floors in Paris, Jack was convinced that he had two left feet and envisioned Sofia landing on the floor in a heap should he be required to attempt a formal dance under the gaze of a room full of wedding guests. Tonight, for the *seguidillas manchegas*, the guests would take turns in presenting Sofia with a gift of money, symbolizing a future of prosperity and financial security for her and Jack, and in response, she would dance with them.

For the next few hours, raucous laughter accompanied the clinking of glasses and the consumption of whisky, wine, cava and enough food to feed a small army. Prior to dinner, plate after plate of tapas were passed around: marinated anchovies, garlic prawns, olives and spicy sausage served with bread. Eventually, the guests were ushered into the gallery, where they were seated and served numerous courses including paella, cold meats and fish baked in a creamy sauce. More whiskey, more wine and more cava was consumed And then, of course, there was the wedding cake, as well as an assortment of almond shortbreads, fruit flans and air light *miguelitos*

Jack could barely remove his eyes from Sofia, who was radiant and bubbling with delight as she laughed, danced and accepted hugs and kisses from her friends and family. He recognised a number of guests - those who'd visited the gallery when they'd returned from Paris, and a couple whom he now knew to be Sofia's closest friends and who'd been regular visitors to the finca over the past few weeks to assist with the wedding preparations. Today, their fascination with Jack was unconcealed. They smiled and giggled at him and asked Sofia questions which, from their cheeky looks, he knew concerned him. Later, she told him how the joke of the evening had been that their babies would hop like kangaroos and she would need to make a pouch to carry them in.

A steady stream of guests approached, handshakes from the males – including Mario who smiled broadly as he slapped Jack on the back, offering best wishes to him and Sofia. There were kisses from the females accompanied by *'felicidades!'* or halting attempts at the English 'congratulations!' Their warmth and smiles emphasised how pleased they were to see some happiness come Sofia's way. Those more proficient with their English laughed as they attempted to share their own stories about Sofia and quizzed Jack about his life in Australia.

Jack found himself returning smiles to everyone: his rudimentary comprehension of Spanish - functional in the presence of Sofia and Andrés - suddenly, totally inadequate amid the chattering of their guests. He repeated his Spanish welcoming phrases, adjusted to male and female, young and old, so many times that they started to blur and he wondered if he was getting them right, but nobody seemed to mind.

Old friends grabbed Sofia for a dance. Old boyfriends? Cousins? The jealousy that Jack had once harboured was gone and he did not mind whom Sofia danced with at all. She was his wife, and he knew, without doubt now, the extent of the love they had for each other.

Looking around the room, Jack could see the touch of Sofia's hand on everything. Mistily, he gazed upon her and could barely believe that they were married. Sofia was now his wife! While she was constantly being lured away by friends and family or to check on the progress of the various courses, she returned to his side every few minutes to give his arm a squeeze, her eyes bright with happiness.

After dinner, Sofia and Jack circulated the floor, arm in arm. He carried a very full basket while she selected from its contents - an assortment of brightly wrapped *detalles* - gifts of sweetly perfumed lace handkerchiefs for the ladies and cigars and small bottles of wine for the men.

Additionally, Sofia pinned bright red flowers on the single women – strangely, upside down, and Jack questioned her eyesight.

'It's an old Spanish custom, Jack. Don't worry. They will all be trying to lose their flowers as quickly as possible. The first girl to lose hers will be the first to marry!'

As the evening wore on, a nostalgic air pervaded the room. The band sang songs of love and passion in deep, heartfelt tones while couples swayed together, their arms wrapped around each other. Jack held Sofia close – for these dances she was his alone, and he was not sharing her anymore. A change in tone caused both he and Sofia to look to the stage. There, to Jack's surprise, Andrés had joined the band, singing with a deep, rich voice. At the end of the song, he retired the microphone as a light wheeze caused him to cough. Jack knew Andrés loved music, his light hum frequently resonating through the studio as he stood at his easel, but he had not realised just how fine a voice Andrés had until now.

~

It was in the early hours of the morning before the guests finally started to leave, and Jack felt so tired, he could barely hold himself upright. Arm in arm, he and Sofia farewelled their friends and family, thanking them for sharing such a wonderful day. Andrés surprised them as, with moist eyes and a shaky smile, he shook hands with Jack and clasped Sofia to him in a tight hug before bidding them both good-night and setting off down the road. With his friend, Antonio, on one side, Stefan on the other and his overnight bag slung over his shoulder, he called back that he would see them in a day or two.

As Jack and Sofia entered the house, it was clear that guests had not confined themselves to the reception area. From the moment they stepped through the front door, they were immersed in a sea of decorations. Streamers, banners and boughs of orange blossom lined the halls. With a sudden movement, Jack scooped Sofia into his arms, and ignoring her laughing cries of 'Put me down! We'll both fall to our deaths', he ascended the stairs, carried her to the bedroom at the end of the landing and nudged the door open.

This room, first shared by the twins' parents and then, for almost two decades, their father, had stood empty for the last four years. Beyond an occasional dusting, the room had remained unchanged. Jack had rarely entered it. Once, when he first arrived, he had helped Sofia move a small chest of drawers to his downstairs room, and together they'd leaned against the broad south-facing window, opened to allow fresh air to enter. Positioned at the finca's highest point, it offered commanding views of the orchard and the Mediterranean.

Following a discussion with Andrés, Sofia had agreed that the room was right for her and Jack, and she'd spent hours sewing bright curtains and a colourful bedspread, polishing the timber dressing table until it gleamed and even hanging one of Jack's recent paintings on the wall behind the bed. However, there was no sign of Jack's painting now, for in its place hung a colourful banner, and the bed before them was swathed with still more orange blossom, amid which he unceremoniously dumped Sofia, triggering another surge of uncontrollable laughter.

'*Espero que no duermas bien esta noche, amigos,*' she gasped. Tears ran down her face as she pointed at the banner, the edges of which were decorated with dozens of tiny footprints and the word '*corretear*' repeated across its surface.

Jack looked at her quizzically as she wiped tears away and tried to control her mirth before translating – 'Hope you don't sleep too well, tonight, friends!' She pointed to the word '*corretear*' – 'Pitter-patter!' – and again dissolved into hysterical giggles. Jack fell onto the bed beside her, cradling her in his arms.

'Let us hope so,' he said softly as he brushed the hair from her forehead, before kissing her slowly and deeply.

Since their first night lying together in Paris in a little hotel room illuminated only by a flashing neon light, Jack and Sofia had spent hours entwined in each other's arms. They had both relished her nightly visits to his darkened room and looked forward to afternoons when they'd lain on the brightly coloured woven rug under the orange trees during siesta. However, this special night, their wedding night, held an indescribable magic of its own. Jack laughed as tiny petals, secreted within the bedlinen by Sofia's mischievous friends, floated into the air when they pulled the cover back. His senses, bombarded with the perfume of orange blossom yet again, knew this beautiful scent would forever remind him of the day he and Sofia were married.

CHAPTER 13

*J*ack and Sofia agreed to delay their plans for a honeymoon. The Spanish spring was a busy season for the gallery, and in any event, their life together was joyful and already they felt like they were on a continuous honeymoon. Besides, although the words were never directly spoken, neither he nor Sofia would contemplate leaving Andrés for even a few days; the return of his intermittent dry cough was a constant reminder of his precarious state of health.

The roadside swarmed with visitors as the summer warmth lured increasing numbers of tourists up the hill to walk the castle's ramparts and take photos of the sea. Many stopped in at the gallery to peruse the local art and crafts, purchasing gifts for their families or selecting personal mementos of their holiday on the Costa del Sol to take home. As the demands of baking for the gallery increased, Jack often assisted Sofia in the kitchen, cheerfully washing dishes, checking biscuits and transporting trays across the courtyard for an almost insatiable flow of customers.

A steady stream of income was derived from regular sales of 'bread and butter paintings,' as Jack and Andrés referred to their pictures of

Spanish dancers, Malagian scenery and yard animals. Increasingly, both were making time to develop more substantial pieces – often experimental, inspired by modern Cubist or Post-Impressionist works and which would take a number of attempts and several weeks to get right. Andrés' style had changed recently and his paintings were becoming increasingly wild – Fauve-like, according to Sofia – with lines and colours that stirred emotions Jack found confusing, although he always nodded encouragingly as Andrés explained the meaning behind his work. Had Andrés' declining health and the subsequent emotional reactions inspired these paintings, Jack wondered.

Jack ambitiously planned a series of portraits depicting daily life around Spanish fincas – aspiring to achieve the translucency of Sorolla as he depicted the dry Spanish summer and the languid manner of rural workers meandering up the steep hills, walking beside donkeys that strained under the weight of the baskets tied across their backs; women with white aprons strung around broad hips, scarves draped across their faces in protection from the sun's burning rays, feeding the large, screeching fowl who pecked the hardened earth for scatterings of seeds and vegetable scraps from the kitchen.

As the heat of summer gave way to autumn, the demands of the orchard increased. Jack and Sofia worked tirelessly, pruning orange trees, cutting away dead branches and checking for signs of insect infestations whilst Andres pottered in the back garden before making his way into the studio for an early start.

Thoughts of a baby, his and Sofia's baby, was ever on Jack's mind, but a pregnancy remained elusive. In the months after their marriage they'd discussed 'their baby' often, as if by the act of their wedding, a pregnancy would automatically follow. This had not been the case, though, and even though Jack found himself counting the weeks between Sofia's bleeds, his hope rising each month, he learned to keep his excited anticipation to himself, for despite Sofia's explanation that women in her family never fell pregnant easily, her downcast manner at the onset of each bleed reflected her deep disappointment.

Cool, fresh breezes suggested that winter would be early, calling for jumpers, a scarf for Sofia, and a constant monitoring of Andrés health for they were determined that no infection would come his way. Thankfully, it was not so cold as the previous year, and before they knew it, the coolness in the air subsided and spring was upon them again.

The gallery was at its liveliest, and daily there were visitors from France, England and America making their way up the mountain, keeping Sofia busy with her baking, while Jack and Andres painted. Jack and Sofia both believed that Andres was looking well, these days. Thinner, perhaps, but his pallor had diminished as his mornings in the sun gave him a healthy glow.

Jack looked up at Andrés as the loud voices of tourists drifted from the carpark. Voices that sounded different from the usual accents of the British, French and Italian tourists.

'Australians,' Jack remarked, immediately putting down his brushes and walking to the door, almost expecting to see his parents again. Australian visitors to the gallery were rare and always a source of interest, both to Jack and to the tourists, who were invariably surprised as well as intrigued when they found an Australian living so far from home. Today, it was two couples, their open-roofed Model T Ford visible through the gate as they walked into the courtyard. The vehicle was conspicuous for the ill-assorted pieces of luggage that had been jammed into every crevice and Jack wondered how they had all fitted into the small vehicle.

As he approached them, Jack was surprised when the taller of the men said, 'And you must be Jack Tomlinson?'

'Yep, that's me, mate,' he replied, shaking the man's hand with an enquiring expression.

'Margaret said we'd find you here, but apologies, I'm being rude – Justus.' He waved towards himself, and turning to the others, indicated, 'Lillian, John and Polly. We are on a bit of a tour and Margaret insisted that, if we made it so far as to Malaga, we had to look you up…see what you're up to… Spoke highly of you, she did. And your mate here.' He nodded towards Andrés, who had silently followed Jack out from the studio to observe the new arrivals.

Jack led them across to the gallery, introducing them to Sofia who quickly oriented them to the gallery items on display. They immediately began moving around the room, ignoring the tables of crafts, instead drawn to the paintings on the walls. He recognised the stance of artists viewing work, as opposed to tourists. It was in the approach, he decided: standing back to take in the whole and moving in, eyes squinting, head tipping. Jack knew they were studying brush strokes and colour blends, perspective and compositional features rather than the aesthetic details of the image, and in doing, so they were attempting to discern the techniques the artist had used.

'Whew…a Matisse, very nice,' noted the small man who had been introduced as John. He continued, 'And quite a collection of Picassos. Everybody is talking about him these days. Jury is out as far as I'm concerned. I'm not altogether sure if he is a genius or a madman.'

'Aren't his paintings of women just too strange?' Polly added in agreement. 'And to think how talented he was as a child. We saw a collection of his works at the Prado.'

'Have a look at this, Justus,' the tall, thin woman – Lillian – called across the room. Justus joined her, standing before Andrés' most recent work, a startling eruption of concentric circles in blues and greens, crossed by black lines forming deep vee-shapes, suggestive of bird wings flapping across a golden plain. 'Resurrection,' Andrés had called it – 'the birth of an olive tree.' Andrés had explained the painting's message to Jack just last week, describing how birds ingested olives and transmitted the seeds across the plains. Jack had thought that the colours were effective, but Andrés' abstracts were not really to his taste. Justus' face was inscrutable as he gazed at the work before continuing around the gallery. He viewed the paintings wordlessly, grunting and nodding here and there, but revealing no indication of his thoughts.

Minutes later, he arrived before a second painting by Andrés – a large work that was breathtakingly beautiful, and of which Andrés was rightfully proud. It was a panoramic image that suggested the township of Malaga through assorted shapes in the foreground, the mid-ground depicting slashes of ultramarine and blazes of alizarin orange interrupted by vivid cobalt blue. Sofia insisted that it had to be professionally framed and submitted to the Prado's annual contest, certain this painting could win Andrés yet another major prize in the esteemed art competition. On each side of the extraordinary canvas hung smaller paintings in the same style. One was of the fishing boats docked down at the wharf in Malaga; in the other, a craggy fisherman and his son, rods in hand, walked along the beach, a storm brewing overhead.

'Marvellous! Extraordinary!' exclaimed Justus, and the others joined him. Together, they analysed the colours used in the wild sky and deep blue sea. Jack indicated that Andrés was the artist, initiating a detailed conversation about Andrés' technique and influences. Justus and his friends quizzed Andrés on the way he'd used his palette knife and the oil mediums that he preferred. They were unanimous in their opinion that Australians had barely begun to appreciate these colourful landscapes, with the majority of the population – critics and public alike – valuing realistic images where the colours and brushwork created an almost photographic likeness of their subjects.

Soon the visitors' inquisitive eyes landed on a series of Jack's paintings, the majority of which had been designed to appeal to tourists. Two, however, had been inspired by the night they'd visited Maria's Den. The first was of a flamenco dancer bearing extraordinary presence. Standing tall; her left arm raised high, framing her face; her right arm extended forward; her facial expression indiscernible – a challenge? disdain? Her black eyes returned the viewers gaze with a piercing directness that was as disconcerting as had been Señora Maria. Jack had deliberately applied every ounce of advice received from

Monsieur Simon, as well as the theories of Clive Bell and Robert Fry, and was pleased with the way his painting had captured the magnificence of the dancer in all of her intimidating glory. The second painting was captivating for the motion that it depicted: a pair of dancers in the foreground, a flamenco guitarist languidly leaning on a set of stairs behind them. Using a bolder colour palette than usual, Jack had been very pleased with the effect he'd achieved.

While both paintings drew many compliments from tourists, the size and price of each rendered them special pieces to be prized by a serious art aficionado who understood the value of quality work and had large walls on which to display them.

The Australian visitors enthused about Jack's work and complimented him on the evocative tone of the paintings. Interested to learn more about his travels, they were surprised to hear that he'd left Melbourne barely two years earlier. He described his meeting with Margaret on the *Ormonde*, how she had taken him in hand, introducing him to her family and effectively redirecting his life from that of a tourist visiting his relatives in London, to a student in Paris and now an artist in Spain. Jack remembered how critical Margaret had been of the male artists in Melbourne and felt a little guilty when they laughed as he described her, clearly familiar with her strong opinions.

'I'd love to hear about the Académie Julian,' Justus said. 'How about we dig through the car and find a bottle of wine for us all to share? There's bound to be something tucked in amongst the suitcases. Does that sound like a good idea?'

For the remainder of the afternoon Jack, Sofia and Andrés enjoyed the afternoon in the courtyard sharing stories, olives, dried fish, bread and wine with the Australian visitors while the rest of Spain enjoyed a siesta.

Jack marvelled at the small world of artists when he realised that, not only did they know Margaret, but also Roger Fry, the Bells, whom he had visited in Bloomsbury, and even Gertrude Stein. They were enormously impressed to hear how Roger and Gertrude had organised an exhibition for both Andrés and Jack, eager to learn every detail.

As the afternoon drew to a close, they walked to carpark to bid the Australians farewell. Justus turned to him.

'So, Jack, will Australia get the benefit of your presence anytime soon?' Justus asked, his piercing blue eyes searching. The question took Jack by surprise and he found himself stammering an incoherent response that combined a shake of his head with an affirmative. Thoughts of his recent conversations with Andrés, compelling him to take Sofia to Australia, collided with her own assertions that she would never leave the finca.

'Well, we are thinking... I am not really sure... Perhaps next year.'

Jack resisted the urge to meet Sofia's eyes even as he felt her jolt beside him.

'Well, you make sure you look me up when you come home, Jack. I will be very keen to see how your painting progresses and learn more about your experiences here in Spain,' Justus concluded.

'Why did you say we may be in Australia next year, Jack?' Sofia asked immediately after the visitors left. 'How could that happen? I cannot leave the gallery!'

Andrés answered for him. 'Sofia, I told Jack he must take you away from here. Maybe not next year. But one day. When I am gone. You cannot stay here. Too much is happening.'

'Rubbish, Andrés. You are not going anywhere. I am not going anywhere. And I sure hope that Jack is not planning to go anywhere, either.' And with a withering glare at the both of them, Sofia stomped into the house, leaving the men looking silently at each other.

Jack felt stricken; he'd never seen Sofia so angry. Shrugging, Andrés smiled feebly at Jack's worried expression. 'It's okay. She'll come around.'

There was no more reference to a visit to Australia that day, but Sofia's displeasure with the men, and particularly with Andrés, whom she blamed for putting such mad ideas into Jack's head, was made evident by her terse exchanges during their evening meal.

However, Sofia's anger did not last long and the conversation was soon forgotten as the days lengthened and the tourist season made for busy mornings whilst the restful siesta, laying arm in arm under the sweet smell of the orange trees, provided a welcome escape from the summer heat.

CHAPTER 14

'Yoo-hoo!' came the call of a familiar voice across the courtyard.

It was October, and having just taken the kitchen food scraps to the compost, Jack was now helping Sofia clear up the breakfast dishes, pleased that it was once again Monday and the gallery was closed for the day.

He'd heard the squeak of brakes from the road, as the early morning bus crawled up the hill and subconsciously noticed that it had slowed down outside the gallery. However, visitors were rare so early in the morning, not to mention the sign's warning that the gallery was not open on Mondays, and so he had taken little notice.

At the sound of the voice, they looked at each other and said in unison, 'Margaret!'

Jack rushed to the door, Sofia close behind, and he opened it, grinning broadly. He had not realised how much he missed this friend who had been such a support to both himself and Sofia during their time in Paris.

'Jack, Sofia!'

'Margaret!' they exclaimed simultaneously, launching into hugs, kisses and talking all at once.

Over two years had passed since they had seen Margaret and yet it felt like only yesterday. She looked different in some ways, every bit a modern woman with her hair cut into a pageboy bob which forced her curls to extend almost horizontal. A baggy cardigan strung across her shoulders revealed a manly-collared shirt, its striped fabric loosely tucked into pleated, baggy trousers with broad cuffs resting high above dainty ankles. Encased in fine slip-on shoes were the feet that seemed to gallantly transport Margaret from country to country, at her whim.

'Margaret! My, my, you look like one of those snooty-nosed society women we see in the newspapers! You know, with polo horses and hounds. You have moved up in the world!'

'Don't you bloody society-lady me, Jack, or I will give you one of my finely practised withering glares. They're killers and are quite the thing in England, only usually I am on the receiving end. Freddie and I traipse around the country estates with their ten bedrooms and maids' quarters and acres of gardens, appraising the art collections of the Who's Who. It's little wonder all the old lords and dukes are going broke and being forced to sell up the family collections, what with their gardeners and house-keepers and chamber maids to pay. Some of those places are enormous. I need to dress respectably, else they might think that Freddie's just a two-bit art dealer, or so he tells me. It's all about gaining their confidence, apparently. *Look after them, and they will have us selling their priceless family collections for ever.* And of course, there is the hope that they will refer us to all of their friends, who are equally strapped for cash.'

'Well, I think you look wonderful – doesn't she, Sofia? It is just so good to see you again! I can't believe that you are here! How did you get here?' Jack wanted to know everything, Margaret's very presence reminding him of how much he enjoyed her company and how much he'd missed her. She was the closest thing to a sister that he'd ever had, and he loved the bond he'd shared with her from almost the minute they'd met on the *Ormonde*.

'Oh, you know – trains, and more trains and then the bus to get me up to here. Tell me about you both. I want to hear about everything and see everything. The wedding, your paintings, the gallery! This place is charming, Sofia – how wonderful, and what a view!'

Sofia nodded, smiling. 'Yes, we love it. It's the only home we've ever known.'

'Well, well! Margaret! Here's trouble.' Andres' grin was broad as he appeared at the doorway. 'I could have guessed that you would be the cause of all this ruckus… How wonderful to see you here.'

Margaret crossed the room excitedly to greet him with a kiss and hug. 'Andres, how are you? You look much better than the last time I saw you, that's for sure.' Of course, he did, Jack thought – the last time Margaret had seen Andres, he'd been lying in a bed at the Hôpital de la Pitié, pale and gasping for each breath.

'I'm very well, Margaret, and so much better for seeing you. How fantastic of you to come and visit us.'

Margaret kept her arm around Andres' waist, beaming back at Jack and Sofia. 'So here I am, together with you all again!' she said. 'Don't let me get in the way. Just tell me what happens and give me a job. I'll need to earn my board because my suitcases are out on the roadside. I'm planning on a nice long stay.'

Sofia laughed delightedly. 'Another woman in the house! How lovely! I need all the help I can get to keep these two layabouts organised!'

'Come on, Margaret. If we head out into the courtyard, Sofia might stop complaining and find us a pot of coffee,' Andres said with a chuckle. 'Then you can tell us exactly what you have been doing that has been keeping you so busy in London – or is it Paris? – these days.'

For the next few hours, the four sat in the courtyard, drinking coffee and catching up on each other. Margaret described some of the changes that were going on in London. The crash of the American stock exchange had spread to England, causing high unemployment in some places, although others seemed to barely feel it.

'It gets a bit hard sometimes. Freddie and I go to these enormous posh houses to look at art collections, while the poor coal miners and ship builders can barely afford food. In some of the towns up north, there are hardly any jobs – and yet other industries are booming. New houses are going up everywhere and I am sure that the number of motor vehicles on the roads increases every day.'

Margaret loved the gallery and immediately insisted that she should attend to it for a few hours each day to give Sofia a break.

As the afternoon wore on, Jack took Margaret out the back to show her the orchard. At the woodpile, Jack wielded the axe, chopping kindling for the kitchen stove in readiness for the next morning. Margaret asked quietly, 'Jack, what is going on with Andres? He looks awful.'

'Yes, his health is declining,' Jack answered in the same low tone. 'Sleeps a lot more these days and his coughing has got worse.' He realised with alarm that, in Margaret's eyes, Andres declining health was even more drastic than he and Sofia had realised.

'I wish there was something we could do. Apparently not, according to the doctor. Andres is quite resigned to his fate. He just wants to enjoy what time he has without being morbid. In saying that, I think he is trying to prepare Sofia for the future. He jokes about dying often, much to her annoyance. She won't hear him speak of it. Refuses to discuss it, even with me. She's going to be a terrible mess when he...' Jack stumbled at the words and Margaret nodded sadly and patted his arm.

'I know, Jack, it is awful. Such a lovely, talented man,' she said. 'It's so unfair. Poor Sofia. She'll have lost all of her family and she's what – only twenty-four?'

Jack nodded. 'Yes, it's awful. Little wonder she refuses to talk about it.'

'Well, Jack, if Andres wants to get on with living, then let's enjoy this time together. The time to be morbid will arrive soon enough, I dare say.'

True to her word, throughout dinner, Margaret had them in stitches describing how she had started some commissions, painting - of all things - pets! She shuddered. Her very first cat portrait began quite by accident.

'I was looking after Michelangelo – Freddie's beloved cat,' she informed Sofia and Andres, 'and just began, you know, sketching. And then my sketch turned into a painting, which of course, Freddie just had to hang on the gallery wall. Not because I am a great painter, of course, no…just because he is nuts about anything to do with that great fiend of a beast. Well, then, of course, one of his old dames spotted it and had to have her cat painted, too…and so it went on. Now, not only am I the go-to person for cats, but also dogs, and anything else that people with far too much money can think of. Last week, I was commissioned to do an enormous bloody parrot sitting on its owner's shoulder. The human was placid enough, but the darned bird scared me witless, squawking and glaring at me whenever it decided that I'd ventured too close. "He won't hurt you, love…he's just excited!" the old biddy kept saying to me!'

Later they took Margaret into the studio and showed her his and Andres recent works.

'What a lovely big studio!' She glanced around at the overcrowded room, where finished paintings leaned haphazardly against the walls.

'Have you been keeping touch with your Parisian contacts?' she asked.

'From time to time. We had a letter from Miss Stein a few months ago and a couple of cheques did come through from the galleries, but we haven't heard anything for a while now. Really, it's near impossible to keep up with it all from here. We did plan to go back soon, but… well, it's not really the right time, now.'

The truth was that conversations about their proposed trip to Paris had been all but abandoned since the wedding. Margaret nodded, her expression thoughtful, and Jack could see that she understood that Andres' health had put a question mark over their plans.

'Why don't we pack some of these off and send them up to London? Freddie would love to show these to his clients. He was thrilled to hear about your exhibition with Roger and Gertrude. When Roger was over at the Grafton, bragging about the exhibition, Freddie was green with envy. You know, they all try to outdo each other with their new discoveries, each determined to be credited for finding the next Picasso.'

Sofia was thrilled by her suggestion.

'What a wonderful idea, Margaret,' she exclaimed. 'I have been worrying about Andres' and Jack's paintings in Paris. It's been months since we heard anything from the galleries there. Perhaps Freddie might know someone who could follow them up.'

'Very likely. They all seem to know each other and I know he has connections all over Paris. How about we send him a list of the galleries in Paris, along with these paintings? He is just as likely to slip across to France himself for a few days. I'm sure he would be happy to follow these up for you.'

The afternoon was spent with the four of them sorting through paintings, and finally, a dozen canvases from each Andres' and Jacks' collections were set aside to be rolled, packaged and forwarded to Freddie.

After dinner that evening, Margaret began questioning Andres about his life.

'So, when did you start painting, Andres?'

'Who were your greatest influences?'

'Margaret, go away and leave me alone,' Andres made a show of grumbling. 'Let's play cards.'

'We need to send some information about you. Freddie will want to give his clients a story about the artist!'

'Tell them anything. Ask Jack about himself.'

'I was just an everyday scribbler,' Jack offered. 'And then I met a crazy lady on a ship,' he said, grinning.

With an exasperated sigh, Margaret persisted. 'Well, at least tell me the prizes that you've won. You first, Andres!'

'Well, Jack has won Sofia, but I am still waiting for my prize. Maybe you will do?' Andres said cheekily, far too playful to take Margaret seriously, and so she gave up, shaking her head in mock disgust before turning to Sofia to gain the information she sought.

Margaret quickly established herself as Andres' daily companion, leaving the 'lovebirds' to 'gaze into each other's eyes', as both she and Andres teased them at every opportunity. Together they developed a balance of work in the studio, as well as rest. She was sensitive to keep from fatiguing Andres and keen to support him as he immersed himself in his first great love in life – painting. Like her, he loved to discuss the latest goings-on, including the gossip of the art world: who was being favoured and who was being ridiculed and the latest outlandish prices that were achieved by various artists.

During the afternoons, while Andres rested, Margaret relieved Sofia in the café, as she'd promised, although Sofia also enjoyed Margaret's company and usually elected to remain with her. Over the course of a week's siesta periods, the two women totally rearranged the gallery and Jack was more than willing to lend his strong arms to help them move tables and supply them with endless cups of iced tea.

Jack and Sofia felt that it was a godsend to have Margaret stay with them. Without doubt, she completed the group and even Andres agreed, claiming that now he did not feel so much like the third wheel seated with newlyweds who couldn't keep their hands off each other! On fine afternoons, they ventured out for sightseeing drives to the nearby villages and beaches, avoiding crowds wherever possible, and in the evenings they played cards, Sofia and Andres teaching Jack and

Margaret *Chinchón*, a Spanish variation of gin rummy, and in turn, Jack and Margaret teaching them bridge.

~

It was in the fourth week of Margaret's visit that Andres took a turn for the worse. The day had started the same as every other, with Jack rising early to help Sofia receive the morning deliveries for the café while Margaret drew water, ready to tackle the day's laundry. Breakfast had been as lively as it had been fun; he'd enjoyed bantering with Margaret, insisting that it was her turn to wash the dishes, while she argued back that he needed more practice, for he never washed them properly.

'Can you two children stop fighting for once, or do I have to send you to your rooms?' Sofia glared at them, even as she tried to control her smile, and Jack grinned at Margaret, thinking how wonderful it was to truly be part of a happy, noisy, teasing family, instead of being on the outside looking in, as he'd done all of his life.

'Oh, she started it,' he replied, and Sofia swatted him with her tea towel as he left the kitchen to join Andres in the studio.

Later, they'd met up in the courtyard for a quick morning tea, following which the girls had headed across to the gallery, whilst Jack and Andres returned to the studio.

At about eleven-thirty, Andres mentioned that he was feeling particularly tired and Jack noticed that he looked pale.

'Too much cards last night, mate! Why don't you go and have a lie-down before lunch? Leave your brushes – I'll clean them when I do mine.'

'Thank you. I think that I might do that,' Andres said. 'I'll see you at lunch.'

As he painted, Jack thought about Andres' decline, and when Sofia called him for lunch at midday, he suggested they delay their meal for a little longer to let Andres have a good rest.

'We have a few customers today. I will call you when they're finished,' Sofia agreed, and the next hour slipped by quickly.

It was after one o'clock when Jack stepped back from his painting and decided he could do no more for now. He'd finished the main blocking for the larger shapes of a castle scene: the hill, the outline of the walls and the turrets rising from within, as well as the sky and blue sea in the distance. Next he would add detail – the window sills and foliage, the shadows and reflected light – brushwork that would bring the painting to life.

Glancing at his watch, he frowned. He'd expected that Andres would be up by now. Looking in through the gallery door, he saw Margaret wiping down a table while Sofia chatted to a young couple as she wrapped a small pottery bowl that they had purchased. Slamming doors from the parking bay indicated that another carload of tourists had arrived. Americans, Jack thought, hearing their voices approach.

'I'll get lunch,' he mouthed to Sofia, and she nodded.

As he entered the house, he was conscious of its silence. None of the bustling movement from above that he'd expected, which would have indicated that Andres was awake and rising for lunch. Self-consciously he decided to go upstairs and check - not something that he'd ever done before. Arriving on the landing, Jack stood still and listened. His concern deepened at the sounds filtering through the closed door. Not the steady, snoring type of breathing he might have expected, but rather a rapid panting accompanied by a high-pitched wheeze. Jack knocked even as he opened the bedroom door, and was shocked to find Andres submerged in a deep sleep, sweat beading his pale forehead, his lips forming light puffs with each noisy exhalation.

'Andres.' His voice sounded sharp as he placed his hand on Andres' shoulder, dismayed to feel an unnatural warmth and the damp-ness of heavy perspiration that had soaked through his shirt.

'Uhhh...' Andres emitted a low groan and half lifted his head before letting it drop.

Jack raced to the gallery, where Sofia was serving tea and biscuits to the small group of Americans. Clearly alarmed by his panicked expression, she muttered an excuse to the visitors and joined him, leaving Margaret to take over.

Quickly, he described Andres' condition as they returned to his bedside.

'Oh, Jack!' she cried, after proving unable to rouse Andres despite shaking his arm and calling his name. Without doubt, his condition was serious.

'We need to get Dr. Garamond immediately. Go to the dairy, Jack. Salvador and Jacinta have a phone. They will call him. I will try to cool Andres down.'

Descending the stairs two at a time, Jack ran the couple of hundred yards to the dairy and was relieved to see Salvador feeding a group of tiny calves at the side of his house.

'Andres needs Dr Garamond – urgently. Can we phone him?' To Jack's relief, Salvador immediately appreciated the seriousness of the situation and turned towards the house, calling for Jacinta, who appeared immediately.

'Sofia needs you – Andres is unwell,' he said when she appeared, then asked Jack, 'Was there an accident? Tell me what has happened so I can prepare Dr Garamond.'

'Andres was tired. He was resting and did not wake up as he usually would. He's very hot and his breathing is awful. He looks terrible!'

Salvador nodded. 'I will tell Dr Garamond this. Jacinta, you go with Jack, si?'

As soon as they arrived at the house, Jacinta ran to Andres' bedside, where Sofia was sponging his forehead with a damp cloth. They spoke rapidly and Jacinta instructed Jack to open the windows while she and Sofa rearranged the bed and applied a strong-smelling lotion from a small bottle to Andres' forehead. Although Jack only understood frag-ments of their conversation, he was thankful for the presence of

Jacinta. Her strong, confident hands, used to dealing with all manner of illnesses and birthing amid her herd of soft-eyed beasts, were surely capable of managing Andres' immediate needs until the doctor came.

He went downstairs to let Margaret know of Andres' turn for the worse and asked her to send Dr Garamond straight through to the house when he arrived.

It seemed only minutes later that the doctor appeared, red-faced and panting, carrying a heavy bag. Tutting with concern, he only took minutes to announce the results of his assessment.

'We must get him to the Hospital de San Julian immediately, Sofia. He needs oxygen to help him breathe.'

'Surely not, Dr Garamond. We can nurse him here!'

'No Sofia, we cannot. Your brother has pneumonia – too much strain on his heart!'

'But we can get some cylinders from the hospital, just like we did with Papá.'

'Sofia, that was different. Andres needs medicine. He will be more comfortable in the hospital with oxygen therapy and injections of opium to relax him. The ambulance - it is already on its way.' Dr Garamond's words were firm and he looked to Jack as if appealing for reason.

'Come on, Sofia, let's do as the doctor says. He knows what is best,' Jack said, recognising her stubborn expression, knowing that her mind was working furiously to formulate an argument that would convince Dr Garamond that Andres was safer under her watchful gaze and tender ministrations.

This was exactly the scene Andres had warned him about months ago, Jack realised, when a bout of breathlessness had resulted in a conversation about the poor prognosis he faced.

While Sofia had repeatedly refused to acknowledge Andres' declining health, insisting that he was, in fact, much better, Jack had witnessed first-hand how Andres' cough became so hacking that it took his breath away and he resorted to the bottle of medicine that he kept on hand in the studio. Jack had listened when Andres raised his concerns about what 'His End' might look like, not out of fear for himself, but as always, with the prime concern of sparing Sofia from as much pain as he possibly could.

'Jack, I will not be nursed at home. Sofia will insist that I am – believe me, I know her – but it is not to happen. You will have to be… boss… This, I have already told Dr Garamond. He understands.'

'Sure, Andres. Anything you want.'

Jack remembered how he'd found the conversation terribly confronting, but he'd listened as Andres had explained his decision.

'It was too hard with our father, Jack. Really awful. Sofia and I … we cared for him all through his illness, through the terrible weakness, then the breathlessness and then the bedrest. We took turns sitting and watching him – washing him, changing him, spooning the few mouthfuls of softened food that he managed to swallow, before his mouth became full of painful ulcers. Sofia - she would not give in. She would cook this and that, trying everything to fatten his bones. And then his functions began to go, one by one. Speech went first, and then he could not eat at all. His arms and legs, they were like matchsticks and became stiff and difficult to move, and so we rubbed him, lifted him, rolled him. Still, Sofia insisted that he would get better. She could not accept that he was going – refused to give in. Sometimes you just have to accept these things. That is life. Do you understand me, Jack?'

What could he possibly have said? Of course, he understood, even though it was difficult to hear.

'I knew what Papá wanted. He wanted us to let him go. To stop trying. But there was no reasoning with Sofia. You will have to, Jack. She will not give up on me, so you will have to lead her. If you don't, I will come and haunt you! You will hear doors banging in the night and your paintings - blood will ooze from their canvas - that will be me… *Woooooh hooooooh!*' In typical Andres style, he'd turned the gravest of subjects into a joke, but Jack knew that he'd made a point and that he expected to be taken seriously.

And now, here were the very circumstances that Andres had predicted. His health failing, and Sofia insisting that she would care for him. Jack knew that Andres would expect him to protect Sofia from her own caring inclinations.

True to Dr Garamond's word, the ambulance arrived in a very short space of time, and Jack waited at the foot of the stairs with Margaret while Sofia, the doctor and ambulance officers tended to Andres.

'The Americans, they've gone?' Jack asked. Margaret explained how they'd swallowed the remainder of their coffee and left, perceiving the seriousness of the situation after Sofia's hasty departure and the doctor running through.

In minutes, the ambulance officers wrestled their stretcher down the stairwell and transported Andres into the back of their vehicle.

'I am going to follow the ambulance, Sofia. How about you come with me?' Dr Garamond said. 'Jack, can you drive down to the presbytery and let Father Sebastian know that he is needed at the Hospital de San Julian, immediately.'

After hanging the 'Closed' sign on the gallery door, Jack and Margaret sped down the winding road to the church as fast as he dared to drive. They swept the creaking Suzie onto the side of the road before running to the door of the rectory where, barely twelve months earlier, he and Sofia had stood, telling Father Sebastian about their intention to marry. As Jack prepared to knock, he heard footsteps from within, and to his relief, the priest opened the door at once.

'We need you to come to the hospital,' Jack said. 'Andres is unwell. Dr Garamond said to please hurry.' The urgency in Jack's voice inspired action, not conversation, and Father Sebastian wasted no time. After pulling on his black overcoat and flat wide-brimmed hat and collecting a small boxlike leather case, he followed them through the door.

In the car, he provided directions to Jack, helping him to avoid the busier main streets. Jack tried to ignore the onslaught of emotions that threatened to overwhelm him as they finally arrived outside a plain two-storey building on a hill, its few small windows covered with black iron bars. Almost before he had a chance to stop Suzie's engine, Father Sebastian had exited, followed by Margaret, and Jack found himself almost jogging as he tried to keep up with them. The stocky priest showed remarkable agility as he led the charge, no doubt all too familiar with the layout of the hospital. He led them to a set of narrow garden stairs that traversed the steep bank. At the top, Jack was surprised to pass through an arched gateway into a courtyard, the buildings surrounding it a picture of columns and arches, the garden bearing a beautiful green lawn adorned with statues and water features. To add to the perfection of this location was the centrepiece: a stone fountain ejecting streams of water high into the air, from which they fell with gentle drops into an ornately carved pool.

Jack looked around, his mind grappling with the incongruity of their surroundings - stunning beauty - and the shocking circumstances that had brought them here. Nothing seemed real. He and Margaret followed Father Sebastian up a second stairwell, this one leading inside the hospital. Its beauty notwithstanding, Jack was shocked at the dilapidated state of the ancient building as they hurried over the blue-and-white tiled floor of a wide corridor from whose enormously high ceiling hung iron chandeliers covered in spiderwebs.

Finally, they entered a long, thin room, its walls punctuated by a series of iron beds, each accompanied by a small chest of drawers. The ceiling of this room provided further evidence of the hospital's past grandeur, a magnificent timber vault that soared high above, with still more cobweb-laden chandeliers adorning its upper reaches.

They hurried along the full length of the ward, passing beds bearing all manner of patients, some emitting moans, others watching them with interest; one elderly lady lay so still, her eyes closed, that Jack wondered if she was breathing at all. Fabric screens surrounded a few of the beds, while strange-looking implements sat by others. A bevy of nurses draped in heavy robes and cumbersome-looking veils pushed trolleys, carried jugs and wielded assorted equipment between the beds, performing their duties with an air of quiet efficiency.

'Nuns,' Margaret whispered, and Jack noticed the large crosses dangling down the front of their robes.

At the end of the third wing, a crowd stood gathered around a bed, and Jack could see Dr Garamond deep in conversation with a tall man dressed in a white jacket, as well as Sofia, whose hand was resting on Andres' shoulder. Andres lay prone, his face pale, eyes closed and hands resting listlessly on his chest.

Jack approached Sofia, and she fell into his arms. 'Jack,' she sobbed, and a lump formed in his throat as he held her tightly, determinedly transmitting every ounce of strength he possessed into her quaking body. Over her shoulder, he watched a young nurse approach the bed, the clipped sound of her leather-soled shoes accompanied by the squeak of the metal trolley she dragged behind her, balancing an oxygen cylinder. The senior nurse at the bedside frowned and ushered them aside to make way for the younger one, who quickly attached a small leather and metal contraption over Andres' face and connected it by a tube to the cylinder.

Jack found himself nodding as the nurse fiddled with its metal tap, quietly explaining how the oxygen would help Andres' failing lungs to do their job. As soon as she finished, Dr Garamond beckoned Father Sebastian closer to the bed. He opened his bag, preparing to commence his mysterious spiritual ministrations.

'Sofia, Jack.' Dr Garamond gestured for them to join him with the tall man. 'This is our respiratory specialist, Doctor Bertrand.'

The doctor seemed kind. Looking at Sofia, he spoke in quiet, sombre tones. 'My dear, your brother is very ill. Hopefully, we can give him some relief.'

Sofia nodded, her face white, and she clutched at both Margaret's and Jack's hands and held them tight.

Jack wondered if either of them had observed the doctor's omission of a positive prognosis, and he feared the worst was imminent. He looked at Andres – near whom Father Sebastian stood with a small bottle of oil in his hand, his lips moving quietly as he ran his fingers across the waxy white dome of Andres' forehead. Jack shuddered. Surely this was the delivery of Last Rites, and everybody knew that Last Rites were for the dying.

It was bizarre. How had this day, which had started off so normally – no, better than normal – come to this?

A sudden movement from the bed caught their attention, and Jack's arms tightened around Sofia as Andres' hands clenched and contorted.

Sofia gasped and Jack stepped back, pulling her face into his chest. Margaret's arms went around them both as they created space for the doctors and nurse to work on Andres, to settle him.

Barely a minute must have passed, but it felt like ages, as if time had been suspended. And then Andres was still.

But not the stillness of rest, Jack knew, and from the sound that emanated from Sofia, the sobs that racked through her, she knew it, too. Andres was gone! Could this be real.

With a rapid movement, Doctor Bertrand signalled for Jack to take Sofia and Margaret from the room, pointing to a door to the left of Andres' bed.

On passing through it, Jack was surprised to find a gracefully curved balcony that looked down upon an altar, the rooms focal point, ornately decorated by carvings that were embellished with gold. Dappled light entered the chapel through an overhead window of spectacular proportions, its coloured glass a mosaic of levitating angels - crowned and glorious. It was as though all funds allocated to the upkeep of the building had been concentrated into maintaining this spiritual place. A sanctuary of exquisite, transcendental beauty that doubtless had bought comfort to hundreds of people over the decades – bereft husbands and wives, heartbroken mothers and fathers, distraught children - all desperately calling to their heavenly Father for healing, peace and rest for the souls of their loved ones, begging for answers for themselves.

Margaret and Jack followed Sofia as she sank on her knees before the altar, sobbing quietly. Taking her lead, each knelt at her side, heads bowed. Time stood still as the three remained in silence, lost in their thoughts. Jack thought about Andres' earnest commitment to art, always searching to expand his knowledge and try new techniques, and felt grateful that Andres had enjoyed the Prado's prize as well as that of the Julian Académie. He thought about how Andres applied the same serious approach to politics, urging Sofia to take the issues affecting the Spanish government more seriously, and when that had failed, he'd turned to Jack, warning him of the troubled times ahead. And Jack thought about the Andres who teased and laughed with him – a best friend, a brother – thinking nothing of launching into a handstand to amuse small children or pull rubbery faces at them to make them laugh. For Jack, it had always been him, Sofia and Andres. And lately, him, Sofia, Andres and Margaret. What a wonderful time they'd had – what a friendship they'd shared. He could barely believe that it was over.

Jack listened to Sofia quietly praying. The Spanish words that she whispered under her breath were punctuated by gasping sobs, and tears flowed freely down his face as he felt overwhelmed with sadness for her loss.

Then there was calm … and then Sofia rose. Her tears were stilled and her face resolute. She held her head high as she walked to the door. She did not have time to break down now, for her brother – her twin, her only remaining family member – still needed her, and she had a job to do.

CHAPTER 15

The return trip to the house was perhaps the most awful experience that Jack had ever lived through and he wondered at how he'd managed to drive Suzie up the hill and back to the finca at all.

Sofia sat in the back with Margaret, collapsed against her in silent shock, every so often sniffing deeply, sighing in sorrow. Jack had no words for her – what could be said? – and he was glad for Margaret's comforting arms for Sofia as he drove, numb, wiping the trail of salty tears from his cheeks with the back of his hand, trying to imagine how their lives would be without Andres.

To his surprise, when they arrived home, Sofia walked straight into their lounge room and then back to the kitchen.

'Jack,' she said quietly. 'Can we move the table into here, please?' She pointed at the space she had in mind, and he looked at her quizzically.

As it turned out, they were not going to be living without Andres for long at all – Sofia had plans to bring him home the very next morning.

'No, surely not.' He looked towards Margaret, wondering what she thought of this plan. Had Sofia gone mad?

'Yes, Jack,' Sofia said, her voice sad. 'It is the Spanish way.'

Over the next few days, Jack realised that he was the only one who found it bizarre to have Andres' body lying in the open casket that rested in the living area, dressed in the same black pants and embroidered shirt that he'd worn to Jack and Sofia's wedding the previous year. Even Margaret acted as though it were the most normal thing in the world, and she and Sofia took to talking to Andres throughout the day, asking him if he'd slept well when they rose, pressing a stray hair against his smooth forehead and patting his shoulder or touching his cold, waxy hands when they spoke to him. In the evenings, they agreed they should have their supper in the lounge, as though Andres might feel left out if they sat in the dining room eating. In time, Jack got used to it, the eating and talking, even laughing, washing dishes and sweeping the floor, with Andres there, large as…well…death. And as the lights were turned off for the night, and they prepared for bed, he found himself joining the girls as they called out their goodnights to him.

Over four days, it seemed that half the population of Malaga trekked up the hill to stand silently, caps in hand, heads bowed over Andres, their right hands forming the sign of the cross. There were long hugs and kisses for Sofia's cheeks and the shaking of Jack's hand as mourners expressed condolences. Eyes were damp and hearts heavy for the many losses Sofia had experienced in her lifetime.

The most surprising visitor was Pablo Picasso, arriving in the early evening just as Sofia was lighting lamps and Jack was closing the gallery doors.

'This is such sad news,' he said. 'Andres was a very talented young man, Sofia. Spain has lost a great artist.'

Turning to Jack, he took him by the shoulders and kissed him on each cheek.

'Eh, you have lost a very dear friend, just as did I, once… So, the grief begins.'

～

Jack could not deny that Sofia seemed increasingly peaceful as the days wore on, and it was as though Andres body lying in the lounge room gave her time to tend to him and to adjust. By Friday, the day of Andres' burial, the shock caused by his sudden illness and death was all but exhausted, and their emotions had subsided to sad acceptance. The church was full and Father Sebastian was resplendent in his final duties for Andres, and the wake lively with stories as friends and family remembered the man they'd all loved.

～

In the weeks following the funeral, the lounge was returned to normal. They tearfully farewelled Margaret at the station, and then, together, he and Sofia returned to the silence of the house, now so utterly empty of bantering and laughter and purpose. It was then that the reality of Andres' death set in.

He and Sofia did their best to move forward and adjust their daily routines for two people instead of three. They tried to plan things, and to make jokes and laugh, but the house, even though it was not large, felt too big for them. Often, he found Sofia standing, quiet tears streaming down her face.

'I miss him, Jack. I just miss him.'

He'd hold her close as lumps formed in his throat. 'I know. I miss him, too,' he'd answer gruffly.

For Jack, the silence of the studio was unbearable. It was Andres' studio, every corner of it a reminder of the past, of the world that, first the twins' father, and then Andres himself, had created. Where once

Jack had felt at ease, sharing their space, now he suddenly felt like an intruder. He, a stranger to the land, alive, opening Andres' and his father's cupboards, using the benches that they'd built, moving their stools, touching their easels.

He tried to paint, but the emptiness around him was distracting. He kept looking over his shoulder, as though an apparition of Andres might be standing there, watching him, and he could not concentrate. He'd find himself sitting, staring and achieving nothing. Sometimes he just gave in to the tears that seeped down his cheeks, the overflow of sadness. He missed his friend greatly.

And then, as unanticipated as Andres' death, there was an equally rapid decline in the gallery's trade. Over the course of two months, the number of people venturing up the mountain to visit the Castillo de Gibralfaro or to buy lunch or paintings was reduced by half, and then a quarter.

Sofia was confounded at first, but then word leaked through that the lack of tourism in Malaga was the result of political turmoil in northern Spain.

'There has been fighting up north, Jack.' Sofia shared the news that she'd heard from Jacinta that morning when she'd walked down to fill her milk urn at the dairy. 'The miners up there went on strike and it has turned out bad. There has been violence – even murders. Now people all over Spain are fearful and tourists are staying away.'

Although they had some savings, Jack knew their money would not last long, and he racked his brains to think of ways that they could improve their income. It bothered him terribly to watch Sofia work her accounts, struggling to keep the finca profitable, and to see her once buoyant spirit all but collapse.

'Perhaps I should find some work in Malaga,' he suggested, and Sofia agreed with him. Anything would help. However, all his attempts to gain employment led to disappointment as, one by one, business owners shook their heads apologetically. Already they were in the uncomfortable position of having laid off their own employees, many of whom had provided years of loyal service. With no work prospects, Jack spent his days pottering around the finca, tidying and attending to repairs around the house and yards, unable to face the quietness of the studio and force himself to paint pictures that had no buyers.

Increasingly he thought about Andres' warnings; those conversations where he'd insisted that Jack must take Sofia to Australia to escape the coming troubles, but when he raised the idea with Sofia, she violently opposed him.

'No, Jack. We cannot leave the finca. Not now!'

'Why not now?' he asked, but she just lifted her shoulders obstinately and turned her back. She spent hours in the gallery, cleaning its benches, reorganising its shelves, rehanging pictures. Blindly – irrationally, even - she insisted that the hardship would be short-term and that they would see their way through. So vehement was Sofia's opposition that Jack could do little more than watch as Sofia juggled their dwindling finances to pay bills, and more weeks slipped away.

Jack began to feel more alone than ever. Unable to improve things, he wondered what Andres would have done and wished that he could ask him. His feelings of helplessness were coupled with guilt for not being able to contribute more, to slow the depletion of their reserves. Surely, as her husband, it was his job to be providing for his wife, not watching her struggle to provide for them. What was worse for him, though, was when his guilt and helplessness insidiously transformed into a still, seething anger towards Sofia because she refused to discuss alternatives.

It was on a Friday afternoon that their crisis came to a head. Jack had been working in the orchard, glad for the sun on his back and the distraction of physical labour as he'd picked oranges from the heavily laden trees and hauled overflowing bins up to the courtyard. Heaven only knew what they would do with the accumulating fruit. Perhaps it would be best to just leave the baskets at the gateway. Someone would surely enjoy it. Returning to the gallery, he found Sofia angrily sweeping the sweet biscuits she baked each morning, once sold by the platefuls to visitors, into a tin, tears streaming down her face. 'Nobody for three days, Jack. Three days! We have not sold a painting for over two weeks. What am I going to do?'

Enough was enough and Jack's anger reached its peak, finally erupting. 'Perhaps, Sofia, you mean what are *we* going to do? Well, I will tell you what *we* will do. We are going to Australia. This is not good for you or me. I need to look after you. I cannot keep hanging around, picking fruit and fixing doors and fences. There is nothing left to fix. What sort of man does it make me, not being able to provide for my wife? I have work in Australia. Family. It will be a fresh start for us. Perhaps' – Jack struck at Sofia's deepest longing with the finesse of a bullfighter driving a final thrust deep into the heart of his prey – 'if we can get beyond this endless worry, the baby we both long for may finally arrive.'

To his surprise, Sofia did not argue. Instead, tears rolled down her face, and she hugged him tightly, repeating over and over, 'I'm sorry, Jack, I'm sorry. I have not been thinking of you. I have been selfish.'

Holding her close, his hand gently stroking the tears from her cheeks, Jack realised just how exhausted she was and knew, without doubt, that taking her to Australia was the right decision. For her, for him and for them.

PART II

HOMECOMING

CHAPTER 16

'There they are!' Jack waved vigorously to his parents, surprised by the emotion that captured his breath and made his heart race, as he stepped onto Australian shores after almost four long years away.

The dazzling brightness of the blue sky and the predominance of Australian voices surrounding him immediately plunged him back into the world in which he had grown up. So, too, did the familiar silhouette of the Melbourne skyline, the bustling energy of Port Melbourne's dock – reminiscent of when he'd boarded the *Ormonde* for London to visit Aunt Elizabeth and Uncle Robert back in 1929. And yet it felt somehow different. Jack knew the changes were not geographical but, rather, in himself. The boy who had left on a brief holiday was returning, now a man who had seen places and had experiences beyond anyone's expectations. He'd been dazzled by the great city of London as a tourist, wandered the streets of Paris as an art student, and best of all, had enjoyed married life in the gentle domesticity of southern Spain.

Jack knew that, when he had left Australia, he'd been a lad with no ideas about what he wanted to do with his life; that it was his parents who had directed his decisions. Now, he was a married man with a purpose. Taking Sofia from the world she knew and loved – he was determined to bring the laughter back to her eyes. To make her excited about their future - as he was because, although he may well have responsibilities, Jack was also a man of optimism, and at this minute he was bursting with excitement about this new beginning.

Holding Sofia's hand, he pulled her closer to him as they weaved through the river of bodies and suitcases leaving the pier, all equally intent on connecting with their waiting relatives or boarding carriages at the railway station.

Jack looked forward to living closer to his parents. They were the only direct relatives he and Sofia had now, and even though William and Marian had expressed their reservations when he'd announced that he was marrying Sofia, the weekly letters his mother had sent since their marriage indicated that they had come to terms with Jack's choice. Now they would really get to know Sofia - her sweetness, calm intelligence and caring manner. Jack had no doubts that they would love her as the daughter they never had.

From the moment Sofia had agreed it would be best for them to move to Australia, renewed energy had entered their lives. They'd spoken endlessly of the journey, arrangements that needed to be made, what to keep and what to leave behind. To Jack's relief, Sofia was reconciled to the idea of selling the finca and leaving Spain.

'The finca means nothing to me now, Jack. Nothing,' she'd said sadly. 'Dad and Andrés are gone. I thought we needed to keep the gallery in their memory. But I was wrong. We cannot live with our memories. We must live for our future, together.'

She'd asked hundreds of questions about Melbourne and his parents' home. It was a conversation that had consumed them as they'd travelled through France and back to London to board the *Ormonde*, murmured in quiet voices as they lay together in the seclusion of their little cabin, arms around each other, swaying to the rolling swell of the ocean. They'd continued their discussions over meals in the beautiful dining room, and still more as they'd walked the decks of the great ship. Although the initial plan to move from Malaga to Melbourne had been borne of necessity, Jack was surprised by the anticipation that had grown within him as memories of Australian life flooded back through their discussions. Things he had taken for granted, had not even thought about for years: Port Phillip Bay with its many popular beaches, Brighton and St Kilda close by. The city of Melbourne with its movie theatres and trams, like those they had seen in Paris. He spoke of Melbourne's distinctive seasons, the biting winter squalls forcing residents indoors before cosy fires, the joy of spring where you would hear the chirping of baby birds in the trees, bees buzzing amid the riot of colourful flowers. He described summers, hot and dry, similar to Malaga, where high temperatures sapped energy through the day and made sleeping difficult at night. Autumn's beautiful sunlit days, the slightest chill in the air, the trees transformed, their leaves changing overnight from green to yellow, red and gold, finally tumbling to form a carpet upon the ground of leaves so crisp that you could hear them crunching as you walked. And, of course, the Australian bush with its majestic gum trees and lazy rivers. The forests - Ferntree Gully and Healesville - where, if you were lucky, you might encounter a male lyrebird, the master of impersonation, with his spectacular tail splayed as he performed on the enormous mound he'd built for his mating ritual, his flapping feathers attracting the female birds. The warble of magpies, surely the most beautiful songsters of all the birds; majestic eagles drifted in lazy circles, tiny dots high in the sky, carried aloft in the thermals.

Initially, he and Sofia planned to live with his parents until they found a house of their own. Jack pictured this as being near his parents', maybe even within walking distance. A quarter-acre suburban block with a shed in the backyard that would serve as a studio for him to paint. They would have chickens, maybe even a dog.

Sofia started to imagine the opportunities also and she shared her dreams with Jack. Maybe she could find work at an art gallery in Melbourne, perhaps as a curator. One day, they might even have their own gallery. Everything seemed possible.

As she'd voiced these ideas, Jack nodded enthusiastically, though he rather hoped Australia would finally give to Sofia the baby for which they both longed. He could picture it, even as he dared to dream. Returning home from work, their house cosy, fire blazing, rooms filled with the wonderful aroma of Spanish risottos, omelettes and Sofia's *almendrados,* fresh from the oven. The ultimate joy fulfilled, a family of their very own. An infant in arms, toddlers ambling about on chubby little legs, young children whom he would teach to draw and paint. Sofia would croon to their babies in Spanish. Little ones would climb up on kitchen chairs and help her make *paella* and *tapas.* Jack was certain that he and Sofia would have a noisy, happy family where children were surrounded by loving parents and grandparents, unlike the quiet, lonely existence he had experienced as an only child or - heaven forbid - the motherless childhood that Sofia had endured.

These images occupied Jack's mind with a primal longing. Certainly, while they were Sofia's dreams also, he often marvelled that people always spoke of a woman's yearning for children, rarely acknowledging the powerful strength of a man's paternal desires.

'Jack,' his mother cried, tears in her eyes as she reached up and hugged him tightly. 'You're home! Finally!'

William shook Jack's hand, clearly pleased to finally see the son he'd not laid eyes on since their surprise visit to Malaga – what? almost two years earlier!

'Sofia, how lovely to see you again. Welcome to Australia,' Marian said with gentle enthusiasm. She and William stood smiling at their new daughter-in-law, clearly unsure how to greet her.

With a sweet, somewhat nervous laugh, Sofia bridged the awkward moment by stepping forward and hugging them each in turn. 'Thank you. It is so wonderful to be here,' she said.

Recognising the shy smile that operated as a shield against Sofia's nervousness, Jack reached his arm around her, giving her shoulders a gentle squeeze. He imagined how strange this moment must be for her.

'You must be exhausted, love. How was the voyage? Not too rough, I hope. I hear the crossing can be terrible at this time of the year.' Marian's string of quickly spoken English phrases proved difficult for Sofia. Jack answered for her. 'Oh, very long. Lots of ocean. Lots of food. I am sure we both put on half a stone.'

'Oh, yes! Dad and I were the same when we travelled across to see you... It seemed as if there was nothing to do but eat and gaze out over the endless stretch of water. It was beautiful, though – we did enjoy it.'

'Well, let's be on our way. The car is this way,' interrupted William, waving to his left. Jack and Sofia followed through the slowly thinning crowds to the Model T Ford, safely located in a small carpark, some distance away. The odour of its gleaming, freshly waxed panels and sparkling chrome were evidence of the pride of place the car continued to hold in William's life.

Inhaling the salt-laden air of Port Philip Bay and looking around, Jack marvelled at how each place had its own feeling. Australia, even in autumn, had a crisp, sharp colour that seemed artificially bright. He thought back to the bleakness of London, where, even in spring, a heavy fog had lingered over the Tilbury docks, filtering the world through a grey mist when they'd drifted down the Thames in the early hours before dawn to begin their ocean crossing to Australia a few weeks earlier. Malaga had a dusty golden hue, broken by the brightness of white buildings clustered tightly together, united by colourful flowers cascading from pots and balconies, all set against the turquoise backdrop of the Mediterranean.

William's driving was significantly more confident now - Jack could not help but notice - as his father slid between two vehicles without hesitation, merging into the traffic that snaked away from the port. Peering out of the window while distractedly answering his mother's questions, Jack could see subtle changes in the surroundings. More litter on the wide streets as they drove along St Kilda Road. Several shops with raggedy 'To Let' signs posted on their dusty windows.

'Hey, Sid's Bakery is closed,' he exclaimed as, turning left, they passed the row of Chapel Street shops that were part of his earliest memories. Of holding his mother's hand on their early morning walk, or 'helping' her pull the wicker shopping trolley she'd always used to transport their groceries home. Of the soft sugar-coated jubes that were slipped into his small hands by smiling storekeepers, a kindly wink suggesting it was their little secret and the sticky gingerbread men purchased from Sid's for afternoon tea.

'Yes, Jack. Businesses have not been doing so well these last few years,' his father replied. 'I daresay you will notice a few changes.'

Marian picked up where her husband left off. 'It's been awful. Holden has laid off hundreds of workers. So has the wool mill. I don't know where it will all end.' Suddenly, collecting herself, she changed her tone. 'Never mind. Enough morbid news. You are home now.'

Jack smiled quietly at Sofia, squeezing her hand. His mother's words seemed to imply that, with his return to Australia, its troubled economy would miraculously rebound.

In no time at all, William turned the vehicle into Copelen Street. Jack's heart leapt as he absorbed the beautiful tree-lined street of his childhood before his father turned the vehicle again, this time into the entrance of a red brick two-storey home with gracious white columns supporting the roof of its large, curved porch. Around the front garden, more changes were evident. Always his mother's pride and joy, the garden had been perfectly manicured by old Tommy Stoppel for years. On Thursdays and Fridays, Tom had mown their lawn, removed weeds and carried out his mother's instructions for new garden beds. He'd pruned roses and planted out the annuals – pansies, carnations and snapdragons - their colours selected to provide a delightful show in spring, their perfume attracting bees and birds, their cut blooms filling Marian's assortment of crystal vases throughout the house. Now, an air of untidiness prevailed. Hydrangeas, always trimmed when any leaf dared to erupt outside predetermined parameters, grew haphazardly. Peeling paint exposed the raw timber of the garage door, which Jack climbed out of the car to open. There was no evidence of Mr Stoppel's toil and he wondered to what extent his parents' lives had been affected by Australia's economic troubles.

Entering the house, Jack was reassured to find the inside largely unchanged. The mahogany table in the entrance hall, with its shapely turned legs that a tiny Jack had loved running his fingers down, gleamed, its polished surface complete with its customary crystal vase of freshly cut rose-buds from Marian's garden extending a gracious welcome to visitors crossing the threshold. The red velvet lounge suite, purchased the year before Jack's departure, looked as new now as it did the day his mother had directed the delivery man to position - it just so – and then, on that same evening, unhappy with its location, she'd had Jack and William rearrange not just the suite, but all of the furniture in the room until it was 'just right'. The rosewood piano in the corner, where a reluctant eleven-year-old Jack had practised scales until his fingers ached, and he'd complained bitterly until his mother had finally agreed that the daily practice sessions were a form of cruelty and the lessons had ceased. All appeared the same, as though Jack had never left.

However, he immediately noticed a heavy, musty odour. Sofia, standing beside him, was lightly sniffing, a slight frown revealing her puzzlement. He realised it was the odour of carpet, a smell that had receded from his memory over recent years. The finca had terracotta tiles throughout, providing warmth in winter and coolness to their bare feet in summer. Sealed with linseed oil, thoroughly swept every day, and mopped with a string mop dipped in steaming hot water every Saturday morning, the floor always had a fresh citrus fragrance. Jack tried to recall a single place in Malaga with fitted carpet and realised that he could not think of one, instead recollecting the brightly coloured cotton rugs scattered across the living area floors and at their bedsides.

'I made the blue room up for you,' Marian stated and Jack knew she was referring to the bedroom that had always been designated 'for 'visitors,' although Jack could not remember a time that the bed had ever been slept in. It seemed a strange arrangement, to be sleeping in the guest room of his parents' house. He would have felt more comfortable in his own room, although on reflection, he recognised that the room at the opposite end of the stairway to his parents' bedroom, was much more suitable than his smaller childhood room right beside William's and Marian's.

Encouraging Jack and Sofia up the broad staircase and along the hall, Marian showed them the spare blankets in the box at the foot of the bed, the fireplace set with kindling should they wish to light it and the cupboard with a row of coat hangers at the ready for when they unpacked. Jack was touched by his mother's efforts to make things nice for his and Sofia's homecoming, noting the set of finely crocheted doilies that lay on the glass-topped dressing table, along with a small crystal vase holding three fresh rosebuds, no doubt snipped from her garden that very morning.

'Thanks, Mum,' he said, hugging her briefly. 'It's lovely to be home!'

She beamed back. 'It is wonderful to have you home, Jack. We have missed you so much. The house has felt so empty without you.'

Looking at Sofia, Marian patted her hand gently. 'Lovely to have you both home. Anyway, I'll leave you to freshen up. When you are ready, come downstairs and we'll have a cuppa.'

Again, Jack was warmed by his mother's kindness towards Sofia and relieved that his parents' manner since they had picked them up from Port Melbourne suggested that the prejudices and concerns they'd raised when he had first announced his love for Sofia, his intention to marry her, had diminished over time.

That evening, over a dinner of roasted beef, gravy and a combination of baked and boiled vegetables, Marian attempted to respond to the news that had only been addressed in letters.

'We were so sorry to hear of Andrés …passing away…'

Sofia shook her head, her eyes filling with tears. 'Hola… Yes…

Thank you,' she said haltingly. 'It was all...too sad. Losing Andrés ... this I did not think would ever...come...happen.'

'No. A terrible thing for you.' Marian was aghast at the tears forming in Sofia's eyes that her words had triggered. She and William moved their conversation to safer areas, such as the job that Jack would finally commence at Goldsbrough Mort & Co. Jack's father described some of the changes that had taken place in the company. The world-wide Depression had created many layoffs due to a decline in wool and cotton exports. Jack was troubled by this information, acutely aware of the dire circumstances that had been created in Malaga as the Spanish economy had ground to a halt.

'Surely, Dad, I can't be turning up to take a job when so many others have been laid off! People would be furious!'

'Eric promised you the position three years ago, and as far as he is concerned, it is still yours. You will need to do something about that damned hair, though.' William's abrupt words caused an unexpected awkwardness and reminded Jack that his appearance was not that of the neat, well-groomed son that they had raised.

'Yeah, sure, Dad. I'll make an appointment this week.'

Sofia joined in the conversation where possible, but Jack was conscious that her limited English was challenged by the rapid ebb and flow of his parents' speech.

'Slow down, slow down,' he laughed. 'Sofia is not used to listening to Australians chattering like magpies. You will need to speak a little slower for her.' Jack was almost sorry for that advice, for then Marian and William began speaking slowly and loudly, as though Sofia were deaf. Laughing about this later in the privacy of their room, she explained, 'It's not just how fast they talk, Jack. It is the phrases! "*Swaggies, blowies* and buckleys"! I daresay I will get used to it in time!'

CHAPTER 17

*O*ver the next few days, the house at Copelen Street had a steady stream of visitors. Some were old school friends of Jack, intrigued about the changes they could see in his life.

'So, you're an artist now, mate?' said Steve. 'Good for you. You certainly have the talent for it.'

'Well, not for now,' Jack had replied ruefully. 'Fronting up to the office next week. Dad's got a job lined up for me.'

'I suppose it's lucky for you, really. It's not as though the Positions Vacant columns are full of jobs these days, especially ones for artists! Mind you, things have got a little better than they were two years ago.'

'Yes, I am a 'very lucky fellow', so Dad keeps telling me.'

'Jack, it will be okay,' Sofia said. 'You will be back to painting soon. I know it.'

'Well, let's hope so. Australians are not so focused on seeing young men become artists. We're more men of the land, or aspiring to be managers in factories or offices. Doctors and lawyers. And we certainly love a man who puts on a uniform. Artists – they're not so highly esteemed.'

His friends, male and female, were intrigued by Sofia, for she was the first Spanish person they'd ever met. They smiled at her, not sure what to say to this exotic beauty that Jack had brought home, and congratulated them on their marriage.

A second wave of visitors consisted of friends of his parents, who dropped in on a range of pretexts, but everyone knew it was really to see Marian's new Spanish daughter-in-law. Most offered warm, welcoming greetings to Sofia and congratulated Jack on his beautiful wife. Some could not resist a comment on the expectation of the pitter-patter of little feet, or the stork or any other euphemism that represented an impending pregnancy – comments for which neither Jack nor Sofia had responses. They also longed for the pitter-patter that had featured on the poster Sofia's friends had mounted on the wall above their bed on their wedding night. However, so far, a baby was proving elusive.

Marian laughingly admonished her friends. 'Leave the poor girl alone!'

Jack had no doubts that his mother was thrilled to hear others ask the questions that she longed to ask herself, but did not dare.

At the end of their first week home, William suggested that Jack come into Goldsbrough, Mort & Co on Saturday morning to get the lay of the office in preparation for his start on Monday. His phrase confused Sofia.

'You will be laying somewhere, Jack? I don't understand…' she asked later that evening.

'No, I will not be laying down on a couch or the floor, or anything else,' Jack explained. 'Just getting to know everybody and finding out what my job will involve.'

At 7:00 am Saturday, Jack stood looking at himself in the clothes that Marian had set out for him – navy trousers, white shirt, tie and matching jacket as well as a shiny pair of black leather shoes - for his re-entry into the workforce. Sofia laughed at his neat attire. The trousers that he'd worn as an eighteen-year-old were somewhat tighter than they had once been, but still fit, while his shirts proved too small and had to be exchanged for one of William's. His hair, cut the previous day at William's barber by the station, barely reached his ears and was now neatly combed and held in place with a generous application of Brylcream.

'You look very handsome. Like a new man…a stranger.'

'You are saying that I, your husband, am not handsome? You want a stranger trussed up in a suit, with pink ears flapping like cormorant's wings for all to see?' Sofia giggled.

Jack was sure he vastly preferred the baggy cotton pants and soft paint-splattered leather boots that he'd worn in Malaga. Frowning at himself critically, barely recognising the man before him in the mirror, he turned to Sofia. 'All we need is to tie some strings to my arms and legs and then I can be a puppet, dancing to everyone's tune.'

'Jack, it will be a…okay… Soon we will get our own home and you will come home, put on your pantalones and boots, and paint in your studio. And I will promote your paintings to the best galleries in Melbourne and make your reputation known. In no time at all, you will be a famous *artista, si?*'

Sofia was articulating the plans she and Jack had discussed repeatedly in the weeks before their journey to Australia, but to him, the words sounded like a distant dream. The dream of another person that Jack could not relate to anymore. He had barely painted in the months since Andrés' death and then there had been weeks of travel across the world. Now, in his parents' home, the notion of painting was unimaginable. He had an uneasy feeling that 'Jack the artist' had been left behind in Spain.

After completing his first week at Goldsbrough Mort & Co, Jack tried to ignore his mixed feelings about the turn his life had taken. Sure, he had accepted the job because he was determined that he would earn a living to support himself and Sofia as they settled into their life together here in Australia. It was not that they did not have any money, for the sale of the finca and gallery had raised over eight hundred pounds, Sofia repeatedly reminded him.

'Your money, Sofia.'

'Our money,' she'd insisted.

'Definitely not. Your father built the home and gallery for you and Andrés. I will provide for our needs. You save that money for a rainy day. You never know when you might need it.'

Given that Sofia had already lost her father and brother, Jack restrained himself from expressing his real fear. What if some accident or illness befell him and he was not able to provide for her? Then, Sofia would be glad to have her own money. For now, he would meet their needs.

However, just as he'd known back in 1930, he had no real interest in clerical work. Jack chided himself for the ungrateful thoughts when they arose, understanding that he was lucky to have a job at all. Not everyone was so fortunate. Melbourne's city streets were lined with men holding signs, offering themselves for employment. Others walked aimlessly to pass the day, and still another group, sat hunched on corners or in alleyways, a worn scrap of a blanket or oversized coat hanging off their shoulders, a flagon of cheap sherry or even a bottle of methylated spirits, deposited between their spindly knees. Some of these were missing limbs. Legs. An arm. Small jars sat on the ground in front of many - a few pennies visible. War heroes? Jack considered how, as a school boy, he'd barely noticed them. Perhaps there were more these days, due to the depressed economy. Now, he viewed them through the eyes of an adult. What an embarrassment, he thought as he walked past them on his first morning. Were these the brave soldiers of the war, he'd been taught about at school? Those who'd fought at the Dardanelles or Gallipoli? Abandoned, and now, lining the city streets with their broken bodies? Jack noted the manner of the people rushing by, their faces averted from the men who sat with army hats low on their foreheads, staring at the ground. He searched in his pocket for the ha'pennies that he carried to buy his daily papers. Tomorrow, and every day there-after, he would make sure he had a supply of coins on hand to place in the jars.

Given the dire economic circumstances, Jack was both surprised and relieved that staff in the financial records department of Goldsbrough Mort & Co were so accepting of his presence in the office; given a job that others, more skilled and surely more deserving than he, would have died for. Men and women alike had greeted him warmly, some joking that they'd thought the legendary son, Jack, was a figment of Mr Tomlinson's imagination. He shook dozens of hands as he was shown around the maze of offices and introduced to clerks, secretaries, brokers and managers, before finally being led to his workspace – an oak desk with drawers on each side and a row of small compartments along the back, thankfully positioned near the only window in the room, a large, airless office lit by flickering fluorescent light. A tinge of mould underscored the stench of cigarette smoke that drifted through the room, loose papers and coffee rings marred the horizontal worktops, the vertical surfaces were lined with deep shelves bearing enormous ledgers, and still more papers spilt over three large metal trays set on a table just inside the door.

He was paired with Frank, an experienced accountant whose job was to teach Jack how to draw up ledgers and maintain records. Frank was both likeable and a good teacher, but Jack was horrified to find the simple task of writing difficult. For all his skilful wielding of paintbrushes in recent years, the act of manipulating the fine-tipped fountain pen to rule lines and enter tiny figures into neat columns proved challenging and he was embarrassed at how often he marred the ledgers with unsightly ink blots on his first day.

The volume of papers to be sorted and order forms matched to invoices was stunning. Frank was patient as he instructed Jack on the process of creating monthly invoices and transporting the completed paperwork to the room across the hall, where lines of secretaries toiled to fold papers, stuff envelopes and record addresses, ready for mailing to clients that spanned the globe. At the end of each day, after hours of concentration, Jack was exhausted. He found the routine monotonous, with little to show for his efforts beyond the neat pages of carefully added numbers, whose totals were then transferred to various other ledgers as daily, weekly and monthly records.

It was not his job to question or evaluate, only to maintain accurate records, which quite possibly might never be looked at again. At five o'clock every afternoon, after placing his pen on its stand and neatly filing his last invoice, Jack pushed his chair into place, slipped his arms into his jacket, placed his hat on his head and left the office. Walking the block to Flinders Street Station, he gave a ha'penny to one of the many lads whose singsong cry, 'E-rald, E-rald!' rang through the station as they waved evening editions of newspaper in the faces of pedestrians racing for trains, expertly making the exchange of paper for coin without breaking step. Jack then strode down the ramp of Platform Seven just in time to catch the 5:27 to South Yarra, occasionally bursting into a jog to launch himself through an open door of a slowly departing train.

The carriage's polished brass racks were crammed with coats and briefcases, while passengers, too late to gain a seat during the peak hour rush, stood gripping the leather hand straps. Jack usually chose to stand in the doorway, his feet firmly planted shoulder-width apart, bracing himself against the rhythmical lurch as the train sped along its tracks, attempting to read the headlines from his newspaper, the large broadsheet carefully folded to avoid intruding on the space of his fellow commuters. Sometimes he liked to just gaze out the door, trying not to feel like a stickybeak as he sought movements in the backyards of the homes bordering the railway tracks: women collecting tubs of laundry off the clotheslines, men chopping wood for the evening fire or bowling a cricket ball to a small batsman, children making the most of the dwindling daylight to swing on the rotary clothes hoist or play with their dog. These glimpses of the minutiae of days in the lives of strangers, as always, fascinated Jack.

Arriving home each afternoon, Jack's routine was equally predictable. Opening the door, he was welcomed by the aroma of dinner cooking on the stove: lamb chops and mashed potatoes, stewed rabbit or, perhaps, rissoles.

In her third week, Sofia insisted that it was her turn to prepare dinner. Accompanied by Marian, she walked from shop to shop, seeking the ingredients she needed. Eventually, they found rice as well as an array of fresh seafood. Marian watched dubiously as Sofia selected mussels, octopus and fresh bream fillets with the deliberation of a chef who aspired for a Michelin Star. Back at home, she immersed herself in preparing the fragrant lemon seafood risotto that had been Jack's favourite in Spain.

To their credit, William and Marian did their best. Politely picking through the rice on their plates, turning over morsels of indeterminate sea creatures, they chewed tentatively, bewildered at the novelty of holding a fork in their right hands, which usually wielded their bone-handled knives. Their conversation became stilted, interrupted by gulps of water and hesitant toying with the food, indicating that the adventurous approach to unfamiliar culinary experiences, evident at Malaga's seafood restaurant and Nerja's olive festival, did not extend to their dining room. Spanish food was unpalatable on their home soil, apparently.

'Oh, Jack. They hated it. I feel so awful!'

'No, Sofia, you mustn't feel bad. They're just not used to eating foreign food. It would have seemed very strange to them.'

'They seemed to like it when they were in Malaga!'

'Yes, but they were on holidays then. Everything was strange! They would have been feeling relaxed – adventurous, even… They might feel ready to try something next time…What about one of your stews?'

'Of course. I wanted to make something uniquely Spanish as a treat. But, like you say, it was probably too different. Perhaps they would like a *fricandò*.'

Jack nodded his agreement. The Spanish beef and mushroom stew was something his parents would like for sure, he thought.

The opportunity for Sofia to cook another Spanish dish never arose again for, when she offered to prepare their evening meal the following week, Marian politely declined.

'No, dear, you do not need to cook. You will have plenty of time for that when you and Jack have your own home. In any case, William enjoys his meat and vegetables and working men must eat well.'

Sofia accepted the rebuff and did not offer her culinary services again. Instead, she made herself busy with the housework, assistance that Marian gratefully accepted, for twelve months earlier, with the Australian economy showing no signs of improvement, William had announced that they needed to reduce their expenses. Who knew how long the hard times would prevail? So, Nina, who had come three times a week to help with the housework, had been relieved of her duties. So had Mr Stoppel and now the tasks of trimming branches, mowing, edging and general tidying of the garden fell to William on the weekends.

Sofia assisted in the house as much as possible, pleased to be busy and happy to fill her days working alongside her mother-in-law. Marian had a kind manner and was easy to be with, although for Sofia, who had managed a household as well as the finca's gallery since she was seventeen, Marian appeared anxious and indecisive. She constantly sought Sofia's opinion on small matters – whether Sofia believed the floors looked clean enough or if she thought that today they should do the flowers. Clearly, Marian had relied heavily on Nina.

Sofia's welcome assistance began at the dawn of each day when the clip-clopping of hooves and clinking of bottles announced the morning milk delivery. Lying in bed, she and Jack listened to the footsteps on the front porch, followed by the clinking of glass, as pint-sized bottles were settled into the milk basket. The cue to rise, Sofia headed down to the kitchen, where she helped Marian prepare breakfast for the men.

Each day of the week had its routines. Monday was, by tradition, clothes washing day for women across Australia.

Sofia enjoyed helping Marian work the electric copper each week. It was the one job that Marian was fastidious about, and commencing immediately after breakfast, together they scrubbed and soaked stains with velvet soap before proceeding to wash – first, the whites and then, the household clothing and then, finally, the bed-linen - in boiling water, before rinsing each load not twice, but three times, before pushing the items through the mangle and then hanging them onto the clothesline.

'Jack, did you know that you can tell if someone is ill, or slovenly, or having some sort of emergency, just by looking at their clothesline?' Sofia asked him one morning.

'What on earth do you mean? Do the pillowcases flap some sort of signal in the breeze?'

'Well, Mrs Jasper, over the back - her washing was not out until early this afternoon and Mum said that never happens. Should be out by 9 am at the latest, so something must be wrong! She thought that she would ask around, to see if anything had happened... And Mrs Howard, you know, next door - well, her clothes are always grey. Mum would like to tell her that she should be doing an extra rinse, but she thinks that Mrs Howard would take offence.'

'Surely not!'

'Well, she might think that Mum is being critical.'

'No, I meant surely you women are not gazing over the palings to read the washing, like some gypsy woman reading tea-leaves!' Jack laughed. 'That's terrible. Fancy having to worry about silly things like the neighbours counting the bedsheets on the clothesline!'

'I never thought about such things in Malaga. We did not have neighbours close enough to even notice what they were doing with their washing. I daresay they would be just as critical if they had half a chance. I know that there was always competition about who cooked the best risotto.'

CHAPTER 18

*T*uesday was ironing day, and although Marian still had flat irons that she set on the stove to warm, she had recently purchased an electric iron as well. Working together, she and Sofia had the linens and garments starched, ironed and hung or folded before lunch. Wednesdays were always downstairs cleaning, Thursdays upstairs. Surfaces were dusted, floors were vacuumed and timber surfaces were polished.

Mid-mornings, the sharp double-beep of the bakery van could be heard drawing closer and closer, its familiar sound drawing women to the kerbside, where they'd wait for the baker to open the rear doors of his van to release the aroma of freshly baked bread, sticky iced finger buns or sultana-filled Boston buns laden with a thick spread of creamy snow-white icing and topped with coconut. Sofia was amazed at Marian's capacity to time the arrival of the van, listening as the beeping grew louder until it turned into their street and Sofia frequently accompanied Marian down the driveway to stand with the neighbours on the footpath, waiting their turn to purchase a high-top loaf.

'Jack, you have married a whirlwind! She never stops! I feel awful.' Marian expressed her concerns to Jack – Sofia was doing too much, washing, cleaning the bathrooms and vacuuming the floors, leaving the easier tasks of dusting and polishing to her mother-in-law.

When he asked her about it, she replied, 'What else have I got to do all day? I will go mad if I'm not busy.'

After a light lunch, usually a ham and pickle sandwich followed by a slice of moist fruit cake, or perhaps a finger bun they'd bought fresh from the baker's truck that morning, Sofia had adopted the habit of going to the shops. There she would purchase meat and vegetables for their dinner. At first, they had made the short walk to the shops together, but quickly Sofia had discovered that Marian found the walk tiring and happily volunteered to undertake the trip alone. It soon became a daily practice for Marian to write a list of the items they needed on a notepad and Sofia would be on her way, enjoying the walk in the autumn sunshine.

'Butter – lamb chops – carrots – pumpkin.' Marian pronounced the English words slowly, relishing her role in teaching Sofia the essential vocabulary of Australian housewives.

Sofia equally enjoyed these moments, savouring the closeness that she had developed with Marian – loving her as a mother, even. She giggled as she repeated the words back, enunciating each syllable carefully, and as she walked to the shops, she glanced between the slip of paper and her route, avoiding the shrubbery overhanging the footpaths and committing her shopping list to memory. She was determined to master the ability to request one pound of lamb chops and half a pound of parsnips and carrots without mishap or the embarrassment of being forced to hand the notepaper to the shopkeeper in the manner of a small child.

When the sunshine allowed, the women spent an hour in the garden doing some light weeding or planting Marian's bulbs and annual seedlings. Sofia, spying the lawnmower in the garden shed, was quick to drag it out and began pushing it up and down the lawn, much to Marian's horror. Ignoring her protests, Sofia persisted in mowing sections of the extensive lawn throughout the week, laughingly declaring, 'We Spanish women may look frail, but we're as tough as old mules and work twice as hard.'

Marian would shake her head helplessly, preferring not to hear her daughter-in-law likened to an old mule, but appreciating her spunk and accepting that William's and Jack's weekends would be made all the lighter for Sofia's efforts.

In the evenings, Jack and Sofia sat together at the dining room table, scouring the daily newspaper's 'To Let' columns in search of their own home to rent. Plenty of houses were advertised, but in William and Marian's eyes, there was always a reason why they were unsuitable. 'Jack! You couldn't live all the way out there,' Marian would exclaim. 'You would have to take two trains to get to work. It would be dark before you got home!'

William would shake his head on the house inspections. 'Too much damp in this wall,' or 'That chimney is dangerous, bound to catch fire.' And so, time passed by and no house proved acceptable. The truth was that William and Marian enjoyed having Jack and Sofia living with them. Not for their assistance in managing the daily household chores, although that was certainly welcomed, but rather, for the company they provided in the large, echoing house. William enjoyed the occasional early walks to the train station with Jack and sharing the ride into the city, although usually the responsibilities of William's position took him to locations across Melbourne and beyond, meeting clients and finalising contracts to export wool, cotton and wheat to England.

All too soon, the colourful autumn leaves receded into memory as a series of bleak, wet, windy days set in. Winter had arrived. Jack shivered as he left the house in the pre-dawn darkness, puffing a haze of white fog on exhalation. He pulled his collar high and tightened the knitted scarf around his neck. Most days it proved to be a flimsy barricade against the icy air. With his hat pulled low and his gloved hands pushed deep into the pockets of his coat, he'd set off to the station, glad for the days when it wasn't raining. If it was, he'd have a fight on his hands battling the wind to maintain a firm grip on his umbrella.

Returning at the end of the winter days, Jack briskly walked through darkened streets, where intermittent pools of gold spilt from the electric streetlamps. He peered into the houses he passed, observing the strips of light that seeped through the window edges, where drawn curtains formed shields against the chill of the black night air. Jack pictured the inhabitants within, cosily huddled before crackling fireplaces with bowls of steaming soup and crusty buttered bread, while their bedsheets were warmed with rubber bottles filled with boiling water.

The drabness of winter was inevitably replaced by the vibrancy of spring and Jack was very conscious of the suddenness with which the season burst forth. Spring had always been his favourite time of the year, forming an explosion that attacked his senses and making him want to reach for his paintbrushes. Colourful scent-filled gladioli, chrysanthemums, hydrangeas and lavender formed a show in the front yards of the houses he passed as he walked to and from the station each day. The bare limbs of plum and peach trees sprouted delicate tissue-like blossoms along their spindly branches. The heavy boughs of ancient oak and mulberry trees came alive, thronging with the hum of bees at work. The air was filled with the sound of high-pitched chattering and chirping from the dozens of small birds who hopped among the boughs, skilfully weaving grass and straw nests in readiness for the eggs that were about to be laid.

The buoyancy of spring was not confined to the natural environment and Jack observed the transformation of his fellow commuters, whose spirits had been subdued during the dreary winter months, when, smiles and greetings were brief as heads remained lowered by necessity, eyes fixed firmly to the ground, feet ever ready to leap dank puddles and traverse overflowing gutters. Now, an air of sociability infiltrated the train system. Commuters strode up and down the ramps with heads high. Ladies wore bright dresses and pearl-buttoned cardigans. Men appearing lighter on their feet, released from the heavy woollen coats and scarves that had enveloped them through the cold, wet winter. Smiles and greetings were exchanged as they declared the loveliness of the season.

Stepping off the train on one such fine afternoon, Jack felt a surge of pleasure at the sight of Sofia waiting for him by the iron railing at the station exit. Recently, as the daylight hours lengthened, she had begun walking to meet him after she'd assisted Marian with the dinner preparations - comfortable in the knowledge that the beans were topped, tailed and floating in salted water laced with a dash of bicarb to draw out the green; the carrots and Brussel sprouts were peeled, ready for a vigorous boil; the meat was laid on the tray, ready for the heavy iron skillet, or set in a roasting dish for baking in the large green Aga, the enamelled cast iron wood-fuelled stove that was the pride of Marian's kitchen.

'You'll never find me,' he'd laughed, when she'd first suggested she come to meet him, back in mid-August.

'Of course, I will. I'll know you by your hat!' Sofia loved Jack's new grey fedora, commenting on how handsome he was, when he nestled it onto his head each morning before he left the house.

'Sofia, thousands of men walk down the platform, each wearing a grey fedora.'

'Yes, but none so tall and dashing as you, my handsome husband,' had been her reply, and as she'd predicted, from the very first afternoon, she'd been able to pick him out of the crowds that descended the ramp each afternoon, from twenty yards away.

Today, Sofia's eyes held a light that Jack had not seen in a while. She beamed broadly as she approached him. Something had happened, he knew. Feeling his face form a grin as the space between them closed, he greeted her with strong arms pulling her close, which produced smiles from the river of commuters flowing around them. Maybe she had found a house? Perhaps she was...late...and the baby was on its way at last!

'Hello, sweet lady. What have you been up to that has put such a sparkle in your eyes?' he teased.

'Just happy to see my husband,' Sofia teased him in return, tossing her head with a swaggering motion. He stepped back and looked into her face enquiringly, for he recognised that something was afoot.

'Jack – I met the most interesting people today.'

CHAPTER 19

*J*ack tried to think of who could be visiting his parents' house that could be so interesting - then remembered, it was Wednesday, and she'd planned a trip into the city, that morning. Sofia had recently established a habit of going into the city, usually on Wednesdays, enjoying the freedom to wander from Collins Street to Bourke Street, meandering through shops. And then there was the wonderful maze of lanes running between the city blocks, full of fascinating little boutiques - milliners and haberdasheries, shoe shops and dress shops. It had started mid-winter, when Sofia had explained her need to buy a warm coat to ward off the chilly breezes on her daily walk to the shops.

'We'll go into town,' Marian had decided, pleased to have an excuse to spend a whole day shopping with her daughter-in-law. They'd caught the train to Flinders Street Station and spent the morning wandering through Georges, one of the largest department stores Sofia had ever seen. For lunch, they'd lined up behind pearl-clad women bearing trays loaded with sandwiches, cakes and tiny pots of tea at Coles cafeteria, and then they'd finished the day by exploring the tiny boutiques selling umbrellas, gloves, shoes and dresses along

Swanson Street. As well as a coat, Sofia bought shoes for both herself and Jack, a beautiful hair comb and a stylish hat that Marian insisted was just right for her.

That night she'd spoken excitedly about the sights. She had not realised that Australian cities had such vibrancy and was amazed by the endless choices of fashionable clothing and shoes available in Melbourne. Way beyond anything she would find in Malaga, and quite possibly more even than Madrid!

'Well, we're not all koalas and gum trees,' Jack had retorted, pleased that Sofia had been so intoxicated by the vibrancy of Melbourne's streets and feeling a little guilty that he had not taken her on a shopping trip before now.

'I know, Jack...but I just hadn't realised how big it was... Also, there is an art store! I only saw it quickly as we were going back to the station, but I would have loved to have gone inside.'

She described the tiny store tucked in a back lane and how it was like the shop where Andrés and Jack used to buy paints and brushes in Malaga. Her words were a catalyst that stirred up memories. Jack was suddenly overwhelmed as he recollected a time in Spain where paint tubes, brushes and canvas were the lifeblood of each day.

Two weeks later, he had not been surprised when Sofia told him she wanted to go back into the city again. She was apprehensive - she wanted to go alone this time, but did not want to offend Marian. Furthermore, she was sure that her mother-in-law would insist on accompanying her. 'I just want to explore, Jack. Roam here and there, as my fancy takes me. Perhaps, find an art gallery, somewhere. Mum would not be interested in that.'

'Go on Wednesday,' Jack had suggested. 'Mum has morning tea's with the church. She won't want to miss that!'

The following Tuesday, when Sofia had announced that she was going to catch the train into Melbourne on the following morning, Marian was aghast.

'But you couldn't possibly go alone!'

'Sofia will be fine,' Jack interjected, knowing better than anyone how capable his wife was and confident that she would be well able to navigate the short train journey and walk around the city safely, in broad daylight. He reminded his parents that Sofia had both kept a house and run an art gallery and café before coming to Australia. An afternoon in the city, alone, free to wander where she wished, would be good for her, he thought.

Since that day, Sofia had returned to the city on a number of mornings, enjoying the freedom of wandering the streets for a few hours, before returning home to help Marian prepare dinner.

~

Linking arms with him, Sofia launched into a breathless explanation of her day's adventure.

'I was walking along Elizabeth Street and turned into Little Collins Street, you know, where that tiny little umbrella shop is. I don't know how I'd missed it, because I'm sure I've been down there before.'

'Probably, distracted by the shoe shops, I suppose!'

Sofia punched him in the arm, for he was always teasing her about buying shoes ever since she had bought two pairs for herself and a pair for him on her first trip to the city with Marian. She continued, 'A little place, the Meldrum Gallery, with a bookshop tucked in one of its back rooms. *The Beckoning Bookshelf* – managed by the nicest, the most beautiful, young girl.'

Jack smiled as Sofia spoke so rapidly that even he, who was used to her 'Spanglish', as he now called it, struggled to understand her words. 'Hey, not so fast,' he said, pleased to see the joy radiating from her and noticing how lovely she looked with her eyes sparkling and her hands waving.

'Hel...en. Her name was Helen,' Sofia continued, slowing down her cascade of sentences. 'She was so nice, Jack, and so patient. She did not mind my accent at all.'

Sofia's words made him frown. Throughout his childhood, Jack had blindly accepted the policy, 'Australia for the white man'. His father had always been very outspoken on the subject whenever it arose in the media. 'Foreigners would work for lower wages,' William had explained to him. 'The standard of living for Australian families would decline.' Additionally, he'd explained to Jack, how people from non-English speaking backgrounds had different ideas. Different customs. They would never fit in to Australian society and really, would be much happier living in their own country, with their own kind. William had explained these were the reasons for why the government's policy that focussed on accepting white-skinned people, only. Those who spoke English, and therefore would adapt to Australian society easily. As a schoolboy, his father's words had made perfect sense. And then, in Malaga, when Jack had told his parents that he planned to marry Sofia and had been met with such hostility, he had questioned William's attitudes. Sofia was no threat to Australian workers. She was a beautiful young woman that he loved. He'd assumed that his parents would be as charmed by her as he was, and thankfully, despite their initial reactions, they now loved Sofia for who she was, as the daughter, they'd never had. But over time Jack, had discovered that not everyone was so welcoming or friendly, toward her. There had been times when salespeople scowled at her accent, feigning ignorance of her requests, intentionally refusing to understand her. Even on her recent trips into the city, she'd experienced insults. A shopkeeper had advised her that the dresses hanging on the racks were not to be tried on before purchasing, when the presence of change rooms indicated that was utter nonsense. On another occasion, Sofia had entered one of the hairdressing salons to make an appointment, only to have the attendant almost push her onto the street, insisting that this was not the right place for her and pointing up the road to a salon in Bourke Street where Sofia "would be much more comfortable."

Constantly, even amongst his workmates, Jack observed negative attitudes being directed toward non-English speaking people, as well as to the Aboriginal people in Australia, and he couldn't understand it. After all, hadn't he been the foreigner in both Paris and Spain? Hadn't he seen dark skinned people working in restaurants? Performing on stage?

Jack's mind returned to focus on Sofia's words as she excitedly described her day. '...she introduced me to Jim. He owns the gallery. We talked about paintings for ages! Jim said that I could come and put in a few hours there anytime I liked. Not for pay, of course – there is no money - but I could go in and help set up when they have exhibitions and things. He said we should come along and meet everybody.'

Before Jack had time to ask who 'everybody' was, Sofia elaborated. 'There is a whole group of them, Jack! Men and woman! Meldrumites, he called them. Passionate about art. It is their whole life!'

'Meldrumites...I am sure Margaret knew them. I remember she thought that I was a Meldrumite once. On the ship, when I first met her...'

Sofia rummaged through her bag distractedly. 'They have classes in the city. Evening classes, too. I had a flyer... darn it, I must have left it behind,' she said, frowning.

While a part of Jack missed the years in Paris and Spain when he'd devoted most of his time to painting, his work on Goldsbrough Mort & Co's ledgers kept him busy. Occasionally, he found himself doodling with the runs of ink that oozed from his pen onto the desk pad and allowing his mind to roam beyond the office walls. At these moments, he'd chuckle to himself as he looked through the small, dusty window by his desk. Just like the poet Banjo Patterson, he mused, who'd recorded his visions of his mate Clancy living a life of freedom, driving mobs of cattle through forest and plains, with the night sky a blanket, a swag for his bed, a campfire for warmth and cooking, and a steaming mug of tea poured directly from his tin billy. A life that was free of shackles that the poet envied for, just like Jack, Banjo was confined to a tiny city office, '*facing the round eternal 'tween the cash-book and the journal*'. While it was not Patterson's bush dream that Jack sought, his mind occasionally meandered back to Malaga and the freedoms of the Mediterranean lifestyle that he, Sofia and Andrés had shared.

Sofia's elation at meeting the Melbourne artists made her words sing, her steps light – as she skipped alongside him relaying the day's events. Jack could not deny that his interest was aroused. It would be wonderful to meet with some artists here in Australia, he agreed. And certainly, it was time for them to move beyond the world of his parents' home.

The following Wednesday, Sofia again visited Meldrum Gallery, this time returning with the flyer outlining the painting classes on offer. Jack read it with interest, his eyes resting on lessons that were being offered on Tuesday and Thursday evenings. The name of the teacher - Justus Jorgensen – caught his attention. He tried to recall where it was that he'd heard that unusual name.

Sofia, bearing the same joyful manner of the previous week, informed Jack that they were invited to join the artists for dinner on Friday night and Jack smiled at her hopeful expression as she reached out to turn the flyer in his hand over, revealing the words scribbled on the back of the page.

'See? The Latin Café – Exhibition St, Friday night. At 6:00 pm. They meet up there for dinner, each week.'

Touched by Sofia's enthusiasm, Jack nodded. Her excitement at meeting with the artists was palpable and made him wonder how she really felt about her life. Days spent as a helpmate to his mother, cleaning, shopping, cutting the vegetables for meals and accompanying Marian to morning and afternoon teas and charity events where he could imagine her politely smiling at the older women trying to follow the conversations around her. He knew that family – his family – was important to Sofia and appreciated her efforts to be a loving and dutiful daughter-in-law. Nonetheless, perhaps it was time that they began making plans for their own life, beyond the so-far futile search for a house to let and - where better to start than to connect with these artists Sofia had stumbled onto?

'Okay. Could be interesting. Let's meet up with them.'

'This Friday?' Sofia asked, squealing with delight and reaching up to kiss him when Jack agreed.

William and Marian could not conceal their surprise when Jack told them that he and Sofia were going into the city on Friday evening, where they would be meeting up with a group of artists. However, despite their raised eyebrows, the only comment came from Marian and was about the meal.

'Italian food! Here in Melbourne!' she said incredulously. 'Who on earth would have thought?'

CHAPTER 20

*W*aiting for Sofia to emerge from the sea of people gathering at the entrance of Melbourne's Flinders Street Station, Jack could almost inhale the exhilaration emanating from the crowd. Usually, at this time of the day, the city's pedestrians were all on the move. Departing the city like an outgoing tide, they'd converge upon the station, surge up the stairwell, crash through the arches towards the turnstiles, sweep into the inner cavern of the enormous interior and finally, they'd spill down the stairs and ramps leading onto the trains waiting to transport them north, south, east and west of the city.

This evening was different. It was as if a giant stopper had clogged the entrance of the station, and looking around, Jack wondered if perhaps half the population of Victoria were congregated here. He was forced to move a few steps along the railing for the third time as people jostled for space. For certain, the convenient location 'under the clocks' – so named for the row of clocks set above the Station's entrance – was where Victorians always linked up with their friends when they were meeting in the city. Jack could recall numerous times, as a young child when he'd stood holding his mother's hand while waiting to connect with William or an acquaintance of hers. And as he'd got older, there were the Saturday afternoons when he'd waited on these same stairs for his friends from school, before walking to Woolworths for bags of humbugs or barley sugar prior to going on to the movies. Tonight, it was the busiest Jack had ever seen.

Being Friday, it seemed everyone was ready for an evening in the city. The incoming arrivals were conspicuous by their dress – decked out in their best clothes for a night at the movies or having a special dinner. Those, like himself, employed in the offices and shops within the city, were in their work clothes. The two groups filled every square inch of the steps while they waited for spouses, sweethearts and friends. Adding to the crush on the stairs were the regular commuters, keen to be on their trains and travelling home as speedily as possible, visible as they muttered expletives and not-so-gently pushed through the stationary crowds obstructing their path. At this minute, Jack had no difficulty believing Flinders Street Station's reputation for being the busiest station in the world.

Continuously scanning the sea of faces around him, Jack had just begun to wonder if he and Sofia would ever find each other when, suddenly, there she was - her face flushed - at his side. He took her hand and they crossed the busy intersection, where they were swept along the street amid a stream of pedestrians.

'This is just like Paris!' Sofia exclaimed as a cab pulled up, releasing a finely dressed couple onto the pavement in front of them. Jack agreed. Certainly, the bustle of motor vehicles, cabs, vans and even the occasional horse-drawn carriage jostling along the roadway was reminiscent of their time in Paris, barely five years earlier.

Their timing was perfect. Just on six, they turned down Exhibition Street, arriving through the open doorway of the Latin Café, where they were greeted by an Italian man, dapper in his black suit, with smiling eyes and an enormous moustache.

'Welcome, friends, come on in. I, Camillo, will find you a seat. Follow me'.

'We are meeting friends…artists,' Jack said and Camillo nodded in reply as Sofia searched the room for a familiar face. Jack had a distinct sense of being thrust back into the world of Montparnasse as, following Camillo, they squeezed between chairs and tables crammed tightly together, amid clinking glasses, hazy smoke-filled air and a cacophony of spirited conversations.

'You want Jorgy, heh?' Camillo called over his shoulder, leading them to a narrow staircase that creaked threateningly as they ascended. At the top, a door opened into a dimly lit room where half a dozen tables were pushed together, and perhaps, twenty people were seated, chatting among themselves. The overflowing ashtrays and heavy layer of smoke drifting to the ceiling, as well as the scattering of wine carafes across the tables, indicated that the gathering had been in progress for quite a while and everyone seemed very relaxed.

'Hope you are all behaving yourselves!' Camillo roared. 'I don't want to see any more naked ladies dancing on the tables! This is a respectable business, you know!' He winked at Jack, his laugh booming. 'My customers downstairs would be disappointed if they thought there wasn't an orgy up here.'

Conversation interspersed with laughter, filled the room. Looking around, Jack was relieved that everybody appeared to have their clothes intact, but was still surprised at the sight of so many eccentric people gathered in one place. Men sported long hair and small beards, a rare sight on the conservative streets of Melbourne. Women wore loose-fitting blouses adorned with long strings of colourful beads. A man with a bright green velvet jacket caught Jack's eye, nodding a greeting.

'Sofia,' a voice called and a young woman made her way towards them. 'I was hoping you would come! And you must be Jack.' The smile Jack received was dazzling, and as she tossed back a mane of auburn hair and looked at them both with wide, clear eyes, he had to agree with Sofia's description of this girl, who could only be Helen. She was quite beautiful. 'Come, sit down here, where it's quieter,' she said, leading them to the back where a few empty seats remained. A small man sat at the table, gazing into his wine glass, oblivious to the smouldering ash ready to fall from the cigarette dangling from his lips. Beside him, a lively, dark-haired lady with a wide smile – the same smile as Helen, Jack noticed – nodded at them as she shifted her chair to make space.

'Welcome,' she said. 'Always lovely to meet young people.'

Helen introduced the couple as her parents, Mervyn and Lena Skipper.

'Don't worry about Dad,' she said, nodding at Mervyn. 'He's not too happy tonight…had a bad day at the paper. Here, would you like a glass of wine?'

Accepting glasses of the red wine Lena poured, Jack observed the scene around them, surprised by the range of ages of those present, including a girl of about sixteen, whom Helen introduced as her sister, Sonia, and a boy who looked to be about fourteen, her brother, Matchum. Jack smiled as the boy grinned cheekily at him before opportunistically draining his mother's wine while she was distracted by the new arrivals.

'Merv, great article,' a voice called from farther up the table, eliciting a wry smile, accompanied by a raised glass, from Helen's father.

'Good,' said Helen with a relieved expression. 'He'll like that. He's had a bad time at work lately. There was a bit of a reaction to one of his articles today and his boss is not too happy with him.' She explained that Mervyn wrote for one of Australia's leading papers, *The Bulletin*. Articles about the arts and theatre. The problem was, it appeared, that Mervyn did not necessarily write articles that conformed to popular opinion.

'There are always debates about art. So tedious. The mob at the National Gallery criticise Max Meldrum at every opportunity, and by association, us, since Justus – our teacher – was so close to Max – his prize pupil and all. Of course, if Max didn't draw so much attention to himself, always arguing black's white and white's black, perhaps there wouldn't be so much hostility towards him, or us. I swear that man came out of the womb arguing. Mervyn understands him, though –

don't you, Dad? – does his best to set them right.' Helen looked at her father fondly.

Jack was impressed. *The Bulletin* was one of Melbourne's most prestigious newspapers, read by everyone. To hear that these people – the Meldrumites – were getting write-ups immediately elevated their status in his eyes, even if it meant that they were being criticised. Jack knew from his conversations with Margaret that there were always controversies about art. Especially between the conservatives and the modernists. And here was Helen's father, a staff writer at the heart of the fray! He wondered if his father had read any of Mervyn's articles.

Helen quietly pointed out a number of the people in the room, beginning with the man seated at the head of the table, deep in conversation with a young fair-haired lady to his right.

'That's Justus,' she said. 'His old friends call him Norway. His wife, Lil – she's not here tonight – she calls him Peachy. To us, he is JJ or Jorgy, although a lot of his students call him Master. I think he'd like us all to.' Helen laughed loudly, causing Lena to frown and shake her head. Changing her tone, Helen continued, 'Really, he is amazing. A wonderful teacher. All he cares about is art. And now building too, of course. He has no time for the critics. Says that most of them couldn't even hold a brush, so who gives two hoots what they think?'

Surprised, Jack prodded Sofia, harder than he intended, whispering, 'I remember him! He came to the gallery. He was with that Australian crowd!'

Sofia peered towards Justus and nodded in agreement and Jack marvelled at the coincidence.

He couldn't hear the words Justus had spoken, but whatever he'd said raised a chorus of replies.

'I'll be there.'

'Me too.'

'Be there at about ten.'

'Sorry, we can't make it this weekend'.

Quizzically, Jack looked towards Lena, who filled in details. 'We've all been going out to Eltham on the weekends – east of

Melbourne – helping Jorgy create his artists' colony. It's wonderful! You've never seen anything like it!'

Helen added, 'It has been great fun. All of the students come along and we dig and mix mud and pull nails out of old floorboards. It's amazing how quickly it's all coming together! Sonny and I work in the garden, don't we, Sonia?'

Jack felt a little bewildered. Creating an artists' colony? Mixing mud. Perhaps he'd misunderstood. He thought that these people were painters.

Lena's eyes sparkled with enthusiasm as she resumed the conversation. 'The land is beautiful. Nine acres. Justus and Lil bought it about a year ago, thinking that it would be a nice place for us all to go and camp on weekends. A place to get away from the city and focus on our painting. But then, of course, like everything Justus does, he got a bit carried away.'

Helen picked up the conversation. 'He'd seen all of these buildings in Paris and Spain. Made dozens – no hundreds – of sketches. Cathedrals that were centuries old. Church windows, ancient doorways, gargoyles. There is nothing like them here in Australia! So, of course, once he owned the land, he decided to build a shelter. And in deciding to build a shelter... well, his ideas just got increasingly elaborate. And so it began.'

'It sounds very interesting. We saw some wonderful old buildings in Paris, too,' Jack said, well imagining how a person could be enthused by the extraordinary architecture on the other side of the world. He thought of La Ruche, that crazy three-storied tower in the Passage Dantzig that looked like a giant beehive, and the gothic buildings around the Académie Julian, with their carved doorways and ornate stonework. Certainly, they were inspiring creations.

'You'll have to see the buildings we've created in Eltham,' Lena said. 'No ordinary structures – extraordinary, rather. Justus did once train as an architect! He knows what he's doing. Now he's utterly gripped by the idea of creating a unique environment for artists, one that inspires creativity. A place where we can forget about stifling, mundane routines and devote ourselves to our art. A place where the very buildings are masterpieces – where the designs, stonework, carvings and even the very plastering of walls are completed by artisans.'

Lena described how the dream was rapidly being transformed into reality, as recycled materials were combined with mud and stone -the buildings like nothing Jack and Sofia would have ever seen.

'No. I can't say I've ever seen a building made from mud,' Jack said. 'I can't even imagine what it would look like.'

'We, also, have mud buildings in Spain, Lena,' Sofia said. 'Remember, Jack? The dairy, as well as some of the barns on the mountain. Adobe. Centuries-old.'

They listened as Lena described the first building that had been completed, specially built for Justus' wife, Lil.

'It's hardly cost anything to build. The wonderful old leadlight windows, oak doors, fireplaces – even the iron staircase – all came from Melbourne's wrecking yards.' Lena told them how demolition companies were now flooded with second-hand materials, thanks to a growing obsession for tearing down wonderful old buildings and replacing them with 'modern monstrosities'.

So enthusiastic was she that Jack found himself nodding in agreement at her invitation for him and Sofia to come out to Eltham and see the buildings for themselves.

He returned his gaze to the man who commanded such admiration from Lena and Helen. Justus' voice was quiet and yet steeped with authority, and the voices around the room were subdued into silence.

'… the relationship between the Master and the artist is critical,' he asserted, and Jack immediately thought of the kindly French master, Monsieur Simon, at the Académie Julian and how helpful he'd been in developing Jack's knowledge and skills.

Justus continued, rising in volume as he illustrated his argument. 'If a violinist insisted on being a soloist, there would be no orchestra. And if a simple fool with a brush and canvas dabbles with his paints in solitude, how can he develop and grow?'

Jack found himself agreeing, acknowledging that he had been a simple fool when sketching on his own. It was because of the influence of Margaret, the tutelage of Monsieur Simon, the inspiration of Andrés and other students, and of course, the encouraging words of Picasso, that his skills had developed.

'The guidance of an experienced Master is essential if a person with mere talent is to be transformed into an artist of true merit.'

Now, holding the attention of everybody, Justus expanded on his theme to include the role of employment in the life of an artist, and Jack's attention escalated when Helen, sitting immediately to his left, became the topic of the master's oration.

'For the artist, a job is an irritating inconvenience, suffered to pay for life's necessities. The true artist has no interest in fads and fashions that waste money. His only desire is to express himself on canvas and develop his skills. This is best served by basic employment that makes no demands on an artist's time or thoughts. Helen, here - she used to spend hours every day playing with horses. Feeding them. Brushing them. Riding them. She had not planned for the animals to take over her life. These things happen slowly. They are insidious. Before she knew it, all Helen's time and money were wrapped up in a pair of damned nags. So, I asked her, "What do you want to be: an ostler, or an artist?" Of course, the answer was obvious. My simple reminder served to redirect her priorities. She is now liberated from playing servant to dumb four-legged beasts and can focus her thoughts and energies where they belong. These days, her work at the bookshop, where she dusts shelves and arranges books, requires little attention and allows her mind to be free for more important things.'

The students nodded in assent and Jack found himself nodding with them – indeed, how quickly life could get in the way of painting!

He felt chastised, recognising how he had willingly allowed meaningless activities to take over his and Sofia's lives to the point where their time, not to mention success, in Paris had receded, and was now little more than a distant memory.

With these thoughts, Jack could see the value of a Master in an artist's life, one who recognised his students' needs and so was able to provide skilful direction to keep them focused. A Master who was alert to the world's entrapments.

Just before they left, Jack approached Justus, who looked at him keenly.

'So... Jack is back,' he said, chuckling with delight. Jack was stunned. Justus had remembered him, after all this time!

'Sit down. Tell me, how is your painting going? You were very good, I remember.'

Taking the now-empty seat beside Justus, Jack explained how he and Sofia had returned from Malaga earlier that year, following the death of Andrés and the hard times that had fallen upon Spain. How he had not found time for painting since their return to Australia as he was fully occupied, working as a clerk for Goldsbrough Mort & Co.

'Well,' said Justus authoritatively, taking the matter of Jack's life in his hand in a single sentence, 'we'll have to get you out of there. What do you want to be? An artist or a rich man's pen-pusher, counting his gold for him?'

Sofia nodded, clearly agreeing with Justus, who laughed at Jack's confused face.

'Never mind. One thing at a time. How would you like to join the classes? Perhaps Thursday evenings?' he asked.

'That would be wonderful,' Jack replied. 'Definitely. I'm ready to start straight away.' He was surprised by the wave of desire that washed over him, to again hold a brush and breathe the pungent, oily smell of paint. He had neglected his art for far too long.

'Wonderful,' Justus answered, looking pleased. 'Helen will give you the details. We are moving the lessons to Queens Street as of next week. I'll look forward to seeing you there. Don't be late. Six o'clock start.'

CHAPTER 21

The next morning, over breakfast, Jack and Sofia told William and Marian about their evening with the artists.

'You might have heard of them, Dad. The Meldrumites. They learned their methods from a man called Max Meldrum years ago. They are very good. They even get write-ups in *The Bulletin*.'

'The Meldrumites!' William blustered, shock evident in his voice. 'Everybody has heard about the Meldrumites. The papers were full of them. It was a couple of years ago now. Tied up in some murder. A terrible to-do. A young woman's body found, not too far from here.' William dropped his voice, his next comment for Jack's ears only. 'Her boyfriend was a prime suspect – some artistic type who had not one, but two, women. The case went on for weeks. All everyone could talk about was the Meldrumites and their depraved lifestyle.'

Jack was shocked, but disbelieving, insisting that the people they had met were nothing like this. Families. Married. Their children also artists. Very respectable.

'That must be another group, Dad. Justus can't be the only one of Max's students who has set up a Meldrumite art school.'

It could be the only answer, Jack thought, and his parents agreed, somewhat doubtfully. What did they know about the art world?

The following week, Jack packed his canvas bag for his first lesson with Justus. Sofia had insisted on using some of her money, untouched since they arrived in Australia, to set him up for his painting lessons, and for once, he did not refuse her. As he carefully arranged the new canvases, shiny glass bottles of linseed oil and mineral turpentine, the clean wooden palette, an assortment of hog hair and sable brushes and the set of Winsor and Newton oil tubes they had bought together, anticipation swept over him. He wondered if he would remember how to mix colours. If he would be any good. Would he still be able to recall the techniques he'd learned in Paris?

All through his workday, Jack anticipated the lesson, and determined not to be late, he arrived at the Queen Street studio at five to six, having walked around the city block twice since he'd finished work to pass the time.

'Tell me all about it, Jack. Everything!' Sofia insisted, when he arrived home after nine-thirty.

'It was…all right,' he replied. 'Just dabbed... Nothing special.'

'Stop it, Jack, you are teasing me. I want to know everything. What did you paint? Did Justus like your work? How many people were there?'

Jack relented, admitting to Sofia how good it felt to be painting again. 'I thought that I would be tired after working all day, but not so. And once we started painting, it was like I'd never stopped.'

He explained Justus' theory of tonalism. 'It's all about suggesting the subject rather than creating a photographic image of it. Using tones to create atmosphere. Focusing on the hues of the painting rather than the subject itself. Justus says you can make the most ordinary subject a work of art by creating an atmosphere that mimics nature. He's made some changes to the theories that were originally taught to him by Max Meldrum. Max is furious with him. He blames Justus for luring his pupils away. Justus says we will meet him sooner or later – he occasionally pops in for an argument.'

'Argument? Why would he bother?' Sofia asked. 'In fact, why does Justus let him?'

'Oh, I think Justus is quite fond of the old man. He used to idolise him, and in turn, he was Max's star pupil. The Master didn't say too much about their falling out, but he did say that, when he went to Paris and saw the modern works there, he could no longer see paintings in the same way as Meldrum did. Meldrum couldn't take it.'

'The Master?' Sofia raised her eyebrows, smiling.

'Well, that's what everyone calls him during the lessons. It's catchy.'

Sofia demanded a second-by-second account of the painting Jack had started, now resting on one of the racks which lined the wall of the Queen Street studio and then she asked about the other students.

'Quite a few new people, plus a couple from the Café Latin. That young fellow, Helen's brother - he was there and what a character he is!'

'Character? He's just a boy. What do you mean?'

Jack described that Matchum, despite his broad shoulders and mature manner, was just twelve years old.

'Twelve! I thought that he was at least fifteen, maybe even sixteen!'

'Yes. As did I. He told me that he is a prisoner of Justus – forced to attend the classes.'

'Surely not. No one would make a child go to painting classes, would they?'

'Well, in this case, it seems that he has been made to go. He's been running wild, truanting, spending his days in the company of riff-raff and getting into all manner of strife.'

'What sort of strife?' Sofia looked concerned.

'Nothing illegal. Well, not too bad... He's rather proud of his exploits. Tearing around the city in billy-carts and sneaking into cinemas. Wild boy stuff.'

Sofia listened with interest as Jack continued.

'A couple of weeks ago, the police brought the rascal home two nights in a row, until finally Lena decided she'd had enough. Justus suggested Matchum attend the art classes day and night, keeping the lad both busy and supervised. Seems Justus is a bit of an amateur psychologist. Anyway, he was confident that he could unlock a creativity in Matchum that could be used for good, rather than evil.'

'Sounds like a good plan.' Sofia nodded approvingly.

'It was so funny. Like a floor show. Matchum doesn't care what anyone thinks. Argues with Justus about everything. Matchum never stopped baiting him.' Jack started to laugh, explaining. 'Tonight, Justus gave us photos of the Princess Bridge. He told us to turn our pictures upside down before painting them so our minds would only see the lines and shapes. It reduces objects to their actual forms, so, when we paint, we are not influenced by the subject and any pre-conceived ideas of what we think we are supposed to be seeing. Clever, really.' Sofia agreed.

'So, what does Matchum do? Sets up his canvas against the wall and stands on his head to paint. Justus didn't know whether to be annoyed or laugh and the rest of us were in stitches. One things for sure - Matchum was not going to shift. Did a fine job of his painting too, I have to say!'

Returning to the Café Latin two weeks later, Jack and Sofia felt more at home as the group greeted them like old friends. This time, he recognised a few fellow students from his art classes, whom he introduced to Sofia. Quickly, they fell into conversation with Clarice, a softly spoken woman who Jack had noticed immediately when he'd arrived at his first lesson. She'd been standing at the front of the room, talking with Justus, the two analysing the large canvas on the table between them. He hadn't had a chance to see the painting, for following right behind him were two men, Don and Larry, who'd immediately spotted Clarice's work and called across to her – a comment about street-walking before sunrise. She'd seemed embarrassed and had quickly put the painting away.

Chatting together, Jack and Sofia discovered that they had common ground with Clarice, for she, too, lived with her parents, only hers were elderly and very ill.

'The only time I get to paint is in the morning.' She rued. 'You will no doubt hear about me – the crazy-lady of Beaumaris! I get up before daylight, and pulling my painting trolley behind me, I head to the beach. They all talk about me – even the artists,' she looked around the room, pointedly. 'I don't care what they say … in fact, the early morning mist creates some of the most brilliant effects – you'd miss them if you weren't up before sunrise.'

'Have you exhibited,' Sofia asked her, with interest, but Clarice just rolled her eyes.

'Every year, but really, I wonder why. Nobody buys my work, and the critics – they just want to focus on me and my trolley, out while it's still dark. I am just a novelty to them.'

Clarice was fascinated to discover that he and Sofia had lived in Paris and Spain, clearly envious of their opportunity to travel and asked dozens of questions.

All too quickly, the evening quickly drew to a close, ending with a conversation about Eltham, and a show of hands for who was going out to the artist's retreat the next day to work on the site. Jack and Sofia looked at each other, quizzically, and Lena noticed.

'Come on, you two- you will love it. How about I pick you up, you can ride out to Eltham with us. Here, write your address down for me. We'll see you about seven-thirty.' She handed them a scrap of paper and pencil, from her bag. Laughingly, they agreed. It would be fun, they thought.

CHAPTER 22

*J*ack and Sofia smiled at each other, as the Skippers'
vehicle crept towards them, its colour – bright turquoise –
decidedly uncommon, its chrome, gleaming in the early
morning sunlight. Numerous arms extended from its windows, waving
to them as it drew into the curb.

'Plenty of room if you don't mind a bit of a squish,' Lena called
from the driver's seat as Mervyn leapt out to take the picnic basket
Jack was holding. He placed it in between himself and Lena in the
front.

'It will be safer here – Matchum! Take care!'

Matchum, ignoring Lena's instruction, made space for Jack and
Sofia in the rear seat by diving over its back, collapsing into the boot
and folding his long frame into the small space, already crammed with
picnic rugs, two thermoses and a wicker hamper. He began singing in a
deep baritone, with a smile and wink at Jack.

Laughing, Sofia and Jack squeezed in beside Helen and Sonia.

'Beautiful car,' Jack said, inhaling the aroma of freshly polished
leather, and immediately, Sonia launched into the story of her mother's
purchase.

'A green car, Mum had to have. Green, but not just any old green. Not the green that the factory produces. Not the green that Australians are buying by the hundreds, as quick as they drop off the assembly line. No sir-ee,' Sonia announced, enjoying the attention of retelling the story that had no doubt been shared a hundred times. 'Mum had to have *turquoise* green. So, when the poor man arrived for the official handing over, producing the keys for the brand-new - chrome so polished that you could see your face in it - "green" car, expecting Mum to fall over him rapturously, what does Mum say?'

Sonia deepened her voice and adopted a commanding tone. '"Take. It. Away. That's not the green I requested. I want turquoise green. T-U-R-Q-U-O-I-S-E."

'That poor man. You should have seen his face! Nonetheless, what Mum wants, Mum gets. So here we are, gadding about in the only turquoise Holden in all of Melbourne. Little wonder everybody stares at us!'

Everybody laughed. Even Lena chortled good-naturedly at her own expense, clearly delighted to be described in such eccentric terms. Sonia continued to chatter non-stop, describing the various characters that turned up for the Saturday working bees to wield shovels, cart rock, toss mud and dig shitholes under the direction of 'the Master'. She emphasised the title with exaggerated reverence and Jack wondered if she was having a dig at Justus. Evidently, her mother thought so too, as more than once she turned around and said warningly, 'Sonia – respect, please,' to which Sonia just laughed. In less than an hour, the turquoise marvel pulled up at the Eltham Bakery where they all piled out to buy rolls, still warm from the oven, and three sticky fruit buns to take to the colony.

'You touch those and I swear, I will skin you alive, Matchum,' Lena warned, hearing rustling from the rear of the car.

While waiting for the others to finish their purchases, Jack and Sofia absorbed the picturesque little town, with half-a-dozen shops open for Saturday morning trade. Railway tracks, flowing to and from a bluestone station, ran parallel to the main street, which had a typical village atmosphere. Quaint, even, with a butchery, general store and news agency. Hills in the distance completed the picture in blues, greys, mauves and greens. Jack felt stirrings of a desire to paint and Justus' vision of an artists' colony in this beautiful rural setting made perfect sense.

∽

Barely five minutes later, the Holden ascended a bumpy dirt track before turning into a cleared area where numerous vehicles were already parked. A group of men were busy emptying the contents of a van, its side emblazoned with the words 'Whelan the Wrecker' in large red letters. Jack watched as they unloaded an enormous window frame, complete with coloured glass, fittings and sill. Heavy, judging by the number of men carrying it across the yard. He instinctively walked over to help, and with a grunt of welcome, a small dark-headed man shuffled his grip to allow Jack to join in. Guided by Justus, the window was placed in a storage shed much like a stable, made of timber poles, an iron roof and three sides lined with old weatherboards.

Justus was outwardly thrilled with the find. 'Did you ever see anything like this, Jack?' he asked. 'Beautiful. And to think it was being thrown aside to make way for some hideous modern façade! It's criminal. Never mind. Their loss is our gain. Thanks to Whelan …' He turned to an older man who was incongruously dressed in a white shirt, black bow-tie and old fashioned billycock, walking toward them. Jack noted Whelan's limp, which may have limited his mobility but had not diminished his capacity as supervisor, for it had been his continuous instructions, transmitted in a lilting Irish accent, that had guided the transfer of the frame from the van to the shed, without mishap.

'Jim Whelan – otherwise known as Whelan the Wrecker. He looks after us. Always ferreting out treasures that some fool has cast aside. Knows exactly what we're looking for here. Thanks for bringing the windows out, mate. Much appreciated.'

'Thanks to you!' Jim responded. 'I hate to see stuff like this left to rot in the yards. Within a week the glass is broken, the wood ruined by the weather. These windows are priceless. Works of art. They don't make them like this anymore. Makes me feel good to see them being used. Now, Master, you'd better show me where you are up to. It's been months since I was here.' And with a nod to Jack, Justus led the old man back towards the buildings.

Jack inhaled deeply, relishing the unique fragrance of the Australian bush, the pungent, organic odour of dew-laden soil enriched by layers of decomposing leaves and the acrid smell of burning wood, bound by the scent of eucalyptus. Morning birdsong filled his ears as a choir of magpies, parrots, mynas and pigeons sang and whistled.

The Skippers led Jack and Sofia to an open area behind the storage shed. The source of the acrid smoke became evident – the remnants of a campfire, with a smouldering log as the centrepiece. Wooden camp chairs were strewn around and two makeshift tables had been created by setting old doors on forty-gallon steel drums.

The clearing was like a camping ground, with half-a-dozen tents and as many caravans around the perimeter, a large open fireplace in the centre. A lean-to, constructed from sheets of old corrugated iron and log poles, was positioned to one side, providing a rustic shelter for a timber bench that held what looked like the remains of breakfast. The two young woman washing dishes in a tin basin smiled. 'They're all out the back, Lena,' called one, her wave directing them down the hill.

Trailing behind the Skippers, Jack and Sofia looked around, intrigued by the piles of timber and rock, buckets, shovels and corrugated iron as well as buildings in various stages of completion. They stopped where a group of men and women, unfamiliar to Jack, was cheerfully working together. Two women were loading shovelfuls of dirt, water and straw into a metal mixer. With a 'That'll do it,' a young bare-chested man grasped a handle and turned it firmly, the spinning action blending the mixture into a thick slurry. Jack noticed a series of large wooden moulds laid out on the ground in neat rows, dried rectangles stacked beside them. 'Mud bricks,' he pointed out to Sofia, fascinated.

To the right, a second group of people was hard at work. 'Coo-eee!' called a loud voice, and glancing up in surprise, Jack realised that it was Matchum, now standing high above, looking over them with a cheeky expression. 'Careful,' Lena called to him, but she did not seem overly concerned at the sight of her youngest son balancing precariously on the roof beams. Matchum joined two men Jack recognised from the art classes – Joe and Henry – fixing rafters in place with heavy hammers that shook the framework every time they pounded the nails home.

Justus appeared at that moment and called for Matchum to come down immediately, but Matchum just smiled back, his hand to his left ear as though he could not hear. Relieving Henry of his hammer, he began pounding nails into the rafter with gusto, making so much noise that to continue calling up to him was pointless. Justus shook his head, turning sharply away with an impatient wave of his hand.

Lena laughed. 'They are always fighting. Two of a kind, each thinking that he is always right. Matchum is the only one here who dares to defy the Master. It's only because he is clever that he gets away with it,' she said, a hint of pride in her voice as she spoke of her feisty and capable young brother.

Justus turned his attention back to Jack. 'You look like you would be good at removing nails from floorboards.'

'Happy to help with anything, just show me the way.'

Justus laughed. "That's the spirit. Every little bit helps.' He led Jack and Sofia towards a pile of old timber boards that appeared to have been retrieved from a demolition site, already being worked upon by a sandy-haired man of similar age to Jack, to whom Justus introduced him, as well as to a hammer.

'Ian Robertson,' the young man said, wiping his hand and smiling as he extended his hand to Jack.

~

Justus then turned to Sofia. 'How about we get you to help Sonia and Helen in the garden? Would that be okay?'

Justus walked her to the place where Helen and Sonia were already at work, laying out shovels and rakes. They led Sofia through a maze of bushes to an area next to a dam that had recently been dug and was now half full of water. Walking over to the edge, Sonia expressed surprise at the rate it was filling, clearly pleased that water would be on hand for the vegetables about to be planted.

'We are going to be self-sufficient,' she explained, and when Sofia looked puzzled, she expanded. 'We'll grow all of our vegetables, have chickens to produce eggs and a cow for milk. The carrots and potatoes are in already. Today, we'll get the cauliflowers, beans, snow peas and spinach seedlings in. Next will be tomatoes. We'll grow everything we could ever want. There will be no need to buy anything at all.'

Helen added that Lena had already bought a Fowlers' Preserving Kit for the colony's kitchen, in readiness for the day when they would bottle fruit and make pickles and chutney from their garden's harvest.

Sofia was fascinated, and while saying nothing about her own experience maintaining the vegetable garden in Malaga, preserving olives and even tending to chickens at various times, she was very pleased to be assigned to work in the garden with the Skipper sisters.

At one o'clock, a bell rang, sounding the cue for everybody to down tools and head up the hill for lunch. Cane hampers and metal coolers magically appeared from the tents and the tables were quickly loaded with cold meats, pies, fruitcake, cheese, bread and buns, creating a feast that was shared amid much laughter and cheerful conversation.

Joe and Henry, the roof workers, called out for Jack and Sofia to come and join where they were seated, with two women, on logs forming a triangular seating area under the shade of the trees. Joe introduced Tess and Roxanne, who had spent the morning making mud bricks. He explained how he and Tess – his fiancée, it emerged – came up most Friday nights, set up their tent and stayed for the weekend, working on the colony's various building projects.

Chatting with the group, Jack noticed the frequent references to Justus as 'the Master', as well as the deference the students showed towards him. Jack was beginning to believe that not only was Justus a masterful teacher, with wide-ranging skills and a passion to share his knowledge, but perhaps even a genius. Certainly, Justus' mind looked to the extraordinary – to what others might deem impossible – and was able to make it happen.

He noticed how, in the same manner as Monsieur Simon, Justus moved from group to group, jovially inquiring about the progress of various projects, nodding with a serious expression as students posed questions, making suggestions and resolving problems they had encountered throughout the morning.

Eventually, the Master joined the group under the trees, sitting quietly at Jack's side and nodding as Joe described his job as a plumber through the week, an artist at night, explaining that his real interest was in alternative building materials, particularly mud brick. He and Tess hoped to build a place of their own, in the not-so-distant future, on the block of land they had recently bought, also in Eltham. The hours spent working on Justus' projects, provided them with the skills and knowledge they needed. Just like the buildings here, Joe's dream was to create a unique home, a work of art in itself and which would be half the cost of a traditional house. He planned to avoid years of being beholden to mortgage payments, determined to be financially free as soon as possible and so, able to devote more time to his art.

Justus asked Tess and Roxanne how the mud bricks were going and if they needed more bales of straw brought over. He then turned to Henry, tilting his head to listen as the student described a series of stone gargoyle figurines he was hoping to acquire. They were perfect for the Gothic style of the buildings, Henry thought, and Justus nodded his approval. 'They sound wonderful! Let me know if we need to use the van to cart them out here.'

'So, what do you think of our artists' colony?' Justus asked Jack and Sofia.

'It's amazing,' Jack said. 'I've never seen anything like it.'

'Come along, I will show you around.' Jack detected the pride in Justus' voice as his vision for the colony was being transformed into reality before their very eyes.

Minutes later, they stood before a large mound of earth, recently excavated from the side of the hill and the cement mixer where Jack and Sofia had watched Tess and Roxanne working earlier. *So, this is how a mud house is built*, Jack thought, as Justus explained in detail how not only mud bricks could be made, but how the mixture could be used to make a whole wall by pouring it directly into a cavity formed by timber panels placed about twelve inches apart.

'*Pisé de terre*,' Justus said. 'Also known as rammed earth. The technique, like mud brick, is centuries old. Used the world over. You probably saw some of these in Spain.'

Sofia nodded. 'Many of the older fincas have adobe structures in Malaga. They're wonderful old buildings. So cool in the summer heat.'

'Ah, that's right. Adobe in Spain. People here have no idea. We've got a few critics who are just dying to see our buildings wash away in the first big rain. They think it's all a great joke. We'll show them a thing or two.'

Next, Justus led them to 'Lil's House', the house that Lena had described to them, where Jack and Sofia saw the impressive finished effect of *pisé de terre* first-hand.

'It is amazing!' Jack said, now understanding why Lena had been so impressed with the building. It was truly beautiful, with enormous dormer windows opening over the valley, ornately carved timbers decorating the doorways and a steeply pitched roofline covered in slate. Jack recognised the European influence and was not at all surprised when Justus explained how the design was modelled on homes he had seen in Burgundy. When they walked through the front entrance, Sofia gasped with delight as she laid eyes on the terracotta floor, reminiscent of her home in Malaga, and Justus beamed with pleasure at her obvious appreciation.

A movement from within the room caught their attention; a lady seated in a wicker chair put a finger to her lips, gesturing at the narrow bench on which a sleeping child lay. Quietly, she set down the book she was reading and rose to greet them, her smile warm as she led them to the dining area. Jack wondered at the slight limp evident in her gait.

'This is my wife, Lil,' Justus said, his voice lowered in consideration of the sleeping child. 'My love and helpmate, and of course, the mother of little Max.'

'Sleeping like an angel now. He's been a terror all morning – into everything.' Lil's smile suggested that she was not overly troubled by the mischievous antics of the child.

'It was Lil who bought this piece of paradise,' Justus said. 'She has always supported my painting. Understood that, for me to produce my best work, I need to be free of petty worries and distractions.'

Jack watched Lil, who was gazing at Justus, her fondness for her husband evident in her contented smile. Justus continued, 'It is fair to say it has been Lil's work – first as an anaesthetist and now as a counsellor – that has allowed our dream for an artists' colony to take shape. Given me the liberty to create, without worrying about how to pay every damned bill. I don't know where I'd be without her!'

Jack consciously filed this information as a further example of the high moral standing of the group whose virtue had been challenged by his father. Surely the Meldrumites could not be so terribly fallen with their leader such a happily married man.

Being shown through the wonderful rooms with heavy beams, arches and interior stone walls, Jack felt as though he had stepped back in time, for the building seemed centuries old. Lil opened a door to reveal the 'armoire' they had brought back from France, cleverly designed to conceal the kitchen sink and shelves. Then, holding their conversation as they returned through the tiny sitting room where Max slept, they ascended an ornate iron staircase which, Justus explained, had been salvaged from the Bijou Theatre in Bourke Street.

Pleased with Jack's interest in the buildings, Justus returned to the theme of his oration the first night he and Sofia had visited the Latin Café: that to be a great painter, one must understand form – it didn't matter what the material was. It made sense to Jack that working with timber, clay and stone would develop an artist's eye for texture and the natural shapes of such materials.

∾

After completing their tour, Justus announced that it was time to get the brushes out. He put out a call for the students to gather around and demonstrated his methods for painting a westerly view of the landscape.

'The important thing about *plein air* painting is to be able to reduce the scene before you to its simplest form. You have to make decisions about what matters and what you are going to ignore.

'The dam, for instance.' Justus pointed across the slope. 'Pretty, yes, but the horizontal features do not offer enough variation to make for an interesting work.'

Of course, Jack thought. Verticals and diagonals were essential for any work of art. He remembered the day Monsieur Simon had walked them through the Louvre, asking them to sketch the shapes of the famous portraits. Circles, squares, triangles. That was all they were allowed to draw. No colour. No shade. Just shapes, which were then analysed for their pleasing composition.

Justus' voice broke through his thoughts. 'You either have to search for a better angle, or consider a new scene.' All eyes were on the Master as, with a few careful strokes on his canvas using a blue-grey mix, he produced an outline of distant hills with Lil's House set before them. 'See here the horizontals and the diagonals. Some trees in the foreground will add the vertical shapes we need – not all of them…just a few.

'See how the combination of verticals, horizontals and diagonals work together, their proportions to each other and the spaces they create. Are they pleasing? Could be a nude, could be a house, could be a pile of vegetables…could be nothing…an abstract. It's always the same. If the composition is wrong, no amount of colour and shade will make it right.'

Some of the students, those who had quickly set up portable easels when the call to paint was made, mimicked the technique. Others, like Jack and Sofia, stood in silence, watching as Justus, now the consummate teacher, truly the Master, held his audience spellbound while he imparted the process for blocking, emphasising the tonal approach that set Meldrumites apart from the traditional artists. As Sofia later told Jack, Justus made it all seem so simple and exciting that even the most inept person would be inspired to paint.

That night, snuggled in each other's arms, they discussed their day.

'I'm sorry, Sofia. I don't know how I could have allowed our lives to drift so far away from painting,' Jack murmured, his mind now clear. 'I just never knew anyone lived like that here in Australia! Devoting themselves to art, the way Justus and Lil do. I thought that artists in Australia just painted for a hobby. Or taught in schools. Unless they were famous, that is.'

'I guess it's just like Spain,' Sofia replied. 'Our father, he was determined to paint full time. And he did, eventually. Once we earned enough income from the gallery. With our homegrown vegetables and fruit, we did not need to buy so much.'

'Those buildings at Eltham! They are amazing! I think Mum and Dad would be a bit shocked at houses made of mud, though! A little rustic for their taste, I'd say.'

'They were wonderful, Jack. Truly extraordinary. I was thinking…' Sofia looked at him. 'As we were driving… There is a lot of land out there. Perhaps, instead of looking for a place to rent, here in the suburbs, we could look at some land… Maybe there is an old farmhouse we could lease?'

Jack considered Sofia's words. 'Perhaps, one day, we could buy a farm. Or at least a small country block of land. I could still travel to work from there. The train runs into the city every half hour or so.'

~

Long after Sofia's steady breathing indicated that she'd fallen asleep, Jack's mind remained active. He considered how, on returning to Australia, he had delegated the art world in which he'd been immersed for over four years, as an aberration. How, on coming back to his childhood home, he'd reverted to the Jack of his parents' expectations - a man who worked hard from nine-to-five to earn a wage. And in doing so, he'd lost all sight of life as an artist, the life that Sofia so well understood. Now, after just one day spent working alongside the Meldrumites, guided by the inspirational leadership of Justus, Jack realised that it was time for changes. No more could he allow painting to be confined to a weekly art lesson. And beyond painting, he felt a stirring of excitement for the Master's plans for the colony. Jack was glad that Sofia shared his enthusiasm for the life that Justus and Lil were creating.

'They have the life I always imagined that we would have, one day, Jack,' she'd told him. 'Like my childhood in Spain, where lessons and painting, buildings and gardens filled our days'.

CHAPTER 23

*O*ver the next few weeks, Jack and Sofia continued their Friday
night visits to the Café Latin and travelled out to Eltham with
the Skippers.

They thrived on the stimulation of those days spent outdoors –
relishing moments when an almost tangible buzz filled the air
following the collective effort of many hands to achieve monumental,
seemingly impossible tasks: to raise four enormous corner poles ready
for its roofing timbers, to fit a fragile casement window into a second-
storey room, or to lay the last slate tile onto a steeply pitched roof.
They basked in pleasure when Justus expressed his approval: admiring
Jack's makeshift ladder built from half-a-dozen tree branches, or
praising Sofia when she showed Helen and Sonya how to set up an irri-
gation system that would trickle water from the dam to their vegetable
garden bed.

It pleased Jack to know that Sofia enjoyed spending time with the
group as much as he did. Her bond with Helen deepened, and each
Wednesday evening she gave him an account of her visits to the city
– of the hours she spent at the Beckoning Bookshop helping to
arrange books or minding the shop, allowing Helen to slip out and

attend to any needs beyond the store. Above all, she relished her conversations with the younger woman – her first real friend in Australia.

'She has had such an interesting life, Jack,' Sofia told him. 'Her parents have travelled the world and lived in the most interesting of places. Always drawn to the arts...although Helen did not sound so very impressed by that. She says that all they used to do was drink excessively and gadabout to parties and theatres. Their house was open to anyone – mostly painters and writers – talking a lot of drunken nonsense about how good they were, trying to outdo each other with their intelligence and wit.'

'They don't seem like that at all,' Jack replied, although he had to admit it was easy to imagine Lena as the centre of attention, filling her home with artistic types. She certainly seemed to revere Justus.

'Helen says it was Justus who set Lena and Mervyn straight. Gave her family some direction. Now the Skipper family has a purpose. Their life is not just about self-indulgence. S can't wait until they all move out to Eltham.'

There was a second reason for Jack's satisfaction in seeing Sofia deepen her friendship with Helen. Over recent months, news of Spain had started appearing in the morning newspapers, first bought to their attention by William.

'What are all of these strikes and nonsense going on in Spain?' he'd asked. 'It all seems terribly violent. Even priests have been killed!'

Sofia had been horrified and had spoken of the events for days, worrying about her friends and relatives who still lived in Malaga. Hoping that they were okay. Hoping that Father Sebastian was safe.

She began searching for news, reading descriptions of Spain's growing tensions. When Jack came home from work she'd show him the articles, desperate to clarify their content, for while Sofia could

sound out many English words, many remained difficult and others had
no meaning at all.

During his three years in Spain, Jack had been somewhat aware of
the increasing tensions Andrés had flagged, and certainly, they'd experienced hardship during their last months before coming to Australia.
However, it was only now, on the other side of the world, as he read
articles in Australian newspapers, that Spain's complexities became
clear to him.

The lives of the working classes had become impossibly unstable
and the Spanish leadership was in turmoil. The Republican government
that the people had swept into power, believing they were the answer
to modernising Spain, had made gains, certainly. Now in Spain, education was free, people had the right to divorce and women were entitled
to vote in elections. However, Spain's economy was again faltering,
and as unemployment rose and poverty increased, its workers were
turning their backs on the very Republicans they'd so strongly
supported. Furthermore, although the workers had once agreed the
Church was too powerful, that its dominance needed to be limited,
those very same people now believed that the Republicans had gone
too far. Spiritual loyalties resurged across Spain, as workers became
deeply offended by the Republican Party's treatment of the church that
they loved; angered when their beloved nuns and priests were banned
from teaching in the schools and when church buildings – centrepieces
of village life – were confiscated.

Each group advocated their solutions but reaching a consensus was
proving impossible. Newspaper articles describing Spain's high unemployment, violence on the streets and the burning of churches were
upsetting, but even more worrying was the repeated suggestion that a
civil war loomed.

'War, Jack! This is terrible. What will happen to Aunt Jovita and
Stefan? To all my friends. I can't stop thinking about everyone.'
Together, he and Sofia deciphered the articles - Jack providing insight
into the journalist's meaning, Sofia describing the context of who, what
and where. They searched for any references to the Costa del Sol and

Malaga, and Jack could only imagine how distressing it must be for Sofia to hear that her country was in such turmoil.

'Andrés was right, Jack,' she repeatedly said. 'I shouldn't have argued with him. We are better off here in Australia. Spain is not a good place for us to be. Andrés knew this was coming and he wanted to look after me.'

These days, while no less concerned about events in Spain, Jack and Sofia found distraction from the woes of the world as their days became increasingly immersed in Justus' plans for the colony, which stimulated conversations that had no end. At night, heads on pillows and arms entwined, they fell asleep mid-sentence, and in the mornings, on awakening, would continue where they'd left off.

CHAPTER 24

*O*ut of the blue, a letter arrived at South Yarra. The envelope thick with its wad of folded pages, the contents a muddle of paragraphs that were pure Margaret, her voice distinctive in the large, sprawling handwriting that outlined her various travels. From London to Paris, she described how she'd attended art classes for almost six months. She'd signed up at the Académie de la Grande Chaumière where, she stressed with a slash to underline the words, s*imply anybody could enrol, for a few francs a week. No talent required.* Margaret made no attempt at false modesty: from here on she was now going to boast to anybody that would listen that she, too, had studied with the Parisian Masters.

Eventually, she wrote, *'the wolves beat at the door'*. She described how financial pressure had forced her to return to London, where she was now living next-door to Freddie, in Gordon Square, house-sitting for his neighbour and regularly meeting with the windbags and egotists at the Café Royal, all intellectualising about some rubbish or other. She stated that she was now as insufferably skilful at bragging with the best of them. Jack laughed as he read, imagining Margaret at the tables of the café, jousting with the artists and disdaining the foolish socialites that clung on to the periphery of the art world. Ever honest, Margaret's letter took a turn to the serious, explaining that despite all her learning, she now found herself cornered into the role of pet-painter, something at which she had proved to be surprisingly good.

'I have to accept that I don't have a single skerrick of your talent, Jack. In fact, I find it ridiculously unfair that you have more skill in your little finger than I will ever have in all ten of mine!!! But I guess I should be thankful that there is an endless market for people to have their wretched animals immortalised on canvas and I am quite the go-to person at present! A quick worker, not too expensive... The offers keep rolling in. I try to increase my prices to put them off, but amazingly, the old cat-mad biddies always find a friend who is willing to pay to have their precious Snowy, Isabella or Dorothy's portrait painted.'

Margaret explained how, finding herself in Surrey a couple of times, she'd dropped in on Aunt Elizabeth and Uncle Robert and whiled away the afternoons eating his aunt's boiled fruitcake, drinking endless cups of tea, and of course, playing a couple of hands of whist for old times' sake. All the while, talking every angle possible about 'their boy Jack and his sweet Spanish girl.' How she'd sat with them listening as they'd marvelled at his extraordinary talent and reminisced about the time he'd spent with them in London, astonished at the opportunities he'd had in Paris and Spain – who would have thought he'd have fallen in love! – hoping he was well, and how glad they were for Marian, who was so fond of Sofia. How lucky she was to have such a sweet daughter-in-law.

'I now feel like an official member of your family, Jack. I know all of your news – they even read your mother's letters to me ... you would be amazed at the things they talk about... when's a baby coming?... worries about your weekends - now spent, building houses out of mud under the spell of a crazy artist. I told them that I knew Justus, too. Did you know that I had lessons alongside him back in Melbourne, a hundred years ago? I think that I reassured them that he was okay...

just a bit eccentric. In honesty, I think that the man's a nutter, but I spared them that bit of information.

'Don't be surprised if you see me standing on your doorstep, suit-case in hand, looking for a bed one day,' she'd written in the concluding lines of her letter. 'The truth is, for all of the excitement of Paris and London, I miss the easy pace of life in Australia. The beaches and sunshine. It's winter here now and unbelievably cold! As I slosh through the puddles in darkness, morning and afternoon, my hands so frozen and numb I swear my fingers will snap off and I won't even notice, I ask myself - what on earth I am doing here?'

And then, in true bossy Margaret style, she had finished with the line, 'And I now also ask myself, what on earth is Jack Tomlinson, artist extraordinaire, doing taking Sofia to wallow in the mud with that lecherous egotist, Jorgensen, and his latest nonsense? I might have to come back just to sort you out!

Lecherous? Jack wondered at Margaret's word choice. He'd heard of Justus being described as many things, but never lecherous.

CHAPTER 25

*a*t the Queen Street classroom in mid-October, Jack set up beside Matchum, knowing that if he set up anywhere else, the young lad would inevitably move to join him and maintain a constant flow of chatter while they painted together.

The lessons were enjoyable and Jack had adapted his style to include the tonal aspects that Justus promoted. He felt pleased with his current work – a village-scape, really, its main subject Eltham station in the early hours of the morning, enveloped in a fine mist.

'Hey, Jack. I was thinking…Do you reckon that we could farm kangaroos at Eltham? You know, build a big fence along the edge and run them in… We could grow grass there, that'd bring them… Then we could skin them and make coats or something.'

'What was Spain like? Did you go running with the bulls? I'm going to do that one day – maybe even go to a bullfight – maybe even be a bullfighter! I'd be fast – they'd never catch me.'

'Give it up, Match.' Justus' voice sailed across the room repeatedly. 'Let Jack have room to think without your endless yakking driving him crazy, for heaven's sake.'

Justus may as well have been talking to the wind for all the notice Matchum took of him, but Jack didn't mind. The constant flow of outlandish ideas from the young boy, who in many ways was so much older than his years, was refreshing after his long, dreary day at the office, totalling numbers and filling ledgers that he was convinced served no real purpose for anyone.

The lesson ended at 8:30, and tonight, as Jack wiped his brushes in turpentine after setting his painting on the large rack at the back of the room to dry, Justus invited him upstairs to his private studio for a chat.

Opening a bottle of wine, he offered Jack a glass before launching into his favourite topic: the Eltham building site, of course. 'It was never meant to be called "The artists' colony." We just fell into calling it that, for lack of a title. I'm thinking about naming the site Montsalvat. How does that sound?'

Jack didn't know what he thought, but agreed. 'It certainly makes me think of Paris. Of Montparnasse and Montmartre. That's where the artists seemed to gather in Paris.'

Justus nodded. 'It was suggested to me, only a week ago. You are quite right – it does have French associations. But there's even more. Montsalvat was the home of the Holy Grail in the legend of King Arthur, and also in one of Wagner's operas – *Parsifal* and also in *Lohengrin*. It means "Mount of Salvation."'

It was a good name for the colony, especially given that it was set on a slight rise just out of Eltham. Not exactly a mountain, but it was a hill of sorts. Jack felt flattered to be asked his thoughts, although he recognised that he was only a sounding board, for, by the easy way Justus used the new title, the Master had already made his decision.

He listened as Justus continued his musings. 'That is what we want the colony to be: a place of salvation from the bonds of materialism, mediocrity and oppression; things that stifle creative expression. A place where the artists of Melbourne can escape. Where ideas can be discussed freely, philosophies expanded upon. Those conservatives that run the show – the Who's Who of the Victorian Art Society and the National Gallery – they ridicule anything unless it's their idea. Insist on teaching the same old methods year in, year out. Young artists need a place to go to escape their small-minded views.'

Again, Jack nodded, although he had no experience on which to base an opinion. Margaret had expressed similar views about Melbourne conservatives; indeed, about male artists in general, when he'd first met her. Jack reflected on his visits to Sussex. In a way, Margaret's relatives, the Bloomsbury artists, lived a little like Justus' dream. In their home, Charleston, the walls and furniture – near every surface – were adorned with paintings. Vanessa and Duncan, the visitors to the house – Clive Bell, Roger Fry, Virginia Woolf – little Angelica, they all lived and breathed art. It was like nothing else really mattered to them. Art was important...paintings were important. Not just nice to look at, but important! A concept that Jack had to admit he still did not fully grasp. Nonetheless, he liked the idea of wonderful paintings that stood for centuries, fascinating people across the world, and the thought of devoting hours – weeks on end, even – to create such works certainly had its appeal.

'...and, for some, Montsalvat will be home.' Jack felt Justus' eyes upon him as the words he'd spoken sunk in.

'Perhaps, Jack, you and Sofia might be right for Montsalvat. I don't want every joker thinking that they will live there – only people who are serious about their painting. The Skippers, of course, are planning to move out of Melbourne to live at the colony - Montsalvat - as soon as possible and there are others who have expressed their interest.'

He cited an impressive list of notable characters who shared his dream: Sue Vanderkelen, the daughter of the Belgian consul, was currently working with Justus on the design of a tower, a project that excited him very much. Betty Roland, the celebrated playwright – recordings of her plays could be heard on the ABC. They each planned on building accommodation on the site, guided by Justus' architectural knowledge, in line with the medieval, Gothic style that would make Montsalvat unique. Some planned to live there permanently; others hoped to create a weekend escape from the madness of the city.

Justus went on to explain the financial structure of Montsalvat:

how presently, fees paid by students for art lessons, as well as donations from wealthy patrons such as Sue Vanderkelen, contributed to the building fund. People like the Skippers helped out with bills. And of course, there was the money Lil earned.

'I would be happy to design a house for you, Jack. You and Sofia could decide what you would need – a studio and a couple of bedrooms, a living area and kitchenette. Together, we would make a wonderful building. Alternatively, you might want to set up a caravan for weekends, move into the Student Quarters when they are finished.'

'We'll certainly think about it,' Jack responded. 'I'll talk with Sofia.' He was again reminded of the Bloomsburys – Margaret included – and their spontaneous approach to life, where important decisions were based on opportunities rather than convention.

'Of course, this is all in the future,' Justus explained. 'But food for thought, don't you think? I can see already how well you and Sofia would fit in. You understand the lifestyle.'

Despite the late hour of his return home, Sofia had waited up, as always, keen to hear about Jack's painting lesson. He quickly gave brief updates of the usual: who was in attendance, what they had done, the progress of his painting. Then, with excitement, Jack told her about the conversation he'd had with Justus at the end of the lesson.

It took an hour, for following the initial telling, Sofia wanted more detail on every phase of Justus' invitation. 'A caravan? Perhaps we could take one out soon. Possibly live in the Student Quarters…' Or to build a place of their own, that Justus would help them design! When were the Skippers going to move out there? Sofia thought soon. The possibilities seemed endless and they talked late into the night.

'I knew he would think you were good, Jack,' Sofia said just before she finally rolled over, past midnight. 'It all sounds just too wonderful…'

Jack agreed. How marvellous it would be - to join the artists! Creating amazing buildings, developing his painting, and best of all, living with people who were passionate about art.

CHAPTER 26

*a*s the sweetness of spring gave way to hot, dry summer, Jack and Sofia continued to meet with the Meldrumites each Friday evening. The routine was simple – Sofia caught the train from South Yarra to Flinders Street Station, where Jack met her under the clocks. Despite the Friday night crowds at the station's busy entrance, he and Sofia now had 'their place' on the lower step to the right and finding each other was never a problem. If they were early, they would first join the artists at the Mitre Tavern, an ancient cottage on Banks Street where the day students congregated after their painting lessons most afternoons, sharing a glass of sherry before crossing to the Café Latin for dinner. Jack had loved the tiny tavern instantly, feeling decades…a century, even…of history clinging to its wonderful stone walls. If only they could talk, there would surely be some amazing stories to be told of the events that had taken place in this dining room.

'Ah, Jack,' Justus had said, spotting him gazing at the arched windows and old oak bar on the first occasion they'd met at the Mitre. 'You are just like me. Fascinated by old buildings. Priceless, aren't they? I suppose it will only be a matter of time before some developer with modern ideas gets his claws into this place.'

'Surely not!' Jack said. 'It is amazing!'

'Haunted, they say.'

Sofia looked startled. 'No!'

'Oh, well, beautiful historical sites often have dark sides too, you know. Thwarted passion, in this case, I presume. It is said that a woman died upstairs - hanged herself. Connie, lover of the esteemed Sir Rupert Clarke. Used to live just across the road from here. Keep your eyes open for a lady wandering the stairs…'

Jack had shivered as Justus laughed. He did not take to stories of death, and even less, to those of suicide. They always reminded him of his conversation with Picasso. Of Picasso's friend, Carlos, who had taken his own life. Of the Blue Period that Picasso had spoken of, and of his unnerving words to Jack. 'One day you will experience grief and then you will understand how to paint the truth.' There was far too much tragedy in the art world, Jack thought. Even Sofia had lost her mother, father and brother. He was very sure that he did not need tragedies to make him become a great artist.

On alternative weekends, Jack and Sofia fell into a habit of travelling out to Eltham; mostly by train, occasionally with the Skippers. There, beyond the brickmaking and gardening, he and Sofia also turned their hands to stone and metalwork, even repairing a leadlight window, each excited to be actively participating and seeing Justus' dream materializing before their eyes.

Jack looked forward to those Saturdays when he was freed from the strictures of work and his parents' home, where painting was deemed pointless for a married man. Glad to escape his parents' expectations for his life. They did not say much these days beyond, 'Oh, so you are going out to Eltham again?' their tone tinged with shades of criticism.

'Of course, we are, Mum. It's what we do. We enjoy it!' It irritated Jack that his parents continued to question the fortnightly routine – it had been in place for months now.

He knew that Sofia also looked forward to those weekends away from the house, discussing what she might cook, enjoying shopping and filling her large canvas bag with rice, fresh vegetables, ham, cheese and herbs. On arrival, she would quickly combine the ingredients and set an enormous pot simmering on the newly acquired Aga stove before heading out to work in the garden. Jack was thrilled to see her so deeply gratified when the amicable crowd enjoyed her meals, ever keen to experience new flavours, singing praises for her cooking and asking her to share her recipes for tapas, bean stews, gazpacho and paellas.

It was obvious to Jack that Sofia had finally found a level of happiness that had evaded her over the last twelve months and he was thankful. Without question, he knew she loved him, but the loss of Andrés, their move across the world from the finca, adaption to Australian life and growing worries about Spain's political environment had quelled the sunny, optimistic demeanour of the girl he'd first met in Paris. It pleased him to see Sofia's Spanish accent, occasionally a source of unwelcome attention in Melbourne's stores, accepted at Montsalvat, or when the art students enquired about Spain, interested in the country of her heritage. Some even expressed their sorrow for the turmoil that was being reported about Spain in the news. Furthermore, Sofia seemed to relish her work alongside Helen and Sonia in the garden, happily weeding and carting water despite the hot days, gaining confidence to share her experience with growing things. She'd found that the Australian summer climate was not dissimilar to Malaga and enjoyed the satisfaction of knowing that her work with Helen and Sonia made a valuable contribution to Montsalvat, particularly after they had enlisted Matchum and Mervyn's assistance to build a chook yard - its feathered harem now producing eggs for them as well as a surplus which was sold to the students each week, contributing much-needed cash to the building fund.

~

While Jack thrived on the closeness he and Sofia shared, absorbed in their present and with their goals for their future gaining clarity, he never stopped dreaming of the day when she would share the news he longed to hear; that a baby – their baby - was finally on its way. They had been married for over four years now, and still, there was no sign of pregnancy. He told himself that perhaps the delay was not such a terrible thing – they had been through a lot with the loss of Andrés, the trip to Australia and then settling in with his parents. He also knew that now, with their weekends spent at Montsalvat, they would find it difficult to maintain their busy schedules, had Sofia been nursing an infant. Jack reassured himself that their time would come. Sofia was only twenty-five, he twenty-three, and as she'd told him several times, women in her family did not fall pregnant quickly, but it would eventually happen.

~

One by one, Jack and Sofia analysed the various students and patrons of the artists' colony they now inhabited. Clarice, intrigued them both, and each week, after Jack's art lesson, Sofia always asked if she'd shown up, but Clarice only attended lessons occasionally. Twice more, she'd joined them at the Latin Café for dinner, and they had enjoyed chatting with her, yet both he and Sofia agreed that there was a certain sadness about her. Was there a lover? A tragic loss of someone dear to her? Helen had told Sofia that Clarice once had a thing with Colin Colahan, news that amazed Jack. Without doubt, the Irishman – who occasionally turned up at the building site with one lady or another giggling on his arm and a bottle of wine in his hand – was full of charm, but he seemed entirely unsuited to the quiet lady so dedicated to her painting.

It annoyed Jack that the men in his class showed such little regard for the paintings that Clarice brought in to show Justus, seeking his opinion. She certainly produced some exceptional works – misty, atmospherical paintings portraying the most unusual subjects, like street-lamps, roads and trams, items that had little appeal to most artists, but Clarice had a way of using them to create intrigue. He thought that her seascapes were quite lovely. The other men did not share his admiration. It was exactly as Clarice had told him and Sofia at the Latin, they thought she was crazy because she rose before the sun, dragging her wooden trolley down onto the beach at Beaumaris, where she painted *plein air*. Perhaps what drew Jack to Clarice was that she reminded him so much of Margaret, being of a similar age, and also, because she seemed to be a victim to the worst of the male-dominated art-world that Margaret had been so outspoken about. Jack admired her brave commitment to her painting despite the obstacles she faced.

Sofia enjoyed the company of Sue, who regularly made the trip out to Montsalvat on Friday afternoons to escape the madness of city life. On arriving at Montsalvat, Sue enjoyed nothing better than to slip out of her fancy shoes, tie a scarf around her hair, pull on an apron and pad around the kitchen barefooted while cooking up a storm for the weekend guests. She'd cheerfully welcomed Sofia's offers to string beans, carve pumpkin and turn the potatoes while she prepared enormous stews and pasta dishes in the open fireplace. The two women's shared love of cooking was a recipe for instant friendship. Sue insisted that Sofia teach her how to make *gazpacho* and *salmorejo,* cold summer soups that were perfect, not to mention cheap, for feeding the ever-growing crowds– sometimes there were as many as thirty dinner guests at the dining room table on weekends! In turn, Sue taught Sofia to make some Australian favourites: Anzac biscuits, lamingtons, and on Justus' birthday, an enormous pavlova laden with cream and strawberries fresh from the garden.

'She's just so happy to be here,' Sofia said. 'So friendly and down to earth!'

'Why wouldn't she be?' Jack laughed, although it rankled him that Sofia was always so appreciative when Australians were 'nice' to her.

'Well, she comes from a very rich family. An important family with all sorts of connections.'

'I suppose, love, that even rich people get a bit fed up with all the nonsense they are expected to put up with. Dressing up to the nines and having to do all of that bowing and curtseying to dignitaries – Sue is probably glad to get away from it all!'

Jack and Sofia both found the Skippers endlessly intriguing, for they'd never met a family who had such blatant disregard for the restraints of society. Lena seemed to lack all maternal instincts, raising her children on a steady diet of loose supervision and scathing condemnation. Any conversation at the dinner table was always infused with her opinions and she was quick to criticise Sonia and Helen for the way their hair looked or the plans they made to go into the city or meet with friends, yet she did not seem to offer them guidance. Jack was conscious of the way she berated Matchum for his outlandish behaviour, but then she would laugh as she related his latest exploit.

Lena's position at Montsalvat was almost that of a private secretary to Justus, her dedication evident in the way that she hung onto every word he uttered, defended his opinions and enthused about his plans. As a wife, her relationship with Mervyn appeared complex. She constantly fussed over his health, for the poor man suffered an endless barrage of headaches and stomach upsets – ailments to which she tended with utter devotion. However, when it came to things that mattered, it was to Justus that Lena turned for advice, consulting with him on all manner of personal things beyond painting, a practice that she seemed to think was a good model for others to follow, as well as acknowledgement of his wisdom and a sign of respect for his authority.

Mervyn was the gentlest-natured of the Skippers, and while full of fun when he worked with Sonia, Helen and Sofia in the garden, said little in the presence of his dominating wife. Sofia told Jack how, when they'd built their chook pen, Mervyn had proved surprisingly competent, ensuring it was fox-proof and that the nesting boxes for the eggs were cosy. 'Really, Jack, you would never have thought it, but I wonder if it isn't from Mervyn that Matchum gets all of his clever ways?' she said. They agreed that, in the presence of Justus, Mervyn was quite overshadowed, but on his own, he was actually a very capable man.

Both Jack and Sofia admired the Skipper girls' open and assertive personalities. Helen had recently turned nineteen and Sonia was seventeen. Jack was not surprised when he heard that they had been taking care of themselves since they were quite young.

'Every couple of weeks, Mum gives us each a pound.' Helen told them. '"You know what you need," she tells us. "You are old enough to choose your clothing. No good, me buying you things that you wouldn't like."'

For years, they'd been free to go where they liked, and without any curfew, they'd often stayed out until all hours of the night. Both Sonya and Helen had developed clear-sighted views about life that they expressed regularly. Their strong opinions, which they coupled with their mother's outspoken scorn, were as humorous as they were shocking – touching on subjects most adults were loath to discuss, including the wandering hands of married men, sex and contraception. They had plenty to say about the Master, both in praise, fully supporting his non-conformist view of society, yet also in annoyance at Justus for his overbearing opinions – encouraging Lena to sell their wonderful Norman Lindsay's – and the way he mocked their father at the dinner table. They had good minds and showed insight into all sorts of things – artistic pursuits, of course, having been surrounded by them from when they were young children, but additionally, the works of philosophers such as Jung and Adler. Sonia had recently applied to Melbourne's Institute of Technology to undertake an upholstery course and had been furious that they'd denied her application – all because she was female. Perhaps because Jack and Sofia were closer to them in age than most of the adults in their world, the two sisters seemed to enjoy coming to their van for a cup of tea and a chat, confiding in Sofia and treating Jack as a big brother. He loved to tease them and they, him.

The antics of the wayward Matchum provided endless amusement for everyone and both Sofia and Jack enjoyed his visits to their van. He invariably gravitated to wherever Jack was working and loved to sound out his latest ideas, encouraging Jack to share in their creation.

'Let's make a watercourse, Jack. We can use stone to build channels. How about we build a windmill from all that scrap metal that's lying by the driveway?' Matchum enjoyed making Sofia laugh with his displays of exaggerated charm, knowing that she was always good for an almond biscuit or one of her delicious churros to appease his boundless hunger.

Perhaps the richest source of conversation was Justus himself. He had ideas on simply everything which he loved to share. From expounding his theories on tonalism, to directing students in the building projects, to providing them with personal advice his wealth of knowledge was boundless. One tactic he enjoyed was to impart information via 'Dialogues' – sharing his complex insights on all manner of topics, the content of which was recorded faithfully in Mervyn Skipper's notepad in readiness for typing, later that evening. Dialogues became a regular Sunday night event, sometimes delivered impromptu, from Justus; at other times, read aloud from the notes that Mervyn had faithfully recorded. Jack found his views about the world he knew were constantly being revised as he listened to Justus' discussions on topics including society, politics, sustainability, materialism and psychoanalysis. The Master loved a good debate, and equally frequent were his passionate tirades about art, architecture and design – views that were impressed on the students with a charismatically delivered conviction that was impossible to refute. While often overbearing to the point of offensive, Justus managed to balance a cutting sarcasm that could leave a table of guests in subdued silence with a captivating charm that had his audience spellbound. Despite the lash of his tongue, Jack never stopped listening or learning from the great man, whose vision for Montsalvat had no bounds.

As well as conversations about the Montsalvat artists' colony, Jack and Sofia discussed the many things they were learning about: the good sense in companion planting of tomatoes and basil, chives and lettuce, couplings that helped to eliminate the multitude of pests that nibbled away and spoiled vegetables; the pros and cons of breeding turkeys; and the benefits of recycling construction materials, which, while fiddly, allowed one to make unique and beautiful buildings while saving so much money.

And together they made plans, united in a determination that art must be central to their future. Sofia confided in Jack her hope that she might resurrect her curating skills. Perhaps Justus would let her set up an art gallery at Montsalvat! Should they buy the caravan Jack's work-mate, Peter, wanted to get rid of? It was old, but very well built with a neat little kitchen stove and it seemed weatherproof. Peter was even happy to tow it to the site for them if they would like it. Then they could travel out on Saturday mornings and stay until late Sunday.

Jack asked Justus whether it would be okay at his Thursday art class.

'Of course, Jack. I have been hoping that you and Sofia would decide to set something up out there. We will find a nice place on the ridge... I know just the spot for you.'

When Jack had asked about the weekly contribution, Justus

referred him to Lena. 'She'll work something out. Lena takes care of all that. Pays the rates and works out how to apportion the costs for everything fairly. Don't forget, we could plan a more permanent building for you and Sofia. Build you a nice little studio and living area. Just say the word. The students would help – they enjoy the work - and it gives them experience for when they're ready to build their own homes one day. What goes around, comes around.'

'We have been talking about it,' Jack admitted. 'We both love the idea of living out at Montsalvat one day.'

'Perfect. Just let me know. We have got quite a pile of materials accumulating now. Windows and doors from Whelan and I have got onto some beautiful mudstone in Eltham. We could build you a place in no time!'

CHAPTER 27

*J*ack and Sofia loved their weekends at Eltham. Excitement escalated amid the artists as each task was completed and simultaneously, whenever an idea for something new and innovative presented itself. The latest project was the most ambitious yet: a building that would be the jewel in Montsalvat's crown – The Great Hall. It was an ambitious project, a mediaeval manor that was to be created from mudstone and rock. It would have huge slabs of slate on the floor and fabulous exposed beams, that had been sourced from the dismantling of some of Victoria's oldest bridges. Justus insisted that their rusted iron fittings - the bolts and screws that had once held the bridges together - must remain intact, heightening the ancient effect that he desired. He planned an enormous open fireplace, large enough to take full logs or perhaps even a pig that could be turned on an iron spit and served up at a banquet. The entrance doors were to be studded and imposing, and huge leadlight windows would run from floor to ceiling. Justus told them about the staircase he'd found, as well as a set of matching casement windows, now carefully stored in the main shed. Weekly, Whelan the Wrecker arrived at

Montsalvat, updating them all on the array of items his keen eye had spotted, some in buildings that were yet to be dismantled. Ideas for the proposed furnishings were analysed, the topic dominating dinner conversation for weeks – exquisitely carved chairs, each one a work of art in itself; an enormous table that would seat twenty people. No idea was too outrageous. The design had been fully drawn out and lay on the dining room bench for all to see. Already, a team of young men had made a start on its stony foundations.

Increasingly, Jack and Sofia were finding life at Copelen Street difficult. Firstly, the daily routines and conversation of the Tomlinson household were extraordinarily dull compared to the stimulating debates and creative world of Montsalvat.

Worse, though, was the burden of mounting criticism directed towards 'his new friends' and 'the Master' that Jack found increasingly difficult to deflect. His parents were convinced that Jack and Sofia had an unhealthy obsession with Justus Jorgensen and his vision.

'Who is this man?' William grumbled. 'Anyone would think he walked on water, the way you go on about him all of the time.'

Jack repeatedly described Justus' goal – his desire to create a place where artists could be inspired, his architectural genius. He described how clever Justus was, how his views were exciting and progressive, how even some of Melbourne's elite were fascinated by Montsalvat. Notwithstanding, Jack deliberately omitted the Master's more controversial views – dinner conversations in which words like 'nudity', 'sexual intercourse' and 'homosexuality' were bandied across the broad table without a blink. For all his praise for Justus, his parents remained unconvinced and William began to assert heated counter-theories undermining Justus and all that he stood for.

The extent of William's opposition to the Meldrumites was revealed when, following some investigation of his own, he renewed his attack on their morality. It was a Monday evening and the dinner plates had just been cleared. Surreptitiously, William asked Jack if he knew of a Colin Colahan, to which of course Jack said yes, he had visited Montsalvat several times. He was a very nice man.

'Well!' William slammed a copy of a newspaper article on the table with the triumph of one revealing a winning hand in a game of poker. 'Read this. I think you need to learn a little more about this charlatan you are so besotted with.'

Jack glanced at the article, which was dated over five years earlier – a summary of the court proceedings from the case of Molly Dean's murder. Horrific details of the event were described. How Mary 'Molly' Dean, a Meldrumite, was found battered and naked. Strangulation. Frenzied stabbing. The work of a lunatic. One of the suspects: no less than Colin Colahan. Damning statements cited Colahan's morality or lack thereof, his multiple lovers and illegitimate children, and of course, the sordid details of the night Molly died – the young model's body found behind garbage bins in Elwood in the early hours of the morning. The article declared Molly Dean had attended the theatre with Colahan the night of the murder, a fact that Colahan had never denied. While Colahan had been exonerated by his rock-solid alibi, a damning question mark hung over his name, and by association, the Meldrumites had been forever tarnished in the eyes of some and the event was an easy weapon in the arsenal of the conservative art world who rejected all forms of modernity. The newspaper article included specific references to Justus Jorgensen and his students by the reporter, its emotive language suggesting that he'd been whipped into a state of thrilling frenzy over the unsolved murder.

Jack and Sofia agreed with William and Marian, that, of course, it was a terrible thing. But they were quite sure that Colin was no murderer!

Whilst an uneasy truce on the topic of Justus was reached, Jack recognised that his parents would only ever view the Master as a charlatan – they were blinded to his creative genius. He and Sofia stopped talking about Montsalvat at the dinner table, preferring to confine their enthusiasm for their weekends, as well as their future, to their bedroom chats. In the mornings, Marian would comment, 'You two must have a lot to discuss – I swear you were talking all night,' no doubt sensing that plans were under construction and anxious to know the details.

CHAPTER 28

The final straw came on a Saturday afternoon in early January. Jack and Sofia had been reclining under the ghost gums of Montsalvat, thankful for the cool breeze sweeping across the building site, after a long yet satisfying morning spent raising the last of the roof joists on Justus' studio. Always a milestone in the construction of any building, the roof-raising was a symbolic event that implied it was all but complete, even though weeks of work remained to finish external cladding, interior fittings, the installation of windows and doors. The sense of camaraderie among the group was strong, as male and female, young and old, revelled in their shared achievement, glad that it had proceeded relatively smoothly. Unfortunately, the pleasant mood took an unexpected turn when a nasty outburst between Justus and Mervyn erupted.

'For heaven's sake, Mervyn. What is it now? Another one of your "headaches"?' Justus' voice carried across the gathering of workers eating their lunch, his tone dripping with unconcealed disdain. Mervyn, who had been notably absent throughout the morning, had arrived in a dishevelled state and approached Lena, who abandoned the leg of lamb she had been carving into fine slices to go searching for his Luminol tablets, for he could not find them anywhere and he felt that his head was going to split apart.

Sneering at Mervyn, Justus' attack continued. 'These headaches are a lot of hogwash. You just do this to get Lena's attention!'

Justus' aversion to illness, and his belief that it was psychosomatic, were legendary. Even Lil, who suffered from a mysterious malady that left her with an assortment of strange symptoms – temporary blindness, agonising pain or complete numbness, sometimes even an inability to walk – received little sympathy and even less practical support from her husband. Lil did not complain about this, for she too shared the belief that illness was a body's way of trying to gain attention or manipulate a situation to its advantage.

Today, Justus added insult to injury by assaulting Mervyn's professional life – ridiculing his weekly column in *The Bulletin* and accusing him of being bourgeoisie, an insult of enormous magnitude to the Meldrumites. Usually, Mervyn walked off quietly when Justus was on the attack, but evidently, he had decided that he was having none of the Master's tormenting today, and everyone was astonished when, red-faced and spluttering, he fired back.

'Don't you talk, you narcissistic hypocrite! You are always happy to bend the rules whenever it suits you without regard for anyone else's feelings. Perhaps it's time for you to start focusing on your own family and stop interfering with the lives of others!'

Gobsmacked, everyone watched as the show continued. Mervyn was not finished.

'And what is this about your telling Sonia she can't go and see Gracie Fields? Since when were you her father? I gave her the tickets and it's up to her how she wants to use them – so you can mind your own bloody business!'

With that, Mervyn turned on his heel and departed, and the group was plunged into an awkward silence.

A silence that was interrupted by the jolly toot-tooting of a car's horn and a cheery call floating down from the carpark.

Looking up with a sinking feeling, Jack observed his father –

somewhat dressed down from his usual weekend attire, although unable to relinquish his mandatory tie – carefully stepping across red, sun-baked earth where loose gravel could be deadly. His hand supported Marian, who was a sight to be believed in her straw garden hat and with a red scarf loosely draped over a bright, flowing floral dress that Jack had never seen before, no doubt trying to appear 'arty'. Together they approached the group, which still reeled from Mervyn's outburst. Marian's laughter tinkled, unsuccessfully hiding a hint of nervousness, as she sought Jack and Sofia, now sitting to attention under the trees. William explained how they'd come for a drive to see first-hand the lure of the endless working bees in Eltham which commanded so much of their son's time. While he attempted to sound relaxed and charming, to Jack his father's words sounded embarrassingly like veiled criticism.

Wondering how much of the fracas between Mervyn and Justus his parents had heard, he wrestled with a dozen competing reactions, from feigning a friendly greeting and showing them around the colony to being furious at their invasion into this space.

Of course, he opted for the former, walking towards them, smiling broadly, as though their unexpected arrival was a perfectly natural thing. Justus joined him and Jack was overwhelmingly grateful for the Master's capacity to switch from dripping sarcasm to honey-smooth charm in a heartbeat. To all appearances, the ugly exchange with Mervyn had never happened. Justus seamlessly adopted the role of gracious host as soon as he realised the invaders of his private sanctuary were Jack's parents. All too frequently, stickybeaks appeared at the fence, people on a weekend drive who came to gawp at the sight of women wearing men's trousers as they heaved wheelbarrows or hewed stone in a most unladylike fashion. They'd comment loudly on the primitive living conditions of the tents and caravans, like it was some sort of freak show. While the students had learned to ignore the intrusions, Matchum loved the opportunity to run towards them, whooping like a red Indian or screeching like a wild beast, giving them something to remember as he chased them away. Jack was relieved that Matchum, subdued by the altercation between his father and Justus, restrained himself today.

Indeed, all reactions to the ugly scene between the Master and Mervyn were quickly set aside as Justus took William and Marian under his wing, and now in his element, extolled his plans for the property as he led them from one project to the next. Trailing behind, Jack marvelled at the Master's genius, his capacity to sum up the sceptical nature of his parents and temper his vision for the colony into a language that even the most conservative person could understand. Jack found himself captivated yet again as Justus' words constructed images of painters, glassworkers and stonemasons, working side by side. Leading them to the site of the Great Hall, Justus explained how this central gathering space would include the best of mediaeval architecture, his words painting a vivid image. Although Jack had heard it a dozen times before, it never failed to thrill him to envisage the massive carved timbers, fireplace, flagstone floor, enormous lead-light windows and the balcony which would look down across the valley. Already in place were the towering posts and framework for the roof, foretelling the impressive proportions of the proposed building, for those who had eyes to see.

However, it soon emerged that Jack's parents did not have eyes to see, nor were they as captivated by Justus' charismatic persona as he had hoped.

CHAPTER 29

*M*onday night, following dinner, William cleared his throat before beginning to speak, his voice quiet and controlled.

'I'm worried about you and Sofia. I fear you've got yourself tangled up with some sort of cult.'

'A cult! What nonsense,' Jack responded, shaking his head.

Not to be deterred, William grilled him on Justus' income. How did he purchase the land? What was the financial structure of Montsalvat? What did the artists who were giving up their time and energy hope to get out of Justus' 'dream'? Jack fielded the barrage of questions as skilfully as he could, explaining how everybody pitched in, offering what they could to support the building fund. How most of the materials came at little cost from Whelan the Wrecker. To Jack, his father's statements were examples of the bourgeois values that Justus so frequently disdained – where money was the measure of value, controlling people's lives and preventing them, particularly those who were artists, from achieving their potential, instead enslaving them to social expectations so that they worked at meaningless jobs in order to line the pockets of rich people.

Marian chimed in, suggesting that Jack and Sofia could better use their time by creating their own home, prettying a place up for the family they would have one day, rather than wallowing their weekends away in mud and stone.

The debate quickly reverted to his parents' major concern: the dubious morality of the group, and how by association with the Meldrumites, Jack's and Sofia's own reputations would be tainted. They scolded him: surely he must know the value of a good name – how it could be easily lost and very hard to regain. How links to the Meldrumites may even impact his opportunity for promotion at Goldsbrough Mort & Co. And then William began an attack on individuals, claiming that the men were scruffy with their long hair and scraggy beards, the women unfeminine, wearing trousers and digging in mud. What sort of environment was Montsalvat for young children?

Jack could barely contain his outrage at the criticisms his father levelled towards his friends. 'You are just worried about what your associates will think about us,' he fired back, 'Just because you choose to live a life dictated by conventions and which measures success by the accumulation of material things, it does not mean Sofia and I have to.' Jack's words echoed the phrases so frequently bandied around the Montsalvat dinner table.

'Well, let me remind you that it is your privileged upbringing that has allowed you to gain an education and a good job – that funded your trip to Paris where all of this damnable nonsense started.'

'I know, Dad... I understand.' Jack felt chastised. 'But I am not a child anymore. Paris opened my eyes to other ways to live. There, people are free to centre their lives around art. It is not seen as...odd.'

'Well, that is not the way of Australians,' William retorted.

'Yes, but that is not all Australians. There are many Australians, like Justus, like the Skippers, who do live for painting. I am happy now. Sofia and I are happy. We love our days out at Eltham.'

Rising abruptly, Jack pushed his chair back and left the table, and Sofia rose and followed him.

Standing in their bedroom, Jack shook with anger. Why should he and Sofia have to justify their decisions to his parents? He knew that they were never going to change their opinion of Justus, no matter what Jack said. Certainly, Justus was not perfect. Jack knew as well as anyone that the Master could be demanding and petulant, scathingly critical and intolerant of other people's viewpoints. Only last week he had listened as Justus derided artists who wanted to exhibit their work. Jack had been confused. *How on earth does an artist sell his work, if he doesn't exhibit?* he'd wondered. But he also knew that Justus had an extraordinary mind. There was nothing that he could not do. His genius operated on many levels and Jack preferred to focus on the talented visionary rather than Justus' petty aberrations.

When Sofia appeared at the door, Jack released his frustrations.

'They're so small-minded and judgemental!' he said. 'They think that, unless a man is working five and a half days a week to earn a wage and focused on owning the fanciest house in the street, he is a bludger. And women! They are expected to be content raising children and caring for the home!'

Sofia nodded as she listened quietly, and Jack understood that she was torn. She never liked to hear him criticise his parents.

'They just don't understand the lifestyle, Jack. They cannot help it. It is hard when none of their friends are artists. They are all professional people, whose children are following in their footsteps. People like that never understand artists. It was the same in Spain, you know. Even for Andrés. When he finished school, his teachers all told Dad that Andrés should be getting training. That he had a good mind that shouldn't be wasted…good enough to go to university, even.'

Jack did not doubt Sofia's words for a minute, remembering Andrés' keen interest in Spanish politics and his concern for the lives of the working classes.

'Dad used to say "Andrés, just ignore them. They don't know what they are talking about." Dad knew, more than anything, that Andrés needed to paint. Yes, he was clever, but…'. Sofia's eyes filled, thinking of the wonderful artist her brother had been, and Jack pulled her close to him, his hands stroking her hair.

Her words reminded him of the conversation he'd with Margaret's cousin, Ness, all those years ago, when he was deciding whether to follow Roger's plans for him to go to the Académie Julian in Paris. She'd warned him about the challenges that came with being drawn into the world of art. How people, particularly families, would question him. Mind you, Jack thought, the crazy world of the Bell household, with Bunny and Duncan, Ness and Clive, Vita and Virginia and all their complicated relationships…there was perhaps good reason for why their families found them odd.

'You know, Sofia, I don't think that they will ever understand. After the war, and now, having just come through these last few years of depression, people like Mum and Dad just want security. The security that comes with a steady job and money in the bank. They will never understand that life can be about other things.' Jack considered how his and Sofia's choices were upsetting his parents.

'Maybe it's time for us to go and live in the caravan. What do you think? I can catch a train from Eltham to the city just the same as from here.'

Sofia agreed without question, relief in her voice. 'Yes, Jack. It is like we are trying to live two lives. I hate seeing you always arguing with your parents about this. They have been so lovely to me. But sometimes I feel a little guilty. As if I am the one who led you astray.'

'No, Sofia! You are the best thing that ever happened to me! You understand me!'

'It will be wonderful to live at Montsalvat, in our little caravan, Jack! Like we are really starting our own life together here in Australia.'

Jack agreed. He couldn't wait for the time when they would be free, no longer under the shadow of constant criticism from his parents.

CHAPTER 30

$\mathcal{M}$arian could barely hold back her tears when, two weeks later, Jack and Sofia loaded their suitcases into the boot of Lena's car on Saturday morning, this time to live at Montsalvat for good. Bravely kissing their cheeks, she kept her smile bright, clearly determined to take an optimistic approach to this change while hoping and praying that they would return home after they had gotten over this 'mad arty aberration,' as she'd described it to her inquisitive friends at their last morning tea.

William limited his farewell to a stiffly enunciated statement: 'I'm sure you know what you are doing.' His tone betrayed his serious thoughts to the contrary.

'We'll see you very soon,' Jack replied, giving his mother a gentle hug, ignoring his father's words. 'And, as Sofia promised, she will be back to give a hand with the housework. Not tomorrow but next week. We'll stay the night and have a good catch-up then.'

Jack did not want this departure to be seen as such a big deal. Really, they were only going to be an hour or so away. It was not like they were travelling to the other side of the world.

As they climbed into the vehicle, Sofia called a final reminder to

Marian not to tackle the bed linen on her own – it would be much easier if they did it together.

The engine ignited and the car lurched forward. Jack looked back to where his parents stood together, noticing his mother's hand clasping William's, and he considered how forlorn they looked, desolately waving at the departing vehicle. *Anyone would think that we are off to a funeral*, he thought, then shook his head, reassuring himself that his parents would soon adjust to the change. He reached out for Sofia's hand and gave it a squeeze, unable to suppress a surge of excitement as the car turned the corner and they were on their way. Finally, at long last, they would be living at Montsalvat!

On arrival, warmly welcomed by Justus, they felt even more confident that they had made the right decision. Their sense of belonging was immediate. No longer just transient visitors – weekenders – they could now call Montsalvat 'home'. Jack carried their suitcases into the van.

'Off you go. I will be alright, here!' Sofia's eyes were bright with enthusiasm and realising that she was excited to arrange their possessions and set up the tiny space – their first real home together in Australia – Jack laughingly left her to it.

'Why do I feel like you are trying to get rid of me?' he teased. 'Let me know if you need anything. I'll just head over to The Hall and see where things are up.'

Walking outside, Jack marvelled at how different life suddenly felt. He and Sofia had been staying in the van on Saturday nights for almost two months now, but knowing that they were here for good, not simply packing their small case for one night and returning to Copelen Street the following afternoon, was thrilling beyond belief.

PART III

MONTSALVAT

CHAPTER 31

*L*ife at Montsalvat was everything Jack and Sofia had hoped it would be. It was wonderful waking each morning to the sound of birds rustling in the trees, their calls to each other heralding the dawn. The very air was infused with a sense of richness – organic odours rising from the heavy dew, the sweetness of nectar drifting in the breeze, the pungent smoke wafting from the open fire, bacon sizzling in an early riser's cast iron pan. Jack felt inspired by living so close to nature – nothing went unnoticed when it was separated only by the thin plywood caravan wall. Each morning, as he stepped out of the van in the greyness of daybreak, he felt the beauty of it all - the freedom that the bush exuded along with its power to inspire creativity.

Living conditions were rustic at best, but they didn't mind at all. The 'dunny' was a tin can surrounded by a screen of canvas supported by tent posts and tree trunks, offering users meagre privacy. The can filled quickly and the men teased each other constantly, debating whose turn it was to bury the foetid contents. Men and woman alike were encouraged to walk to the gums on the outskirts of the property to relieve their bladders amid the trees – reducing the load in the can. Together, Jack and Sofia discussed strategies for cleaning, both for clothing and dishes, as well as for their own daily wash. When their stays at Montsalvat had only been single nights, Jack had set up two washbasins on a bench outside their van, one for the few dishes they used in the van, the second for face washing and teeth cleaning. They'd been happy to stand beside their large metal basin morning and night, shivering as they sloshed soapy water onto themselves from top to toes.

Now that they were living at Montsalvat permanently, a more satisfactory arrangement was needed, and Jack got inventive. He purchased the bits and pieces that he needed from the hardware store in Eltham – a long rope, which he tied to a rock and flung over a tree branch, the metal handle of a canvas bag which he attached to the rope and a shower-rose with which he fitted the bag. The rose swivelled to allow the water flow to be controlled. Each evening, as soon as he arrived home, he carted a steaming bucket of hot water from the outdoor fire. This he poured into the canvas bag before hoisting it just above head height. By careful use, he and Sofia were able to have a few minutes each to soap up and rinse away the day's grime, and they both agreed that the bush shower was as good as any they'd ever used before.

They quickly found that the Montsalvat week was divided into distinctive routines – weekdays and weekends.

The weekdays, for all intents, began mid-Monday after the day-trippers and weekenders had returned to their work lives, and it lasted until Friday evenings. Even Justus was absent from Mondays to Thursdays, preferring to reside in his and Lil's home in Stanley Street, Brighton, the location far more amenable for his painting lessons in the city. The core group of mid-week residents included Lil, the Skippers and Jack and Sofia. While nobody ever said it, Montsalvat's atmosphere was definitely more relaxed without Justus' dominating and exacting personality overseeing their activities.

Jack and Mervyn departed for work in the city each morning,

leaving the women to divide their days between shared tasks in the kitchen and garden, and attending to their own personal washing and housework. Then they'd meet back in the kitchen in the late afternoon, taking it in turns to prepare the evening meal.

He and Sofia loved the calm, predictable routines of the weekdays. They started by drinking a cup of tea in bed, enjoying the intimacy of their little nest, as Sofia called their caravan. By six o'clock, they were up, Sofia preparing breakfast in the communal kitchen, while Jack collected two large buckets of water for her from the galvanised tank that collected rainwater from Lil's roof. Most days, he got a ride with Mervyn to Eltham Station, and from there, they caught the train into Melbourne. Enjoying the daily commute, he'd think about the house he and Sofia hoped to build and drew small sketches of floor plans and the exterior façade, developing ideas which he'd discuss with her in the evenings.

At first, Jack had felt guilty about leaving Sofia alone for the long days, knowing that she worked physically hard in all manner of weather, while he sat in the comfort of an office. 'Jack, I love it,' she told him. 'Do not worry about me at all.' Her healthy glow and broad smile reassured him that she was, indeed, the happiest he'd seen her since before Andrés died.

He managed to shorten his lunch hour, allowing him to leave the office at four-thirty in the afternoon, and when he was back at Eltham early enough, he'd meet up with Sofia, Lil and the Skippers at the Upper Plenty Pub for a pint of beer, a ritual that the residents of Montsalvat had developed the previous year.

'A good chance to mingle with the locals,' Lena said. 'Let them see that we don't have two heads.'

Jack could immediately feel the benefit of sharing a beer with the men at the bar. The suspicion some Eltham residents held for the Montsalvat artists was widely known, their fertile imaginations conjuring up all sorts of outlandish images and turning rumour into fact. The stories eventually circling back to the artists, of rampant nudity and free love. The regulars who drank at the pub laughed as they shared the latest rumour in circulation on the streets of Eltham about the goings-on at Montsalvat with the artists, and the publican was always welcoming and interested in the progress of the buildings. Additionally, the pub was a good place for connecting with tradesman, who were keen to chat, curious about the alternative construction techniques employed 'up the mount' and happy to provide services at a reduced price for cash-in-hand work.

Each afternoon, Jack listened to Sofia's account of her work in the garden, caring for the chickens, turning the compost, establishing trees, fighting weeds, and setting up a small yard suitable for Montsalvat's newly acquired cow, Freda, that Sonia tended and provided milk for coffee, rice puddings and custards. He loved to see how fulfilled she was, excited by the way each project would take Montsalvat yet another step closer to the self-sufficient lifestyle Justus advocated. As an added bonus, recently, Sofia and Helen had taken on the responsibility of caring for Justus and Lil's son, Max. This allowed Lil to supplement Montsalvat's income by offering a counselling practice in town and Sofia had felt a sense of privilege, entrusted in caring for Justus and Lil's little son. Her stories became full of the two-year-old's antics, how he'd cried when she stopped him from pulling out the row of strawberries that were just going into flower or been sick after eating unripe peaches. It made Jack happy to see Sofia enjoying those hours spent caring for Max. Increasingly, she had been becoming disappointed by the onset of her period each month. Jack was disappointed too, in honesty, however, he was prepared to be patient. Sofia had told him, after all, that her own mother took almost five years to fall pregnant with the twins, so perhaps it was family trait.

Dinner at Montsalvat was always at seven and both he and Sofia enjoyed those mid-week meals where, in the absence of Justus, the conversation took on an air of family banter. The Skippers provided the pivot on which many conversations turned. Matchum, Helen and Sonia teased Mervyn relentlessly.

'Dad, you were up all night last night banging away on that typewriter. It's a wonder any of us got any sleep at all.' Sonia had said.

'Why on earth do you need to type them, when you've got Justus' oracles recorded in your notebook.' Matchum had asked.

'Matchum,' Lena warned, looking apologetically at Lil, who just laughed.

'My notes are sketches, only. When I type them, I am able to add the detail. Plus, they are a lot clearer, for when they needed for future reference,' Mervyn replied.

Jack's expression must have revealed his surprise that Mervyn had made a practice of typing up the copious notes he'd record of the Master's utterings. Helen told him that there were dozens of the books, all stored in suitcases.

'What on earth are we going to do with all of those notebooks when you die, Dad?' Sonia asked.

'Sonia, don't say that,' Lena chided.

'You'll all be fighting over them when I'm gone,' Mervyn retorted. 'They'll be worth a lot of money one day!'

'Helen can have them,' said Sofia.

'Good grief, I don't want them. They might make good fire starters, though.'

'We can hang them in the dunny,' said Matchum. 'Although we'd end up with black arses.' He adopted a formal radio newsreader voice: 'This arse was officially wiped by the pontifications of Justus Jorgensen, as recorded by Mervyn Skipper.' They all laughed, even Lil.

Lil seemed more relaxed in the absence of Justus, or perhaps it was that she expanded to fill his gap, her sharp intellect and delightful charm heightened as she joined the discussions, often providing insights from her experience as a psychologist. Lil believed that many problems that beset people's lives sprang from unhappy marriages, unwanted pregnancies or illicit lovers. She was convinced that in the majority of cases, depression and hysteria could be treated by immersion in creative pursuits, and as a consequence of her therapy, the numbers of students attending Queen Street painting lessons increased. With delightful humour, she shared anecdotes of her day's work at the dining room table, having them in stitches. The wife of an influential

Melbourne family had found her daughter in bed with a girl had wanted to know if Lena could cure the daughter of lesbianism. A businessman who in a pickle, suicidal, his issue: a beautiful wife whom he loved dearly, and an indiscretion that had led to a pregnant office-worker. Truly, he'd only slept with her once! She'd told him she was safe! Now the office-worker was threatening to arrive on his doorstep and tell his wife.

They vied with each other, each determined to guess which of the weekend visitors were behind some of the more outrageous stories.

'No, no, I couldn't tell you that,' Lil laughed. 'I'd lose my licence. No one would ever trust me again. I promise, it's no-one you know!

'I will tell you though, that I do have a client who is going to move out here. Arthur. He's just started lessons with Justus. He's come down from the country. Had a solicitor's practice, but it wasn't working for him. He's very nice, but has been through a bit. He's fragile.'

'Once he starts slipping and sliding in the mud-heaps he'll soon forget all about being fragile,' Helen said decisively, sharing Lil's and Justus' disdain for fragile personalities.

On these evenings, especially when the banter got particularly irreverent, Jack often found himself glancing at the empty chair on the end of the table. No one ever sat in it in Justus' absence. Even when he was twenty miles away, imparting his considerable wisdom on both painting and life to his students in Queens Street, his dominating presence still lingered here in the dining room.

The weekends at Montsalvat were considerably livelier than weekdays. The population could quadruple with the arrival of Justus' Queen Street students, as well as a growing number of individuals who shared a fascination for the model of alternative living that Montsalvat offered. The first carloads usually arrived on Friday afternoons, a second influx on Saturday mornings and still another wave arriving on Sundays. Some people came for a single day, others set up camp for the weekend, and still others stayed for weeks. There was always a mix of new and familiar faces at Montsalvat. The regulars, such as Joe and Henry, Tess and Roxanne, and in addition, a string of Toms, Dicks and Harrys, often accompanied by their girlfriends. They arrived with high spirits and enthusiasm; bottles of beer and wine; guitars and harmonicas. All had been seduced by Justus' dream and were quick to don gumboots to puddle in mud; and heave beams, windows and roofing materials into place. Spellbound, they listened with a combination of admiration and awe as the Master extolled topics of anti-establishmentism, bourgeoise values and artistic freedom.

When he was home, dinner was always treated as a symbolic affair that Justus took very seriously. His place was the large chair, hewn from recycled timber, positioned the end of the table and to all intents, giving him the air of a medieval lord. Lil took her seat at the opposite end of the table and everybody else sat through the middle. Justus believed that the evening meal served to unite the colony and a setting where any problems should be addressed. All were expected to be seated on time, and while mid-week meals may have been vastly more relaxed in the absence of Justus, they were considerably more interesting when he was present.

Justus thrived in the presence of an audience – for him, the more the merrier – for the gatherings around his table endorsed his status as Master of Montsalvat. Sue, as the self-appointed weekend cook, usually assisted by Sofia, was less impressed by the influx of diners that Justus invited without forewarning. With increasing frequency, she was expected to stretch the meal to feed as many as thirty mouths, which occasionally meant that Montsalvat's residents went hungry. She would fume, chiding Justus for his thoughtlessness, and the way that he kow-towed to the socialites.

Sofia agreed with her, and complained to Jack, 'They all arrive in their fancy cars and fine clothes and clean leather boots, but you can see them turning up their noses at our living conditions. And Justus - he pays more attention to them than he does to us, yet we do all the work.'

It was true, Jack knew, but it didn't worry him. 'Justus is just buttering them up, hoping that they will make a big donation or provide some sort of grant. You know what he's like. It's all about Montsalvat to him. The buildings – the dream. He's proud of what we've accomplished here and wants to share it with anyone who'll listen to him.' He always believed it was important to defend Justus.

'No, Jack. Justus just loves being the Lord of the Manor; we his devoted subjects!' Sofia insisted.

Despite the frustration that the large numbers of guests may have created, dinner table conversations were usually at their most eventful on Sunday nights, well-lubricated by the Brown Brothers red wine that Sue siphoned from drums to bottles, which were sold by the glassful to visitors.

Throughout the meal, conversation was informal, but after an hour or so, a hush would fall over the table in anticipation of the Dialogue, about to be delivered.

Those who'd worked on the building site all day usually preferred a simple reading selected from Mervyn's extensive body of concisely structured notes, for Justus' orations could be long winded. Many found it a challenge to battle heavy eyelids in an effort to remain interested, but not Jack. He had no difficulty remaining alert, for he was ever keen to learn Justus' thoughts on everything from Chekhov and Voltaire to Socrates and Plato, after which there would be discussion from the table.

At other times, Justus would launch into a social commentary – his favourite topics being human weaknesses; particularly those of self-deception, contradiction and inconsistency.

'He just opens your eyes, doesn't he?' Jack said to Sofia one night. 'I've asked him to recommend some books for me to read!'

'Then, in the absence of the Master, you will be able to sprout wisdom to us all at the dinner table on week nights,' Sofia replied, and even though Jack suspected that she was teasing him, it did not stop him from visiting the Master in his studio, spending hours in deep discussion. On his bedside table, he began to accumulate a pile of books recommended by Justus, which he read by the kerosene lamp late at night.

'Heavens, Jack, it does get a little tiring,' Sofia complained one Monday morning, after they'd sat up until midnight listening to the Master thunder on about love and marriage. 'Does love trump marriage, or does marriage trump love? Is marriage even important? Is art more important? In the end I wasn't sure what the Master thought. I'm glad he didn't ask me any questions. You couldn't possibly disagree with him or he would cut you to ribbons!'

Jack did not disagree with Sofia. He never spoke at the table, only nodded, preferring to listen carefully, then ponder over the Master's words for a few days rather than make some half-baked comment that would reveal his lack of understanding.

Sometimes dinner conversations turned to the personal lives of the students and no topic was off limits. Justus would question a couple's decision to get married or dissect a relationship difficulty that had been brought to his attention.

'So, what's eating you two?' Justus asked one evening, turning to newlyweds Dave and Glenys. The hapless pair were seated halfway down the table already overflowing with the weekend entourage. A nice young couple, they'd been arriving on Friday afternoons and setting up their little two-man tent for the past six weekends or so. The day had been particularly hot and their relentless, uncharacteristic, nit-picking had been noticed by everyone.

'Nothing…' Dave stammered as a dozen faces turned towards him expectantly, if not somewhat sympathetically.

'Come on! Out with it. You have been hissing at each other like a pair of rattlesnakes all day.'

Glenys looked at Dave hesitantly. 'Dave spent the last of our money on a pair of work boots this morning. I don't know how we are going to buy food for the rest of the week!'

Dave frowned. 'Well, you didn't tell me that you had bought new curtains. If I'd known that, I might have done things differently...'

'Curtains,' Justus repeated. 'What on earth would you want to waste money on curtains for, Glenys? Of course, you wouldn't be alone. Thousands of people seem to need to waste their money, rushing off to the Myer sales, adorning themselves or their houses with cushions and curtains or some other silly fashion just to impress others.'

Turning to Dave, who now looked a little subdued, for everybody could see Glenys glaring at her husband with thunder-filled eyes, Justus continued. 'It seems to me that you have more problems than money, heh! What do you think, Lil? Sometimes in marriage it takes time to work things out. Misunderstandings, petty differences, priorities – these are the little annoyances that are hugely distracting. Especially for an artist.'

By now, Justus had the whole table's attention and his words, intended as a lesson for Dave and Glenys, were evolving into a serious oration. Jack expected that Mervyn would snap out his notebook and start recording the Master's words at any second.

'What matters is that they are resolved quickly, so that your minds are not clogged with petty emotions that stifle creativity. Lil and I had just the same such problems when we were in London, didn't we, Lil?'

Jack inhaled with anticipation and looked at Sofia. A glance around the table revealed the rapt attention of the Skippers and Arthur, Lil's lawyer-client who had recently joined them at Montsalvat permanently, and whose smooth, educated voice had qualified him for the role of reading Mervyn's typed notes on the nights when the 'Dialogue' was presented as a reading. Even Dave and Glenys looked intrigued, no doubt pleased that the focus of Justus' monologue had shifted from themselves to an account of his and Lil's personal life.

'We were in a little flat in London. No money. Lil was working as an anaesthetist then, while I painted. They were lean times and Lil became very ill. Well, as things happen... I just lost all sexual interest in her, and consequently took...Janine...that was her, wasn't it, Lil?... the young woman who modelled for me?...as a lover.'

'Lynette.' The tone of Lil's interjection as she corrected Justus was indiscernible.

Jack reached for Sofia's hand, squeezing it, as Justus shared his solution. 'I thought about this, of course, realising that something had to be done. And then it came to me. Lil should become my model! She agreed, and after painting a series of nudes of her, my love and sexual attraction was reinvigorated!' Justus looked triumphant, as though he was the genius of all marriage counsellors. All eyes turned towards the now-silent Dave and seething Glenys to see their response to the implied solution – that if he worked on a series of nudes of her, their marital problems would be resolved, although to Jack, the Master's solution hardly seemed to address the more pressing issue of their financial crisis.

'Really, Sofia! That was a bit personal, don't you think?' Jack said in a rare moment of criticism of Justus, as he drew Sofia close to him in their small bed later that night.

She replied, 'Don't you ever dare to breathe a single word of any problems we have, or we'll find ourselves being dissected by Justus over the dinner table, and he will no doubt have you painting nudes of me!'

'Well,' Jack teased, running his hand suggestively down her back. 'I do know that you make a wonderful, prize-winning subject. Remember Paris?'

Sofia looked up into his eyes in the light of their kerosene lamp. 'That was not a nude, Jack. I was wearing bedsheets. And...' She sunk back into his arms. 'I certainly do remember Paris!'

Jack held her tightly, caressing her body as he remembered that wonderful night together – and the beautiful portrait that it prompted, which had won him the Julian Prize for portraiture at the student exhibition.

~

It had been a terrible shock when on a cold wet Sunday afternoon Joe and Roxanne arrived at Montsalvat to deliver the news – Clarice Beckett had died overnight. Jack was shocked to the core, and Sofia cried. She'd only met Clarice three times, but there was something about Clarice that had made Sofia's heart ache. Jack understood, for he felt it too. How could she have died, so suddenly. She was barely forty-years of age. Surely not suicide! But no, illness, for it turned out that Clarice had contracted pneumonia and it had been all over for her in a few short days. Jack could not explain the depths of sorrow he felt for the loss of Clarice's quiet existence, and he believed it was important for he and Sofia to show their respect for her by attending her funeral.

CHAPTER 32

*S*ofia, true to her promise, joined Jack on the morning train to Melbourne each week, alighting at South Yarra Station while he went on to Flinders Street. In the evening, he returned to Copelen Street, and over dinner with William and Marian, they discussed the latest happenings at Goldsbrough Mort & Co, Marian's garden, and the letter that had arrived that very day from Aunt Elizabeth…anything other than their lives at Montsalvat. On Tuesday mornings, after Jack left for work, Sofia finished cleaning the upstairs rooms before helping Marian remake the beds with fresh linen. Following a long lunch with her mother-in-law, she then walked to the shops to fetch groceries. They finished the afternoon sitting in the sunshine with a cup of tea and fruitcake in the garden, before Sofia hugged Marian farewell. It was time for her to walk to the station.

'Sofia, love…I am sorry about all of the fussing over the last few weeks…'

'It's okay. I know that you were just worried about us. We are fine, though…really fine!'

'Yes, I can see it now. Jack looks so happy… I just don't understand it, really. I would never have thought that Jack would like such an outdoorsy sort of life…living in a caravan and all… Who would have thought…?' Marian's words trailed off and Sofia had hugged her tight, hearing the quaver in Marian's voice.

Carrying their small overnight case back to the station, she met Jack at Richmond, and together they travelled home to Eltham. As they did, Sofia updated Jack on her afternoon.

'She just seems so lonely.'

Jack listened as Sofia told him about his mother's parting words.

'Yes, the house must feel empty now that we've gone. Never mind. We will be back next week. Anyway, soon enough we will have some grandchildren for them,' he said, feeling optimistic that now, with them happy and settled out at Montsalvat, the baby they both longed for might finally appear.

CHAPTER 33

*I*f Justus - omniscient and omnipresent, striding about Montsalvat, directing and instructing everyone in his midst, ever the Lord of the Manor – was larger than life, the persona of Max Meldrum had taken on legendary proportions in the minds of many of Justus' students, and Jack was no exception. It was Max who had inspired the word 'Meldrumite', a term Jack first heard from Margaret when he'd met her on the *Ormonde*. It seemed that he'd since heard the word used a thousand times in the form of verb, noun and adjective. *Meldrumite* was attached to the technique that produced misty atmospheric paintings which focused on tone, rather than colour, line or subject. It was equally used as a term of scathing criticism when the traditional Melbourne art establishment decried the methods Max had taught. Worst of all, though, the collective noun ascribed to those who adhered to Meldrum's techniques - *Meldrumite* - had been associated with all manner of scandals, real and imagined. Beginning with Colin Colahan's tenuous connection to the gruesome death of Mary Dean, it now applied to Justus' followers and the 'Artist's Colony', even though Max Meldrum had no role there.

Behind the title was the man himself, a fiery little Scotsman who had once played such an influential role in the shaping of Justus. Adding spice to the legend of Max Meldrum were stories about the wedge that had grown between him and Justus. For most people, the events leading to the division were unknown. However, that a rift existed between the two men was undeniable, and Justus clearly rued it. He often fell into nostalgic mutterings, bemoaning the friction that had developed between himself and his old master. Mostly this would occur during a Sunday dinner when one of the city visitors raised Max's name, asking Justus if he'd spoken to his old master recently, or relaying a story about some event that Meldrum had recently attended. Justus was always affected and frequently plunged into a sea of self-pity that was proportionate to the quantity of Brown Brothers claret he'd consumed. Jack often wondered about the relationship Justus had with Max Meldrum. In honesty, he wondered if his relationship with the Master possibly mirrored that Justus had shared with Max. The Master had implied this.

'He was a good man, Jack. Passionate about art. All fired up and ready to take anyone on. That is what I liked about him,' Justus said to him one afternoon. 'You remind me of myself when I was younger. When I was eager to listen and learn everything that Max had to share with me.'

'How did you meet him?' Jack asked.

'Oh... I had been going along to Melbourne's National Gallery School for a couple of years. Learning from Fred McCubbin – you've heard of him?'

Jack hadn't.

'You should see his work. He is very good,' Justus said. Jack thought that he must look him up for it was rare for Justus to praise an artist. 'Anyway, one day a few of us went to a lecture organised by the Victorian Artists' Society. "The Voyage of Culture," they called the speech, and what a voyage it has taken me on!

'We students - we did not know what to expect. Sure, we knew there was going to be controversy. Our lecturers told us that Meldrum had made public accusations against the National Gallery, but really, we did not have any idea what was coming. Well, we found out soon enough for out he came, preaching fire and brimstone, shaking his fist and deflecting the challenges from the floor as quickly as they came, in his feisty Scottish accent.' Justus laughed at the memory.

'Meldrum was up there lampooning the Melbourne Gallery School for their outdated teaching methods – anyone would think that he was preaching from a pulpit. There was nearly a riot. The Gallery teachers could not accept that Max, the ex-pupil on whom they'd bestowed a scholarship and sent to Paris, would dare to come back and challenge them so. They reckoned that Meldrum was a madman, but to me, he was a breath of fresh air. I immediately threw in my position at the Gallery and went and knocked on Meldrum's door. Asked him if he would give me lessons. And that is where it all began.' Justus' voice quavered with nostalgic longing.

'There was a group of us. Colin and Clarice, Jim Minogue, Archie Colquhoun, Percy Leeson, John Farmer. The Meldrumites…that is what they called us, and the name has stuck ever since.'

'So, how did you come to fall out?' Jack asked hesitantly, hoping that he wasn't opening up old wounds.

'Well, first off, a couple of us decided to go to Europe and Max believed that we'd abandoned him. Took our departure, personally. Then he decided that he missed us so much that he'd come to England and join us - but it wasn't the same. We'd seen the art there, Jack. You know... You've been to Paris…. Seen the paintings at the Louvre. The Gauguins and the Picassos, we loved them, and Max didn't like that we loved them. We were supposed to share his disdain. It's all about his ego, really. He was angry because his student grew up. The student can't stay a child forever, can he now, Jack?

'And then, when I came back to Melbourne and started teaching, I adjusted the technique that Max had taught. Well, Max was furious. He'd spent a lifetime developing his theory on tonalism and I'd dared to deviate from it.'

∼

It was a thrilling experience for Jack when he finally met Max. It was very early on a Saturday morning and he'd been working on a land-scape just outside the van. Stepping back, he'd perused his work, pleased at the way he'd invoked the atmosphere of the early morning mist drifting across the open fire and the sun capturing the droplets of dew on a spiderweb strung from a snowy-white branch of a ghost-gum. So absorbed, he didn't notice the approaching men until the sound of voices distracted him. He was surprised when he saw Justus, accompa-nied by a man whose height barely reached the Master's shoulder. The man was familiar, and it occurred to Jack that he'd been present at Clarice's funeral.

'Jack, I was hoping I would find you up! I'd like to introduce you to my old teacher, Max Meldrum. Max, this is Jack – a fine young artist, and if I may say so, after your own kind.'

Jack wiped his hands on a cloth before reaching out and shaking the man's hand, surprised that Meldrum's small stature contrasted so greatly with his considerable reputation.

'Not bad, boy, not bad,' said Meldrum as his eyes scrutinised the painting. 'What training have you had?' The words came out like the bark of a snappy terrier.

Jack described how he'd spent the year of 1930 at the Académie Julian in Paris, studying with Monsieur Simon.

'Puh,' waved Meldrum. 'All that modern rubbish. You stick with what you're doing. And if you want to learn from a real artist, you're welcome to my studio at any time.'

With that, he turned back to Justus. 'Well. You'd better show me your latest pile of rocks, I suppose...' How odd it looked to see Justus kowtowing to another man! And it seemed, as the morning wore on, that everybody was a little quiet, conscious of the presence of the 'mighty Max Meldrum' in their midst.

Not all was to Max's pleasure, it emerged, for raised voices erupted from Justus' studio around ten o'clock. Words like 'murderer,' 'immoral,' 'obscene' and 'ungodly' rang through the crisp, clear air, before the red-faced Meldrum stomped out and without looking at anyone, strutted to his car and took off with a roar.

Nobody saw Justus for the rest of the day. He buried himself in his studio, and at the dinner table, he was silent on the matter. Certainly, nobody was game enough to ask what had happened to upset Max.

CHAPTER 34

*W*hile Jack worked within the confines of his office at Goldsbrough Mort & Co, Sofia spent her days working amid the fertile soil of Montsalvat's vegetable garden. There, along with fresh carrots and spinach that now furnished their dinner plates each evening, she reaped all sorts of interesting information. Regularly, she updated Jack on all manner of fascinating revelations – some of which they found deeply shocking.

'You won't believe this, Jack,' Sofia said one afternoon in late October.

'I believe every word my sweet wife tells me,' he replied, his eyes twinkling as he swept her close to him.

'Not this, you won't. Not in a million years.'

Jack leaned back, looking into Sofia's eyes, his curiosity aroused.

'Would you believe that Helen is Justus' lover?'

'No way!' Jack could barely believe his ears. 'He must be a hundred years older than her! Lil would never tolerate that!'

'She is. Mervyn told me that's the reason why Meldrum has finally turned his back on the Master – because he is disgusted with Justus' behaviour. Apparently, it started years ago…when Lil was pregnant. That's why Meldrum was so angry with Justus. He saw paintings of Helen – nudes – in Justus' studio and put it all together! That's why he departed in such anger.'

'Mervyn knows?'

'Oh, he doesn't like it. He was just about shaking with anger when he told me.'

'Why on earth would he be talking about such a scandalous thing?' Jack found the information impossible to process.

'Helen was in one of her moods. You know how she gets. Snappy and…well, even nasty. You should have heard how she spoke to Mervyn. Then she just threw her spade down and marched off. Worst I've ever seen her. That's when he told me. Said that it must get to her sometimes, Justus being married and everything. No life for a young woman to be tangled up with a married man.'

Jack was deeply troubled by the story and could barely contain the agitation that stirred within him, for, hearing that the man he respected – almost idolised, in truth – could behave so reprehensively, was beyond shocking. Sure, Justus had admitted to an affair way back when he and Lil lived in London. Deplorable as that was, Lil seemed to have forgiven him; she and Justus seemed happy together, and it was in the past, long before the Montsalvat dream. This was not the Justus that Jack knew and held in such high regard. The Justus he knew always advocated self-responsibility and discipline. True - he rejected conservative views of marriage, because he believed it served men and acted as a shackle to women. However, despite the tale he'd once shared at the dinner table about the young model that he'd had an affair with, nothing the Master said implied that he still believed that it was alright for married men to take lovers! And Helen – so young! She would have been – Jack calculated – nineteen when it started – and Justus over forty!

'But Max is almost three. Are you saying this has been going on all of these years?'

Sofia - curiosity overtaking polite discretion - had asked Helen if Mervyn's revelation was right, and Helen had been quite happy to furnish her with details. She relayed this conversation to Jack.

'It was an accident, really,' Helen had explained to Sofia. 'I was going through a bad patch, still trying to find myself. Mum, so strong-willed and domineering, always had me on edge. Nothing I ever did was right. And then Justus made me give up my horses and focus on painting. He didn't realise how much they meant to me. I truly loved those horses – was quite at a loss after they went. Honestly, I hit a patch of depression. You know, felt ugly, useless, confused. So, as always, Mum consulted with Justus and Lil, and they all agreed he should paint me. A nude. They believed that, if I saw myself "*au naturel*," I would appreciate my beauty and bounce out of depression.

'What Mum and Lil did not anticipate was that the Master's therapy involved bouncing me around his bed!' Helen had laughed as Sofia listened, astounded.

'Not that Mum cared, of course. She's never been hung up on sex or cared about social judgements. She just wanted to be sure that I was still using contraception. Lil had given me an IUD years earlier after I'd turned sixteen – just in case. Probably never imagined that it would be Justus' seed we were barricading.'

'Lil!' Sofia's mind, focusing on Lil's role as a doctor and psychologist, had disregarded her position as Justus' wife. 'What on earth does she think of all this? Does she even know?' she questioned Helen, barely believing that regardless, of her physical frailty, the strong, intelligent woman, who'd already forgiven Justus' dalliance once, would tolerate this second transgression. Surely, she was as shocked as Sofia by the unexpected outcome of Justus' 'therapy'.

'Oh, she's okay. Probably glad to be rid of the burden of marital duties. She's not well, you know. She and Justus seem to have an arrangement,' Helen replied, dismissing any concerns Lil could justifiably harbour.

Sofia had persisted. 'But what about you, Helen? Don't you want to be married? Have a family?'

Helen pondered the question. 'Really, I am not so sure about what I want. To be an artist, I suppose. To garden. To paint. Of course, what I'd love is to have my horses back. Justus says "We'll see," but I'm hoping he'll let me one day.'

Jack listened with a sickening sensation as Sofia recounted her conversation with Helen. 'I felt so sorry for her, Jack. I don't think she understands what she's doing.'

'Well, not our business, I guess,' he replied in a clipped tone, although inwardly, he was in turmoil. Over the following weeks, he could barely look at Justus without picturing Montsalvat's leader enticing Helen into his studio while Lil and Max lay sleeping, only yards away. It shocked him to learn that this had been going on for years and he had been utterly blind to it.

Justus must have sensed the coolness in Jack's manner towards him when, over the next couple of weekends, he to failed seek him out in his studio in his usual fashion,. In hindsight, it was evident that Justus, ever shrewd, had made enquiries to determine the reason for Jack's aloof manner toward him. In his usual style, he opted for a public airing, framed by way of an impromptu 'Dialogue' one Friday evening, forcing the issue into the open.

Sated by Sue's excellent beef bourguignon, to which the Brown Brothers claret was a perfect accompaniment, Justus called for everyone's attention before commencing one of his favourite themes – an attack on social mores. A deft diversion in the opening sentence narrowed down the topic and the subject of marriage came under the microscope.

Justus decried how 'this entrenched social institution' had served men across the centuries so very well and yet, in doing so, demeaned women. It delegated a wife's possessions, decision-making and freedom, more often than not, to small-minded, unimaginative or uncaring husbands. Girls had little more to look forward to in life than the joy of servitude to housekeeping and the art of breeding children, whether they liked it or not.

Jack listened intently to the Master's theory, with an ominous sense that tonight's oration was directed towards him. When Justus' story took on a more personal twist, Jack's heart began to race and his breathing grew heavy.

'Marriage does not have to be a shackle,' the Master pontificated, his voice increasing in volume as his thoughts gathered steam. 'Women should be free to pursue their passions. Look at Lil. Unrestricted, she has been able to work as an anaesthetist, doctor and now, as a psychologist. She has been free to develop her talents in a marriage of mutual support.'

Justus cast a benevolent smile toward Lil, as he spoke. 'Our mutual respect and understanding have always been the bedrock of our marriage, our love as husband and wife.' Turning his attention to Helen, Justus patted the silent young woman's hand. 'Yes, Helen and I may share a closeness; however...' Justus returned his gaze to Lil, before finishing, 'this does not impinge on the happiness of my marriage, nor my love for my wife!'

While omitting loaded words like 'mistress' and 'lover,' Justus had utterly extinguished the hope Jack had desperately clung to, that the story of Helen's relationship with the Master was false. Shocked by the relationship existing at all, Jack was now mortified by its open discussion at the dinner table, with the accompanying assumption that it would be accepted. He could barely look at Justus.

'What this is' – Justus leaned forward, dramatically, as if divulging the secret of the ages: the solution for ensuring all marriages would be as happy as his and Lil's – 'is...consideration!

'Lil's acceptance of my needs demonstrates her love for me. How could a husband not love his wife in return for such consideration?'

Jack assumed that it was a rhetorical question and was in no state to respond to the man, whose piercing gaze landed upon him. Instead, he glanced from one woman to the other, wondering if they shared the same enthusiasm for Justus' theory of 'consideration.'

Lil's status – seated in a position of honour at the opposite end of the long table to her husband, mother of his child – was indisputable. The Master's Wife. She bore a dignified expression, head high, eyes focused on Justus, her thoughts inscrutable.

Helen's demeanour was more transparent. Shifting in her seat, she looked down at her plate, ignoring the measured looks now being directed towards her. How must she feel as Justus extolled the deep love he and Lil shared to the audience? Jack recognised, with a flash of insight, that Helen did indeed hold an exalted position among the students – seated at Justus' immediate left. However, with tonight's subject centred on the sacredness of love between a husband and his wife, Helen's role as his lover was significantly and publicly diminished, and Jack understood why the beautiful young woman's moods sometimes swung from gaiety to sullenness, without apparent cause.

With Justus' long-winded oration finally complete, silence fell over the room.

Reaching for Sofia's hand under the table, Jack squeezed it firmly, knowing from the stony expression on her face that a thunderous fury was brewing. Mervyn also looked like a volcano ready to explode, his fists clenching in powerless rage, his mouth opening and shutting like a goldfish. First Lena, his wife had been enchanted by Justus's vision, championing everything he said, almost to the point of absurdity. Now, Helen, his own daughter, had fallen under the Master's spell.

Jack could only imagine how Mervyn must feel, forced to listen to Justus' pompous self-justification for seducing Helen. However, angry as Mervyn appeared, he retreated from the battle before it had even begun. He must have concluded that Justus was simply too accomplished in the art of verbal sparring to take on. Indeed, they were all familiar with the consequences of disagreeing with the Master: how he'd come back at the hapless victim with a barrage of oh-so-reasonable questions, probing and searching for technical weaknesses in their arguments, skilfully twisting and sharpening their words into fiery darts which he'd direct straight back – never missing his mark. The final outcome was always the same; Justus, cool as a cucumber and with that damnable smile fixed on his face - exhilarated by the sparring - his opponent crushed, seething with frustration and anger. Nobody knew this better than Mervyn, who had been Justus' victim on multiple occasions.

CHAPTER 35

$\mathcal{I}$t was on a Wednesday afternoon, almost twelve months after they'd moved to Montsalvat, when Jack arrived home to find Sofia tight-lipped and flustered. 'What happened?' he asked, but she just shook her head silently and refused to meet his eyes.

'Come on, Sofia. Tell me. Something has upset you.'

Relenting, she told him how, after she and Helen had cleaned up the breakfast dishes that morning, Helen had started to wash the newly laid terracotta floor tiles.

'She was washing them with milk, Jack! Milk!' Her eyes widened with astonishment, tears glistening. 'There were flies everywhere. The air was thick with them.' Sofia shooshed her hands in rapid sweeps, as though beating off imagined flies. 'I asked her why on earth was she using milk, and at that moment, the Master came in and stood watching us. I asked again why she was washing the floor with milk. It was so hot the milk was practically curdled! Well, Justus intervened. He said that it was he who had directed Helen to use milk. That it was the best thing for cleaning the tiles. Truly, Jack, I could not help myself. I laughed and laughed. Once I started, I just could not stop! I told Justus that I had been washing tiled floors all my life and had never heard of anyone using milk to get them clean! Honestly, it just seemed so funny. Anyway, Justus was not amused. He said that we were not in Spain and did not do things the way Spanish peasants did!' Sofia breathed deeply, collecting herself. 'I was dumbfounded. I didn't know what to say! So, I just nodded and left them to it.' She again paused, holding her hand to her mouth, half-laughing, half-sobbing, before continuing. 'That would have been enough, but later in the morning, Justus came here to the van for a chat. I thought he was going to tell me off for interfering with his instructions about the floor, but he wanted to talk about us.'

Sofia's voice broke as fresh sobs arose. 'You and me, Jack. He asked if I supported your art. Did I want to see you truly happy and fulfilled? He said that if you were happy, then I would be too, and so on. I told him we were very happy, but he said that you must be getting tired, travelling to Melbourne each day. That I must have money from the sale of the gallery in Malaga and perhaps I should use it to pay our accommodation fee, so you would not have to work and could devote yourself to painting. Jack, I didn't know what to say. I told him that I would talk to you.' She looked at him expectantly, seeking reassurance.

Pulling her close, Jack hugged Sofia tightly, upset to see her so distressed. 'It's okay, love. Don't worry about Justus. He's just mad about art. I'm doing fine, travelling back and forward - the train doesn't take that long. I will talk to Justus, set him straight. Like I said, your money is yours. I am your husband and I will look after us. We have plenty enough to get by.'

Jack refused to hear of Sofia spending her money – over four thousand pounds - a fortune really, currently secured in the Commonwealth Savings Bank's vaults. As far as Jack was concerned, Sofia was his wife and it was his duty to provide for her. The three pounds, six he earned each week was more than enough for their needs. Sofia's money was to be kept 'for a rainy day,' he'd often told her, and many a time when building work came to a halt due to the wet weather, they'd lie snuggling in the van, cocooned in the cosy warmth from its kerosene heater. And as they listened to the blistering winds and deluge pummelling the thin plywood roof, Sofia would laughingly suggest they go out shopping and spend some of 'her money' now that it was raining.

Later that evening, Jack drew Justus aside and assured him that his work with Goldsbrough Mort & Co was no trouble. Indeed, he rather enjoyed his days getting out of the office and travelling the countryside. Justus' response was one of light indifference.

'It was just a thought, Jack, but of course, it's up to you and Sofia. It is good for wives to feel that they are supporting their husbands, helps to bond the marriage. Certainly, you and Sofia know what is best for yourselves and will make your own decisions.'

Justus' response made Jack suspect that Sofia had misunderstood the Master's comments. However, that night, assuring her that he'd spoken to Justus and was sure that he did not mean anything, Jack felt her body stiffen in his arms.

'No, Jack. Justus was rude. He was goading me. Justus thinks he has a right to tell everybody how they should live their lives!' She turned away from him and gazing at her back, and Jack knew that Justus was not the only one with whom Sofia was annoyed.

Eventually, the turbulence caused by the string of misunderstandings and disclosures of recent weeks eased, and life reverted to its usual happy pace. However, Jack was increasingly conscious of Sofia's tendency to criticise Justus. It seemed that almost everything the Master said or did was wrong, and Jack felt caught between supporting Sofia's viewpoints and defending the enduring admiration he felt for Justus. Indeed, Jack wanted Sofia to be happy and to feel supported by him. However, unlike her, he accepted Justus' imperfections, believing that there was far more value in the man, and their lifestyle here at Montsalvat, than harm, and he was sure that Sofia did, too. He knew how much she loved their cosy little van and in the evenings her conversations were peppered with news about the garden's progress, or the exploits of Max.

Beyond her criticisms of Justus, Sofia did have a second subject of ongoing concern which she voiced with increasing regularity.

'Jack, what about your art? You never seem to find the time to paint these days.'

It was true. Between his work in Melbourne and the weekends dedicated to the building programs - short of the Saturday afternoon 'lesson' from Justus, frequently cancelled due to the pressing demands of the construction work - there was little time to paint. Occasionally, rising early, he had a dabble, but in honesty, he hadn't completed a painting in months.

'It's okay, love. Getting the buildings finished is the priority at present. Once everything is in place, we will all have time for painting. I've learnt so much; it's been wonderful – how to make mud-bricks and position roof beams, digging the well... Where would I ever have even seen those things, if it weren't for the building projects? I'll get back to painting soon.'

However, while a part of Jack was keen to be painting, what he most loved about his days at Montsalvat was the joy of working side-by-side with the young men, experiencing the connection he felt with the extensive 'family' that he'd longed for all of his life. Together, analysing the land and marking the layout of a new building. Discussing the accuracy of their string-lines and angle measurements to ensure they were square. Heaving and grunting, as they raised enormous logs into position and the collective swell of pride at seeing corner posts standing straight and true. Reviewing the design – should the window be here, or here? – and negotiating the tricky problems, such as how to transfer the latest load of enormous windows from the back of Whelan's truck down to the dining room without breaking a single pane. Or, what to do about the kookaburras that had taken nest below the ridge of Lil's House, their cackling laughter ringing through the site each dawn and dusk, reminding everyone that they were the kings of the bush, reigning supreme as they overlooked the workers from their lofty height.

Additionally, and what Jack did not admit to Sofia given her recent disenchantment with Justus, was the pleasure he derived from his hours spent one-on-one in Justus' studio. To Jack, the Master's intellect was awe-inspiring, and he was constantly amazed by the enthusiasm the older man had; ever analysing, questioning and trialling art theories and practice. Jack loved learning from him, be it about methods used by painters of old, or some new-fangled idea. Furthermore, what intrigued Jack was the way the Master always seemed to come at things from the opposite direction to ordinary people; he'd see things that others needed to be shown and revelled at any opportunity to do the showing to Jack.

CHAPTER 36

*W*alking back from the station, in heat retained from the uncharacteristically warm spring day, Jack admired the glow of the setting sun as it filtered through the tall trees, their branches rustling in the evening breeze, a light scent of eucalyptus drifting in the air. It was just after six-thirty pm – and he was a little later than usual. With increasing regularity, Mr Gilmore had taken to inviting him to sit in on Goldsbrough Mort & Co's weekly meeting. Jack enjoyed these gatherings, listening to the regional managers as they discussed issues related to the wool trade across Victoria – the quality and quantity of wool, buying and selling prices, transport issues and the grievances of various clients. Sometimes, it was decided that Jack should escort one of the wool agents into the rural regions to meet with an anxious client, answering their questions regarding the company's accounting processes. It was a compliment, really, and Jack knew they were considering him for promotion to a role in the auditing department that would provide him with increased responsibilities, as well as a wage rise. Jack didn't mind at all.

Contrary to the concerns that Justus had expressed, Jack quite liked his journey into Melbourne each morning. Although utterly bored with his clerical duties, his interest in the wool trade had grown as the rows of figures before him developed meaning. Now, Jack was able to interpret the invoices, and from them, identify the various clients by their names. He could recognise those who were producing exceptional quantities of the finest grade wool, as well as those who were fledgling producers. He enjoyed interpreting the records, observing rises in his clients' yield or quality of the annual wool clips.

Turning into Montsalvat's gateway, Jack was surprised to see Sofia in the evening twilight, running towards him, smiling with barely contained excitement. He felt his smile expand in response to hers and caught her in his arms, wondering what had happened to cause her excitement.

'Come, Jack, come with me,' she whispered, leading him to their van, the glow of their kerosene lamp visible through its small windows. Bewildered, Jack wondered what Sofia had in store. He was even more puzzled when she sat him down on the narrow bench and straddled his legs, her arms around his neck, her forehead against his.

Jack laughed. 'So, who can I thank for this special attention from my beautiful wife?' he asked, as his hands moved gently over her shoulders, breasts and arms, his lips on hers - as always, loving their softness.

'We'—kiss—'are'—kiss—'going'—kiss—'to have a baby!' The last words came out in a rush. Jack held his breath as he pulled back, looking searchingly into Sofia's eyes, as if hardly believing what she had just said. Then he whooped in excitement.

Lifting her as high as he could in the low-ceilinged van, he threw his head back and laughed before pulling her close again.

'Really? How do you know? Are you sure? When did you find out?'

It was everything that he had waited to hear. Often, he'd observed children and their parents, brothers and sisters, extended families. From his vantage as the only child of a quietly spoken father and gently doting mother, the lives of families with lots of children seemed loaded with boisterous excitement. Laughing, squabbling, yelling confusion. It all seemed so…fun…and connected.

In contrast, Jack always felt his aloneness amplified. He'd imagined what it would be like to share a bedroom with a brother, someone to build a train set with, or look together out the window into the night, making shapes out of the stars. Perhaps they would tell ghost stories, or go fishing together, or play cricket. Or wrestle, or kick footballs, back and forth.

And now, he was going to have his own family. He and Sofia would be three. A child to swing up onto his shoulders, gallop around like a horse, give 'whizzeees' – holding a little arm and leg and spinning a squealing, giggling little body around like an aeroplane. Jack was ecstatic.

The dinner bell interrupted their joyous moment, and Jack leapt up. 'Come on, let's tell everybody about the baby at dinner!' He could not wait to shout to the world that his first child was on the way – finally, he was going to be a father!

Lil was the first to congratulate them, saying how wonderful it would be for Max to have a playmate. Justus, looking surprised, shook Jack's hand and smiled benevolently at Sofia. The Skippers expressed their good wishes with kisses and hugs, Matchum decreeing that he was now to be known as Uncle Match, and Arthur patted Jack on the back, announcing that the occasion called for a toast.

Jack had thought his life had hit perfection in the months he and Sofia spent in Malaga after they were married, until the grief of Andrés' death cast its dark shadow. The trip to Australia and living with his parents had offered them the novelty of changed circumstances, and then meeting the Meldrumites and subsequently joining the artist' colony at Montsalvat gave both him and Sofia a sense of belonging, which they loved. However, the anticipation of their first child, their very own baby, eclipsed all of his previous experiences.

Each morning Jack bounced out of bed to make Sofia a cup of tea before setting off to the station. He could feel the spring in his step as he walked. Jack was a man with a family on the way and had responsibilities to meet. With a broad smile, Jack was quick to share the good news with anybody who'd listen, and his joy was contagious. Everyone, from the station master to the baker and publican, familiar with the happy-go-lucky young man and his beautiful Spanish wife, regularly asked how Sofia and the baby were doing.

The long days of summer provided extra hours of sunlight, and during weekdays, they relaxed outdoors, resting in low-slung canvas chairs, sipping glasses of Sofia's refreshing sangria, while they listened to the impossibly high-pitched chorus of cicadas. An easy camaraderie persisted among the Montsalvat residents.

On weekends, when it was too hot to be lugging bricks or hewing stone on the building projects, the Jorgensens, Skippers and anyone else about had taken to escaping to the cool of San Remo. Besides offering welcome relief from the dry heat of Montsalvat, the little seaside village at the mouth of Port Phillip Bay provided great painting opportunities. Seascapes became an obsession and there was much excitement as everyone enthusiastically gathered together their paints, canvases and easels, loaded up the vans and headed off for the weekend. Justus was determined to purchase a block of land in the area and met with real estate agents, accordingly.

Thanks to a touch of morning sickness, combined with relishing any opportunities for time alone, Jack and Sofia had not ventured to the seaside so far, volunteering to stay home to ensure the animals had food and water.

Jack's love for Sofia felt like it was expanding with her waistline. He delighted in pulling her close to him, feeling the bulge nestled between them. Rubbing his hands around the contours of her belly as they lay in bed at night, he hoped to transmit his deep paternal love to the child within.

Sofia moved his palm across the tightly stretched skin. 'Feel there, Jack. He is hiccoughing,' she said, or, 'Can you feel his foot kicking me?'

They gazed endlessly at her growing bump, which rolled and distorted at will, with both amusement and fascination.

As the heat of summer gave way to cooler autumn days, building projects were attacked with renewed vigour, and Jack enjoyed pairing with Matchum, who maintained a constant flow of chatter and was forever laughing and whistling as he worked. Helen and Sofia needed a fence to keep Freda out of their vegetable garden and with their shirts shed, leaving their backs exposed to the sun and tanning to a deep gold, hair shaggy and golden tipped, they looked every bit like brothers as they felled trees, stripped away the outer layers of bark and branches, and then sawed the bared trunks into lengths – posts to hold the fencing wire. Frustration set in as their posts tilted first to the left and then to the right, no matter how much they'd tried to pack the holes, drawing the attention of Justus.

'What good are those,' he asked, looking at the dozen five-foot lengths they'd prepared.

'Well, they are only fence-posts – not as if they are designed to hold up a roof or anything,' Matchum replied, grumpily.

'No point in doing all that work and standing them in a holes so shallow that they fall out in the first rain,' Justus retorted. 'The posts will need to be six-foot, at least. One-third in the ground, two thirds out. You want that fence to stand for fifty years – at least! That's unless you're planning on doing the work all over again in a couple of years. Pull it out and start again, boys.'

Together, he and Matchum worked tirelessly to finish the Student Quarters, the building planned to accommodate the weekend students, who camped on the grounds of Montsalvat. When Justus had suggested that Jack and Sofia might like to relocated to one of the cabins, the two rooms offering them more space than the caravan, now that they had a baby on the way, they had readily agreed. With Sofia's rapidly expanding waistline, they were already were feeling cramped in their vans tiny living space. The cabin would offer warmth through the winter, and comfort for Sofia as she arose in the night to attend to the newborn, for there, they could have a small fireplace.

∼

In the first week of March, Jack and Sofia were excited to move their belongings from the caravan across to their new rooms. Sofia, now so rounded with her bulging belly that Jack had taken to calling her 'his little Spanish olive,' was thrilled to be able to arrange furniture, put their clothing into chests of drawers and set up the crib in readiness for the baby.

Her contentment was complete when Jack and Matchum returned from a trip into Melbourne the following Saturday morning and between them, hefted a large plywood box into the room. Sofia gasped in surprise as she looked from Jack to Matchum in disbelief and then turned her attention to the box, tears sliding down her cheeks as she lovingly stroked its side.

'My Spain,' she whispered. 'Thank you, Jack.'

It was the tea chest they'd transported from Spain to Australia over two years earlier. Sometimes, on her Monday visits Mum and Dad, Sofia had squeezed into the small storage space under the stairs and pried the brass tacks off the lid to remove one item or another. Afterwards, Jack always noticed how quiet she became, lost in the memories of a life on the other side of the world where the orchards, gallery and painting formed the pivot around which daily routines had revolved. The contents of the chest were all that remained of those days. Paintings and articles that held memories that were deeply personal and which roused a terrible sadness for Sofia, now that both her father and Andrés were lost to her.

Today, however, the sadness of Sofia's past seemed to be less troubling, perhaps because she was so enveloped in the joy of pending motherhood. Jack watched as she laid out a set of paintings, speaking at once to both the baby in her womb and to him, and he knew that this was her way of sharing her family – the grandpa and uncle who were so close to her heart – with their child. She seemed at peace.

Selecting four paintings, her brother's and father's Malagian scenes of the seaside and the finca, Sofia announced that these needed to be framed. Jack knew that these paintings would form the basis of the first stories their baby would learn, in the manner of a children's illustrated book, and he could almost hear Sofia's soft voice bringing to life the rippling Mediterranean Sea stretching to the horizon, its waters so greeny-blue it was hard to tell where one colour started and the other ended; the craggy slopes of the finca, lined with olive and orange trees; the donkeys laden with baskets trekking up the mountain; large roosters pecking on the roadside; and a sun that blazed so hot it sent everybody indoors for the afternoons. And their child would learn the stories of two immensely talented artists, Abuelo and Tío Andrés. Grandpa and Uncle Andrés. Over time, their cherished paintings would be revealed, each with its own story, and although their child might never set foot on Spanish soil, its heart would surely beat to the pulsing rhythms of the fandango, and its vocabulary would be peppered with the Spanish words Sofia would speak.

The newspaper articles Jack read on the way to work each morning, buried deep within the international pages of *The Argus,* claimed that a civil war encompassing all of Spain's regions was but a hairsbreadth away. However, Jack knew that the Spain their child would learn of, was one of wonder and happiness. Not the lost and broken Spain of the present, its north and south, posturing as though in a deadly dance of bull against matador, its outcome likely to produce equally tragic results.

There seemed to be an unspoken understanding that the Picassos, Sorollas and Matisses would not be displayed, or even mentioned. It was as if both Sofia and Jack knew that these paintings were not for Montsalvat walls, best left buried in the depths of the chest, along with the lace tablecloths embroidered by Sofia's mother, the ancient family Bible which held details of their wedding date, as well as those of Sofia's parents and grandparents, neatly folded birth certificates, wedding certificates and death certificates, the delicate parchments perfumed by the dried sprigs of orange blossom lying between their yellowed pages, and the blue and white glazed platters and silverware that Jack and Sofia had received as wedding presents. Time for these another day.

With all of the reminiscing that the presence of the chest aroused, it was not surprising that a conversation about Margaret ensued. Jack had not heard from their old friend in ages – the last time being a very belated reply to his own letter, sent over a year earlier, updating her on the news of their meeting with the Meldrumites, his lessons with Justus and how they hoped to move out to Eltham and live at the artists' colony one day.

Twice since, Jack had written to her, sending his letters to Charleston, Sussex, hoping they may be delivered to Margaret via her Aunt Vanessa. The first was sent after they'd moved out to Eltham to live at Montsalvat; the second, when they had news that Sofia was pregnant. They had no idea if she'd ever received either of them.

To their amazement, it was as if all of their talking and thinking about Margaret garnered the power to conjure her very being into their lives for, the following Saturday, they were enjoying the quiet of the wintery sunshine, pleased that everyone had headed off to San Remo on a painting expedition, when they were surprised to hear a voice calling 'Yoo - Hoo' from the carpark.

Jack looked at Sofia quizzically and wordlessly strode across to the open doorway, peering up the hill. Could it be...?

The woman standing in the vacant carpark was unmistakable: tall, smartly dressed, her baggy pants whipping around her legs in the morning breeze, her long white tunic top out of place in Montsalvat, where everybody avoided white clothing at all costs, her hair swept up in a cap of sorts decorated with a spray of bright orange flowers, a burst of curls erupting above her left ear.

'Guess who?' he cried, launching off the doorstep at high speed and returning a few minutes later with a beaming Margaret at his side.

'Sofia, look at you – how wonderful!' Margaret exclaimed as she awkwardly manoeuvred to hug Sofia. 'When are you due? You are enormous! Must be so uncomfortable... Do you mind if I touch? It's about as close as I'll ever get to a newborn, I expect!'

For the next hour, they chatted non-stop, Jack and Sofia listening as Margaret described her journey back to Australia.

'I'd had enough of London – damned near froze my bloody arse off,' she said, the broad Australian accent, so distinctive, even in Jack's ears when he was living in Paris and Spain, now replaced by rounded British vowel sounds. 'Those winters are just too ridiculous. There was no way that I could bear another. Then dear Freddie looked at me one day and said, "Margaret, what are you doing love? Is this really what you want with your life? To paint cats, dogs and birds?"'

Jack and Sofia both laughed at Margaret as she adopted an effeminate British tone, mimicking the words of her cousin.

'He was leading up to making me an offer to join him at the gallery. The Grafton needed another buyer and he thought that I could be trained up. I do have a talent for spotting up-and-coming artists, you know!' She looked at Jack pointedly.

'But then, it was like I was hit by a lightning bolt. Certainly, he was right. If I had to gaze into the eyes of another Siamese cat, I was going to go stark raving mad. I swear they were daring me to make a mess of my painting. Intimidating, it was! Like they were in a battle of wills with me, and I knew that they were winning. As soon as Freddie said the words, I knew, precisely, what I wanted. To go home to Australia. Catch up with my dearest friends, Jack and Sofia! Bask in the sunshine! Go swimming at Beaumaris! – Clarice is still there, isn't she? Have you met her yet?

Margaret was shocked when Jack told her that Clarice had died the previous year. 'She's been like my big sister,' she explained. 'She always used to encourage me... "We women, we need to stick together," I wanted her to come to London with me back in 1920, but those awful parents of hers. I am sure that they pretended to be sick, just to tie her down. Oh… It's just too awful; poor Clarice never received a skerrick of encouragement from anyone, her whole life!'

Jack and Sofia listened as Margaret came to terms with Clarice's death. More than ever, he regretted never having asked Clarice if she'd known Margaret. Not only did they know each other, but they'd once been close! He would have love to have heard Clarice's stories about Margaret!

'Did you see her work, Jack? She was an amazing artist – truly gifted. Even Max saw it, and he never thought much of women painters – even those who were his own students!'

Jack nodded, remembering the misty scenes depicting the streets of Melbourne with T-model Fords drifting through them, and Clarice's extraordinary seascapes. He wondered what Roger Fry and Gertrude Stein would have made of her paintings. What a shame she had not made the trip to England with Margaret. How different might her life have been.

'She did have an exhibition once, but those critics – they just ripped her to shreds, poor girl. Showed no understanding of her work. Honestly, who do they think they are? I feel so sad for her. I was sure that a day would come when her talent would be recognised. Now… well, it's too late, isn't it?'

Margaret was keen to hear details of Clarice's funeral and glad to know that Jack and Sofia had attended. She was pleased to hear that Max had attended, too, but not surprised that Justus hadn't.

'No, he wouldn't have. Hates death… always did.' she said.

'What are you doing now, Margaret?' Sofia asked.

Recovering from the shock, she continued describing her own movements.

'Well, when I made up my mind that I was coming home, Freddie linked me with some contacts, in a flash. Friends of his who own a decorating business – fabrics and wallpapers. I started work there, two weeks ago. It's not too bad. Apparently, Australia is mad for wallpaper these days. They seem to like my style.'

Margaret looked around the room, not a scrap of wallpaper in view on the mud-brick interior surfaces. She glanced at Jack's easel in the corner. 'So, what are you up to, Jack? Making your mark on the art world here in the Antipodes?'

'Well, I paint a little bit, usually early in the mornings. Most of my time is taken up with the buildings these days. Mind you, as Justus says, all creative endeavours help to round out the artist. It's inspiring just to be among so much talent. Here we've got stonemasons, cabinet-makers, lead lighters and writers. Artists, too, of course. Plus, the building and garden projects.'

'You are right though, Margaret,' Sofia interjected. 'I keep saying the same thing! Jack should be painting much more.'

'Fair go, now – I can't be working all week, helping out with Montsalvat, looking after my expectant wife and painting as well,' Jack replied. 'Anyway, I learn plenty from Justus. The man's a genius. Come on, Margaret, we'll show you around. Nothing's happening here today. Everyone's gone down to San Remo for the weekend.'

As they weaved through the various buildings, Jack gave a detailed account of the evolution of each, from Lil's House to Sue's Tower to the recently finished Student Quarters, where Jack and Sofia now lived and the half-completed Great Hall. An assortment of other buildings – sheds, Justus' own quarters, a dairy – were also in various stages of completion.

'So, this is what the old bugger's up to,' Margaret said. 'Not surprising, really. He was always mad about buildings. I remember him back in Meldrum's studio. Did I tell you I went there for a while? Back when Max was giving lessons in Brighton. I had an almighty row with him - Max, that is - because he told me that there would never be a decent female painter. The nerve of him! Justus, of course, was his favourite – always had his head in the clouds, raving on about one idea or another. Mind you; this is pretty impressive. I feel like I am in a seventeenth-century village in France. And look at those gargoyles!'

Margaret stayed well into the evening, sharing cold sliced lamb and salad with them. They reminisced about their time together in Paris and Spain, and Sofia revisited her tea chest.

'Margaret, you have these,' she said, selecting a pair of Andrés' paintings of the Malaga harbour – the blazing gold and brilliant azure looking out of place in the dusty pisé walls of the room, and pushing them into Margaret's hands.

Of course, Margaret refused, saying they were Sofia's, and of course, Sofia insisted.

'He would have loved you to have them. We have plenty. These are set aside to be framed as soon as I can get into town.' Sofia showed Margaret the group she'd selected only two days earlier. 'You were very special to Andrés, not to mention helpful to us at that awful time. He died happy, knowing that his works were hanging on walls in Paris, New York and London, thanks to you! And now they can hang on the walls of Melbournites.'

Tears were shed as Sofia and Margaret reminisced over the time she'd shared with them in Malaga. Those pleasant days when they'd lived in harmony, the boys painting while Margaret helped Sofia with the house and gallery. And then it had all come to a horrible end. Jack was eternally glad that Margaret had been with them through it all.

At seven, he walked her to the station. 'Thanks for coming to see us. It's so good to see you again,' he said before hugging her. 'We must catch up soon. Perhaps Sofia and I can meet you in town, or you could come out again after the baby is born?'

'Definitely! I'll be back, Jack, of that you can be sure. Can't promise that I won't get into a row with Justus, the old rascal. But I will try to be on my best behaviour.'

CHAPTER 37

*E*ven in Sofia's final weeks of pregnancy, she insisted they continue their weekly visits to Copelen Street, enjoying the afternoons sitting in the garden with Marian, delighted with 'Mum and Dad's' enthusiasm for their first grandchild. Hours passed as they discussed the baby's pending arrival and Marian insisted on buying endless baby clothing: nighties, booties and bonnets now overflowed the small chest of drawers in their cabin purchased in readiness for the baby.

'Jack, what are we going to do with this?' Sofia said, laughing as she showed him the latest acquisition that Marian had given her that morning. A beautiful lacy jacket with a row of tiny pearl buttons down its back, a soft shawl and little booties to match – snow-white, knitted from the finest of wool; and utterly impractical for a 'bush baby'.

'Mum is so funny,' she told Jack when he asked how her day went. 'She doesn't want me to do anything. Always worried about the baby!'

Jack started as Sofia's statement triggered a long-forgotten memory. He was a small boy, playing with his wooden horse at his mother's feet, while she and their housemaid, Nina, transferred a load of steaming sheets from the copper to the mangle. He loved watching the soapy laundry pass through the spinning rollers, exiting in long, flattened ribbons, steam rising, ready to be rinsed in clean water and then to make a second pass through the rollers to wring excess water from the linen, before it would be hung on the line.

Suddenly his mother had clutched at the concrete basin. She'd gasped loudly, her face contorted in pain before she slid to the floor. He remembered the thumping sound her body had made, her white face resting close to where he was sitting, a bright red stream of blood oozing from her mouth, the sight of which had frightened him, more than anything.

'Are you right, missus, are you right?' Nina had cried anxiously before her strong hands, pale pink on the palms, black everywhere else, had reached for Jack. Clutched tightly to her ample bosom, he was jolted against the heaving padding as she'd ran to the telephone.

There had been a flurry of activity as men in uniform had arrived. By then, the blood flowing from his mother's mouth had settled, but her blue skirt had blossomed with clusters of red flowers; their blooms growing and running into each other. Efficiently, the men lifted her onto their stretcher in a quick, smooth movement and slid her into the back of their ambulance, and then there had been silence. A grey shadow cast over the house, empty of its usual cheerful bustle; even as Nina played quiet games with Jack. Each morning, she set out crayons for him to draw a picture that would be delivered to his mother, something to cheer mummy up, while she rested in hospital. Jack remembered how Nina would make him a vegemite sandwich and slice his apple into tiny wedges and how, after lunch, she would lay with him on his brand-new big boy's bed, humming to him until he drifted into his afternoon sleep. She reassured Jack that the blood he had seen exiting his mother's mouth was no problem – just a small cut to her tongue which she'd bitten as she had fallen. Just fainted, he was told. 'It sometimes happens when people get too hot.' He recalled his father's unusual presence in the kitchen and how he'd looked puzzled as he'd turned the stove's knobs to the right and then to the left to reheat the meal that Nina left each day. Those meals were served half-burned and half-cold, messily plated – his father clumsy and inept at the tasks that women seemed to perform effortlessly from the time they were young girls. Jack recalled the grim atmosphere that hovered over the dining table as he and his father had eaten, William frowning when Jack unsuccessfully wielded the large spoon from bowl to mouth, spilling peas across the floor – where was his own small spoon that his mother gave him? More than anything, he remembered the silence as his father, overwhelmed with fears for Marian's health, had no words for a three-year-old Jack.

How could he ever have forgotten this momentous event? Jack wondered with a shudder. Although profound, it had been meaningless to him as a three-year-old. Indeed, he'd had a terrible fright, and then he'd fallen into self-pitying misery – his mother gone from him for weeks. He'd missed her. Cried loudly and often, he supposed. The memory had been long buried and Jack had never made any connection between his mother's collapse and a thwarted pregnancy until this moment. A wave of sadness for Marian, and horror for himself and Sofia, rippled through him. He decided they were fears best kept to himself.

'Mum worries about everything,' he answered Sofia. 'Humour her, love. She would feel awful if you so much as broke a fingernail while you were doing her housework. Sit with her in the garden and talk about babies. She'll love that. Betty's there now; she'll help Mum with the housework.'

'What do you know about Betty, Jack?' Sofia asked.

'Nothing, really. She'll be from one of the homes. Perhaps a mission. That's where she would have been trained so she could work as a housekeeper.'

Fortunately, an upturn in Melbourne's economy had allowed Marian to employ a girl to come into the home three mornings a week to help with the heavier housework. Employed for almost two months, Sofia enjoyed speaking to the young Aboriginal girl, who had a quiet manner and shy smile, though she found her story confusing. She told Sofia that she'd been taken from her family when she was seven - removed from a loving family, according to Betty – and raised in a Children's Home. Her father was a 'white fella', a railway worker. Betty knew less about her mother. Indian, she had always believed, although in recent years she'd realised that her mother was most likely, Aboriginal. That would account for why she had been taken from her family. Betty told Sofia that lots of Aboriginal children were removed like this, it was quite common. Over a few weeks, Sofia gleaned that Betty and her two sisters had been collected from their school by police officers one afternoon, despite the protests of their teacher. 'The police!' Sofia had questioned, shocked. 'Whatever for?'

Betty had no idea why; however, she did know that it was commonplace. There were lots of children like her at The Home, all with the same story – a train trip, or perhaps a ride in a car; a meeting with a lady or a man, or both, who would then take them to The Home. If they cried for their Mummies and Daddies they were beaten with a cane switch. Some children were told that their parents had died; others that their mothers didn't want them. The children were constantly reminded that they were the 'Lucky Ones'. They were receiving training and would get jobs. They would have a good life. Betty was convinced that the stories she'd been told were lies. She was determined that she would find her family, but so far, she'd had no luck.

Sofia tried to make sense of Betty's story, each week returning with more questions; however, the housekeeper had become teary when Sofia asked things that she couldn't answer. 'Where was her house? What was her mother's name? Did she remember her surname?' These facts that had long since slid from Betty's memory. She wasn't even sure if she had been called Betty before she'd been taken. Seeing her distress, Sofia changed the subject, but later she asked Marian what terrible thing must have happened for Betty and her sisters to be taken by the police.

'Oh, it's for the best,' Marian explained. 'Betty will have a much better life among white people. Civilised. She will be able to earn a living now that she is trained for service.'

When Sofia asked, 'What about her family? They must miss her. They haven't seen her in years,' Marian shrugged the question aside.

'Children need to be kept warm and fed, not brought up in humpies in the bush,' she'd replied, her pursed lips indicating that that was the end of the subject. Sofia wondered if the statement was directed at her and Jack, and their rough living conditions at Montsalvat, because the house Betty had described did not sound anything at all like a 'humpy in the bush.'

More than once, Marian asked how Jack and Sofia thought that they could possibly manage an infant in the primitive conditions of Montsalvat. 'Perhaps it's time to look for your own home, somewhere closer to town,' she encouraged Jack hopefully, when they'd announced that Sofia was expecting a baby. 'Sofia could get a girl in to help.'

William also took Jack aside, expressing his concerns, even offering financial assistance if it would help. How was Sofia going to manage a baby without running water and medical assistance on hand? Wouldn't a house in the suburbs, complete with electricity, be more suitable?

'Dad! Eltham's not a desert! We do have a doctor and even a baby health clinic.'

'Yes, but what if there is an emergency?'

'Well, the colony has a car. And Lil - she is a doctor - and she's always on hand if we were to have a problem, and in any case, there won't be any problems!'

He and Sofia had repeatedly extolled the benefits to children who were fortunate enough to grow up in the bush, using Justus' and Lil's Max as an example. Now three years old, the little boy was robust and as strong as a young bull, flourishing in the healthy fresh air and with the freedom to wander unrestrained on the grounds of Montsalvat.

He did not mention his own misgivings about the 'can' down the valley for toileting, constantly overflowing and always overdue for emptying, or the thought of Sofia carting buckets of water from the well to wash nappies.

Despite the bravado Jack had adopted when deflecting William's and Marian's misgivings about the lack of amenities at Montsalvat, he was thankful when, at seven months into her pregnancy, Sofia finally stopped heaving wheelbarrows of manure to the garden beds, using the pitchfork to turn soil or carrying the heavy watering cans across the yard to ensure the seedlings had their daily drink. Instead, she limited herself to the weekday kitchen routines, spending more time with Lil and Lena. Companionship with the older women spurred a whole new collection of stories which Sofia shared with Jack each evening, both humorous and thought-provoking. Lena, never maternal herself, was suddenly full of advice on the nuances of pregnancy.

'Don't you let them put you to sleep after you go into labour,' she warned Sofia.

'Whatever do you mean, put me to sleep?'

'Oh, twilight sleep is all the rage at present. These doctors, they think that if you sleep through the delivery of the baby, it will be less painful and you won't remember a thing. It's a lot of rubbish, isn't it, Lil?'

'Yes, Sofia. I agree. Tell the doctor that you won't be having any needles. You and the baby will be much better off for it. They'll want to give you morphine and scopolamine. I am sure that it's dangerous.'

Jack and Sofia discussed the advice, and while much about the prospect of labour was a mystery to them, they agreed that it would surely be better to be awake and alert during the delivery.

Sadly, as Sofia's pregnancy advanced, the sullen moods that occasionally engulfed Helen increased in frequency. At first, Sofia had been shocked by the sudden outbursts or icy silences from her friend, so different from the open chatty manner of the younger woman she'd first known. Upset, Sofia had confided in Jack that she thought that she may have upset Helen.

'I don't know, love. Perhaps you should just ask her if everything's okay. Give her a chance to talk about it.'

However, the next day, Sofia found Helen's mood back to normal, as though nothing had happened, and when she'd asked if there were any problems, Helen just laughed and told her not to be silly, and Sofia decided that she must have imagined things. But she knew she had not imagined the cutting criticism when Helen had accused her of using her pregnancy to avoid work one day, when Sofia sat down for a few minutes because she'd felt dizzy. Jack was furious.

'She's got no right to speak to you like that, Sofia! Don't you put up with it! Should I speak to her?'

However, Sofia had considered Helen's circumstances. 'No, no, Jack. It is time for us to be understanding.'

'Understand what? That she is being nasty to you and getting away with it!'

'Jack, think about it. What has she got? A feeble sham of a relationship with Justus. How will Helen ever get married and have a family of her own while she is captured under his spell?'

Jack, preferring not to dwell on Justus' unscrupulous behaviour towards both Lil and Helen, listened silently, while Sofia continued, 'I think her moods are springing from her own unhappiness. She is sick with jealousy for what we have, Jack. I'm sure of it. Envious of our marriage and the baby. I feel so sorry for her.'

'I must say, she looks damned awful these days,' Jack offered. 'Is she ill?'

Sofia shrugged. 'She doesn't seem to be looking after herself at all. I don't know what is wrong. She smokes non-stop, and today, it was so strange. She left her feet bare, did not put her shoes on at all, even when I encouraged her to. And it was so cold! I am sure that she hasn't brushed her hair for days. I suggested to her that we go shopping – get some new dresses – her clothes are falling to rags, but she said no. Justus doesn't believe in wasting money on clothes. Huh, it's not as if he pays for her clothes, anyway. Helen has her own allowance from Lena. Who is Justus to tell her how she should spend it? I could shake that man!'

Jack was sure that Sofia was right. Helen's relationship with Justus did not make any sense to him at all. He thought about the bold, cheerful girl that Sofia had introduced him to, barely three years earlier, and considered how much she'd changed. These days, Helen seemed to be enslaved to Justus, always adhering to all manner of instructions he gave her, and neither he or Sofia could see what she gained in return from the man. Only the week before, there had been an ugly moment in the dining room when Helen had been unable to respond to the bell and serve dinner.

'Don't let this happen again, Helen,' Justus insisted, ignoring her protests that she had been unwell. The debate had gone on and on, Helen imploring Justus to be understanding, or at least tell her what she was supposed to do should she be so ill as to be unable to attend to her duties, but he'd simply maintained his stance that she must be obedient and do his will.

'In the future, when the bell rings, you must answer it.'

'But I couldn't!'

'Don't whine.'

'I'm not whining.'

'Helen, there is nothing to compel you to stay here, but while you are here, you will obey me.'

And the worst part of all was that, while everybody had listened and felt sorry for Helen, nobody had said a word.

Sofia was right. They should feel sympathy for Helen, knowing the impossible position that she was in. 'You are the most forgiving, understanding woman in the world,' Jack said, hugging her.

Sonia's reactions to the pregnancy were the opposite of her sister's, although Sofia saw less of the younger Skipper girl these days, for her work as a stonemason kept her busy. Sonia had developed a real talent for belting hammer against chisel, chipping away stone to create Gothic corbels, lintels and sculptures, based upon the sketches that Justus drew for her.

She was thrilled that her work was being used to decorate the buildings and gardens of Montsalvat, and perhaps even more pleased when Justus asked her to show some of the young men who came out to Montsalvat how to carve the stone.

'You should see their faces,' she told Jack and Sofia, her own face glowing with triumph. 'Weren't expecting some girl to be teaching them how to beat a rock into shape!'

Always sweet to them, Sonia had been excited about their baby right from the beginning. As a regular visitor to the Queen Victoria Markets, she constantly brought home gifts: tinkling rattles for a tiny fist to grip, fine woollen booties to keep little feet snug and a lovely crocheted blanket to adorn the cot, the granny squares worked from the softest of yarns, its colour; lemon, edged with a snowy white that would suit a boy or a girl.

May turned into June and each afternoon, as Jack walked home from the train station, he wondered what the day had brought for Sofia. She'd had a few bouts of mild contractions which fizzled into nothing, but each episode renewed their anticipation of labour, which was surely going to be any day now. The thought filled Jack with a combination of excitement and dread. Would Sofia have an easy time of her delivery? Would it be quick? Would their plan to telephone him at the office should her contractions commence in earnest, giving him time to get to the hospital, unfold as planned? And then he had to contend with the unwelcome reflections that intruded at the most unexpected times. His mother's miscarriage. Her mother's death. These thoughts he cast aside as quickly as they arose, but Jack could not deny the current of anxiety left in their wake, and he looked forward to the day when their baby finally arrived safely. By the end of June, Sofia's sleepless nights, rounded face and slower movements all foretold that the birth was only days away. Perhaps even hours, and Jack hesitated before leaving for work each morning, worried that the minute he'd step out of the door, Sofia would collapse into labour, with nobody there, to help her.

'Jack! It won't be like that. Don't be silly,' she'd said to him. But he wasn't so sure. The truth was that neither of them knew much at all about the business of childbirth.

CHAPTER 38

Sofia's labour started slowly, beginning with a dull ache in her lower back that caused her to stretch and reach behind her, as she tried to massage the offending area. Lena had bought a box of pears; sweet and almost ripe – perfect for preserving – and together, she and Sofia sliced them in neat crescents to be stewed in a spicy syrup and then sealed in sterilised Vacola jars.

'Ooh, I think a little person might be saying it's time to come out,' Lena said, when Sofia put down the paring knife and arch her back for the third time in an hour.

Because Sofia had already experienced a couple of false alarms, she reserved her judgement, although the cramps did seem particularly persistent this morning. However, by four pm, the steady rhythm of cramping was undeniably labour. The pains started deep in her lower abdomen, gathering intensity as they rose upward, causing her swollen bump to tighten with such pressure that she was sure it would crush her baby. She held her breath as she clung to the back of a chair, waiting for it to pass. This kind of contraction would have had her phoning Jack's office had she not known he would already be on the train home, she later told him as she relayed in minute detail the events of the afternoon. By 5:15, she'd begun doubling over every five minutes or so, the intensity of the pain like nothing she could have imagined. Sofia knew it was time to be heading to the hospital, but she desperately wanted to wait for Jack.

And so it happened that on an early June afternoon, Jack had entered the kitchen of Montsalvat to find Lil and Sonya standing beside Sofia, who looked pale and exhausted, collapsed on the low seat before the fire. A rug had fallen to the floor, used when she had been shivering with cold minutes earlier, and now cast aside as she was feeling overly warm. As Jack walked through the door, Sofia looked up at him, her tired eyes flashing a glimmer of excitement. 'Oh, Jack,' she said before suddenly pushing herself upright, and leaning against the table, closing her eyes and inhaling deeply.

For almost a minute, an atmosphere of quiet intensity filled the kitchen, all eyes on Sofia as she bore out the contraction. Sonia rubbed her lower back and Lil, with a shushing gesture towards Jack, focused on Montsalvat's small green enamel kitchen clock. The intensity receded like a slow outgoing tide with Sofia's eyes finally opening, her breathing returning to normal, Sonia's hand withdrawing, and Lil making a brief note on her paper.

Lena appeared. 'Mervyn's getting the car,' she said.

Jack could not believe how useless he felt, nor how glad he was for the presence of the women, each presenting a picture of calm competence.

'Just in time, Jack,' Lil said. 'Sofia, do you think you will be all right to walk to the carpark?'

Sofia nodded, standing, at which very moment, a sudden rush of fluid ran down her legs.

'Well, Jack, the baby is definitely on the way! Are you ready?' Lena said, as she mopped the fluid with towels she'd set aside earlier for that very purpose.

Jack knew that he would never forget the next hour for as long as he lived. The combination of helplessness and fear as he silently supported Sofia on her left, while Sonia took the right side; Lena and

Lil bringing up the rear of the procession. Lil's keen eyes scrutinised every step Sofia took and Jack was thankful for her medical training. He listened in surprise as the women laughed and joked with Sofia and was amazed when she laughed in reply, the procession moving all the while towards the carpark that today seemed to be twice its usual distance. He marvelled at how, without fuss, Lil tapped his shoulder and waved a signal to pause, reacting to Sofia's faltering step and indrawn breath, signs that were meaningless to him. He watched in fascination as, without instruction, Sonia stepped in front of Sofia and commanded her to 'Lean against me.' As the contraction hit, he heard Sofia whimper softly. Once it subsided, their slow trek to the carpark continued, finally ending at the Skipper's Holden, which Mervyn had thoughtfully driven to the closest point possible. Its engine was humming as Jack followed Lena's instructions to sit in the back before positioning Sofia against him. Lena then climbed into the front while Lil wished Sofia good luck and told her to keep her legs firmly closed until she arrived at the hospital. These women certainly seemed to know their stuff, Jack thought.

The few minutes it took to drive to Belgrave Hospital seemed endless, and when they finally arrived, Jack had gathered his wits sufficiently to point out the wheelchair in the emergency department doorway. Lena commanded Mervyn to fetch it, and he did even better, returning with a look of triumph, the wheelchair, a male wardsman and a cheerful nursing sister following. A picture of reassuring competence in her blue-striped dress and winged veil, wielding authority like an army sergeant, the nursing sister had Sofia whisked out of the car, into the chair and out of sight within seconds. The Skippers departed home after telling Jack that they would cool the champagne and cut the cigars, and he paced the floor outside the labour room, glancing impatiently at its broad, foreboding door. After twenty minutes, he started knocking on the white panel, desperate for information about Sofia's progress. He was repeatedly reassured that the midwife would let him know as soon as there was any news and told to sit tight. It was clear that fathers were not a welcome addition to the labour ward.

At 11:30 pm, a tightly bundled infant with bright blue eyes and a lusty cry landed in Jack's arms.

'Look after this little tiger,' the nurse said. 'Just a few more minutes and you can see Mrs Tomlinson.'

Jack's throat constricted with emotion and tears filled his eyes as he peered at the angry little face, framed by the blue swaddling, its mouth opened, the sound of a tiny engine roaring emitting from its depths.

'Shhh....' The croon came naturally and seemed to work, for within seconds the wailing engine stalled and a pair of curious blue eyes momentarily studied him, before closing. Jack examined the tiny eyelids that formed perfect arcs; dark eyelashes resting on sweet, smooth, rounded cheeks. A button of a nose and a little mouth that repeated tiny sucking movements. So utterly perfect! He sat gazing at the baby for almost ten minutes. His baby! His and Sofia's! Now, at last, they were a family!

'You can come in now, Mr Tomlinson.' The nurse's words interrupted his reverie and he followed her through the doorway and along the corridor.

'We've moved her back to the ward now. She is doing very well.'

Sofia smiled at Jack as he approached the bed, her hair now brushed with loose curls cascading over her shoulders. She looked beautiful, her yellow nightgown fresh, her eyes glimmering with jubilation that almost masked the residual pallor in her cheeks from the ordeal of childbirth. She reached out to take the baby from him.

Jack again felt tears threaten. He was overwhelmingly relieved to see Sofia looking so well, for the hour of pacing in the labour room had proven to be fertile ground for haunting memories of tragedy to fester, particular those of her mother's death in childbirth.

'He's beautiful,' he whispered. 'You are beautiful. Are you okay? Was it too terrible?'

'No, Jack. No, it was okay. He is a big baby and he did not seem to be too anxious to get here, but Sister Lambeth gave him a firm talking-to!'

'Still Scott...?' Jack asked, referring to the name they had decided upon should their child be a boy.

A few months earlier, he had suggested they call a boy Andrés, but Sofia had resisted.

'Too much sadness. How about Scott?'

During the later stages of her pregnancy, she had been enthralled by *The Curious Case of Benjamin Button*, determinedly mastering the English text and only occasionally needing to check the meaning of a sentence with Jack. F Scott Fitzgerald had written it, and Sofia had recalled the kind young man, straddled with that horrible wife, whom they'd met in Paris, almost six years earlier. Jack was in full agreement, remembering the author's compliments for both his and Andrés' paintings, how genuine he'd been in his wishes for their success. Now, that evening in Paris was a distant memory. A time when none of them could have foreseen the path ahead of them: Andrés, tragically gone; he and Sofia married, residing on the other side of the world, living on an artists' colony. Calling their baby Scott would be a way of resurrecting a little bit of the 'Paris magic' into their lives.

CHAPTER 39

*S*cott proved to be a delightful baby with an ever-present, gummy smile and bright, watchful eyes. He eagerly clung to the arms reaching down to lift him from the mat Sofia laid out on the kitchen floor or alongside her in the garden. For hours, he'd chuckle at flapping curtains or when outdoors, the leaves waving against the blue sky, hands clutching at the air before him, tiny feet kicking his blankets free. Scotty hated their stranglehold on his limbs. However, he was prone to bouts of colic. Despite endless doses of gripe water, the best solution to relieve the pains was to hold him upright, where he happily nestled his head into a willing shoulder as his eyes became heavy. The blue eyes he was born with rapidly evolved into liquid pools of dark brown, inherited from his mother. Sofia claimed that, when Scott gazed at her with that solemn expression, he looked just like Andrés, and they frequently reflected on how sad it was that he would never know his *tio*, the uncle with the gift for entertaining small children, who would have adored him.

It was hardly surprising that Matchum extracted Scotty's first smile, for he spent hours making faces at the infant, determined to claim victory to that particular milestone. As weeks turned to months,

Matchum loved hoying Scott into his arms, shouting 'Come to Tío Matchum,' adopting the Spanish title for uncle and disregarding Sofia's laughing protests that she'd just put Scotty down to sleep, or just fed him, or just quietened him. As Scott began to move, Matchum delighted in chasing the crawling baby under tables and having him squealing by playing monsters and tickling games and hide and seek.

That is, unless Jack was around, for he claimed Scott at every opportunity – holding him, feeding him, bathing him and changing him. Jack prided himself on being the one who could settle Scott best, when colicky tummy pains had him screaming, administering the gripe water then placing him over his shoulder and rubbing his tiny little back.

While Sofia was never far from him, Scott was happy to be passed around to Lil, Lena, Sonia and Arthur - even Mervyn, who demonstrated a real knack for handling infants. They all reached out to take little Scotty, as he became affectionately known, from Sofia's arms at every opportunity.

Even Justus was happy to bounce the baby on his lap on occasion, looking every bit as proud as if he were Scotty's grandfather, smiling fondly at the latest member of his growing family. However, the minute that Scott's smile faltered, Justus quickly passed him back to Jack or Sofia.

The weekends bought a new round of pseudo aunts and uncles for Scotty as the Queen Street students arrived with clothing and toys. They loved calling to him while he crawled among them in the dry grass, sucking on leaves, dirt and insects, chuckling as he dodged from reaching arms that attempted to halt his movements.

Justus' interest in Freud's psychoanalytical theories extended to raising children, and he believed himself and Lil to be experts on the subject. However, Justus' refusal to see Max disciplined did not prove to be a popular child-rearing model, for everyone suffered Max's screams that rang across Montsalvat whenever he didn't get his way.

Nonetheless, oblivious to his own child's very evident shortcomings, Justus regularly offered advice. For one, he thought Sofia's visits to the clinic, operating in Eltham every Tuesday morning to check on the local babies' weights and administer injections, were unnecessary nonsense.

'What's with this running back and forth to the baby clinic?' he asked Sofia one morning as she settled Scotty into the large pram, ready to walk him into town. 'All they'll do is look for problems and tell you that you aren't doing things right.'

'No, Justus, they are very helpful. Plus, I love talking to the other mothers and seeing all of the babies play together.'

'Well, Lil never needed any battle-axe nursing sister telling her how to raise Max,' Justus said.

Sofia ignored his rude comments.

'I'm not going to let him tell me what to do, Jack. He may think he can have Helen and the other women under his thumb, but not me. Thinks he's an expert on everything!'

'No, love, don't worry about him. You make your own decisions. Justus just likes to have an opinion about everything. Now that he's had his say, he'll leave you alone.'

Jack knew how much Sofia enjoyed her weekly visits to Eltham to attend the Baby Health Clinic. There she'd seek solutions for Scott's continuing colic, check whether she should be worried about a new rash and measure the progress of his weight, length and teeth formation against the nurse's charts. She loved this time, spent sharing stories about sleepless nights, and comparing Scott's development milestones with the other young mothers.

'The nurse is no battle-axe at all, but sweet and kind. And I love watching Scotty play with the other babies. He loves it too!' Sofia persisted.

Jack smiled his agreement, for he enjoyed the stories Sofia brought home to him each week after her visits to the clinic and was glad to see her making friends with the local mothers. Often, when they were down the street together, Sofia would introduce him to Muriel or Lillian or Elizabeth and their infants. He wished that Justus would confine his thoughts to art and the building projects, sometimes. Then life would be perfect.

Notwithstanding, Jack and Sofia agreed with Justus' and Lil's advice that babies should be allowed to free to crawl around on the grass and climb up against rocks and tree stumps, unrestrictedly exploring their environment without endless fears about germs and things that might scratch and bite.

Winter days gave way to the fineness of spring and then the long, hot days of summer were upon them again. By mid-April, Scotty was standing up, his chubby little legs wobbling as he clamoured around and got into everybody's way, but nobody cared. He was happy and healthy, and as Lil had hoped, proved to be a great playmate for Max. He drew out a rare sweetness in the five-year-old, who was frequently prone to tantrums.

Jack knew, without doubt, that he was a lucky man. He had a lovely wife and a beautiful, healthy baby, and he adored them both. Coming home each afternoon was a joy and he loved everything about being a husband and father.

He and Sofia continued their Monday visits to his parents' house, where Marian had set up a cot for Scotty in Jack's old bedroom. He enjoyed seeing his parents in their role as grandparents, and occasionally he and Sofia spent whole weekends with them, giving William a chance to play with his little grandson. Jack saw a different side to his father these days, as he produced a tiny cricket bat and laughed delightedly at Scotty's attempts to hit the ball that he rolled along the ground to him, or let Scotty hold the garden hose and help him water the plants. Each week there were new toys for him – a little scooter or a spinning top. Marian loved to buy Scotty picture books, reading them to him before giving them to Sofia to take home to Montsalvat. Sometimes Sofia would leave Scotty with Marian for a few hours and slip into the city for some shopping; other times, she would put him in the pram and walk the streets.

'Jack, I met some Spanish people today! They are lovely!' She told him about the older couple, Geronimo and Lavito, who had a small restaurant in Russell Street. He'd laughed when she'd insisted that he come with her to meet them and heard the pride in her voice when she introduced him. Jack had been excited for her, seeing her joy at connecting with Spanish people who treated Scotty with such affection, as though he were their grandchild.

Occasionally, they met up with Margaret, or she came to visit them. She insisted that Scott must call her Aunty Margaret, and was delighted at his version – Aunty Marty. He loved her, squealing as she swooped on him and cuddled him, telling him that he was her very own special baby!

'I'm not a baby,' he giggled as she tickled him.

'Yes, you are, you are my very own special baby, and I am taking you home with me!'

'No, you're not,' he'd wail, even as he laughed, knowing that she was teasing him.

'Yes, I am... I need a little boy at my house... I'm lonely living there all by myself... You have to come and keep me company!'

It pleased Jack to know that Scotty was surrounded by so many loving people, between himself and Sofia, Matchum, Sonia and the rest of the Montsalvat community, his parents, Geronimo and Lavita, and of course, Margaret. His boy was strong and robust, with his sturdy little legs running everywhere, following Max into one form of mischief or another.

Sofia did, however, draw the line at Scott being offered sips of beer – a common practice at Montsalvat, where Max had been receiving mouthfuls of foaming amber since he was old enough to smile a toothy grin and lisp 'Thip...thip...' to anyone who'd listen. As he'd got older,

Justus often perched Max on his knee, where he'd sit sipping a glass of beer mixed with lemonade, through a straw.

Sofia did not support the practice, however, which Jack learned in one swift lesson.

It had been a long morning, with a group of men working on Montsalvat's front fence, digging holes for posts and setting the rails ready for palings to be attached. Justus had decided that he was sick of the sightseers who drove up the hill and into the grounds for no good reason and had thought that a fence might slow the stickybeaks down.

The day had been warm, and at mid-afternoon, the men paused to enjoy a cold beer under the trees. That was when Max and Scotty had appeared, immediately climbing onto their fathers' laps. The sight of Max sipping from his father's glass inspired Scottie, who'd turned to Jack, his hands reaching for his beer, and Jack had indulgently allowed him a tiny sip. It caused Scotty to cough, his eyes watering, unused to the fizzy amber liquid.

'That'll put hairs on the little man's chest,' said Jimmy, a friendly fellow who had been part of the building team for about six weeks now. He had taken quite a shine to the young boys, loving to play like a monster, roaring at them and chasing them when they least expected it.

Before Jack had a chance to reply, Sofia's voice cut through the air like a knife. 'What are you doing, Jack? Here, let me take him!'

He jolted, surprised by her uncommon display of anger.

'This is not to happen, Jack. Little children should not be drinking beer. Scotty, time for your nap.' Scotty screamed his protest as Sofia grasped him firmly and set off down the hill, and Jack shrugged as he looked into the sympathetic eyes of the men. 'Oops. I suspect I haven't heard the last of that,' he said sheepishly.

Later, apologising for this uncharacteristic public outburst, Sofia told him that it was not suitable for small children to be drinking alcohol. Furthermore, she was sure that many evenings when Max fell asleep on the floor among the legs of the adults at the table, nights when Justus threw the snoring child over his shoulders and carried him off to bed, the boy was more than a little drunk.

he construction of buildings at Montsalvat progressed with extraordinary speed, enhanced by the high-spirited enthusiasm and muscle power of Justus' art students. Jack was amazed by the Master's unfailing ability to induce a continuous stream of wide-eyed devotees to Eltham, all inspired by his progressive anti-establishment views, delivered alongside theories of colour and tone and interspersed with scathing tirades against the Melbourne art establishment. Arriving by the carload, they eagerly attacked all manner of tasks with zeal, encouraged by the sight of the buildings rising out of the Australian bush like a medieval European village.

From their shiny-eyed ardour, Jack knew that Montsalvat had evolved to mystical proportions. It was as if their very own utopia was emerging before their eyes. They were disciples to a dream that was intertwined with the charismatic personality of the Master. Justus was Montsalvat. Montsalvat was Justus.

Jack understood their devotion to both Justus and his vision, for he, too, felt it. Certainly, Justus was always at his best and most brilliant when he had a gathering of these fresh young minds around him, sounding every bit the embodiment of a modern-day oracle.

Nonetheless, Jack and Sofia were learning more about the darker side of Jorgensen's leadership. For example, should anyone else be opinionated or charismatic, Justus would cut them down without a thought. His oldest friend, Colin, who often joined them for Sunday dinner, would have the guests in fits of laughter, regaling them with improbable tales of his time in Paris or some love affair that had gone badly, when suddenly Justus would rebuke him sharply. While the diners fell into embarrassed silence, Colin always laughed good-naturedly, never taking offence. Not everybody's armour was so resistant to the piercing thrusts of Justus' tongue, though, and repeatedly Mervyn fell prey to this spiteful aspect of the Master's personality.

Jack and Sofia often spoke of Mervyn, and Sofia, having spent many hours working in the garden with him, was particularly concerned about the gently-spoken man.

'He's lost his family, Jack,' she'd lament, and Jack could not deny the truth of this. Lena, mad about art, always nodded enthusiastically in agreement with anything that the Master uttered, be it about painting, the building programs or matters affecting her own family. Her devotion to Mervyn was beyond question – at the first sign of illness, she was quick to coddle him like a dependent child, rising like a rescuing phoenix and gliding into action to minister to his ailments. But it was apparent to all that it was Justus whom Lena respected. It was his opinion she sought when deciding whether Matchum should be allowed to go into Melbourne with the local lads for a night out or whether Sonia should apply to the technical college to do an upholstery course; matters that really should be decided by herself and Mervyn.

It was clear to Jack and Sofia that Mervyn had never fully recovered since the nasty altercation back in October, on the day Marian and William had unexpectedly arrived at Montsalvat. Ever since that time, on the nights when Justus was home, Mervyn sat quietly at the dinner table, avoiding drawing attention to himself, lost in his thoughts. To his credit, Justus did make some effort to be pleasant. He'd thank Mervyn for typing up the dialogues and ask how his work was going. Perhaps it was this kindly interest Justus displayed that inspired Mervyn to let down his guard, one fateful evening.

Jack was surprised when Mervyn chose to speak up during dinner, clearing his throat before his soft voice commanded the attention of the table.

'Justus, I've got news for you,' he ventured. 'I'm resigning from *The Bulletin* – I'm going to start a paper of my own.'

'Really? What makes you want to give up a good job like that?' Justus asked, and Jack immediately recognised the sarcasm lacing his words that foretold this conversation was not going to go well.

It was easy to see that this was not the reaction Mervyn expected and the poor man became flustered and incoherent in his efforts to explain the decision.

'Well, I hate the job. It is nauseating, attending endless plays and films, most of them nonsense or just plain tedious. I can't bear the thought of sitting through them any longer, much less having to write some commentary on them.'

'What? Do they bore you? Or perhaps it's that your writing is boring and no one is interested in what you have to say anymore. Have people stopped reading your articles, Mervyn? Is that what it is? Heavens, who could blame them?'

Jack squirmed. He hated it when Justus behaved so cruelly and hoped the conversation would quickly revert to a more pleasant subject. Trying to think of something to say that would divert the Master from his attack, no words came. However, Mervyn found words, which he furiously flung across the table at Justus.

'Why do you always ridicule everything I do?' he cried, spittle flying off his lips.

'Because you are ridiculous, Mervyn. Look at you – red in the face and behaving like a child. How do you expect me to respect you when you go on like this?' Justus had slipped into possibly his most malicious persona, a picture of smug, relaxed calm, and Mervyn was inflamed to breaking point.

'Damn you, you bastard! Damn you!' Mervyn cried, his chair

scraping and keeling, precariously, as he pushed away from the table and rushed from the room.

Jack rarely reacted to the Master's behaviour at the table, but tonight he could not help himself.

'That was a little harsh, Justus, don't you think?' He could feel the stillness settle over the table as everyone looked from him to Justus. Spats between Justus and Mervyn were frequent, but Jack? Nobody had ever heard him question the Master before. He sensed Sofia stiffen beside him and sensed that she was holding her breath.

Jack, however, knew he was on solid ground. Justus' words had been cruel. Mervyn was a good man. Something needed to be said. He did not falter as his gaze met Justus', patiently awaiting a response, refusing to look away as the older man returned his examination through hooded eyes. Seconds passed, and the tension at the table increased, yet Jack did not care. He'd asked a question and he wanted to hear Justus' answer.

Jack did not know whether the Master truly realised that he had gone too far with Mervyn, or whether he'd not wanted to offend Jack, but he managed to look contrite and self-deprecating.

'Oh, he brings out the worst in me every time. Always whimpering and complaining.'

'Mervyn's a decent man, Justus. Very helpful around here. He's done wonders, helping Sofia and Helen down in the garden. And he spends hours, creating notes for you – The Dialogues. He deserves some respect.'

'Yes, Jack. You are quite right. Lena…apologise to Mervyn for me, will you? And tell him that it's a good idea to quit *The Bulletin*. It's a rubbish newspaper, anyway.'

It was a double-edged apology, but Jack knew that it was about as good as Justus would ever offer, and accepted it.

It was only a matter of weeks before Mervyn again instigated a dinner table debacle, this time directed towards both Justus and Arthur Munday. However, such were the circumstances that it was Sonia who became the subject of Jack and Sofia's musings.

Rostered onto dinner duties, Sonia had carefully placed a large platter of roasted vegetables on the table when Arthur playfully reached out and patted her on the backside. Mervyn's reaction was immediate. 'Keep your dirty paws off my daughter!' he hissed, his face reddening.

Arthur just laughed, holding his hands up to Mervyn in a gesture of retreat, and Sonia said, 'Dad…it's okay. Art did nothing wrong!'

'Well, he's always ogling you. It's not right. He's twice your age.'

Justus, perhaps taking the comment a tad personally given his relationship with Helen, could not help himself. 'Give it up, Mervyn. Sonia is a beautiful young woman and ripe for picking. It will be good for her to have a lover.'

Mervyn's response was physical. Slamming his chair back with a clatter, he rose quickly – almost staggering, he was so angry.

'I refuse to listen to such lecherous rubbish! It's obscene!' he shouted. 'It's not right for you old men – married men,' he emphasised, glaring at Justus, 'to be preying on young girls in this way.'

When Sonia returned from the kitchen, she seated herself next to Arthur, rather than taking her usual place, and it occurred to Jack that for the last few weeks this had been where Sonia sat. Her look towards Munday, a reassuring smile, said it all, and Jack's heart thumped. Could Sonia be involved with the good-looking, Arthur Munday? Apparently so!

That night, lying side-by-side, Jack and Sofia considered this latest revelation, amazed that the girl – for indeed that was all Sonia was – could have fallen for Munday.

Although much older, Munday was undoubtedly charming. And he had been working closely with Sonia over the last few months while she taught him the skills of stonemasonry. Nobody had thought a thing about it. Just about everyone had attempted to convert rock into artful decorations under Sonia's tutelage; the girl had proved to be a total natural. She had a gift for reading the raw stone and seemed to know just where the blade should be applied and how much pressure to allow when whacking the heavy mallet against the head of the chisel. As a result, carvings, albeit bearing varying degrees of finesse, adorned Montsalvat's buildings and grounds. Half-completed heads, distorted and fractured, lay abandoned in the rock pile, roughly hewn urns and decorative tiles served as garden ornaments and better works – mostly Sonia's – decorated the roofs and doors of the many buildings.

But Sonia and Munday as lovers! He was twice her age! All of the Montsalvat residents were privy to Munday's history of depression. His attempted suicide. That was why he'd come to Montsalvat. To heal. He donated the sale of his legal practice to Justus, in return receiving art lessons and a home for the rest of his life.

Jack had never really felt close to the ex-lawyer, yet he liked the way the scruffy, outspoken younger Skipper girl was always quick to speak up against injustices and defend her beliefs. She had become quite attached to both him and Sofia, and often joined them in their van for an hour or so after dinner, to chat over a cup of hot cocoa. She was endlessly fascinated by Sofia's heritage and loved to talk about his and Sofia's time in Paris and Spain.

For a seventeen-year-old, Sonia had spunk in spades. She often had Jack and Sofia in fits of laughter with her outrageous opinions and total disregard for social conventions, status or gender. While perhaps not quite so beautiful as Helen, Sonia – thankfully - also lacked the moodiness of her older sister. He and Sofia learned that life in the Skipper family was not the ideal they'd imagined. Although sisters, Helen and Sonia had shared none of the closeness Jack would have expected, when they were young. Sonia had been a loner, close to her father perhaps, but she and Helen had argued so much as young girls that Lena had sent them to different schools.

'I think Sonia is looking for someone to show an interest in her.

That is why she comes to us – we don't judge her. Sonia feels safe here,' Sofia said to Jack. 'Really, for all of Lena's openness, I believe she neglected her children. Left them to their own devices while she focused on her art and social life.' It was clear the girls had grown up in an adult world with little supervision, and often, Sonia sat at Jack and Sofia's small table, rocking Scotty from side to side while regaling them with stories of married men who'd pursued her, trying to steal a kiss or fondle her well-developed breasts, when she was as young as fourteen. Lena, busy with her art, friends and trips to plays and concerts, or tending to Mervyn's health needs, lacked both the time and interest to take the responsibility of raising her daughters too seriously. Far easier to treat Helen and Sonia as adults, giving them a pound a week to manage their wardrobe and learn life's lessons by experience rather than thoughtful and protective maternal nurturing

Sofia was speechless when Sonia explained that, just like for Helen, her mother had taken her to Lil to discuss contraception when she'd turned sixteen; that Lil had fitted her with a diaphragm and encouraged Sonia to wear it 'like a piece of clothing, just in case.'

Feeling it her duty, in the manner of an older sister, Sofia questioned Sonia's attraction for Munday at the first opportunity.

'Well, it's not so much that I love him,' Sonia explained. 'It's just that he is someone I can call my own. He likes me. The town boys aren't interested in me. I'm far too wild. That's what their mothers tell them. Of course, they're happy for a grope. Wouldn't dare to be seen with me in public, though. Anyway, they're so dull. Not a brain between them.

'Arthur is sweet. He takes me seriously when I talk. Plus, now I'm with him, the old geezers keep their paws to themselves.'

As Sofia relayed Sonia's words, Jack felt saddened by the situation. Surely, Sonia should have a boyfriend that was closer to her age. 'It's all a bit difficult, really, Sofia. She's happy. Arthur's happy. I guess it's up to Lena and Mervyn to work it out with her. Not our business!'

~

Jack lay awake for the fifth night in a row, sleep being elusive, as his mind raged in turmoil, struggling to comprehend the recent disclosures of the colony.

The light knock on the door came as a surprise, and he moved quickly, hoping to answer it without disturbing Sofia. However, always a light sleeper, and even more so since she had the responsibilities of motherhood, she sat up as he went down the stairs.

Opening the door, Jack found Sonia silhouetted in the darkness. Her voice sounded strange as she spoke, quivering, her words edged with barely restrained anger.

'Is Sofia up? I need to speak to her.'

Appearing at his side, Sofia nodded quietly. She ushered Sonia to the table while Jack found a candle, which he lit and placed between the women before turning to leave.

'Jack, stay. Please. I would love your advice on this, too, if you don't mind,' Sonia asked, and Jack sat on the wooden bench beside Sofia.

They never discovered whether Sonia had abandoned the advice she'd been given to wear her diaphragm regularly, or if it had utterly failed in its purpose. Regardless, at nine-thirty that night, across the candlelit table, Sonia revealed to Jack and Sofia that she'd not had a period for almost two months. And judging by the nausea washing over her as soon as she placed her legs over the side of the bed each morning, it was clear that she was pregnant.

Jack was amazed, as much by the manner of Sonia's disclosure, as he was by the news itself. Her matter-of-fact approach to the pregnancy and her lack of regard for the contempt she'd encounter carrying a baby out of wedlock surprised him. Certainly, she'd been listening to lively discussions about sex all of her life. Furthermore, she'd learnt to disdain ill-serving social mores. Nonetheless, finding herself pregnant could not be easy, and Jack admired Sonia's determination to take responsibility for her actions – hers and Munday's, that was - and stare boldly into the eyes of anyone who dared to scorn her. She explained to Jack and Sofia how a baby born to loving, caring parents had all that mattered, and 'who gave a damn about what the gossips may say?'

The anger that Jack had noticed when Sonia had first arrived and whose embers had flickered amid her controlled retelling of the facts returned. Nothing to do with the pregnancy, which Sonia was resigned to, but rather, the root of her anger sat squarely with the 'father-to-be' with whom, Sonia admitted, she'd just had a blazing row.

'Of course, you'll have to get rid of it," she'd relayed, her voice adopting a pompous, superior tone that Arthur had used when she had told him of her condition.

'What am I? A dim-witted child who cannot deal with my own problems?' Sonia asked, looking from Jack to Sofia. 'And then, if that wasn't enough, he said that I should tell Justus!' She had again mimicked Arthur's patronising tone. '"He'll know what to do!" he told me.

"Tell Justus? What has he got to do with anything?" I asked Arthur – pathetic man! Can't form a single thought without asking the Master's permission!'

Jack and Sofia had listened and the trio drank hot cocoa and talked well into the night, mainly about the joy babies brought and how nice it would be for the two-year-old Scotty to have a little mate. Sonia had no misgivings about the unexpected pregnancy. It was Arthur's pathetic response that had made her furious.

Nonetheless, Sonia did go to Justus the very next morning. That evening, again seated at Jack's and Sofia's table, she laughingly relayed the outcome of the meeting, explaining how, standing at the door of his studio as he worked on yet another self-portrait, she had just wanted to run. Her greater fear was not of disclosing her pregnant state but, rather, of interrupting the Master at work!

'You know what he's like when he's painting,' she said. 'It's like baiting a lion in its den. I wondered why I was bothering. 'But, like a fool, I knocked and waited. *"Yes? What do you want?"* he called out to me, without so much as looking up from his easel. *"I'm pregnant,"* I told him. I didn't see any sense in beating around the bush. Do you?" Jack and Sofia didn't know what to say. 'Well - he was quiet for a minute then said, in that barking manner of his, *"What do you expect me to do? I have no interest in domestic matters. I am not a counsellor, nor an obstetrician."* That's just, exactly what I'd thought he'd say; that it was none of his business, and I told him that I agreed - it was between me and Munday. That it was Munday who'd sent me to speak to him. That I was quite happy to sort it all out for myself. And so, I left him to it. Rude man! Really, he might have shown a little bit of interest, don't you think?'

Jack did not know what to think. Everything about Sonia's pregnancy was wrong, to him. Everything about her relationship with Arthur was wrong. He had never thought much of the man, and at this minute, wasn't sure that he didn't despise him.

After Sonia had left, Jack and Sofia continued to discuss her situation between themselves. 'Good on her for being so brave about it,' Sofia said. 'What a shame Munday is not showing a bit more interest. I'm sure he could have handled this so much better.'

'Yes,' Jack had replied thoughtfully. 'Although I cannot help but think that, while Sonia is pleased Justus is staying out of things, my guess is that we haven't heard the end of it yet.' And he was right.

It was the following Friday evening, the table full as the first of the weekenders had arrived, when the matter of Sonia's pregnancy received a public airing. Jack was not surprised. He had warned Sofia that Justus, who always had an opinion on everything, would have something to say.

As the meal finished, the Master launched into his usual monologue. Slow to warm up, he rambled from one thought to the next. This time about the colony and his image as the leader, renowned in Melbourne's art circles. The importance of reputation for the Meldrumites. How the memory of the 1930 tragedy still lingered in some minds, quick to resurrect the scandal of Molly Dean's murder at any opportunity.

As Justus continued, his monologue converged towards a clear and present dilemma. An unmarried woman in their midst, pregnant. Sonia. Whether she and Arthur should marry. Alternatively, should she be forced to leave the colony?

'Sonia, if you don't marry Arthur, you will have no rights to the baby at all. It will be Arthur's,' Lil offered. "You don't want that, do you?'

'Why on earth would she marry anybody, if she doesn't bloody-well want to?' Sue asked.

Mervyn, not happy with Justus, Arthur or Sonia at this stage, looked at his daughter. 'Well, love, you've made your bed... I guess now you're just going to have to lie in it.'

Justus, who had been silent while others bandied their opinions across the table, spoke. 'I think that there is only one solution - you will have to leave, Sonia. We cannot have the reputation of Montsalvat ruined by the presence of illegitimate children.'

The table went silent as everybody absorbed his words.

'Justus, this is Sonia's home. You can't just throw her out.' Sofia, shock in her voice, could not restrain herself.

'Yes, Justus. If people want to talk, let them. It is Sonia's and Arthur's business. No one else's' added Sue.

'Have you thought about a termination?' Lil suggested. 'I'm sure that I could find someone who would do it.'

'No, no, Lil. That would not be right,' said Justus. 'There's nothing to it, Sonia. You and Arthur will have to get married.'

After half an hour of going nowhere, Sonia had finally had enough. Looking across the table at Munday, who sat low in his seat, his shoulders hunched, his face long, eyes lowered in helpless misery, and who hadn't contributed a single word to the discussion, she exploded.

'Do you want to marry me?' she asked, eyes blazing.

Looking at Sonia with a baleful expression, Mundy's silence spoke louder than any words.

Sonia concluded the matter. 'Well, I don't want to marry you, either. And I won't. Nor will I be getting rid of it, so stick that in your pipe and smoke it.' And with a withering glare directed towards Justus, she stood up and swept out of the room, plunging the table into stunned silence.

'I could have cheered,' Sofia later told Jack, and he agreed. It was a memorable moment at the dinner table of Montsalvat, that was for sure.

Funny how the sun, moon and stars lined up because, over the next few days of quiet whisperings, coupled with stony silences as everyone wondered about Sonia's fate, a second controversy erupted, so extraordinary that it cast a new light on the impossibly awkward situation.

CHAPTER 41

The patter of soft rain woke Jack in the early hours of Saturday morning, its drumming steadily increasing in volume until it became a thunderous deluge against the roof's corrugations. He listened to the water flowing down the metal channels and spilling onto the ground below, transforming the bare soil outside their doorway into slimy mud.

Racing outside, he placed their wooden chairs under the eaves and collected pots, toys and the cane wash-basket and moved them to shelter. He and Sofia watched the rain pour from the sky. The saturated earth could hold no more water and the puddles grew larger. Linking, they formed rivulets, meandering as they streamed across the yard, and hopefully, made their way into the dam – where the water would later hydrate the cow, chickens and garden.

There would be no building work today, Jack knew, and glad to settle into their cabin for the day, he built a fire in the small pot-bellied stove while Sofia mixed a heavy batter, which sizzled as she dropped spoonfuls onto their heavy iron skillet. By eight am, they sat close to the fire, cups of hot tea in their hands, a plate full of buttery drop-scones dripping with golden syrup before them. Scotty drove his small wooden truck across the tiles while making a vrooming sound, and Jack sighed with satisfaction. For all of the dramas that seemed to befall the lives of others, regularly played out at the dining room table, his and Sofia's life within these four walls was simple. Rustic, perhaps, but good. Happy. Maybe today he would put up some shelves for Sofia and draw a plan for a bench he wanted to make for her, an indoor washstand for their small kitchen. Then they could eat their breakfast here, rather than going across to the kitchen.

Sofia's contentment mirrored his own, even as they revisited the heated conversation that had arisen over the table last night. Both were shocked by the varied reactions to Sonia's pregnancy. That Justus would even think that Sonia should leave Montsalvat if she didn't marry Arthur beggared belief. Where would she live? And how on earth could Sonia marry Munday, if he didn't want to marry her? Why would she even want to marry a man who did not want to marry her?

'I think that Sonia should just go ahead and have the baby,' Sofia said.

'Justus won't throw her out…he wouldn't risk upsetting Lena. I'm sure the Skippers' financial contributions will help Justus see reason.'

'And when Arthur sees the baby, of course, he'll want it,' Jack added. He could not imagine any man rejecting his child.

Traditionalists at heart, both he and Sofia were confident that, after the baby was born, a wedding would ensue and all would be made right.

By noon, everybody was outdoors, attending to the clean-up, their old spirit of camaraderie palpable as they worked together, their cheerful banter making Friday evening's dinner-table conflict seem a distant memory. The sunshine and clear wintery sky were glorious and the few students who'd set up camp for the weekend helped Matchum and Jack as they cleaned the mud off the entry of the kitchen, draped sodden canvas tents across tree branches and re-stood the collapsed caravan annexes. For all of the sticky mud underfoot, the deluge had cleansed the roofs and walls and windows better than any elbow grease could have achieved, and every surface glistened. The natural world seemed enchanted as the tiniest of movements set the long grass trembling and tree branches waving, causing a thousand tiny diamonds to shimmer as the sunlight glanced off the droplets on a thousand leaves and an equal number of minuscule cobwebs. If little fairies appeared dancing around the mushrooms that had sprung forth overnight, and elves with pointy green caps had railed at the kookaburras swooping down to garnish the fat worms wriggling through the mud, nobody would have been surprised.

Sofia worked in the kitchen - she and Sue dicing parsnips and carrots, string beans and searing cubes of beef for, following the enforced solitude of the last forty-eight hours, everyone was in the mood for a feast.

Seated in their usual place, Jack smiled at Sofia wryly, and the look she returned implied that she shared his flash of apprehension. It was as though the chairs and the table and the sideboard and even the cutlery and crockery remembered the ugly scene of Friday night, even if the residents may have chosen to brush it aside.

'Here we go,' Jack whispered to her half-jokingly, and the general quiet that descended over the group suggested that they were not the only ones who had a sense of lingering trepidation as they recalled their last meal at this table. However, they need not have worried, for Justus was in a wonderful mood. At his best. Expansive, laughing and joking. Benevolent, thankful for the work everybody had put in that day. He complimented Sue and Sofia on their extraordinary beef bourguignon and even offered to top up Mervyn's wine glass. As the meal ended, Justus cleared his throat, drawing attention to himself – a common occurrence, for he certainly loved his after-dinner dialogues. Tonight, however, he opened by saying that he had an important announcement.

Everybody looked towards him, expressions of surprise on their faces. Justus did not usually prepare his audience for an announcement. Instead, it was a given that everything he said mattered; the very act of him opening his mouth to utter a thought carried weight.

He cleared his throat a second time. Something momentous was at hand, surely, for the Master appeared a little sheepish, as if unsure of how to begin.

He did not hesitate for long, though. Once beginning, Justus' sentences gathered steam. His tone was well-modulated, the volume of his phrases rising and falling, artfully engaging his audience, arousing their curiosity, persuading them to believe in him; to accept the logic that flew in the face of convention; that would have the world shaking their heads and railing at the lifestyle of the Meldrumites.

'And so it is…' came the crux of his endless preamble. 'Montsalvat is going to have a second baby. Like Sonia's, also due in about eight months. The two new additions, added to Jack's and Sofia's Scotty, and our own little Max, will form the solid basis of Montsalvat's next generation.' Justus looked thrilled by his announcement.

'Whose baby?' Jack looked around the table, mystified.

Not Lena's, of course. Surely not Lil's, whose health was unreliable, and what with her counselling practice - would she want another child? Sonia…well, indeed she was pregnant - that was not news. Sofia? He looked at her questioningly as Justus spoke.

'Why Helen's, of course! Imagine! They say that sisters sometimes cycle in the same pattern!' Justus was wide-eyed, apparently enthralled by the marvellous rhythms of nature.

Helen pregnant! Justus' baby? The collective gasp was audible as the news drifted into the air and then settled onto the diners, one by one. Jack looked at Sofia. Her expression was a mask, her face as blank as his own, as if they'd conspired to conceal their reactions for the present time. Sue, seated across from Jack, looked furious and her hand clutched at her knife in an unnatural manner. Did she want to stab someone? Sonia looked startled as she looked at Helen in disbelief. Lena's eyes were directed somewhere toward the salt shaker at the centre of the table, her gaze calm and steady. Jack guessed that she already knew of Helen's pregnancy. Mervyn looked thunderous. His chair rattled as he pushed it back, rose and left the room, his hunched shoulders and stumbling gait suggesting that this conversation - indeed the very act of standing - was simply too much to bear. Lil's eyes were unwavering; fixed on Justus. Steely? Stony? Jack could not decipher her expression, nor could he begin to imagine her thoughts. And Helen? She also gazed towards Justus. Pleadingly? Certainly, she looked less sure of the theory that he espoused with such confidence. She repeatedly glanced downward, avoiding Jack's eyes, and those of anybody else. Was she as stoic and confident to proceed with her pregnancy as Sonia was? Was she prepared to stare down the social conventions that scorned single mothers as if they alone were responsible for the babies that grew in their wombs, judging them as morally depraved and a threat to good, honest clean-living folk? For her, a wedding to Justus to repair the indiscretion was not an option, for he was already married. And then there was Lil for her to contend with, inhabiting the same table – sharing the same man, their children growing up as siblings of sorts, side by side.

It was unthinkable.

Justus didn't seem to think so - and listening, Jack watched the Master's eyes glimmering while he expounded his new, revised theory.

In the blink of an eye, the heated debate over Sonia's pregnancy that had taken place only two days earlier, dividing opinions among everybody to the point where firm rifts had formed, may as well have never occurred. Sonia's plight and the concerns Justus had about the fragile reputation of the colony were now being recast, illuminated by the glow of Helen's pregnancy. The predicament of a new baby, born to an unmarried woman, was no longer a stain on Montsalvat. There was now no need for unwed mothers to be cast into the streets. Instead, Montsalvat would demonstrate to the world a highly evolved social structure. A community where men and women lived together in mutual support, their tolerance for the needs of each other, demonstrating their love was a potent living example of Justus' 'theory of consideration.'

~

The news of Helen's pregnancy rocked Jack to his very core. He'd coped with the knowledge that Justus was having an affair with Helen by ignoring it. By believing that it had nothing to do with him and Sofia. Lil didn't seem to mind, so why should they?

But a pregnancy - that was different. Not the baby. An innocent child didn't worry him. It was the Master's role in it. That he was already married to Lil. That poor Helen could not even marry Justus if she wanted to. The whole mess. No longer would he be able to ignore Justus' appalling relationship with Helen, with her growing belly a constant reminder.

'Bloody old hypocrite!' Sonia fumed when she joined him and Sofia for coffee in their cabin the following evening. 'Happy to lay the curse of womanhood on me, a poor young girl – prepared to throw me and my innocent child out into the world, from the only home we've ever known. Penniless and homeless, with not even a bonnet for the baby. And then, in barely a blink of time, he damned well has the nerve – the *married* Lord of the Manor - his wedded wife sitting across from him - his young pregnant lover beside him – to smile smugly, like a cat that got the bloody pot of cream. The cheek to reframe his appalling behaviour as an example of how highly evolved we are, here at Montsalvat, with our "advanced social order!" He makes me sick!'

Jack agreed. He still had not come to terms with Justus suggestion that Sonia should leave Montsalvat. His claim that Sonya was a threat to the reputation of the artists' colony!

'Poor Helen,' Sofia said.

'Puh… poor Helen! She is silly enough to put up with Justus' nonsense. Let herself be pushed around by him. Honestly, between Mum and her, you would think that the man is a prophet.'

'Yes, but Justus can be very charming when he wants to be,' Jack said.

'Charming! That's one word for him,' Sofia said. 'But I don't care about him. I am worried about Helen. She is still a young girl. We must look out for her. Hopefully, she will talk to me while we are working in the garden. I expect that she's feeling utterly overwhelmed at present.'

CHAPTER 42

*W*hile Montsalvat was a wonderful environment for Max and Scotty to run around in, freely exploring their world under the watchful eyes of a multitude of adults, it was not without risks.

Jack and Sofia were always aware that it was, after all, a building site, with all manner of sharp implements, heavy tools, deep holes, water-filled tanks, dams and scaffolding from which an adventurous child could fall. Add to that snakes and spiders, and the surrounding acres of open paddocks and rearing children in the Australian bush was not for the faint-hearted.

Sofia, nervous of the potential dangers, monitored Scotty's where-abouts closely. Her call – 'Scotty, where are you?' – was repeated throughout the day as he ran wild, usually a dozen steps behind Max. Scotty doted on the older boy, his little chubby legs always trying to keep up. Safety was less of an issue through the week when routines were less hectic and it was easier to manage the boys' movements, but things could get chaotic on the weekends when the number of visitors to the site increased. While the students were quick to claim the little fellow and practice their parenting skills in preparation for the day when they may need them, they were unreliable carers. Scotty would suddenly appear by Sofia's side, his 'babysitter' nowhere in sight, no doubt distracted by all manner of interesting conversations and activities.

All the same, it was not the casual supervision of the weekenders or the dangers of the building site that were responsible for the harrowing February evening, when he was barely two.

It was Tuesday evening and Jack was home early for a change. Today, he had travelled north of Melbourne, towards Woodend, with Charles, a wool agent who'd become a close workmate over recent months. They'd left the office at around eleven-thirty to meet with one of the company's most important clients, Peter Gilbert. Jack loved this drive that ended directly below an enormous geological formation, Hanging Rock. The rock's looming presence was hard to ignore, dozens of golden fingers rising into the sky interconnected by bottomless crevices, into which, if one was to fall, they would be lost forever. The first time they'd driven to Woodend, Charles had shown him the enormous boulder 'hanging' above the pathway, giving name to the area. Jack had hoped it wouldn't choose that day to finally drop from its perch, for anything beneath its path would be crushed in an instant. One of the bonuses of this trip was that Charles detoured across to Montsalvat and dropped Jack directly in the driveway on their way home, hence saving Jack the train journey and walk from town. It had just gone five when he entered their cabin, surprising Sofia and Scotty with his early appearance. Reaching out, he swept Sofia close to him with one arm, Scotty with the other, and squeezed them against him tightly, laughing at Scotty's squeals of delight. It had been a pleasant day and Sofia had spent the morning baking – Anzacs and jam drops – to stock the kitchen's large jars for the week. Max and Scotty, of course, loved her baking sessions, helping to roll dough and form animal shapes to be placed in the oven and were impatient to sample the biscuits as soon as they slid off the flat trays onto the wire racks, growing cool enough for little hands to manage.

Scotty was just about to have his daily wash in the large steel tub

Sofia had filled, and for the next half hour, Jack played with him, making beards out of the soap suds for Scotty and himself. Bath-time completed, Jack turned into the 'tickle monster,' chasing Scotty and towelling him dry before sitting with him to play with the new wooden truck that Grandpa had given Scotty when they'd visited the previous day.

'Okay, my sweet amigos,' Sofia interrupted, 'now we must go across for dinner.' With Scotty perched on his shoulders, Jack walked with her to the communal kitchen, where the boys always ate at six pm. Justus, who was spending more time during the week at Montsalvat these days, had long insisted on feeding the children in the kitchen and settling them in bed before seven, so the adults could eat their dinner at the dining room table without 'petty interruptions'.

On arriving, Lil had the children's dinner ready - mashed potato, rissoles and gravy - and Max was toying with the food rather than eating it. When Jack placed Scotty in his usual chair, the child immediately began squirming, looking at Jack, preferring to continue riding on his father's shoulders than to eat his dinner. 'I suppose they have been eating biscuits all day,' Jack laughed, and Sofia returned his knowing look with a guilty expression.

At that moment, Justus appeared, and noticing Max playing with his food, he frowned.

'Eat your dinner, Max!' he said sternly.

Ignoring his father, Max continued playing.

Raising his voice, Justus repeated the command, in a rare display of impatience toward his son.

'Max. Eat. Your. Dinner. Now! And you'll sit there until you've finished. You can stay there all night, for all I care,' Justus' words immediately prompted a loud bellowing from Max.

It was evident that Justus was in a bad mood. Sofia quickly spooned the potato mix into Scotty's mouth so she could get him out of the kitchen and back to their cabin quickly, glad that Justus' stern manner had quelled any thoughts of resistance from Scotty.

Jack diplomatically distracted Justus from the boys' behaviour by asking how the installation of the iron staircase for the Great Hall was going. The staircase was unique. and Justus had been thrilled when Whelan claimed it for Montsalvat. Circular, the ornate metal pieces had been sitting in a higgledy pile of twisted iron for the past month. They'd intended to install it the following Saturday. However, Justus told Jack, this would not be happening. Today, he'd discovered that the finished measurements of the stairs were smaller than they'd allowed and adjustments were now necessary - an irritation responsible for his bad mood.

Sofia quickly finished feeding Scotty, and with a sympathetic glance at Max, who had still barely touched his dinner despite his father's stern warnings, she took Scotty by the hand and led him away from the table. By six-forty he was washed and snuggled into his little bed, listening as Sofia stroked his cheek and sang '*Arrorró*', the Spanish lullaby that had become a nightly ritual. Scotty hummed quietly, thumb in his mouth, dark eyes gazing into hers until his heavy lids closed and he drifted into a deep sleep.

Back in the kitchen, Max resisted all of Lil's efforts to get him to eat dinner. His wailing had gathered steam and showed no signs of abating, drawing Justus back into the kitchen.

'You eat your dinner now, or I'll tan your hide,' he declared, his shout - loud enough to be heard in Eltham - causing Max to wail louder.

Justus did not often interfere with Lil's management of their son and rarely was Max asked to do anything he didn't want to do, but tonight Justus had embarked on a battle of wills with his five-year-old and had no intention of being beaten. At seven o'clock, the diners were seated, and the meal served, while Max remained in the kitchen, his cries increasing in volume.

Finally, Justus had had enough and left the table to roar at Max, 'Shut this blessed noise up! We cannot hear ourselves think with all your racket!' Silence descended on the kitchen and Justus returned to the table.

Lulled into complacency, the adults chatted for almost half an hour before Lil left to check on Max. She returned immediately. Max was gone!

Rising, Jack, Sofia and the Skippers headed out into the yard, thankful for the dusky twilight, while Justus and Lil said that they would search the house.

For fifteen minutes, Jack and Sofia worked together, calling for Max, first checking around the dam, which, of course, offered the greatest danger, and then searching among the buildings. Darkness was quickly descending and the shadowy shapes began to vanish in a veil of black.

Nearing their cabin, Sofia popped in to check on Scotty and emerged, white-faced. His little bed was empty!

Hearts thumping, they tried to stay calm, knowing that the boys would be together and could not possibly have gone too far away in the short amount of time they had been missing. Surely they were just hiding somewhere! The problem was that 'somewhere' was elusive, and much to Justus' consternation, Lil insisted they call the police. For two hours, police recorded statements, and torches in hand, swarmed through the buildings and grounds of Montsalvat and beyond.

Justus seethed at the invasion, his fury evident in the abrupt replies he gave to the officer's questions. Were there poisons, guns, wells, dams, containers into which the boys may have climbed? Had any strangers been seen around the premises? Who had recently visited Montsalvat? Had any visitor behaved suspiciously - you know – showed undue interest in the boys? How well did Justus know the students who came up each weekend? Justus had the look of a man under interrogation and his responses were loud and defensive. Jack explained to a now weeping Sofia, who believed that Justus was being obstructive rather than helpful, that the Master was as much worried about Max and Scotty as he was about the invasion of police sticky-beaking into every nook and cranny of Montsalvat, and that he just wanted the police to get on with their search, not ask pointless questions.

Feeling his heart beating furiously, Jack tried to control the quiver in his voice as he reassured Sofia that all would be well. He had to believe that the boys would be found very soon and tried to focus on the possible places they might be, rather than all of the terrible things that could have happened to them.

'There's no sign of footprints around the dam,' a young policeman reported. 'What about any old wells on the property?' Jack shook his head.

'We've checked the sheds and all of the buildings. Even that old caravan out the back' said a second officer.

'Have any cars arrived or left since the lads have been missing?' the first asked ominously.

The cars!

Jack half laughed, much to Sofia's astonishment, and ran to the door. 'Max is mad about the truck. I bet he's taken Scotty up there! That's where they'll be, I'm sure of it!'

And at ten o'clock at night, the two little boys were found – snuggled together on a pile of old blankets, fast asleep in the back of the truck.

Relieved, everyone fell into bed, dirty and tired after stumbling around by torchlight for over three hours, and the next morning all they could get from Max was that he didn't want to eat his dinner, as well as a promise that he would never get Scotty out of his bed again.

And all heard the tongue-lashing Lil directed at Justus for being so harsh on Max.

CHAPTER 43

There is inevitably a point when the beliefs to which people attach themselves falter. Sometimes that moment arrives when long-defended absolutes fail to withstand the scrutiny of cold, hard reality; when weaknesses of man or theory, or both, are exposed. Other times, there is a slow erosion of beliefs as contradictions create one crack, human frailty another, and alternative theories emerge, undermining the bedrock of ideology and allowing seeds of doubt to take root. Suddenly, whole philosophies collapse, tumbling like a house built from cards.

Jack and Sofia's commitment to Justus' vision for Montsalvat seriously stumbled in the year of Scotty's second birthday. Jack listened to Sofia's repeated complaints about the Master's behaviour as, increasingly, his dominating manner, public humiliations and petty irritations affected others.

'He makes me so mad, Jack. And not just me. Where are Henry and Joe? We never see them these days. They've got sick of his nonsense.'

'Well, they are both married now, with other responsibilities to take up their time.' Jack tried to make light of the changes at Montsalvat but, with increasing frequency, he failed to find the words to defend Justus' weaknesses.

Sofia seethed for days when Justus repeated the same advice that he'd once given to the Skippers to a lovely older couple – wealthy patrons who regularly supported Montsalvat – that they should rid themselves of their collection of Norman Lindsays, claiming that they were bourgeoisie. Even Jack believed the Master went too far when Dave and Glenys excitedly shared their plans to travel to Europe the following spring. Just like Justus' and Lil's trip only a few years earlier, they planned to tour London and Paris, visit the famous land-marks – see the paintings at the Louvre. They even thought that, just like Justus, they would travel into Spain – to Barcelona to see the imaginative architecture of Antoni Gaudí, as well as the surrealist works of Joan Miro.

Justus' response to their plans was entirely unexpected; although, Jack thought, his reaction duplicated that of Max Meldrum when Justus, himself, had ventured to Europe all of those years ago. For immediately, Justus interpreted Dave and Glenys' travel plans to be an abandonment of their commitment to his teachings and the Montsalvat dream. It was as though they'd personally insulted him and he did not hide his outrage, ridiculing their excitement for wanting to seek inspi-ration from distant horizons and claiming that none of them could survive in the outside world, away from his influence.

Jack and Sofia felt terrible for Dave and Glynis. Already, they'd spent an afternoon chatting with the couple, listening to their plans and answering their questions about his and Sofia's own experiences in Paris and Spain.

Sofia had been excited for them, and Jack could see the look of longing in her eyes as she spoke of her country of birth. Did she want to go back, he wondered? She seemed settled here in Australia, these days, and despite her frustrations with Justus, he knew how much she loved living here at the artists colony with her little family. They were now hoping that a second pregnancy might ensue soon.

'How dare he,' she fumed, and Jack agreed. Justus had no right to control people like this. To make them feel bad about their decisions. He decided to speak to Justus about this behaviour. To tell him that he must stop being so controlling.

Two further incidents shook Jack's sense of allegiance to Justus to the core.

The first occurred on a Wednesday evening when Jack and Sofia arrived at the dinner table a little late, after battling to get Scotty to sleep. He'd spent the morning running around on the dried mudheaps with Max. After lunch, Sofia set Scotty on his little seat on the back of her bicycle. They'd ridden into Eltham to buy fresh bread for their breakfast and some fruit for Scotty to snack on. Returning, Scotty became clingy, crying for no apparent reason, although his flushed cheeks, runny eyes and sniffle suggested he was developing a cold or perhaps he was teething. He became obstinate and contrary; hungry one minute, then shaking his head and wailing loudly the next. Sofia offered first a banana and then a biscuit and slices of apple, but none of these appeased him. When she offered him his very favourite treat, a piece of dried apricot, he threw it onto the floor. Throughout his bath he remained restless, and as darkness fell, all Sofia's attempts to settle him had proved futile. Each time his breathing deepened, Sofia quietly stepped away from him, but, as though sensing her departure, his eyes had flown wide open and he'd set up a loud wailing. Now, convinced that his bright red cheeks and the sticky dribble already soaking through his nightdress were the eruption of his two-year-old molars, Sofia rubbed oil of cloves onto the red swollen gums and offered a consoling breast, onto which Scott latched for comfort rather than hunger, until finally, he settled.

Jack and Sofia arrived at the dining room at seven-twenty, very late by usual standards. Justus, who was in a particularly finicky mood following an argument with the local council officers regarding sanitation at Montsalvat, made a scathing comment about how babies were now dictating the dinner time routine. 'Perhaps, Sofia, you might care for Scotty properly rather than making Jack late to dinner,' he said. The conversation at the table ground to a halt as Justus' words sank in, all present recognising the sharpness of Justus' rebuke which in itself was not uncommon; however, it was extraordinarily rare that Jack or Sofia would be on the receiving end of Justus' tongue lashing. Usually, such a reprimand would draw a quick apology. Tonight, however, Jack's anger was aroused, and quietly seething, he ignored Justus altogether and took his time settling Sofia into her seat, before taking his own place. He forced a grim smile towards the Skippers and accepted the bowl of baked vegetables that Sonia passed to him, which he presented to Sofia, holding it while she served herself. The only sound in the room was the clinking of cutlery as she lifted the vegetables onto her plate. Jack breathed deeply, knowing the volumes of insult that he was casting, by the mere act of ignoring the Master.

Rarely were Justus' commands snubbed in such a direct manner and the tension at the table was electric. Justus looked thunderous for a second. However, he quickly collected himself when he realised that no apology was forthcoming and laughed, diffusing the tension at the table and reclaiming his position of advantage and control.

It was Justus' heartless response to illness just a few weeks later; however, that proved too much for Jack and Sofia.

CHAPTER 44

For Jack and Sofia, the final straw came like a thunderbolt. Jack had not been present, but Sofia's description of the events shocked him.

It was a balmy evening, late March when despite the onset of autumn, the sun's warmth lingered even after the sun had set and the pungent fragrance of eucalyptus filled the air. Jack had remained in Melbourne for a workplace meeting, planning to spend the night in South Yarra with his parents. Sofia always missed Jack during these occasional overnight absences, but was determined to make the best of it. Ensuring Scott was settled early, she'd made her way to the dining room to help with the evening meal. Most people had arrived and were already seated at the dinner table. They made quite a spectacle these days, for both Helen and Sonia's bellies were swelling in unison, and now, at almost seven months pregnant, they looked like a pair of colourful beachballs tumbling around the grounds of Montsalvat in their ballooning maternity smocks.

Sofia had finished filling Justus' glass from the bottle of claret she'd carried into the room, before setting it on the table alongside the bowl of boiled potatoes, a platter of greens and slab of corned beef, and then sitting next to Mervyn. Curiously, Lil's seat at the end of the table remained vacant. The group silently glanced at each other, wondering what had happened.

A slow shuffling was heard and Lil appeared at the doorway. It was evident that she was having a particularly bad day - inflicted by one of her 'attacks' - this time, involving her legs. Sometimes, Lil's vision was affected; other times, she developed numbness in her hands, causing her to drop cutlery onto the floor. In line with her and Justus' shared belief that illness was psychosomatic, such attacks were usually ignored, at least by herself and Justus. More than once, Sofia had quietly asked, 'Are you all right, Lil?', and each time receive the same reply: 'Yes, yes, I'm fine, Sofia. Don't worry about me.'

Tonight, however, Lil's condition was shockingly poor, her gait reduced to a tiny shuffle. It was clear that she could barely walk. And then it was evident that she couldn't, for suddenly she fell to the ground, where she lay still, her heavy breathing filling the room. A nervous silence settled over the table, the diners waiting to see what would happen next.

Justus was first to move, purposely leaning forward to stab his fork into the sliced corned silverside on the platter in front of him, acknowledging its pleasant spicy aroma. From the floor, a slow scraping could be heard as Lil, using her arms in a crab-like motion, inched the body that refused to cooperate, towards her chair.

'It was awful,' Sofia sobbed. 'We just sat there. Nobody said a thing. Nobody! And Justus just kept on eating, as though nothing was happening. Eventually, Lil made it to her chair, but it started to wobble when she tried to pull herself up. I had to do something, Jack; I couldn't just sit there. So, I stood up, to steady the chair for her. But Justus yelled at me - "No." No! That is all he said. So there was nothing for it, but to sit down again, while Lil finally dragged herself onto her seat and ever so quietly asked for a glass of wine. I have never seen anything like it, Jack. It was cruel. Cruel!'

Clinging to him, Sofia sobbed as she continued. 'We have to leave here. I can't stay. This is terrible. Terrible for Scott. Terrible for us. I am not going to raise my son to treat people like that. It's all been a mistake. We must go.' Sofia was so distraught that Jack was sure she wanted to walk out of the door and leave the colony, there and then.

'Shush,' he said, holding Sofia close as she sobbed into his chest. His thoughts ran riot and a sickening lump grew in the pit of his stomach. She was right, he knew. Something about Montsalvat was poisonous. Justus' theories, so right in many ways, were terribly wrong in others. He and Sofia needed to leave and make their own life together, away from the dominating presence of Justus.

Jack anticipated the disappointment Justus would feel. The Master would take their decision to leave personally and view them as traitors. Deserters. He would be angry and question their motives, using guilt and sarcasm to undermine their decision. He would belittle them, just as he'd done with Glenys and Dave. Jack also knew that, when Justus realised that these tactics were not going to change Jack's mind, the Master would revert to charm. Jack hoped they could part as friends and be able to return for visits, perhaps for Sunday night dinners occasionally, as many of the colony's friends and patrons did.

'We will go, Sofia. We will work out a plan and then we will tell Justus,' he consoled her. 'Let's not rush this, though. We don't need to have hard feelings. We will find a place, and then tell Justus that we've decided it's time to move into town. It will be okay.'

CHAPTER 45

*W*ithin two days, they found a cottage on the main street of Eltham, close to the station. Jack would only have a block to walk each morning and afternoon, and while they would be close enough to meet with Helen and Sonia regularly, they would be able to build their own lives together, away from Justus' influence.

As anticipated, Justus ranted and raved, but not to the degree that Jack had expected. Used to the older man's tactics, Jack refused to be intimidated by sarcasm and petulance. And then, also as Jack had predicted, Justus realised his and Sofia's minds were made up and decided to make the best of the situation. Everyone knew that Justus held a strong affection for Jack. Jack himself wondered if the Master saw similarities between their relationship and the closeness the Master had once shared with Max Meldrum. Regardless, it appeared that Justus also preferred to preserve their friendship and he'd been pleased when they'd announced their new home was only five minutes away.

Once a new place to live had been found and the awkward conversation with Justus over, everything fell into place quickly. They planned to move the following Saturday. Arthur kindly offered that they could have the use of his vegetable van to transport their belongings, and Justus suggested that they use Montsalvat's truck for some of the larger pieces of furniture.

Jack took Thursday and Friday off work to help Sofia with the final cleaning and packing of their rooms. Not that there was a lot to pack, or even an urgency to move everything at once, but Jack felt it was better to make a swift break. Also, Sofia had been extremely tired in recent weeks and Jack guiltily reflected on how much the emotional turbulence at Montsalvat had exhausted her.

On Friday morning, Scotty and Max did a final round of the garden with Sonia, who was quite open in her disappointment to see Sofia and Jack leave Montsalvat. Despite her advanced state of pregnancy, she insisted on a final walk with 'my little hombre' – her pet name for Scotty – allowing Sofia to slip into town for some bicarbonate of soda and vinegar to wash the floors and clean the windows of their studio. Sofia was determined to leave the vacated rooms spotless, ready for their new resident, a wonderful glassworker from Melbourne who was keen to take up accommodation at Montsalvat and spend weekends in the creative country atmosphere, focusing on her craft.

'Nobody is ever going to call me a dirty Spanish peasant,' Sofia told Jack angrily, still stung by the comment Justus had made over three years earlier.

While Scotty was being tended to by Sonia and Sofia was preparing for her trip into town, Jack seized the opportunity to have a final chat with Justus, just the two of them, before his and Sofia's departure the next day. Since the initial awkwardness and tenuous truce over their decision to leave, the last two weeks had been busy, and Jack had found little time to spend with the older man. Even though he was appalled by so many of the Master's actions, Jack still maintained grudging respect for Justus, the artist and teacher, and wanted to return their relationship to its old comfortable footing before leaving.

Justus seemed equally pleased to see Jack. He turned from his easel, and with excitement, showed Jack an old book he had stumbled across that outlined the glazing techniques used by painters of the eighteenth century. Justus, ever besotted by the methods of ancient masters, was in the throes of experimentation, keen to employ these same techniques in his own portraits.

This was the Master that Jack admired. The passionate artist, sharing his discoveries with such enthusiasm that his students could not help but be inspired. These moments when Jorgenson's focus was on art rather than on the shortcomings of other people.

Listening to Justus, Jack caught sight of a movement outside the window and walked out onto the balcony. Below, Sofia stood against her bike, trying to hold her polka dot summer dress, fluttering around her legs, in a respectable position. She was ready for her ride into town. Leaning over the railing, Jack smiled down. He wanted her to see that his visit with Justus was going well. Sofia called up to him, but her words vanished on the breeze. Jack shook his head. 'No shoes, today!' he called. It had been a longstanding joke, one that had been resurrected when, a few weeks previously, Sofia had stumbled on a new shop that had opened in Eltham. Returning with a large package, Sofia had revealed to Jack an indisputably beautiful pair of shoes - so dainty and fragile that they seemed to be from another planet. Incredulous, Jack had hesitantly admired their fashionable sling-back and fine satin decorated with embroidered flowers.

'So ... where will you be wearing these?' Jack had asked tentatively, unsure whether Sofia, her eyes dewy with pleasure at the beauty of her purchase, had finally lost her mind, so foreign did the shoes look on the rough-hewn table amid the mud-brick walls and stone floor of their cabin.

With a rare burst of anger, she'd snatched the shoes up, deftly folded the tissue paper around them and stuffed them into the beautiful embossed cardboard box in which she had so proudly carried them home.

'We may live in mud and squalor now, Jack, but I do not plan to be living like this forever,' she'd retorted, and for the next few hours, she'd served Jack with stony silence.

The beautiful shoe-box had vanished from view and Jack suspected it was buried deep in her Spanish tea chest, the resting place of her prized possessions, and they had been silent on the matter. Thankfully, a few weeks later, when Sofia had mounted her bicycle in readiness to cycle into town for shopping, she announced 'I'm just off to get some shoes,' and Jack had known that he was forgiven.

Smiling as he watched Sofia ride away, it pleased Jack to see Sofia's happiness, buoyed by the knowledge that they were leaving Montsalvat, and he wished that they'd decided to move into a home of their own, earlier.

CHAPTER 46

*O*ver the next half hour, Justus continued his explanations, repeating the steps he'd just learned for Jack's benefit, pleased with the transparency the technique promised to produce.

Suddenly, a crash erupted from the grounds below. Walking to the window, Jack and Justus peered through the panes curiously and observed smoke drifting across the courtyard. Simultaneously, they listened as the clatter of heavy footsteps rounding the treads of the iron staircase got louder and Matchum burst into the room.

'Fire,' he cried breathlessly, and turning, beckoned them to follow as he leapt down the narrow circular stairwell, precariously taking the stairs two at a time.

As soon as they stepped outside, the smell of smoke was over-whelming, dense grey plumes immediately making Jack's eyes water.

Matchum swung sharply left towards the Student Quarters where flames were visible. Already the fire had a strong hold on the end cabin.

Helen and Lil were already filling buckets of water from the main tank across the courtyard. Jack raced forward to assist, jolted by the realisation that his cabin was next door, and that fierce flames were forcing their way in.

Relieved that most of his and Sofia's belongings were packed in boxes and set in a neat pile in the front room, ready for their move tomorrow, Jack knew he needed to act quickly. The oils were flammable as were his drawing pads and books, not to mention the timber furnishings and the curtains on the back room windows. He guessed he had a few minutes at best, if they were to salvage anything.

On entering, the studio was filled with smoke and the sound of crackling, emitting from the backroom. Jack glanced through the central doorway, but the smoke was so thick that entry was impossible. He shut the door, hoping to contain the flames and gain a few minutes before the fire spread throughout the building,and, working with Matchum and Justus, they hurled the stacked boxes outside - kitchenware, crockery and painting supplies. Sofia's tea chest, 'her Spain' caught Jack's eye, and Matchum helped him to carry it out. Jack was glad that he'd dragged it from the bedroom yesterday, where it had sat acting as a bedside table for over three years, concealed by the heavy cotton cloth Sofia draped over it, which was usually topped by a small kerosene lamp. Smoke filtered through the doorway, quickly filling the room, making their eyes water and scalding their throats.

'Jack! Matchum! Enough! You need to come out,' Justus called to them when a pile of papers on the kitchen dresser erupted into flames, releasing billowing black smoke into the room.

Stepping back, Jack watched, helplessly, as flames devoured the room. He'd not even thought about what was lost in the back room. Their clothes, certainly. Books, perhaps. Linens. Thankfully, most of their belongings were in the boxes they'd retrieved, and Jack was thankful that they'd salvaged these.

His heart still racing, Jack watched the fire burn when a deadening feeling weighed upon him, a foreboding that something was amiss. In the distance, a figure was cycling towards them – Sofia. He heard her calling, but her words were indiscernible. He looked around for the children. Scotty?

Dread swept over him as his eyes scanned the group. Matchum, Arthur, Lena and Justus were frantically retrieving paint pots, easels, a heavy iron kettle and saucepans from Arthur's cabin, next door. Sonia and Mervyn were clearing objects from the vicinity as they were brought outside. Helen was struggling to manage the hose; its trickling stream proving utterly ineffective against the rampaging flames. Lil stood to the side watching in shock, with Max huddled closely against her.

Sofia called again; her words now clear.

'Scotty? Scotty?' Half-riding, half-staggering, she dragged the bicycle towards him, her face distorted in terrible anguish, breathless as she spoke.

'Scotty, Jack. Did you get him? Where is he? Is he safe?'

Jack stared, his ears refusing to accept the unthinkable, as her barrage of questions assaulted him. His dread would not take form; his mind incapable of digesting the unthinkable. The others stopped what they were doing and listened.

'Scotty's not in there ...' Jack stumbled over the words, willing them to be true. 'No ... He's with Sonia.'

'No, Jack. I told you. He was sick. I put him in his bed.' Sofia's words were overly loud. Caught between a cry and a scream, sobs catching in her throat, a plea in her voice that surely Jack had known this; had acted on the information she'd given him an hour earlier.

Realisation of the tragedy before them dawned, and Jack made a crazed run towards the gaping door where flames blazed at the entry, having already consumed the papers and fabric, now voraciously attacked the timbers, chairs, his heavy easel, the small kitchen table. An invisible wall of scorching heat beat him back.

Matchum grasped him. 'No, mate, you can't go there,' he murmured, winding both arms around Jack's chest to restrain him.

'Scotty! Scotty!' Jack cried, his arms swinging wildly in a futile bid to subdue the flames. Bereft, he looked at Sofia's face, contorted with anguish, accusation, disbelief. Wrenching clear of Matchum's clasp,

Jack again fought to enter the burning building, a howl rising within him.

~

A quiet sobbing emerged as the awful reality sunk in. The Skippers and Arthur stood by helplessly, Helen clutching at her abdomen as if to protect her unborn child from the flames, Sonia moved closer to Sofia, charcoal tears streaming down her face, her left hand attempting to reach out to Sofia, her right hand mirroring her sister's, unconsciously cradling the weight of her own pregnant belly.

Watching in disbelief, dwarfed by the magnitude of the horror before them, the inferno continued. Nobody cared to stop it, anymore.

Scotty, the dear little boy with the mischievous black eyes and cheeky smile, had been in the bedroom. The bedroom that was no more, the building crackling, exploding, collapsing before their eyes.

'Sofia.' Lil stepped forward, first to speak. 'He would have been asleep. The smoke would have sedated him.'

Sofia stepped back, her hands wringing helplessly, eyes wildly searching the forlorn weeping group, the belongings that had been dragged out only minutes before as if Scotty's mischievous little face would miraculously emerge from among them. Her gaze landed on the tea chest.

'The paintings, Jack. You saved the paintings?' Sofia shrieked with incredulity, her words searing through his conscience like a hot knife. 'You left our baby, but you saved paintings!'

Sofia thumped at the plywood chest whose treasured contents also signified her most profound losses. Saved! At the cost of her greatest treasure! The harshness of her blows threatened to crack the old metal seams. Falling to the ground before it, a keening erupted from her throat, timeless and universal. The culmination of loss, shock, despair and trauma experienced by mothers throughout time, vented forth from unfathomable depths. Shocking to hear. Impossible to comfort. A heart-rending cry that would forever echo in their ears.

Jack walked towards her like a robot, masked by his own shock and disbelief, but Sofia's hands rose against him, and the horror blazing in her eyes beat him back.

CHAPTER 47

*G*rief. Three letters embraced by soft consonants. The 'g' a rather beautiful sound. Gold. Glad. Glamour. Glitter. Gleeful. F for Flowers. Fun. Frolicking. Flutter. Sandwich the 'rie' in the middle, and you come up with a mood of unspecified dimensions.

For Jack, grief was a madness. A rage. A fury. Grief relentlessly drummed at his mind, refusing to permit a single thought to settle. His 'G' was damning, cursing Guilt that swamped his thoughts and crushed his spirit, rising to berate him every time sleep cycled to wakefulness. His 'F' had multiple dimensions. Fury, flames, fireballs, fear. Failure. Fire!

Grief jammed his fists into tight balls, their knuckles white with unleashed fury that wanted to pound the stone walls and dry clay, and even the kind faces of those who offered sympathy. Grief poured out of his eyes, coursing down his cheeks like raging wild rivers. Grief erupted out of his lungs in deep, hacking sobs. Grief was the hatred he felt as he looked into the mirror, loathing himself for his error. His irresponsibility. His misjudgement. It seized him, the minute he opened his eyes, inescapable, even if he rolled his head deep into his pillow and sought the oblivion of a few more hours escape. Grief was there when his body pretended to be controlled and rational. When he talked to the police. Explain. Describe. Who? What? Where? Why? *Why? Why?* How does a father qualify the death of his beloved child?

Remarkably, his voice performed on command, answering the questions dutifully. Where did the words come from? Who spoke? Jack, himself, was gone – hidden deep within the fleshy vessel that was his body, curled into a tight ball, while his heart pumped with mechanical efficiency, even though it was broken. His face looked the same, albeit tired and drawn - aged in a moment in time. His legs held him upright, walking here and there on command. His fingers did not fail as they signed this, and wrote that, although a fine tremor persisted. But Jack was gone.

As was Sofia. Sofia? *Why hadn't she come inside and explained? Just because she hated the Master. She could have made herself clear. She could have told him. She should have said that their baby, their little love, their shining light, who trusted them to protect him, was in the cabin.* But no! Jack shook the thoughts from his head. It was not Sofia's fault! He knew that. Oh, to turn back the clock! Undo everything. Such a small thing. Just a second chance to hear her words – those two simple sentences. *'Scott's in his cot. Please check on him.'*

Lil tried to reason with Jack. 'It would not have changed anything,' she implored. 'You could not have reached him. It was very quick. Scotty wouldn't have known anything. He was asleep. The smoke would have sedated him.' Kind words, designed to bring peace and establish understanding - to absolve guilt.

The afternoon passed in a blur. Jack's parents arrived, shock on their faces, their bodies diminished in size and hunched, the weight of the loss too great to bear. Their dear little grandson who'd given them so much joy, was no more.

Margaret arrived later in the evening, shock etched on her face. She held Jack tight and he cried into her neck, racking, gulping sobs, that broke her heart, and she cried with him. When she asked after Sofia, he just shook his head helplessly and sobbed again. Deep in shock, Sofia hadn't wanted to speak to anyone, least of all Jack. In the end, Lil had ushered him away - told him that the police had arrived. They needed to speak with him. Lil had suggested that she give Sofia sedation, encourage her to rest.

'Let's check on her, Jack,' Margaret suggested, and they walked to the Skippers house together, where the found Sofia in Lena's lounge, sitting silently, haggard and motionless, despair in her eyes. Opening her arms, Margaret pulled Sofia to her. Jack's heart broke yet again as he watched his wife trembling against Margaret, unnaturally silent, her eyes dry, as though she had cried every tear that a body could ever muster. She probably had, he thought, for both Jack and Margaret, of all people, knew how much Sofia had already lost in her life.

CHAPTER 48

That night, and then for the next week, Sofia stayed at the Skipper's house. He wondered at her decision to seek solace with the Skippers; for him their household held more people than he could cope with. Likewise, for Sofia, he was certain, what with the swollen bellies of the two young women and a grief so enormous that it sucked the air out of the room, was surely claiming all but the life out of her. However, she insisted on staying and Lena set up a bed for her in their small sitting room, on which she lay though the night, whilst in the day she'd sit, motionless, on their verandah. Each morning Jack walked up the hill to sit with her, but it was unbearable. Always slender in stature, now Sofia appeared emaciated. Her sentences, which had become more English than Spanish over the last five years in Australia, had reverted to mostly Spanish, on the rare moments when she spoke, and even to him, her words were difficult to understand. The silence between them was large, and a terrible awfulness encapsulated them – Sofia felt it too, he knew - for she quickly looked away from him whenever their eyes met, and then she wouldn't look at him at all. Blame? Sorrow? He'd clung to her hand, willing her back to him. But then she'd withdrawn her hand from him, too. Lil finally suggested to Jack that he stay away for a day or so. That she would counsel Sofia. Help her through the dreadful shock she had experienced.

The residents of Eltham were generous in their sympathy, shocked at the tragedy that had befallen the handsome young man and his beautiful Spanish wife. At Montsalvat, the community could barely function. Sombre and wordless, they attended to the essentials. Cooking. Washing. Eating. The carving of stone and hammering of wood and stacking of bricks - creative pursuits that were the heartbeat of Montsalvat – ceased. Minds numbed, their energetic spark extinguished, as they came to terms with the tragedy.

Justus remained absent, closed up in his room. 'He can't cope with anything beyond his control,' Lil explained. 'He never has been able to.'

'Yes, but he should be here.' It was Sonia who had spoken up. 'Men need to be there, through the bad as well as the good.' Her own experiences had left their mark.

'Sonia, Justus is hurting. Believe me. I know him. His sorrow for Jack and Sofia is immense. The loss of Scotty is too dreadful. Justus has no words to express his pain, and so he chooses seclusion,' Lil said.

News of the tragedy travelled quickly and many students from Queen Street arrived to offer their condolences. Sue set herself up in the kitchen, supported by Lil and Sonia, where they made continuous pots of tea, crusty bread and bowls of stew, offering substance to those who had no appetites.

Max, shattered by the death of his little mate, moved around in a daze. Lost amid the hushed tones of grieving adults, he did not know how to occupy himself. Gladly, he yielded to the arms that constantly reached out to him, picking him up and hugging him tightly. It was as though they believed that by the mere act of holding him close, Max at least would be kept safe from harm.

On the day of the funeral, the tiny church in Eltham overflowed with mourners, rocked by the loss. Friends of William and Marian, work associates from Goldsbrough, Mort & Co, people from Melbourne's art circles, brethren in this time of grief, hugged Jack and Sofia and expressed condolences, tears in their eyes. Eltham's locals, the shopkeepers and the young mothers that Sofia had befriended in town stood quietly as the local minister spoke words of spiritual mysteries, hope and peace.

Hating the sight of the tiny coffin, yet unable to remove his eyes from it, Jack absorbed the photograph of Scotty that had been placed upon it and was reminded of another picture, of a little boy who had died way too young. Jimmy, of course. Uncle Robert and Aunt Elizabeth's Jimmy. Jack recalled his uncle's drunken sobbing, what?... twenty years after the death of his son, and for a brief second, he did not feel so utterly alone. He knew that Uncle Robert would understand his feelings. What Jack didn't comprehend is how Uncle Robert bore, not those moments of drunken memories, but rather, the days of sobriety.

The publican opened his doors for the wake, that followed the funeral. However, the deaths of young children do not provide satisfying stories of a life well-lived. After an expression of condolence, lubricated by a quick beer in the pub's lounge, most of the visitors headed back to Melbourne early.

CHAPTER 49

*A*fter the funeral, William and Marian, assisted by Margaret, begged Jack and Sofia to leave Montsalvat, to come live with them, even just for a short while, but they refused. Perhaps it was too soon to leave that which remained of Scotty – the ghostly echo of his little voice as he ran around the yards and buildings of Montsalvat, calling and laughing. Where else could his joyful little spirit be felt?

Instead, Jack returned to the caravan, which had sat empty for the past two years except for a student seeking shelter on a wet weekend and an amorous couple seeking privacy.

In the van, Jack sat still. Alone. A world of solitude. Thoughts – there weren't any. Movement – any motion undertaken by his arms and legs had no bearing on his will, which, if given licence, would command him never to move again. Sounds – indistinguishable; travelling towards him through a pea-soup fog. Hard to hear, if he could be bothered, and mostly, he couldn't. Sights - the face of Margaret reappeared often, each time begging him to leave the van. Walking up with him to sit with Sofia, whose eyes, once sparkling with joy, were filled with vacant sorrow, looking at him for an answer that he did not have.

'Why did you lose our son?' they asked, even though she did not speak.

Others arrived, offering food and drinks. He ate and drank. Lil came and sat. Talking. Encouraging Jack to come and join them at the house for meals. He tried once, but there was too much normality in a world that was not normal.

His parents arrived each morning, desperate to offer some sort of comfort. Worried about the hacking cough that had settled upon him, they brought cough mixture and a vapouriser. The stilted attempts at conversation. The quiet apprehension. Leaving before lunch with a promise to return the next day. Helpless to comfort him as they, too, suffered. The concentration of sadness was too much for the tiny van to accommodate.

Finally, Justus appeared. With a pile of canvases. Paints and brushes.

'Just get it out, Jack,' he said. 'Paint.'

So, Jack painted. Tormented. Self-flagellating. Eyes, accusing. Some with tears. Some cold. Were they Scott's eyes? Desperately crying – Daddy, help! Sofia's eyes? Embittered. Grief-filled. Fathomlessly deep with sorrow. He could barely stand the way they looked back at him as the paint hit the canvas. Sometimes he painted catatonically, staring deeply into the eyes that tortured him. Other times, with fury. Wild slashes. Fiery red. Iridescent orange. Licks of yellow. Furious sweepings of paint blazing across his page.

His parents appeared yet again only this time Margaret was with them. They meant business. His mother cried. His father was harsh, Margaret practical.

'Jack, you are ill. You need to come home.'

'I'm at home.'

'No, Jack. This is no place for you. You need help to get better.'

'I need to be here, for Sofia.'

'Jack, Sofia is gone. We don't know where she is. Do you know where she could be?'

Jack snapped out of himself, albeit briefly. What did they mean, Sofia was gone? How could she be gone?

'She is with the girls. Staying in the girls' house.'

'No, Jack. She left two days ago. We don't know where she went. Caught the morning train into Melbourne.'

A cold tremor passed across Jack's body and he could feel the eyes of Margaret, Justus and his parents upon him.

Margaret spoke. 'Jack, we're packing you up. You need to get into the car and go home with your parents. We need to get you better so you can help me find Sofia.'

'I need to find Sofia,' Jack repeated after her, as he attempted to stand. The movement set off a hacking cough, forcing him to sit again.

Leaning forward, Margaret hugged him, and he could see tears in her eyes.

'Come on, Jack. Time to go,' he heard her whisper, and stepping back, she nodded to Justus and William who took his arms and assisted him to stand.

Reaching out, Jack grasped Margaret's outstretched hand, and putting one foot tentatively forward, followed by the other, they stepped through the maze of paint-canvases strewn around the van; the jumble of clothes, clean and dirty, but mostly dirty; half-drunk mugs of tea – days old – nestled amongst jars of turps and linseed: the palettes, and the plates. Eight days ago, Jack had lost his little boy. Somewhere, at some time since, his wife had vanished, too. Lost? And Jack. He barely knew where Jack was, what he was doing, or why he was leaving this place of memories. Memories of grief in spades, but also those of love. Passion. Of joy and fulfilment with Sofia and Scotty. Seeing his little boy grow sturdy, strong, and brown as a little berry, playing in the mud heaps and chasing tiny lizards, running towards him when he returned home from work in the afternoons, eagerly seeking to be swung up on Jack's shoulders. This place of fresh air and bird-song, where artists gathered under gum trees, captivated by Justus' vision to create not just paintings, but rather, a whole world; one that nurtured talent and provided refuge and freedom to express themselves. A world that Jack knew also held a darker side, that was less about freedom and more about bondage to Justus' extraordinary will. Jack knew that great men with big dreams also bore powerful egos, dominating personalities that had the potential to induce suffering on others as well as themselves.

But none of that mattered for now. Jack only knew one thing. He had to restore what remained of his family. He had to find Sofia.

End of Book Two

In Memory

Shattered Dreams is dedicated to the memory of my brother, Scotty, who died tragically in a house fire in 1968. He was three years old.

DID YOU ENJOY READING THIS BOOK?

If so, perhaps you might consider leaving a review and helping others
to find it!
I would be so appreciative if you would, because
reviews … really … really … matter!

https://www.goodreads.com/book/show/50709050-shattered-dreams

https://www.amazon/dp/B083QZZD26

Thank-you, so much!

PRE-ORDER NOW!

PORTRAITS IN BLUE - BOOK THREE
Searching for Sofia
Available December 2020
Pre-Order Now On Amazon at www.
amazon.com/dp/BO85XtBM99

Make sure you are first to know about the progress of Searching for
Sofia by following me on facebook
https://www.facebook.com/pennyfieldsschneider
or contacting me to subscribe to my newsletter
pennyfieldsschneider@gmail.com

A PARTING NOTE FROM THE AUTHOR

When I came up with the idea of the *Portraits in Blue Series* I had a few simple thoughts in mind.

My central character would be a Melbourne boy - Victoria being the state that I grew up in and Melbourne, a city that I love - increasingly so as I visit as an adult, wandering through the wonderful lanes buzzing with coffee shops, gourmet restaurants amid historical buildings. If you've never been, I encourage you to go!

My story would set in England and Paris as well as Spain, somewhat satisfying my desire to know more about these places, all of which I have been fortunate enough to visit.

Montsalvat (Eltham, Victoria), would be pivotal. Although not revealed until Book Two, *Montsalvat* captured my imagination when I learned of it from my father when I was a young child. I had never forgotten his enthusiasm for this artists' enclave; however, I remembered little more of his comments beyond the name. My research revealed a location with a rich history and it was thrilling to find that Montsalvat still functions as an artists' retreat as well as a tourist attraction and function centre. It is a fine testament to Justus Jorgensen's dream back in the 1930s, when he embarked on his ambitious, alternative building project assisted by his cohorts of art students some of whom remained with him for decades.

Unquestionably, I knew that art would be pivotal to the theme of my story in order to satisfy a desire to deepen my knowledge of the art world. From technical skills to history to famous paintings to the intriguing lives of artists, I wanted to know it all. I chose the 1930s as a period of interest that combined many of the events I wished to embrace. I have loved every minute of research and my thirst to learn more remains strong.

I intended my story to be underpinned by themes of relationships and love. These aspects of the story evolved organically as Jack became his own person and forged his own friendships, while I merely recorded the words of his emotional journey. I hope that you enjoy his friendships and romance as much as I enjoyed writing about them!

From the outset, I also decided that my story would serve as a memorial for a terrible tragedy that occurred in our family, over fifty years earlier. Shocking as it was, I was determined to resurrect a ficti- tious version of events and honour a life that holds precious memories.

With these simple thoughts in mind, I laid out timelines and inves- tigated art movements, individuals and historical events which aligned to give my story both authenticity and accuracy.

Finally, when as a first-time author, I embarked on writing this tale of a fictitious man's life wandering through the streets of 1930s Bohemia, interacting with lives both well and badly lived, I was obliv- ious to the potential legalities or otherwise of such a venture. I will say that I deliberately aimed to portray those real-life characters with respect, and where irresistible opportunities to include intriguing scandal and unpleasant behaviour arose, I have ensured that such events are on the public record and have used eye-witness accounts as reference points. I have attempted to keep my imagined dialogue within the realms of the perceived nature of such characters. Hopefully, a modern account of such events serves to increase public interest in these lively artists of the 1930s.

Penny Fields-Schneider

Let's Talk about Reading and Writing

I would love you to join me on my writing journey. Subscribe to my monthly newsletter to learn more about the settings and characters in the Portraits in Blue series. Additionally, you will receive freebies including short stories and articles of interest and you will be the first to know when my books are available at discounted prices.

To join just email pennyfieldsschneider@gmail.com and I will send you the links

BOOKS BY PENNY FIELDS-SCHNEIDER

PORTRAITS IN BLUE SERIES

Portraits in Blue - Book Two – Shattered Dreams

Portraits in Blue - Book Three – Searching for Sofia (Due December, 2020)

Portraits in Blue - Book Four - Sofia's Story
(Due 2021)

SHORT STORIES
(Available free to Penny's newsletter subscribers!)

Picasso Blue

Framed

Acknowledgements

Thanks to the many people who have read and critiqued various drafts of the *Portraits in Blue* series. Cassie, Rosemary, Pauline and Jany - your collective feedback forced me to dig deeper to polish my manuscript.

Special thanks to Jacques-Noël Gouat for your unfaltering enthusiasm for The *Portraits in Blue* series. Your time spent reviewing drafts to assist me getting the French components of the story accurate is hugely appreciated. If any inaccuracies remain, they are my own!

Thanks to the wonderful Tarkenberg, who patiently bore the grunt work of editing *Portraits in Blue*. I am so appreciative of all that I have learned through your patient teaching as you've attempted to turn a very green, first-time writer into an author and a rough draft into a somewhat publishable manuscript. I am in awe of your attention to detail and frequently amused by your humour even as you recommended corrections to the manuscript, including revisions to my 75 word sentences!

To my husband and children, my enormous thanks for sharing in my all-consuming creative endeavours. Your support, encouragement and time spent reading drafts and listening patiently as I bounce the multitude of thoughts I have off your well-worn ears are much appreciated!

PENNY FIELDS-SCHNEIDER worked as a Registered Nurse before completing a Bachelor of Arts and Diploma of Education and henceforth, redesigning her life as a secondary teacher. An avid reader from a very young age, Penny has always aspired to be an author. In recent years, she became seduced by the world of art, dabbling with paint and brushes, attending art courses and visiting galleries. Penny aspires to create works of historical fiction that leave readers with a deeper understanding of the art world as well as taking them on emotional journeys into the joy and heartbreak that comes with family, friendship and love.

When Penny is not writing, she enjoys helping her husband on their cattle farm in northern NSW, loving every minute she can spend with their children, grandchildren, friends and family.

Penny would love to hear from her readers and you can join her newsletter or contact her through the following channels

Email PennyFieldsSchneider@gmail.com
Website
http://www.pennyfields-schneider.com

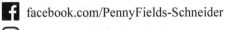 facebook.com/PennyFields-Schneider

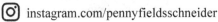 instagram.com/pennyfieldsschneider